The
REDEMPTION

FILTHY RICH AMERICANS | BOOK FOUR

NIKKI SLOANE

For my husband

ONE

MACALISTER

FRUSTRATION TWISTED MY MUSCLES INTO CORDS, MAKING MY clasped hands ache. Before the darkest day of my life, the one where I'd made a terrible mistake, no one would have *dared* miss a meeting with me. I'd had employees willing to sit in on conference calls while they were in labor or waiting for surgery.

Today, Stephen Alby was eight insulting minutes late. It was long enough to send a message of how little he respected me, my time, and my enormous wealth. Of course, that was assuming he was late. I was beginning to wonder if he would materialize at all. I was easily his biggest client, and if this was how he was going to treat me, perhaps I needed to take my money elsewhere.

I refused to let any of my irritation bleed out onto my face and held my posture neutral since I was out in public. It was noon, and the private penthouse restaurant was fully booked for lunch, and although the dining room wasn't large, every person in the space was aware of my infamous presence. Conversations had paused at my entrance then lagged awkwardly as I was seated at my table.

It wasn't the one I preferred, the one by the window, which

boasted a view of the harbor and its position of status to the rest of the room. I no longer maintained that level of clout. Instead, I'd been relegated to the smallest table by the door, away from the center where the most influential executives in Boston took their power lunches during the week. Like me, this table existed on the fringes. My money and the Hale name were enough to keep me on the exclusive guest list and earn me a seat in the room, but scandal had driven me to the outskirts.

The din of conversation dropped once more as someone else unexpected appeared at the entryway and spoke with the maître d'.

Clearly, the woman had never been here before. It wasn't the way her curious gaze took in the floating chandelier at the center of the room that gave it away—it was the soft smile that teased her lips. If she'd taken lunch here before, she'd know this wasn't a place for happy, friendly smiles. Deals were brokered over seared foie gras and scallops. Careers were made and broken by Boston's elite while seated at these tables covered in fine white linens.

Once upon a time, I was the king of this town, and I held court in this room.

It seemed the palace intrigue had continued in my absence, but I was desperate to climb back onto my throne and rise above it, rather than play the game with everyone else.

The young woman nodded as the maître d' spoke, making the waves of her blonde hair shimmer. Her face was familiar, and although it had been years since I'd seen her, it took me only a moment to place the girl. Last time, she'd worn a pale pink bridesmaid dress at my son's wedding. Today, it was a cashmere sweater dress in navy that covered her frame. It pretended to be modest, but the fabric clung provocatively to her breakneck curves.

When she was led toward my table, I set my jaw.

"Mr. Hale, may I join you?" Her tone was warm and confident.

Mine was brusque. "Are you here to apologize for your father's lateness?"

Sophia Alby's smile was unflinching. "I'm sure he'll be here soon. Let me keep you company while you wait."

I didn't appreciate how she lowered into the vacant chair across from me without my approval, but I wouldn't voice my displeasure until the maître d' had gone. I didn't care if I was rude—only that I didn't *appear* rude to the people around us, the people who mattered.

The man nodded as she settled into the seat, then he flitted away. I lifted my unimpressed gaze and pinned it on her. "Miss Alby—"

"You have a problem," she interrupted. There was a strange, off-putting smile fixed on her face.

One of my eyebrows arched so high, it nearly escaped my face. "Is it the girl who just sat uninvited at my table?"

Her unsettling smile widened. "That depends." She crossed her arms and leaned on the tabletop, manners be damned. It was a conscious decision. She'd gone to the same elite school as my sons, which meant she'd had the finest upbringing. Like my family, the Albys were one of the founding families of Cape Hill—the wealthy hamlet outside of Boston where we lived.

How old was she? Younger than Royce, which meant approximately twenty-five, perhaps twenty-six. I'd invited enough scandal into my life, and the absolute last thing I needed was to be seen having lunch with a pretty girl half my age. Irritation swelled inside me like the bell curve of compounding interest, and it darkened my tone. "It depends on what?"

The girl drew in a sharp breath. She wasn't as intimidated by me as she should be, but she wasn't entirely immune either. Her voice faltered. "On how you react to what I'm about to tell you."

My hot irritation cooled and thickened until I was frozen motionless by the warning in her eyes. It told me to brace myself. Whatever information she was about to divulge, I wasn't going to like hearing it.

"Well?" I demanded.

Her pink lips pressed together while she assembled the thoughts in her head. She blinked when the decision was made, and the statement poured from her. "I think James DuBois is planning to write a book about you."

The sounds around us of conversations and cutlery against plates fell silent in my ears. I'd heard exactly what she'd said, but my mind refused to accept it. "Excuse me?"

"James DuBois," she repeated. "He wrote *The School for Scandal*, about the rich parents who bought college admissions for—"

"I'm aware of who he is," I snapped. It was impossible not to know. The marketing budget must have been six figures for the book because it was everywhere. It had spent weeks on the *New York Times* bestseller list.

Moreover, I existed in the same circle as some of the people who'd been named in DuBois's book. Not friends—because few people earned my respect enough to be considered friends—but they were acquaintances, at the least.

The idea of anyone writing a book about me left a sour taste in my mouth, but the thought of James DuBois applying his considerable investigating skills to my life made my chest tighten to the point of discomfort.

"No," I snarled. I'd suffered enough scandal for three lifetimes, but there was more still hidden in my past. I wouldn't let him near me and had plenty of resources to ensure he dropped it. "I won't allow it."

Miss Alby's face skewed. "You can't stop him."

"My money says otherwise."

She sighed like I was being foolish. "I mean, sure, you can make it difficult for him. Send the cease and desist letters, get the lawyers involved. But the story will come out, whether you want it to or not."

The band around my chest tightened further, making my breath go shallow. I despised both my reaction and the truth I begrudgingly knew she was speaking.

"How," I kept control of my voice, since it was the only thing I could control at this moment, "did you come by this information?"

She tipped her head down, tucking her chin to her chest, and stared at me with glittering eyes. "I'm not sure what it is, but people have a habit of confiding in me. They like telling me their secrets."

Despite my unease, an unavoidable spark of interest flickered in me. "Is that so?"

"Yes, Mr. Hale." The corner of her mouth lifted. It wasn't enough to classify as a smile, but it threatened one. "I know everything that happens in Cape Hill."

There'd been a time when the same could have been said of me, but that awful morning years ago had changed that.

"Which is why," she added, "you have a problem."

I kept my face plain, but my heartbeat quickened.

After my wife's death, I'd been charged with involuntary manslaughter. The best attorneys money could buy had told me I had a strong defense, even with the video of me pushing her over the balcony railing. They wanted to argue I was in emotional distress after the contentious boardroom meeting. That I feared both my son's and daughter-in-law's lives were in danger. Or that the shove I'd given my wife was simply aggression and a desire for distance, not to send her plummeting to her death.

More than two years had passed, and I still didn't know if any of that were true. I'd lost control of myself, and when I tried to remember that moment, it was only a hazy fog of chaos.

The lawyers wanted to argue my case. They were confident they could get me acquitted, but instead I'd taken the plea deal to spare a trial. I'd already unleashed enough scandal to mar the Hale name—I couldn't risk everything coming out and watch it destroy my legacy.

Yet Sophia Alby was staring at me as if she'd already taken a thorough look at the skeletons hidden in my closet. It made my hand instinctively curl into a fist.

"Whatever it is," my tone was cool, "you think you know about—"

She waved a hand to stop the threat I intended to issue. "What I know doesn't matter," she said. "But controlling what DuBois knows? That does."

It was rare when people surprised me, but she'd accomplished the feat. It took me several moments to adjust to the unfamiliar sensation. "If he were to pursue a story about me, then, you're correct. It would."

She nodded, seemingly to herself, making her golden hair shimmer once more. "So, I came here to make you an offer."

"Ah. This is where you extort me for money."

"Um, no." Her eyes lit with amusement. "I'm an Alby. I have plenty of money of my own."

I was aware, as most of it had come from me.

Money was the easiest solution. It solved all problems, so my patience wore thin. "Then what do you want?"

Her gaze left mine and drifted around the room, taking in the power players of Boston who largely ignored us. When her focus finally returned to mine, there was a hard edge ringing her eyes. Her voice dipped low. "To the world, you're a villain. What if you could rewrite the story and become the hero?"

I drew in a slow, deliberate breath. "That's not possible."

"Why not?"

"Because, Ms. Alby, I'll never be a *hero*." The taste of the word was unpleasant.

I'd accepted long ago that no matter what I did, I'd never be seen as anything other than a villain . . . not by the people who mattered to me. I'd saved Marist's life on more than one occasion, and still she hadn't chosen me.

"You don't actually have to become a hero," she said, as if it were easily solved. "History is written by the winners."

"That may be true, but I fail to understand what you're suggesting. Why would I care about being a hero?"

She grinned. "Because no one wants to read a boring story about a good guy." Her shoulders straightened as she arrived at the heart of her proposal. "I know every secret Cape Hill is hiding. Let me use them to help you shift the spotlight away before DuBois finds all of yours."

I didn't trust her bizarre offer. "And what would you get out of this arrangement?"

Pride flared in her eyes. "I control what information gets out."

I was sure the faint smile that drew across my lips contained no warmth. She wanted to control the narrative so she could weaponize it, and I could respect that. "You want to shift the spotlight," I said, "so you may focus it on someone else."

There was a sharp intake of breath, telling me not only was I right, but that I'd caught her off guard.

"Yes," she said softly.

I was curious to know who she disliked enough it made her willing to face me down. "Who?"

She shifted uncomfortably in her seat. "That's not important."

"And yet your non-answer tells me otherwise." Annoyance

slid hotly down my spine. I didn't care for the way she tried to lure me with information like a worm on a hook.

Her gaze slid away from mine. "Maybe we can talk about it if you say yes."

I cut off my dry laugh before it escaped. "No."

Her attempt to brush off my statement was decent. "You need an assistant."

This was true. My previous assistant was no longer available, and I hadn't found anyone to replace Nigel since I'd been released. But this girl sitting before me was . . . unacceptable. She was too young, too spoiled, too *distracting.* "No. Tell me who you want to destroy."

She frowned, and I found it displeasing on her pretty face. "I don't want to destroy anyone."

I waved a hand to push away her statement. "Tell me who you want to shift the focus to."

She sighed. "No."

"Why not?"

"I have my reasons."

The desire to know was strong, but my irritation outweighed it. "While I appreciate the information you've passed along about DuBois, if you wanted a job, Ms. Alby, you went about it the wrong way."

Finally, the fear I was accustomed to seeing in other people's eyes seeped into hers. "I can help you." She amended her plea by adding, "We can help each other."

This time I didn't bother stifling my incredulous laugh. "You?" I shook my head as my tone filled with condescension. "I don't have any interest, plus I don't need help. Even if I did, I highly doubt you could do anything for me."

Fire burned inside her, narrowing her eyelids. "I have a lot more power than you think."

"Is that so?"

Her ruby red manicured nails flashed as she tucked a lock of hair behind her ear. "Do you remember when HBHC's stock fell right after Royce got his seat on your company's board?"

I clenched my jaw. Of course I did. When I'd been the CEO of the Hale Banking and Holding Company, I'd led my family's company out of the Great Recession and tripled the shareholders' investments. Even now, I monitored every dip and peak in the stock price religiously.

Ms. Alby's expression was proud. "I caused that."

This girl was taking credit for something so far beyond her capabilities it was utterly ridiculous. My voice froze over. "HBHC is the eighth largest bank in the world. If you believe you—in any way—manipulated its stock price, you're not only mistaken, but delusional."

She didn't blink. "I did it," she said, "and it was easy. I repeated one conversation I'd had with Marist to a few key people, and that rumor? It sent your shares tumbling."

My daughter-in-law's name was a trigger, and anger welled inside me, pushing against the dam I'd created to keep myself from losing control. Pressure was building, but I'd have to find release elsewhere later.

I drew in a deliberate, calming breath. "Even if that's true, it'd be foolish to try it again. I still control the largest stake in HBHC, and as I'm no longer on the board, I have more time to pursue my interests." My gaze drilled down into her, and she wilted beneath it. "You do not want to become my focus, Ms. Alby."

"No, I don't," she said.

It rankled that I couldn't do anything about what she'd done. There was no punishment or retaliation I could dole out. It was likely she'd been a pawn in Marist's game, anyway, and I should direct my anger there. Not that I could. My daughter-in-law had done whatever she could to outplay me, and I respected that. We Hales understood it was win at all costs.

My tone was measured and even. "If you're half as smart as you think you are, then you know I'll come after you with my considerable resources if you meddle in my family's business again."

Ms. Alby's throat bobbed as she swallowed hard. "I get it. I just wanted you to understand what I'm capable of. What I can bring to the table."

I clenched my fists tightly then let the tension release, using the action to disperse emotion. "I've heard your proposal." I straightened in my seat and spoke with finality. "And I decline."

Her lips parted in surprise. This was not the answer she wanted, and without it, she looked lost. Until this moment, she'd been so sure of herself, and when her confidence flagged, it exposed her raw innocence beneath. Her father wasn't an attractive man, but luckily, Sophia Alby had always favored her mother and now surpassed her. The uncertainty in the girl's eyes made her look younger, and vulnerable, and the man I'd been before would have exploited it in every way possible.

Instead, I forced myself to ignore her stunned look and glance down at my Cartier watch, which had been an anniversary gift from my first wife. "How much longer does your father intend to keep me waiting?"

"He doesn't know you're here yet," she said softly. "He thinks he's meeting you at twelve-thirty."

"Excuse me?" I'd set this lunch appointment at noon to maximize visibility to the rest of Boston's elite and remind them I still existed.

She pushed back from the table and stood, and I was already halfway out of my seat before I recognized habit had forced me to give her this courtesy I wouldn't have otherwise. At least it allowed me to use my height to my advantage. I towered over her, and it drew her gaze up.

"My father will be early for a meeting with you, so I'm sure he'll be here any minute." She licked her lips nervously. "You'll change your mind, Mr. Hale. You'll find I . . ." She tilted her head and gave in to a shrug. "Well, I tend to get my way. Like when I asked my father's assistant to push his schedule thirty minutes. Or when the maître d' sat me at your table when I didn't have an invitation."

Her words hadn't finished settling on me before she pulled a card from her purse and dropped it on the table.

Brightness lit her eyes, and her mouth widened into a soft, disarming smile. "My phone number and email, for when you're ready." She turned to leave without a farewell.

Competing thoughts warred in my mind as she departed, but when my gaze latched on to the bare sliver of her back, everything else faded. The dress she wore was professional and demure from the front, but like her, it held back a secret from me. I couldn't stop myself from admiring the strip of pale skin and the long line her spine carved down the center of her body.

It was like sculpture. Flawless. Beautiful.

For one long moment, I *wanted* her.

More than three years spent lusting after Marist, despite every attempt not to, so to suddenly feel a tinge of interest for someone else . . .

The power of it made me brace a hand on the back of my chair and grip it so ferociously, I expected it to splinter beneath my grasp. This reaction was inappropriate and unacceptable. The spell Marist held over me was broken, but I wasn't recovered. I was merely a man weakened by starvation, eager for any morsel of food, even if it was to my detriment.

She was just the first woman to genuinely smile at me in years. That was all this was.

Sophia Alby wasn't anything special.

Yes, she'd sat across from me and tried to hold her own

when few people in this world had, but she'd failed to get what she'd wanted from me, hadn't she? I could respect how she tried, but not her failure.

My gaze drifted down to the card on the table and her neatly printed information in black ink.

Had she failed?

Perhaps this had been her opening salvo, a kickstart to negotiations.

I snatched up the card and tucked it into the interior pocket of my Brioni suit coat, intrigued at the concept this could be a game. If so, I'd change the rules to ensure we were playing on my terms and not hers. I'd make it so my win was inevitable.

And I would learn every secret she was hiding.

As my driver pulled up to the house, a strange sensation of wastefulness settled on me. The Hale estate had been in my family for more than a century, and each generation had put its mark on it, adding to the sprawling grounds. My grandfather's addition was the stables, and my mother's had been the hedge maze.

I'd been so involved in my work, I hadn't done much to improve the family home yet. Currently, the only legacy to my credit was that I'd likely be the last Hale to live here. I'd driven everyone else away.

Twenty thousand feet of living space were mine, and mine alone.

Which I despised. My son was supposed to raise his children here, but Royce didn't trust me within a hundred yards of his wife. My youngest son, Vance, had moved out late last year, claiming the commute to Boston was eating into too much of his time. He was in his final year at Harvard Law, and although that was demanding, I suspected my impending return had been a factor.

I exited the car and stood on the marble steps, gazing up at the dark windows of the impressive house. For the last two years, I'd wished for nothing more than to be alone. Now the vast freedom and emptiness were unsettling.

It was cold in the entryway, but that was the way I preferred it. Sleep never came easily for me, which meant exhaustion could strike without warning, and I'd found it easier to fight it off if I wasn't comfortable.

The cold kept me alert and sharp.

There was no staff to greet me at the door, which I also preferred. A man unwilling to hang his own coat was either lazy or inefficient, or both.

It was late afternoon, and the springtime shadows were long across the inlaid hardwood floor. I climbed the grand staircase that branched halfway up in two different directions. A portrait hung there once at the split, but Alice's actions had torn apart our family beyond repair, so I'd done the same to the painting.

The bare space bothered me, but I wasn't sure what to replace it with, and apparently Royce hadn't any ideas either during the time I was away. I reached the landing when a woman appeared at the top of the steps and gave a sharp noise of surprise.

"Macalister," she said.

It was infuriating the way my pulse beat erratically at the sight of her, even with her ridiculous black-green hair.

My body began to heat, but my voice stayed cold. "Marist," I answered.

TWO

MACALISTER

MARIST HALE'S TRESSES WERE THE COLOR OF DARK MOSS, although she would have preferred I compare it to Medusa's snakes. My daughter-in-law was so taken with Greek mythology, I'd read several of her books to try to understand the fascination. She saw herself as the fearsome gorgon who could turn men to stone, which correctly applied in this moment.

My feet were rooted to the carpet.

"Why aren't you at the office?" I demanded. "Are you unwell?"

"I took a half-day." Her gaze darted away from mine. "I didn't think you'd be home until later."

Meaning she'd tried to avoid me. I disliked that, but my enjoyment at seeing her overruled it. "My lunch appointment ran long, so I canceled my other meetings."

No longer frozen in stone, I resumed my climb of the steps. She'd said *I* and not *we*. Was she here on her own?

I asked it casually. "Where's Royce?"

She didn't want to admit it. "Prague."

It explained why she looked so nervous. She'd visited me once a month while I was away, but we'd been surrounded by guards and prisoners and other visitors. We'd never been alone, not since that elevator ride up to the board meeting. I'd taken her hand then in a moment of weakness, and again later that day to help save her life.

We hadn't touched since, and I'd come to terms with it. After I'd helped Royce pull Marist to safety over the balcony, I'd had to let her go completely. She saw herself as Medusa, but I saw her as the powerful goddess Nyx, and if I continued down the dark, wrong path I'd started years ago, she'd be my destruction.

Even if what I felt for her was love, it had to come to an end.

"What brings you here?" I asked, joining her at the top of the stairs.

She eyed me warily as if I might suddenly lunge at her. But then a line creased between her eyebrows. "Lucifer."

I paused. "Excuse me?"

"The cat," she clarified. "He's been throwing up and ripping out chunks of his fur on his legs. Maybe there's something in the carpet in our new place he doesn't like. I don't know for sure, but he hasn't handled the move well at all."

I blinked slowly to illustrate my indifference, and it prompted her to continue.

"I brought him back." She lifted her chin in an attempt to look confident. "He's already curled up on his favorite chair in the library."

"You brought your cat to my house for a visit?" I patronized.

She scowled like I was the one being unreasonable. "This was his home. He wants to stay here."

The word cracked through my mind like a bolt of lightning. *No.* That cat was a constant reminder of her and Royce, and everything I couldn't have. "I do not care what your cat wants."

Marist's sigh was heavy with frustration. "I know you don't, but Royce is hardly home as it is, and once he's the chief operating officer, it'll be worse."

I straightened. "Allen's naming him COO?"

"At the end of the third quarter."

Judging by her guarded expression, she expected me to be upset about this, but . . . I wasn't.

"Good," I said. "He deserves it, and that puts us one step closer to a Hale resuming the top role at HBHC."

My offhanded compliment surprised her.

As a pleased look warmed her expression, it was contagious, and when I felt the urge to soften, I railed against it.

"But the cat leaves when you do, Marist. I hate the thing."

"I don't believe you." She put her hands on her hips, and a triumphant smile burned on her lips. "I saw you petting him once, remember?"

Irritation coursed hotly through my system.

"*Once,*" I emphasized, but it did no good. She'd caught me on one of the rare occasions when I'd decided to stroke the cat behind the ears. I'd found the animal's rumbling purr oddly soothing.

"You were smiling," she said. "And you *never* smile."

I didn't like her accusation. Everything I'd worked toward—all that I'd ever wanted in my life—had vanished in an instant. My entire world had fallen apart.

"I haven't had much to smile about recently," my tone turned cruel, "but I'll take your note and make sure to put it on my schedule."

Tension held her posture stiff. "You don't even smile when you beat me in chess anymore."

"Because you let me win," I snapped. "There's no victory in your pity."

Marist shook her head. "Like I told you last time, you're giving me too much credit."

We stood across from each other at an impasse, and the silence between us amplified in the tense air, building toward a breaking point. I'd lied when I said I'd been forced to cancel my afternoon meetings. I'd come home to achieve release. It meant I needed her gone from my home so I could cast her out of my thoughts, which was impossible to do while I stared at her.

She abruptly whispered it. "I'm sorry I didn't come that last month for our match. I tried to, but—"

"I know." An uncomfortable sensation, not unlike pain, gripped my chest.

One afternoon a month, she'd drive an hour down to the correctional facility in Norfolk where I was held, and we had played our game with the prison's chipped chess set. The first few visits were painfully uncomfortable for both of us. My pride didn't want her to see me like that, but I couldn't deny her. I badly needed the mental escape she provided.

I'd confessed in an email to Royce how her visits were keeping me grounded during a difficult time. They'd become a bright spot to look forward to every month, and he'd indulged me and allowed it. He trusted me around his wife when other people were present, but Royce and Marist had moved out the day before I'd been released, taking an apartment in Boston close to HBHC headquarters.

Either Marist hadn't heard me, or she felt compelled to keep going. "I wasn't allowed to wear any jewelry except my wedding ring whenever I visited. I knew that was the rule." It was unsettling how she sounded ashamed when she had no reason to. "I thought I'd taken it all off, but—"

My gaze slipped down to her right hand and the blue sapphire nested between two diamonds. "You forgot about Julia's ring." I frowned. It wasn't my first wife's ring anymore, it was Marist's, and I needed to correct that. "I misspoke. The ring I gave you."

"I wear it all the time," she said softly, and I appreciated it.

I was intelligent enough to know she wasn't wearing it for me. The ring meant a lot to Royce, but I was pleased, regardless. I'd made several poor decisions when it came to Marist, but this gift wasn't one of them.

She grasped the ring and worried it between her fingers. "They wouldn't let me put it in my car and come back without it." Anger swelled in her voice. "They said I was trying to bring in contraband, and I could try my visit again next month. The guard wouldn't even let me tell you what happened, the asshole."

A different kind of pressure built inside me as I recalled the memory. Violent and dark. I'd waited for hours, worried something had happened when she hadn't arrived for the visit. I'd had no way to contact her or Royce. No way to know if she'd been involved in a car accident on the drive down, or simply forgotten her promised visit. All my freedoms had been taken away, and the powerless sensation was the cruelest form of torture during my two years of incarceration.

"You knew, though?" she asked, relief streaking across her expression.

"One of the guards told me eventually."

He'd bragged about it, hoping to provoke a rise out of me. Every person in the Norfolk prison thought they knew how much I was worth, and the guards often enjoyed flexing their power or reminding me of my lack of status while I was incarcerated.

What they didn't understand was the amount of patience I was used to exercising. My situation was temporary, my time under their rule finite. I was built to outlast because my focus never wavered from the finish line.

But the woman in front of me was no longer my goal. She never should have been in the first place.

Marist subtly pulled her chin down to her chest. It was her 'tell' that she was considering something. Thoughts were weighed inside her mind, and it was obvious when she'd made her decision.

"How about we play now?" she asked. "If I win, Lucifer gets to stay."

Satisfaction rolled through me at her offer. I thoroughly enjoyed playing chess, and winning, and it was even better when stakes were involved. We'd played nearly a hundred matches together, and by my count, Marist had bested me only five times.

This would be easy.

I didn't give her an answer with words because it was unnecessary. She knew well enough I'd accept, and she followed me into the library where the mythology chess set I'd had commissioned for her was on display.

Also on display was the black cat, coiled in a ball on the back of the leather reading chair beside the fireplace. A patch of sunlight from the window lit the creature like a spotlight, but otherwise the room was dark. The animal didn't lift its head when we entered the room, but its vivid green eyes opened and peered at us like we were intruding in its dominion.

Perhaps that was what bothered me so about the cat. It exuded an air of superiority, as if it tolerated my presence and it wasn't the other way around. This was my house, and I was its master. Yes, one could argue it was just a simple animal and elitism was the general culture of cats, but this particular one seemed smart. Cunning. As if it had personally judged me and found me unworthy.

I turned on the lamp on the desk, making light spill across the spines of the books my family had been collecting for a century, and watched as Marist strolled to the chair. She set her fingertips on the top of the cat's head and ran them down along its back, causing the animal to stretch out its legs in contentment.

Bare patches of skin dotted the cat's usually glossy black fur, and I didn't care for the way that looked. Even if the thing was irritating, I could recognize it had been a beautiful creature. This version of it made a foreign sensation creep through me. Dissatisfaction?

It grew worse as Marist continued petting the animal and gazed down at it with a smile tilting on her lips. It was a look she'd never given me. One that spoke about how much she loved the animal.

She'd brought it to my house hoping to ease its distress, willing to put its happiness above her own. When was the last time I'd done that?

Not since Julia died.

My wife's sudden death had taught me how fleeting life could be, and I realized I was in charge of my own happiness. Whatever I wanted, I'd reach for it, and take it by force if necessary. But my ambition had come with side effects and collateral damage.

It was time to reevaluate my goals.

I strode to the side table, retrieved the chess set, and carried it to the desk, depositing it there with a quiet thud while Marist continued to dote on her pet. The cat's purr swelled when she scratched its cheek, and I convinced myself the sound was irritating and not at all pleasing.

I snatched up two pawns, one white and one black, and exchanged them in my hands behind my back. "Choose," I said.

She lifted her gaze to mine, and although she tried to hide it from me, it was obvious how badly she wanted to win the game. It made me uneasy as I considered that outcome. I excelled at many things, but the one thing I hadn't mastered was losing with grace. I thrived on competition, and it wasn't in my nature to give up.

I had on her, hadn't I?

THE REDEMPTION | 21

Marist's attention left the cat and focused solely on me as she walked toward the board. "Left."

I extended my closed left hand to her, turned my palm up, and peeled back my fingers to reveal the white pawn shaped as a satyr. The half-man, half-goat figure was carved from marble, and I was pleased with the weight of the piece. The chess set we'd played with the last time was cheap acrylic.

Everything about this game was a higher quality and far more exciting.

She gingerly took the pawn from my hand as if minimizing the risk of touching me, and a sinister voice deep inside my mind whispered to *make* her do it. Instead, I ignored the voice. We put our pawns on their squares and took our seats across from each other, separated by rows of mythic Greek figures recreated as chess pieces.

As white, she had the advantage of the first move, and she made it confidently. The timid chess player she'd once been in this room was gone, forgotten. I'd taught her well, and Marist had become a formidable opponent.

We were both contemplative in our openings and didn't talk, but as we moved into the middlegame, my competitive nature got the better of me. I looked for ways to distract.

"You're right," I said. "The cat doesn't look well."

"No. He's by himself all day." Marist's gaze trapped mine, weighing me down with her meaning. "He's lonely. I think it'll do him some good to have companionship."

My nostrils flared, and I tightened my eyes with displeasure at her subtext. I wasn't lonely, and even if I were, who was to blame? Everyone had left me. "You're speaking about the cat," I said pointedly.

She acted like she hadn't implied otherwise. "Yes."

Marist had claimed I gave her too much credit, but the opposite was true. I'd spent years underestimating her. Even now,

I'd tried to distract, and she'd reversed it onto me masterfully. I clenched my teeth as she captured one of my rooks, catching me off guard.

That should never have happened. Pay attention.

Sometimes, one mistake was all it took to lose everything.

Thankfully, I was able to get back on track after a few turns, and her eyebrows pulled together in dismay as I took her bishop. She recovered quickly and squared her shoulders, pretending I hadn't undone all the plans she'd made.

It was impossible to tell if she were making conversation, or if there was an agenda buried in her question. "Are you ready for this weekend?"

Confidence ran through my words. "Of course."

I'd invited HBHC's board of directors and their spouses to my home for a morning of skeet shooting on the grounds, followed by a luncheon where I'd announce my return to headquarters.

Immediately after the events of Alice's death, I'd stepped back from the company and put as much distance as possible between us. But I was still the president and the chief shareholder of Hale Banking and Holding, and I would resume working at headquarters, offering my guidance and expertise in a management role.

If any of the men took issue with it, I expected them to make it clear. They could tell me to my face, in my home, how exactly they found me unfit to work for the company bearing my name. I'd use the afternoon to remind nearly all the men who had given them their board seat, and tripled shareholder earnings during my tenure as CEO.

This new position didn't come with much power, yet Royce's reaction had been tepid when I'd explained it to him. However, that didn't mean anything. Like me, my son was excellent at guarding his thoughts. He'd been the one to suggest I wine and dine the board before delivering my news, hoping to make it go over easier with them.

"I'm curious of your thoughts," I said.

Marist's fingers paused on her queen. "About you returning to HBHC?"

"Royce wasn't as receptive as I would have liked."

"Gee, I can't think why that would be." Her voice was dry as she pushed Athena forward, trying to bait me to go after her. But doing so would leave my king vulnerable to an attack by her knight in another set of moves. She pinned her stare on me. "What game are you playing? Are you hoping to get back on the board?" Her voice went shallow, like the idea was so distasteful she could barely utter it. "Are you doing it to try to get close to me?"

"No." The word was forceful enough it disturbed the cat, and its ears went back. "No," I repeated, calmer. "I'm not playing a game."

She didn't believe me. "You're always playing a game."

I used my pawn to take her queen in one swift, deliberate action. Marist's eyes widened as she took in the board, stunned I'd fallen for her simple trap. When excitement flashed through her blue eyes, weakness momentarily took hold. She was so stunningly beautiful, and my son was unworthy to have stolen her heart.

Stop. Enough.

"Check," she said, quickly moving her knight into position.

I could have attempted to run, but I despised wasting time. The outcome was set. I slid my king over one square, and as soon as I lifted my fingers off the piece, Marist was up out of her seat, eagerly moving her rook into position.

Her word was breathless like she'd run a marathon. "Checkmate."

I toppled Zeus over and sat back from the board.

The thrilled smile on her lips froze awkwardly, then died as realization dawned in her. "You . . . let me win."

"Perhaps you give me too much credit."

She shook her head. "I know you let me win."

"How is that?"

She sank into her chair, pleased with the result but not that it'd been given to her. "You're not upset you lost."

I blinked slowly, not confirming or denying it. The girl was clever, and I turned my gaze toward the black ball of fur that would once again be a resident of my home. "Maybe I'm a different man than I was before."

"Maybe you are," she said softly.

The cat sensed I was looking at it and cast its wary eyes on me. It still found me lacking somehow.

Like it didn't believe I'd changed at all.

THREE

MACALISTER

Royce stood at the base of the front steps outside the house, his brown hair ruffling in the late April wind. The sky was overcast and would be a perfect backdrop for spotting the orange clay discs against, and the wind wasn't that strong. Unless it picked up, it was unlikely to disrupt our game.

My son looked tired as he waited for our guests to arrive. He had one arm slung around his wife and his hand sliding up and down her sleeve as if to keep her warm. It was brisk, but not intolerable, and her tailored jacket was wool, so I suspected Royce's gesture was more for my benefit than hers.

He used every opportunity to remind me who she'd chosen.

Lines crinkled at the edge of his eyes. Not with age, as he had just turned twenty-nine—but with exhaustion. The demands our business placed on him would only increase as he climbed in the ranks. I'd done my best to prepare him, or at least what I believed was the best. He'd received far more instruction than I had, but I'd made up for my lack of experience with my drive and determination.

I glanced at the team of staff waiting beside the golf carts to drive my guests down to the field once they'd arrived, and I scowled. The invitation had clearly stated the game was to start at ten. I expected people to be early, and yet no one had arrived.

Royce noticed when I glanced at my watch. "It's early," he said.

Annoyance ran through me. "I'm aware."

"Here comes a car," Marist said, glancing beyond the fountain at the center of my circle drive and down to the long driveway lined with trees.

A black Bentley prowled toward us, and I straightened my posture. Some of these men I hadn't seen since my ousting. A lesser man might have been intimidated, but I was not a lesser man. I was eager to put the past behind us and return to the level of respect I'd once commanded.

I was pleased when the car pulled to a stop and Damon Lynch stepped out, followed by his wife Kristin. Damon had been a fiercely loyal ally when I'd been the chairman. He'd voted with me no matter what because he'd understood his role.

When I went away, he never visited, but I didn't take it as a slight. Partly because we weren't close friends, but mostly because seven months ago, he'd declared he was running for Congress. It was a smart decision to keep his distance from me until I'd paid my debt.

Damon delivered a practiced smile, and it was nearly convincing. He'd make an excellent politician. He was packaged correctly with wealth, looks, a strong background, and little moral conviction. He shook my hand firmly. "It's good to see you again, Macalister."

"Yes," I said quickly. "I wonder if there's any space for Vance at your campaign headquarters."

I didn't mince words, and when I reinforced my point by not releasing my hold of his hand, the smile faded from the future congressman's eyes. "Sure." His voice was less convincing than his smile had been. "We'd love to have him as part of the team."

"Excellent." My youngest son hadn't inherited my head for numbers, but instead his mother's charm. We'd long discussed Vance's future in politics, and my aspirations for him reached toward 1600 Pennsylvania Avenue. Working for Damon's campaign would be the perfect first step in his career.

More cars arrived, and after Royce and I received them, the board members and their wives were ushered to a golf cart and whisked down the lawn, disappearing behind the stables in the distance.

We were only waiting on Mr. and Mrs. Powell when a silver BMW barreled up the drive and sped around the fountain, braking to a hard stop beside me. Displeasure dug into me, and I seized the passenger door handle to reprimand the driver—

The woman who stepped out of the back seat was dressed head to toe in black. Her long coat was wrapped around her, belted at her narrow waist, and poised over a pair of heeled boots that looked as expensive as they were impractical. The single dark hue of her clothes exaggerated the contrast of her honey-colored hair and ruby lips, but I ignored how striking she was. Exasperation twisted so violently inside my chest it was difficult to find words.

"Ms. Alby," I leveled the full power of my gaze on her, "your trip is wasted. My decision on your proposal was final."

Her red lips spread into that dazzling smile I found both enjoyable and infuriating. "I'm not here to change your mind." She skewed her mouth to one side momentarily, reconsidering her words. "I mean, I might be. But that's not why I came."

I still had a grip of the car door, and my fingers tensed to the point of discomfort. My voice was colder than the wind playing with the tendrils of her hair. "What reason brings you here, then?"

"I invited her."

I turned to glare my surprise at my son. Once, he would have lowered his gaze in response, but Royce had found his footing with me. His days of bending to my will were over.

"Why is that?" I asked in careful words, the edges so sharp it made Marist look away.

But Royce wasn't fazed. "She mentioned she was looking for work, and you need an assistant."

I ripped my hand off the door handle so I could ball it into a fist. Ms. Alby and Royce had worked together to orchestrate this setup, and I wouldn't abide. "*No.*"

It was as if she hadn't heard me. Her driver pulled a long bag from the trunk of the BMW, and she took it from him, tossing a polite *thank you* to the maniac who'd screeched to a stop in my driveway. The bag looked designed to carry a shotgun, likely borrowed from her father.

"Why do you have that?" I demanded.

She paused, and her gaze darted to both Marist and Royce. "Aren't we shooting skeet today?"

"Only the men," I said. "The women don't."

"Why?" She blinked. "Afraid they'll beat you?"

Marist made a sound like she'd strangled back a chuckle, but my tone patronized. "Hardly. They're never interested."

"Well, I'm interested. Are you any good?"

Ms. Alby's cavalier question bordered on rude. Of course I was. I excelled at whatever I put my focus on. "No," my chest lifted with pride, "I'm excellent."

"Yeah?" Her attention dropped to the bag, her hands gripping the straps, and she appeared lost in thought. Abruptly, her head snapped up and her gaze locked on mine. "How about a deal? We can play each other. If I beat you, you accept my offer."

Interest sparked inside me, but I squashed it down. "What will I get when I win?"

It was as if she hadn't considered that probable outcome. "Then . . . I won't make my offer again."

"And you'll leave," I added.

She shrugged. "Sure."

I strode toward her and slipped a hand around her elbow, not caring that I didn't have permission to touch her. Her coat was a thick barrier between us, and my touch wasn't harsh, but her blue eyes widened as she stared up at me. She'd shown up uninvited, as far as I was concerned. This was my house, and therefore it would be my rules, and I could kill two birds with one stone.

My voice dipped low. "And you'll tell me whose secret you were hoping I'd reveal."

Her breath caught and hung between her parted lips. Leaving was one thing, but the stakes were suddenly *much* higher for her. Of course, they were nonexistent for me. In the unlikely event I lost, I'd be saddled with an assistant who I would immediately find cause to fire.

I didn't make deals unless I knew I could live with either outcome.

For a moment, she considered retreating, and my curiosity intensified. At best, she could put off the inevitable. I'd find out her secret, one way or another.

I tipped my head down toward the bag in her hands. "Have you shot that thing before?"

She hesitated. "No."

It was as I suspected. She'd shown up with her father's shotgun wearing heels the spring sod would devour, making for poor footing. The recoil from her first shot might knock her right off her feet.

That thought caused a strange feeling, and I didn't care for it. I wanted to win, but for once it seemed unlikely I'd find enjoyment in humiliating someone else. I appreciated her tenacity; that had to be all this was. I respected Ms. Alby for not accepting *no* the first time she'd presented me with her offer.

Her expression firmed up with determination, and she shook off my hold. "All right. Let's go."

We'd made a wager, and it was important to me it be sealed properly. I tugged off my glove and extended my hand.

She gazed at it like it was a trap. But she slipped her soft hand into mine, and as I clasped her palm, an odd thrill radiated out from where we were joined. Electricity buzzed as I held her hand longer than I meant to, and far longer than was appropriate. But it pleased me when a flush washed across her cheeks and her gaze broke away from mine.

Whatever this energy was between us, it affected her even more than it did me.

I let go, tugged my glove back on, and turned toward the waiting golf cart so I could savor her reaction without her witnessing it. It was incredibly flattering to know I could still cause that type of response in a woman, especially one so young and attractive.

"Royce," I said, "stay here to greet Mr. and Mrs. Powell and come down with them." I tilted my head back toward the girl standing awkwardly beside her car, holding on to the bag as if it were already becoming heavy and tiresome. "Come along, Ms. Alby. This won't take long."

My son's face was flat. "No, it won't."

She followed me, her boots clacking against the stone pavers set in my driveway, but when the driver on my staff tried to take her bag to stow it in the back, she pulled it tight to her chest. "No, thank you."

The man couldn't help but grin at her when she flashed her radiant smile. I did my best to avoid it and took the passenger seat up front, leaving the entire space of the back seat to her. Once we were off, rolling quietly down the path that sloped across my lawn, that odd feeling returned.

It was bad enough I was going to embarrass her, but I'd have to do it in front of an audience as well.

"May I give you some tips?" I asked.

Confusion crowded her voice. "Tips?"

"On shooting. It may look easy, but it isn't."

When there was no immediate response, I craned my neck to look back at her. Distrust filled her pretty eyes. "You want to give *tips* to the person you're playing against?"

I frowned. "You said you hadn't shot before." I gave her a logical reason for my concern. "I'd prefer you not injure yourself on my property."

She didn't just smile, she grinned—and it left me with an uneasy feeling. "I think I'll be okay." She pulled her bag across her lap. "But, yeah. I'd like to hear your tips if you don't mind sharing them."

I explained to her how to determine her dominant eye, and that she'd need to keep both open while shooting so she could track the targets as they moved across the field. I told her to lead. "Shoot for where the target will be, not where it is."

I detailed the rules of skeet and how we'd each get a chance at breaking twenty-five clay targets from different positions around the field.

Normally, I enjoyed instructing. But as she listened, she unzipped her boots, pulled a pair of slim sneakers from her bag, and slipped them on. Then her blonde hair was collected in her hands and pulled back into a ponytail.

The uneasy feeling I'd had before intensified.

We rounded behind the stables, and the playing field came into view. Staff had placed outdoor couches, tables, and portable heaters in a semi-circle for the audience of the game, and currently my guests milled about the area, the wives grouped together and the board members evaluating their equipment and safety gear. The golf cart hadn't yet come to a stop before I stepped out and strode quickly toward the board.

"Gentlemen, take your time. I'll be playing separately first until everyone arrives, and then we can start."

Mitch Vanderburgh peered across the grass and spotted my opponent. "Is that Stephen Alby's daughter?"

Damon's critical gaze focused in on her. "What's she doing here?"

"We have something to settle, but it will only take a few minutes."

I didn't give the men time to protest—not that they would—and when I turned back toward Ms. Alby, a band of worry lashed across my chest. There'd been more than just shoes and a shotgun in her bag because she was currently threading her ponytail through the back of a black baseball cap.

She'd set her bag on one of the tables, and I watched with wary eyes as she fished out more items and donned them. Fingerless gloves. Sound protective earmuffs. Anti-glare shooting glasses. The final item was the shotgun, long and black with one barrel stacked on top of the other, and the white Perazzi logo gleamed along the black tubes.

My shotgun and safety gear were already nearby, as I'd warmed up this morning with my staff, and I hurried now to ready myself. Her practiced efficiency told me I'd made a critical mistake, and when she opened the break-action and loaded two shells into the gun, I grew angry.

"You said you'd never shot before."

She stared at me through her yellow-tinted glasses, and a smug smile teased the corners of her mouth. "Not this gun. It's new. It was a birthday present from my parents."

She closed the break with a loud click, the sound putting a period on the end of her statement, and my stomach knotted. People didn't give a thirty-five-thousand-dollar shotgun as a present unless they were sure the recipient would know how to use it.

I clenched my jaw. "I've already warmed up. Would you like to take a few practice shots?"

"Nope." She pointed the barrel to the sky and rested the butt of the stock against her hip. "As host, you're going first."

My mind was filled with outrage at her command and the way she'd mislead me. But my body ignored it and flooded with a much different emotion—pure, hardwired lust. On a basic level, it was the visceral male response to an attractive woman holding an impressive weapon. But above that, it was the power and confidence she exuded. Her expression screamed she planned to destroy me.

Sophia Alby had played me exactly how I would have manipulated her if our roles had been reversed, and as much as I disliked it, it was impossible not to respect it.

It took me much longer to load my shotgun than it should have. Anxiety made my skilled fingers fumble. When it was done, I walked to the starting station and gazed across the lawn to the trap houses that would launch the orange, four-inch clay discs. The one on the left, the high house, would be the first throw, followed by a single launch from the low house on the right.

I adjusted my stance on the temporary flooring that had been put down over the newly green grass. Spring had come, and the flowers in the gardens were beginning to bloom, and I'd considered ripping them all out and paving over the colorful reminders of the wife who'd planted them there. I forced the distracting thought from my mind. The only thing that mattered now was winning. I wasn't about to be embarrassed in front of my own people.

The shotgun wasn't heavy, but tension clung to my fingers as I visualized my shot and stood in the ready position with the gun angled in front of me. I wasn't allowed to bring it into firing position until the bird had launched. I steadied my breathing and focused on the high house.

"Pull," I said loudly.

The orange disc streaked through the sky, and I brought the shotgun up against my shoulder, tracking the bird's path until I understood it, and squeezed the trigger. There was a puff of orange dust as the clay shattered, but I didn't breathe a sigh of relief until the low house launched its target, I pulled the trigger, and a second cloud of orange burst in the sky.

I broke open my shotgun, pulled the empty shell casings out, and reloaded. This time when I called for my shots, they'd launch at the same time, which would cut down on how long I'd have to spot them. Ms. Alby's watchful gaze was locked onto me, but she said nothing.

I settled into my ready position, let out a steadying breath, and called for my targets.

The high house shot was easy, but my tempo was off on the second. I swung the tip of my gun to the right, trying to keep up, but lagged behind the bird. So, when I squeezed the trigger, there was no burst of orange to follow my gunshot. I glared at the gray, overcast sky, trying to will it into existence.

I'd *missed*.

It meant I had to exercise my option immediately—essentially a do-over—from this station. If I'd shot a clean set, my twenty-fifth shot was supposed to come from the center of the field at the end. It was intolerable I had missed, not to mention degrading to have to shoot again from the same spot.

I reloaded, readied, and called, and this time I didn't miss when the single skeet from the low house arced across the field.

As I stepped out of the way, Ms. Alby moved past me to take her position, her determined gaze focused on the field. It was as if I didn't exist and what I'd shot didn't matter. This was what I enjoyed most about the sport—you weren't playing against others so much as yourself.

It always ensured I had a worthy opponent.

The girl's stance was flawless, and I watched with envy as she practiced her nimble switch from ready to the firing position. She repeated the action several times, like a dancer walking through her routine, moving with an efficiency and grace that had undoubtably taken years to master.

There wasn't a sound from any of my guests as Ms. Alby prepared. Not even the birds in the trees nearby dared sing. The entirety of Cape Hill went silent when her shoulders relaxed, her gun resting in front of her like she'd been born that way.

Her voice was strong and clear. "Pull."

She moved so quickly, it was inhuman. I'd seen great shooters before, but the precision she displayed was on a different level. One explosion of orange was immediately followed by another.

Her reload and reset were as fluid and methodical as everything else she'd done.

"Pull."

In less than two seconds, she misted the sky in the same shade as the tulips growing on the west side of my gardens.

A second game of skeet played out inside me, a series of shots launching simultaneously. Concern I was going to lose volleyed against my interest at discovering her enormous talent. Perhaps interest wasn't the right word. It felt more like . . .

Desire, a dark voice whispered.

No. Absolutely not.

For one thing, she wasn't Marist, and another was my commitment to myself. I was no longer infallible—any hint of impropriety would further damage my reputation and possibly push it beyond repair.

It was undeniable the way my blood burned through my

veins, but it was merely my sex-starved body yearning for what it couldn't have. All cravings left unsatisfied went away eventually.

My shotgun seemed unbalanced as I carried it toward the second station, weighed down with the unfamiliar feeling of playing from behind, and the scrutiny of the board of HBHC. The men were solemn, perhaps not wanting to break my concentration. They were aware I had to focus now. On the ride down, I'd worried about embarrassing her, and now I was in danger of looking like a fool.

Or perhaps the men were in awe of her, as I was, and were enjoying the show.

The second station repeated the same pattern as the first, only in a new location, and this time I hit each of the four targets.

As did Ms. Alby, and despite the cool weather, sweat clung to my temples.

We moved around the stations, laid out in the shape of a half-moon, shooting efficiently and not speaking during the transitions. Neither of us missed. Anxiety grew in my center as the number of shots we had left dwindled. I needed her to make a mistake if I had any hope of winning.

"You're quite good," I remarked as she squared her shoulders to the field and began her process. The shotgun moved from her ready position swiftly to her shoulder, and she spotted the places in the sky where she anticipated her targets would be.

It was absolutely a routine meant to clear her mind, like how baseball pitchers often groomed the mound and took a deep breath before delivering a pitch. Consistency was key, so I did my best to derail her concentration . . . but it was wasted. The girl had shut the world out, including me, as determination burned in her eyes behind the yellow-tinted glasses.

Once she finished filling the air with orange powder, she

turned and delivered a glowing smile in response to my compliment. "Thank you."

Two golf carts rolled down the path, one carrying the Powells and the other Royce and Marist. The two pairs climbed out and made their way toward the party watching from the couches.

"What's the score?" Royce asked.

"Macalister missed L two," Mitch said.

If that surprised my son, he didn't show it. "And Sophia?"

"She hasn't missed any."

Marist's expression skewed and while the volume of her voice was normal, she might as well have announced it loudly for all to hear. "Macalister's losing?"

"At the moment," I growled and stomped toward the seventh station beside the low house.

There were six shots left for me, and the game was more mental than it was physical. All I had to do was stay steady and focused, and I would be fine. Ms. Alby would miss; I was sure of it. Things had a way of working out for me, and if they didn't, I found a way to ensure they did.

"Pull," I called.

The shotgun was reassuring when it was firm against my shoulder, and I squeezed the trigger, enjoying the kick of the weapon when it fired. Overhead, the target split in two. I swung the barrel to the left, sighted the next bird and fired.

There was a sharp intake of breath from behind me. As she'd already demonstrated, Ms. Alby's reaction time was faster than mine. It meant she knew what had happened a fraction of a second earlier than I did.

I'd missed.

Again.

Rage poured through my veins like lava, choking up my system and forcing a red blaze to sear across my mind. How the fuck had I missed? I broke open my shotgun with a violent *crack* and yanked out the empty casings, fisting them uncomfortably in my hand for a moment while I tried to compose myself. The discomfort helped center me.

I could live with the consequences of losing our wager, but defeat? That was much harder for me to handle. There wasn't anything I hated more than losing. All the sins like incompetence or betrayal or death were simply different types of loss.

Ms. Alby's feminine voice broke through my haze. "Do you want me to give you a tip?"

It wasn't clear if she meant her offer in earnest, or if she was rightfully throwing my earlier hubris back in my face. It didn't matter. I slammed new shells into the barrels and closed the break with a sharp snap, issuing the word as cold as the weapon in my hands. "*No.*"

My mindset wasn't right. There was likely a voice inside me warning me to slow down and reset, but my pride was an open wound, and the only way I knew how to cover it was to reestablish my skill. To control and dominate.

"Pull."

The game was mostly mental, and she'd already beaten me. When the target from the high house slipped past me—my third missed shot—it solidified my loss for everyone else. Unless she missed four out of her next seven shots, the great Macalister Hale was going to bested by some twenty-six-year-old girl.

I hadn't shot this poorly in years.

No matter how quickly she moved, time dragged by, slowing with each shot she made. We shuffled to the final position in the center of the field, situated directly between the two trap houses. I finished out the round by hitting my final two targets then stood to the side to watch her as she completed her series.

Her legs were wrapped in black leggings, and the hem of her long black coat flapped subtly in the breeze. When she was my assistant, I'd instruct her to wear skirts and dresses. It wasn't just that I liked my employees to look a certain way, but she had a nice figure. She should be using it to her advantage.

Men became weak around beautiful women.

Even I wasn't immune, and Sophia Alby was a beautiful woman. She was focused and hard now, but once the game was over, I suspected she'd return to the bright, infectious girl I'd met at lunch earlier this week, with curious eyes and a mouth that could twist into debilitating smile.

I wanted to despise her as she made her final shots then exercised her option at the end. A perfect twenty-five, which I'd only completed a dozen times in my life. This girl had done it with so much finesse she'd made it look easy.

Across the lawn, the crowd of guests clapped for her. She nodded her appreciation while her spent casings were removed, and the bent, unloaded shotgun was placed across her shoulders. She pulled down her earmuffs to hang around the back of her neck and removed her shooting glasses, fixing her gaze on me.

As she spoke, her gloves were tugged off and pocketed. "Good game, Mr. Hale. Or should I say, boss?"

She thrust her hand out.

I'd lost, and my stomach was a bubbling cauldron of unpleasantness, but I refused to show it. I warmed up my tone just enough to keep the bitterness out as I took her offered handshake. "It's Macalister. Congratulations, Ms. Alby."

That same spark was there when we touched, and her voice went uneven. "It's Sophia. And thank you."

When she tried to pull away, I locked my fingers tighter around her. "Will you play another round?"

Sophia's lips parted like she was going to speak, but she produced no sound. My hold on her seemed to have a paralyzing effect. It gave me a moment to solidify my plan. The only other person here who had skills like us was Damon.

Was she worried I was going to ask to redo our wager?

"Perhaps we can talk Mr. Lynch into joining us," I added.

She practically jolted with excitement, and it broke loose her tongue. "I'd be happy to."

I ended the handshake, turned, and strode toward the crowd. I'd lost the bet, but I'd do all within my power to even the score. If I couldn't defeat her, someone else eventually would, and I'd enjoy seeing it. "Damon, you'll play this next round."

The scowl that crossed his face was unexpected, but no more than his response. "No."

I pulled up short, stunned. I'd issued an order, and although I was no longer his chairman, I still owned the company where he sat on the board. How dare he refuse? "Excuse me?"

"As fun as it was to watch you do it," he said, "I have zero desire to be beaten by a girl who competed in the Olympics."

My heart thudded erratically as his statement hit me, and my accusatory gaze flew to the blonde standing beside me.

Sophia shrugged as if this revelation wasn't important. "That was a while ago." She tried to continue her blasé attitude, but it came out forced. "I didn't qualify for Tokyo."

I heard every ounce of ache buried in her words. She hadn't qualified, but she'd wanted to badly. Her unachieved desire was . . . relatable. My life's ambition had been to chair the Federal Reserve. Now, it was a goal I would never attain.

"Which Olympics?" I demanded. She hadn't medaled. If she had, Damon would have said so, and moreover, I would have known about it. It was stunning I'd overlooked this detail, but perhaps I was destined to miss more than just targets today.

"London," she said.

There was a vague, familiar feeling like I'd known this once, but everyone's children in Cape Hill were exceptional. They were landing full scholarships to Ivy Leagues, or

winning equestrian competitions, or becoming Rhodes schol-
ars. I hadn't begun using her father as my wealth manager until 2014, either.

"She was also an alternate for Rio," Marist said, her gaze
focused on the blonde.

How fitting. My daughter-in-law was fascinated with
Greek mythology, occasionally comparing our family to the
gods on Mount Olympus, but her friend Sophia was an *actual* Olympian.

"Well, I suppose I don't feel as bad losing to you now," I lied.

Her red lips peeled back into brilliant smile.

She didn't believe a word of it.

FOUR

SOPHIA

MACALISTER HALE WAS JUST A MAN, I REMINDED MYSELF FOR THE third time this morning as I stood in the hallway outside his door at HBHC headquarters. He needed food, and water, and sleep just like the rest of us humans. If I cut him, he'd bleed the same red as I would.

But he was a legend in Cape Hill, and two years of prison hadn't changed that. If anything, his absence had made the idea of him grow larger in my mind. When he walked into a room, heads turned like a goddamn king had just entered.

And now the king was my boss.

His office door was only halfway closed, but I banged my knuckles on it and waited for an invitation anyway.

"Yes?" a very male, very irritated voice came from inside.

"It's Sophia Alby."

He sounded annoyed that he had to say it. "Come in."

The office was large, and the view of the harbor out the floor-to-ceiling window was impressive, but the space inside was barren. The shelves in the bookcase behind the desk were empty, as were the walls. There was a sitting area to the right with two gray couches and chairs gathered around a low table, but the neutral colors only added to the vacant feel.

Although the office hadn't been used recently, I wouldn't call it unoccupied. Macalister's larger-than-life presence filled every square inch. He gazed at my black Chanel suit, and a scowl twisted on his lips.

"You're late."

I glanced at my Apple watch. "You said eight, right?"

It was eight a.m. exactly.

"Yes," he said. "Which means you're late. To be early is to be on time."

I pressed my lips together at his lecturing tone and reminded myself I'd signed up for this. I tried to sound remorseful. "It won't happen again."

That seemed to satisfy him, because he pointed to one of the couches. "Sit down."

As I did, Macalister grabbed a leather portfolio off the desk and made his way to join me. He moved with confidence and ease, looking far more comfortable today in his office and a three-piece suit than he had at home wearing a sweater and slacks.

He was as terrifying and exciting as he'd been before Alice Hale fell from the rooftop of this building. The only difference was his once dark hair was now deeply threaded with gray. I suspected he'd been coloring it before, and after the accident he'd decided to let it go. Or maybe he couldn't touch up his gray when he was in prison.

Either way, the look was totally working for him. Macalister was a bona fide silver fox.

He unbuttoned his black suit coat before taking a seat on the couch across from me, put the portfolio down on the cushion beside himself, and set his gaze on me.

Christ, his eyes. They were slightly more blue than gray, and fucking *intense*. I'd told Marist a long time ago that Royce and his brother Vance were hot, but Macalister was the best of the Hale bunch, and it was still true today.

Of course, I'd always been into older men.

Not always.

I frowned at that unhelpful thought. I needed to focus. The first part of my plan was complete, and now it was time to roll out phase two. I laced my fingers together and set them in my lap as I crossed my legs. "Before I tell you the plan, we should talk about my salary."

I might as well have told him I was illiterate. His broad shoulders pulled back, and he looked down his sharp nose at me. "You are getting way ahead of yourself, Sophia." He picked up the portfolio, tossed it down on the table with a loud thump, and it slid to a stop in front of me.

"What's this?"

"A non-disclosure agreement." He settled back into the couch and cast an arm along one of the cushions, looking like a beautiful advertisement for men's bespoke suits.

I opened the folder. It wasn't unexpected he'd present me with one—well, I had assumed it'd come from someone in human resources and not him personally—but this document *was* surprising. It was excessively long. I paged through it and shot him a glance that read, *seriously?*

His ice-blue eyes narrowed a degree. "This is not negotiable. If you want to work for me, you'll sign it."

Was this a tactic to scare me off? It wouldn't work. "I get it. I know things you want kept secret."

The muscle running along his jaw flexed. Was he grinding his teeth? "Whether or not that's true," he said coolly, "anything we discuss or any conversations you might witness during my employ cannot be repeated."

I nodded my understanding and went back to skimming the document. I had no intention of leaking secrets—and every intention of him doing it for me. As I read, I caught movement out of the corner of my eye. He'd reached into his interior coat pocket, produced a pen, and set it on the glass table with a quiet *ting.*

He wasn't subtle in the way he tried to hurry me along, but I ignored it and kept reading.

Finally, I picked up the black pen accented with gold, scribbled my name on the line, and closed the portfolio. "Salary."

His eyebrow arched. "You told me you have plenty of money."

"I do, but I don't work for free."

"I'm not ready to make you an offer." Macalister's hand on the back of the couch was held loosely in a fist, and he ran the pad of his thumb over his knuckles. It was distracting, and kind of . . . sexy. I forced my attention back to his lips as he spoke. "I don't know your qualifications," he added, "nor have I seen your résumé."

I sat up, my back going straight. "The job I'm planning to do for you isn't something that needs a résumé, but I can prove I'm qualified."

He looked bored. "How so?"

"I know why Mr. Shaunessy wasn't at your house on Saturday."

There was no change in Macalister's demeanor, but he couldn't control the way his chest lifted with a deep breath. "He had a prior commitment."

"I bet he did."

Liam Shaunessy sat on the board at HBHC and had an affair with Alice. He'd slept with his chairman's wife. Now he lived in eternal fear of the day Macalister would come and destroy him for it.

This bombshell didn't have the impact I was looking for, so I dug deeper in my arsenal.

"And I know what used to happen," I lowered my voice to a hush, "when a man was promoted to the board at this company."

It was as if I'd cracked a whip. Macalister launched forward, his spread fingertips on the glass as he leaned over the table and put his face just inches from mine. His expression filled with darkness and silent rage, and holy hell, it was gorgeous. "I don't know what she told you, but I'd choose your next words *very* carefully."

It took a second to figure who he was talking about. "Marist? No, she's never said a word to me."

Not that she would. We weren't friends, and I wasn't sure we ever could be. I'd had to make a name for myself at Cape Hill Prep, and I'd done part of it at Marist's expense. We didn't speak about our time in high school, but I was pretty sure she hadn't forgiven me for it. It left us without friendship, but instead a partnership.

I helped her whenever I could. Sometimes it was beneficial, but it was mostly done out of guilt.

Macalister cautiously retreated to his seat, looking relieved this highly volatile information hadn't come from her, but his curiosity took over. "Who, then?"

I wasn't going to waste a bargaining chip. "I'm qualified, and now I want to talk about my salary."

"All right," he snapped. "One hundred thousand." He switched gears so quickly, it made me uneasy.

This was a lowball opening offer, but Stephen Alby hadn't raised me to be a fool. "That's all restoring your reputation is worth to you?"

"You seem to think I'm incapable of doing that without your assistance."

Macalister's glare was a blade of steel, cutting me down to size, and my voice wasn't as powerful as I wanted it to be. "It'll be harder without it."

Anger made his nostrils flare and his eyes burn. "Are you threatening me?"

"No," I answered quickly. "I'm just being real."

I didn't understand why he was fighting this. He had nothing to lose—except some money—and he was the type of guy who wouldn't flinch at dropping six figures. I swallowed a breath and pushed forward.

"I don't want to work for you. I want to work *with* you. Being your assistant is just my cover. It's an excuse for me being around so I can do the actual work."

He gave me an exasperated look. "And that work is?"

"You don't have any friends."

He leveled his imposing stare and hardened. "Your master plan is to, what? Get people to like me?"

He said it with disgust, but in a nutshell, this was the idea. It was phase two.

"That's part of it, yeah. You want to keep something out of DuBois's book? Then you need to make sure no one tells him anything. Friends don't sell each other out." I'd practiced this line on the drive into Boston this morning. It was a backhanded compliment and stripped the concept down to its bones. "Which means the ruthless and intimidating Macalister Hale will have to learn how to be charming."

His short laugh was empty and intended to make me feel small. "I already know how to be charming, Sophia."

My heart fluttered in my chest. Was I about to wake a sleeping giant? "No, I don't think you do. Right now, the only reason someone would go out on a limb for you is because you leave them no choice. You motivate by fear."

His eyes flashed with heat. He didn't like what I was saying, but he wasn't going to argue with it either.

I gave him my best smile and strived for a light, joking tone, even though I was serious. "You can only terrorize people into loyalty for so long." I gauged his reaction, and when there wasn't one, I softened my voice. "Why don't we try it my way?"

His ice-blue eyes went unfocused, and his gaze drifted from mine, shifting to stare out the window at the coast beyond. "Tell me what you want."

It was impossible to know if he meant my salary, or just in general, but I went with the easier choice. "Five million dollars."

Irritation was slathered on his face as his attention snapped back to me. "That's an enormous amount of money for someone who didn't seem to care about it at all the last time we spoke. I am not a fool. You want something out of this arrangement, and I believe you need me far more than I need you." His expression was shuttered. "Perhaps I shouldn't have to pay you at all."

I swallowed thickly. "I'm risking my reputation to save yours."

"One hundred thousand dollars."

He smoothed a hand down the line of buttons on his suit vest, as if he could brush my request aside that easily. Frustration built inside me, threatening to erupt—

"And the remainder of the five million," he continued, "contingent upon DuBois's book coming out and my satisfaction with its content."

I sucked in a sharp breath. Did he realize how enormous the weight was he'd just placed on my shoulders? I gazed at him and his calculating expression. Yeah, of course he did. Making the money dependent on something I had so little control over was stacking the odds against me.

But it'd certainly motivate me to try, wouldn't it?

"Do you agree?" he asked.

I mustered all the courage I possessed and pretended this would be easy. No big deal. "Sure."

Macalister reached across the table, and as I stared at his

offered hand, my stomach flipped over, filling with equal parts of excitement and apprehension. Both times we'd shaken hands on Saturday, there'd been this strange magnetic pull to him. What if it was still there?

Or worse . . .

What if it *wasn't*?

My mouth went dry as I put my hand in his, and when he squeezed, every muscle in my body tightened in response. God, what was wrong with me? This wasn't normal or right. He was so much older, and arrogant to the point he was rude, not to mention . . . maybe a murderer? Alice Hale's death was an accident, but I was currently shaking hands with the man who'd caused it.

My body didn't give a fuck.

Sparks crackled through our connection, lighting me up, and I prayed I could keep it contained. If Macalister had the slightest inkling of my thoughts, he'd throw me out of his office in a heartbeat. I had to get control of myself. Crushes were for teenagers, and I was twenty-six, not thirteen.

I felt weightless when he let go of me, as if he were the thing tethering me to this world, which may have been true. Walking into HBHC this morning felt otherworldly. It was all shiny chrome and glass in the lobby, full of air and light. Up here near the top floor, it was the opposite. Dark wood and deep colors and partitions to create secretive meeting spaces.

"Now that we've agreed on terms, you'll tell me the details of your proposal," he said, looking completely unaffected by my touch from a moment ago. "Specifically, your plan of action."

I rubbed my palms together, trying to dispel the electricity from my body. "First, you need a date."

Confusion splashed through his expression. This was the last thing he expected me to say. "A date?"

I nodded. "I'm not going to dance around it. You seem like

the kind of guy who appreciates it when people get to the point."

"You'd be correct."

My chest lifted as I took a preparing breath. "We need to bring your stock up, and the fastest way is for Cape Hill to see you with a new woman. It vouches for you and shows everyone it's okay for you to step back into their circle."

Macalister contemplated the idea with unease but didn't rule it out immediately. He delivered the statement flatly. "You have someone in mind."

"Yeah." I shifted on the couch. "Evangeline Gabbard."

He peered at me like I'd lost my mind. "I expect Mr. Gabbard will object."

"It's doubtful. He died last year."

Surprise washed through his eyes. "How? Was he sick?"

"Plane crash."

Mr. Gabbard had been working on his pilot's license, and the small plane went down with mechanical problems not long after takeoff. It left his wife Evangeline widowed at forty-seven and—which most of Cape Hill didn't know—saddled with a charity foundation that was a mess and in debt.

"She's attractive," I ticked off her qualifications, "well liked, and age appropriate. And as I understand it, she's in financial trouble. If you start dating, that tells Cape Hill you've moved on."

Even if it was a lie, we'd need people to believe Macalister was finally over his inappropriate infatuation with Marist. Word had spread like wildfire through the town about his declaration of love in front of the HBHC board. A man coveting his daughter-in-law was shocking, but that had been just one scandal in a day full of them.

He nodded in understanding and asked it like he was repeating a homework assignment. "So, I'm to seduce Evangeline Gabbard?"

"Uh . . ." My brain went fuzzy at the idea of him seducing anyone. "I guess that's up to you. I was thinking I'd put my feelers out and see if she wanted to make a deal. You're a finance guy, and she needs help with hers." I pulled my eyebrows together. "I'm not sure she wants to really see anyone yet. It's been a year, and I know there've been some guys interested, but she hasn't taken anyone up on their offer. It makes me wonder if this arrangement might appeal to her." Meaning it could help get people off her back if she was feeling pressure to start dating.

"This relationship would only be for show."

"Yeah."

He ran a hand over his jaw, letting his long fingers trail down over his high cheekbones, and I abruptly had to avert my gaze. The way he looked while he'd done it was violently sexy.

"All right," he said.

My pulse skittered. "I have the greenlight on this?"

He sounded annoyed he had to repeat his approval. "Yes."

"You were easier to convince than I thought you'd be. Most people don't like being set up on—"

"I am not *most people*." Macalister's posture, even when relaxed and calm, exuded confidence. "What I am is practical, and your suggestion makes sense. You approach first. If she's not open to the idea, then I'll step in."

It sent alarm bells ringing in my head. Macalister's imposing, controlling way wasn't a turn-for on too many people.

Just you, Sophia.

"There are other women we could try," I said quickly. "If it doesn't work out with—"

This was a done deal. He rose from the couch, acting as if I were no longer speaking, and strolled toward his desk. "Coffee."

I floundered for a moment, not really wanting any, but also not wanting to be rude. "Um, sure."

He stared at me incredulously, like I was supposed to be doing something.

Oh. My face turned warm, and I launched to my feet. He wasn't asking me if I wanted coffee—he was telling me to go fetch him some. I pressed my lips together. If I was supposed to be his assistant, I had to play the part, didn't I? "How do you take it?"

"Black."

I suspected as much. Macalister was efficient, no-frills, so it made sense his coffee would be the same. My gaze ran the length of the room, double-checking there wasn't a machine or side bar in here. This office was smaller than I would have expected, but then again . . . he'd only started using it today. It looked like it had been vacant for a while before this morning.

I hadn't had a tour yet. I'd been escorted to his office by one of the security guards downstairs, but I still felt stupid asking. "Do you, uh, know where the coffee is?"

He was masterful at delivering a look that said exactly how irritated he was with me. He flung a finger at the hall. "Be pro-active. I'm sure you can find someone out there who knows."

Right. I went to take a step, but when a man appeared in the office doorway, my heart stopped. My legs turned to stone.

The man lifted a hand and knocked his knuckles against the doorframe to announce himself. He hadn't spotted me because his gaze was set on Macalister, and I foolishly wondered if I stood perfectly still, maybe I could avoid detection.

"Tate." Macalister was surprised to see his son's friend, but not unhappy.

Tate Isaacs smiled, and it was a punch to my gut. I'd gotten nearly everything I'd wanted in my life except for two things—and Tate was one of them. I'd loved this boy once so desperately, my heart still ached when I saw him.

And he wanted absolutely nothing to do with me.

He stepped into the office, looking so effortlessly good it was unfair. His gray crosshatch suit was paired with a brightly striped tie, and he strolled forward with his usual swagger.

"Came to see if the rumors were true," Tate said lightly.

A smile threatened in Macalister's eyes. "I told you someday you'd come work for me."

"Yeah, you warned me." He stopped beside the desk with his back to me, and his voice went uneven. "I never got a chance to speak to you after . . ." His head tipped down. "You've every right to be mad, but for me, it was just business with Ascension. I hope you understand."

Macalister waved a hand as if absolving him from his sins. "Of course. I never thought otherwise." It was clear he didn't want to talk about it. "How are you liking the asset management department?"

Tate's posture straightened as if he'd brightened. "It's busy. So busy, it doesn't leave much time for sleep."

"Good. That's how it should be."

The men fell silent.

Now the conversation had nowhere else to go, it plummeted into uncomfortable awkwardness.

"Well," Tate backpedaled and glanced toward his escape, "I just came to by to say hello and I'm down the hall if you need—"

"Yes." Macalister didn't waste time waiting for Tate to finish his polite offer. "Please help Sophia locate the kitchen." Macalister cast a finger toward me and promptly put his attention on his phone.

Tate's dark eyes went wide when he turned and discovered me frozen beside the couch. I couldn't imagine what I looked like. It seemed very much like he couldn't believe what he was seeing either.

"Sophia?" His word was loaded with confusion and distrust.

"She's my assistant," Macalister said.

I shoved a smile on my face. "Hey, Tate. It's been a while."

"Yeah." He smiled back, but I heard the words in his eyes. *"It hasn't been long enough."* He jammed his hands in his pockets. "Kitchen's down the hall. Take a left by the picture of the Seattle branch." He paused and begrudgingly added, "You want me to show you?"

It came out forced and overly enthusiastic from me. "No, thanks."

I left the men in the office and scurried out into the hall.

Thankfully, the coffee system was easy to figure out, and by the time I returned with an HBHC insulated cup full of black coffee, Tate was nowhere to be found.

Macalister didn't bother looking at me as he took the cup from my hand, causing our fingers to brush. That sliver of contact was enough to warrant his attention though. He eyed me curiously as he took a sip.

"I take it you and Tate are no longer together."

I jolted. "What? No, we never were."

He studied me like a math equation. "Are you sure? I recall the way you looked at him at Royce's wedding."

My pulse kicked. Macalister hadn't been in the loop the last two years, but before that? He didn't miss much.

Well, other than his wife's affair.

"Yeah," my tone was curt, "I'm positive Tate and I didn't date."

"Why didn't you?" He acted like his question was innocent when it was anything but. "You're both young and attractive, and you ran in the same social circles."

I was still off-balance from seeing Tate, and hearing how Macalister found me attractive only added to my disorientation.

I'd been a media darling during my Olympic outing and a homecoming and prom queen. I'd spent my high school and college years believing I was the prettiest girl in the room . . .

although never on the inside. Just on the surface. My ego might have rivaled Macalister's at one point, and by the time I'd graduated with my bachelor's in communications from Columbia, I'd amassed over a million followers on Instagram.

But faceless strangers, who could say whatever the fuck they wanted without consequences, had no qualms about picking me apart. And, Christ, they were good at it. Every decision I'd made was second-guessed or shouted down, every flaw I tried to disguise was amplified in hurtful comments.

I was unwanted, either by my parents, or the boy I was hopelessly in love with, or the people who pretended to be my friends. I was no longer the prettiest girl in the room, and sometimes, on a particularly rough day, I wondered if the ugliness I felt on the inside had crept out and was starting to take over.

"I don't know why we never dated," I answered softly. It was the truth too.

Was it possible Macalister would understand how I felt better than anyone else?

My heart raced as I opened it up and displayed it for him. "Sometimes two people aren't meant to be together, no matter how badly one of them wants it." I watched my words soak in. "And I wanted it so fucking much. Like, an unhealthy amount."

Macalister's gaze was fixed on me like he was witnessing a disaster unfold and he couldn't tear himself away, even when he wanted to.

The office was deathly silent, so I barely had to whisper it. "You know what that's like, don't you?"

I wasn't sure how he'd react. Would he laugh off my accusation? Pick something up off his desk and hurl it aside in anger? Calmly tell me I didn't know what the hell I was talking about?

He stood motionless, trapped inside his body. He could have belittled me or worse—he could have exploited my vulnerability as a weakness. But the gravity seemed to press him into place. The moment suspended between us, thickening until it was hard for me to breathe, and yet his shoulders rose as he took in an enormous breath.

He gently laced the word into the quiet enveloping us. "Yes."

His simple confession, spoken in an uneven voice, nearly broke me, yet made me stronger. It was nice not to be abandoned with my lonely ache. Neither of us had to be alone.

I stared at him with my heart pumping in my chest so loudly I wondered if he could hear it, while I marveled at the sight of him in his tailored suit. He was tall and broad, in excellent shape and had a handsome face. He owned the second largest bank in the country, and at the pinnacle of his career, he'd been one of the most powerful people in the world.

But he was just a man.

One who'd lost more in love than nearly anyone.

The magnetic pull to him when we'd touched had been strong, but it didn't compare to the awareness flooding down through my body now. This connection was a thousand times more electric, and so fierce, it stole my breath.

He felt it too because it knocked him backward a half-step.

Macalister's expression filled with panic, but it vanished as quickly as it had appeared. He lifted his chin and pulled his guard back in place, returning to the calm, controlled man I was more familiar with.

"You were right when you said people like to confide in you." His hands hung at his sides, but his fingers curled into loose fists. "I did not intend to say that."

Perhaps the connection had scared him, but it was too late to take it back. It couldn't be undone. But I didn't appreciate the way he peered down at me now like I'd dug this information out of him against his will.

"I wasn't trying anything. I just wanted you to know . . ." I sighed. "I've been there. If you want to talk about Marist—"

His expression turned stormy. "Don't ever bring this up again, you understand me?"

The harsh words stung like the slap of a hand. "Yes, sir."

I'd disoriented him, and he lashed out, desperate for something familiar to cling to. "Tate is who you want me to ruin in DuBois's book."

Oh, hell no. My own hands tensed into fists. "I don't want to ruin anyone, and let's be perfectly clear. If *she's* off limits?" I glared up at his beautiful and infuriating face. "Then so is Tate."

"Fine." Macalister snatched up his coffee and took a long sip. "Go down to Human Resources and start your employment paperwork. I'm done with you for now."

My mouth fell open, but he sat down at his desk, opened his laptop, and I ceased to exist.

FIVE

SOPHIA

Macalister didn't strike me as a cat person, but there was a gorgeous black one slinking down the grand staircase when I was ushered into the Hale foyer. The cat softly meowed its greeting as it hurried my direction like I was its long-lost friend.

I bent down and wiggled my fingers, enticing it closer. "Look at you. What's your name?"

The cat answered with a deep purr and wove itself around my legs, but there was only irritated silence from Macalister.

I ran a hand along the cat's back and was startled to see the uneven patches of fur on its hind legs. Was the cat sick? I straightened and gazed at Macalister, who was still wearing the same suit and tie from the office today.

"What's wrong with your cat?"

"That's Royce's cat," he clarified.

I couldn't picture Royce as a cat person either, plus . . . "Didn't they move out? He left his cat behind?"

Macalister closed his eyes and pinched the bridge of his nose. "The animal had issues, so Marist brought it back. It's temporary."

Interesting. "Does the 'animal' have a name?"

He sighed. "Lucifer."

A smile warmed my cheeks, and I bent once more to pet the purring cat. My tone was sugary-sweet. "Are you a little devil? You don't look like a devil."

In response, Lucifer flopped down on his side and stared up at me with his bright green eyes.

Meanwhile, Macalister's frustration with me climbed toward the ceiling, and I savored the taste of it. I'd officially been his assistant for ten days, and I'd begun testing my boundaries with him like a child did with a parent.

I was a little surprised he hadn't fired me yet.

"Focus, Sophia," he ordered in a dark voice. It sent exciting shivers down my spine. So far, his bark had been much worse than his bite, and I enjoyed getting him worked up. I wondered if secretly he did too.

I turned my attention back to the sophisticated security system as Macalister synced it with my phone so I could come and go from the house in case he ever needed me to fetch him something from home.

And when that was done, he gave me an abbreviated tour. I'd been in his house plenty of times before, but that had been for Royce's parties during high school, or the Hale-Northcott wedding nearly three years ago. This tour took me into the study, and he showed me where copies of important documents could be easily found in case of an emergency.

More importantly, his tour took me up the stairs, down the hall, and into Macalister's most personal space. *His bedroom.*

The ceiling was tall, the walls were painted a dark gray, and the high king-sized bed was covered in oatmeal colored linens. The room reflected its master. It was masculine, impressive, and impersonal. The sitting area was set to one side, and two green chairs were gathered around a low table.

I wanted to be a professional, but it grew increasingly

difficult as he walked me toward his closet and explained his system for rotating suits, shirts, and ties so he didn't wear the same combinations too often. I kept busy making notes on my phone to avoid thinking about him getting undressed here later tonight.

"Have you eaten?" he asked me abruptly.

"Like, recently?"

His displeased look was rapidly becoming my favorite.

"No, I haven't," I answered.

He pulled out his phone and thumbed out a message. "I'll tell my staff to prepare dinner for two."

It came out before I thought better of it. "You want to have dinner with me?"

Macalister went still. "I'm hungry, and it would be rude for me to eat without offering you something as well."

"Oh."

It was an afterthought for him. "Am I interrupting plans?"

I stared at the pattern in his tie, avoiding his gaze. "No."

"Excellent. We can continue our work over dinner."

We were served dinner in the kitchen, which felt only slightly less formal than the dinning room. Macalister's chef was an older gentleman, and the man explained the meal to us with a French accent that was so thick, I probably would have understood more if it had been in French. It was chicken, that much I knew. But it smelled amazing and tasted even better.

We went over Macalister's schedule for next week, and although we *were* working, I had the strange feeling that it was an excuse so he didn't have to eat all alone in this big house.

"You'll wear dresses or skirts from now on at the office," he decreed as he speared a roasted potato with his fork. "If you need to purchase some items for your wardrobe, I'll provide a stipend."

I froze. "Um . . . what?"

His phone was laying face-up on the table, and as he spoke, he tapped the screen and began to scroll. "I prefer my staff to look a certain way. You may call it sexist, but I'm traditional. You're a beautiful woman, and you should dress to reflect that." He picked up his phone and displayed the screen to me. "Tomorrow, you will wear this."

It was a selfie I'd posted to Instagram before I went to an art showing for my friend Penelope. The sleeveless teal dress was fitted and pleated on one side, with a long pencil skirt that ended just below my knees.

That art exhibit had been *months* ago.

"Okay, wow." I didn't know where to focus first. He was telling me what to wear, but he'd called me beautiful, and . . . he'd gone digging deep through my Instagram feed? "Are you following me?"

He looked at me plainly, telling me I'd asked a stupid question. "You're my employee, so yes. Tomorrow, I have a meeting with analytics that will be quite dry. When you come in wearing that dress to check if we need anything, it'll wake the men back up."

"Again, wow." I'd never experienced such polarizing feelings. On one hand, it was kind of flattering, but on the other, hadn't he just, like, broken the law? In my mind, he wasn't really my boss, but in the eyes of the law he was, and he'd objectified me sexually.

"Does what I said bother you?" His blue eyes sharpened as they evaluated my surprise.

Well, well, *well.*

I wasn't the only one testing boundaries, and if he wanted to use me like that, did I really care? I picked up my knife and cut another piece of my chicken. "No, it doesn't bother me."

I liked his displeased look the best, but his pleased one? It was a close second.

"Good," he said. "Have you made any progress with Mrs. Gabbard?"

I swallowed my bite and leaned forward, whispering it like a closely guarded secret. "I passed her your note before recess and—good news—she checked the box for yes!"

Macalister's jaw clenched in irritation, accentuating his high cheekbones. "Excuse me?"

I dropped the schoolgirl charade. "I had lunch with Evangeline this afternoon. She was receptive to your offer, so I've booked you a table at Marquee for tomorrow night. She'll meet you there at eight."

"Good," he answered.

In the quiet that followed, the atmosphere in the room began to shift, and an unnatural tension took hold in his shoulders.

I hesitated. "What is it?"

"Nothing." He tried to ignore whatever was bothering him but failed terribly. Macalister didn't give an inch or show weakness if he could help it, but he sighed. "I'm remembering how tedious dating can be. I do not enjoy making small talk."

Was this his way of telling me he sucked at it? Because that wasn't news to me. "Yeah, I'm going to suggest you *don't* try to make small talk." There was far too much in his life that was a minefield. "Keep the conversation focused on her. Evangeline does a lot of charity work and sits on a bunch of boards. Talk about that." I gave him a bright, wide smile. "I mean, a man who listens and doesn't talk about himself non-stop? Careful. She might just fall in love with you."

Something suspiciously like sadness curled in his striking eyes but was blinked away. "I certainly hope not."

Was he thinking about Marist? I picked up the napkin in my lap and set it on the table beside my plate, wanting to direct his focus elsewhere. "Don't you think Evangeline is pretty?"

She wasn't as beautiful as Alice, but Evangeline was still stunning, and Macalister's second wife had been a snow queen. Gorgeously cold. Evangeline was warm and genuine, and in my opinion, a nice balance to Macalister's brusque personality.

Plus, she was almost fifty yet barely looked forty. They'd make a great couple.

Jealousy pinched inside me, like a rubber band being snapped in the center of my chest. God, I was ridiculous.

"Yes," he said, "I suppose she's attractive."

What a glowing endorsement. "Not young enough for you?" *Shit.*

Shit! Why had I just said that? Macalister's neck flushed, and his eyes went black. "You're straying dangerously close to the line I asked you not to cross."

"You're right," I said quickly. "I'm sorry. Please forget I said that."

"Perhaps you weren't aware that both my wives were only a few years younger than I was when we married."

Embarrassment drove my gaze to the tabletop. Why did I care, anyway? Half the men in this town had trophy wives. But my offhanded comment must have upset him enough that his guard temporarily went down or he felt the need to defend himself.

"Marist was an outlier," he continued in a bitter tone. "She did not make sense, yet no amount of effort could make me see reason."

I lifted my chin and stared at him in surprise. He'd just scolded me for hinting at her, and now he was volunteering this information? It felt like he wanted me to ask. "Have you? Seen reason?"

I wanted him to be over her, because I understood how hard it was to long for someone you could never have. I wouldn't wish it on anyone.

His expression was resigned. "I'm not proud of how long it took me to see it, but yes. If I'd continued to pursue her, it would have destroyed whatever relationship I had left with my sons, and I'd made her a marked woman. If I didn't stop, it was only a matter of time before I lost her too."

Marked woman? I was so confused. "What?"

Macalister drew in a deep breath, and when his intense eyes filled with emotion, the world around us ceased. His voice was unsure, like it was one he'd barely used in his lifetime and didn't trust it to work. "I've loved exactly three women in my life. The first two are dead, and the last nearly died twice. And I'm responsible for it all."

My mouth dropped open, and for a long moment, words wouldn't assemble in my brain. "You think you're," I took a breath, "cursed?"

He lifted his eyes toward the chandelier hanging over the kitchen table. "This conversation is preposterous." He rubbed his fingertips across his forehead, smoothing away the crease that had formed there. "No, I don't believe in nonsense like fate or curses or karma. I trust in math and logic, but I cannot ignore the pattern that has presented itself."

I struggled to understand. His first wife had been killed when she was thrown from her horse and hit her head. How could he think he was responsible for that? "What pattern? That bad things happen to the women you fall in love with?"

He grimaced. "Thank you for making it sound even more ridiculous than it was in my head."

"Wait a minute." I straightened in my seat as I replayed what he'd said. "Twice? I know Marist almost fell off the balcony, but when was the other time she nearly died?"

He opened his mouth to answer but then tilted his head. "I thought you knew everything that happened in Cape Hill."

Displeasure heated inside me. I couldn't stand the idea of

being kept in the dark. *Never again.* "I said almost everything."

He took a moment to contemplate something. "We'll exchange information, then. Tell me who you want named in the book."

Instead, I pushed back from the table, grabbed my plate, and walked it across the enormous kitchen so I could deposit it in the sink. I'd done it to avoid him, but Macalister did the same, probably as an excuse to follow me. His plate clattered softly in the other side of the sink as he set it down.

"This is inevitable. You realize I won't be able to tell DuBois this secret if you don't tell it to me first."

I leaned back against the counter and folded my arms across my chest. "I'd be an idiot to tell you before we know for a fact the book is happening." And even then, the timing would be crucial. I couldn't tell Macalister until I could trust him not to burn me. "We'll know by Aspen."

He repeated it like he hadn't heard me right. "Aspen."

"Yeah, the Food and Wine Classic in June. I've got a friend who works for his publisher, and she said it's on his schedule. You used to go every year."

"Of course. HBHC is a sponsor."

I nodded. "I bet he's hoping he'll run into you there, and if not, there will be plenty of HBHC board members he can chat up."

He looked less than thrilled at that prospect.

"It'll be fine." I faked a syrupy tone. "Once you two meet, he'll only have eyes for you."

Macalister's expression soured further, but I did my best to ignore it and glanced at the screen of my phone. I was twenty-six, and my parents didn't keep tabs on me, but if I didn't text or come home soon, there was the off chance someone might worry.

Doubtful.

"Thanks for dinner," I said.

He only acknowledged my gratitude with a simple nod of his head.

It felt like our evening was coming to a close, and I shifted awkwardly on my feet, waiting for him to dismiss me. But he just stood there with one hand on the edge of the sink and his piercing blue eyes trapping mine, and my pulse climbed with each passing second.

If I didn't break this spell, I was going to do something foolish. I'd find a reason to move closer to him and try to smell if he wore cologne. Or an excuse to stroke the fine silk of his tie. Or to learn what the rough ends of the whiskers edging his face would feel like against my fingertips.

God, I was obsessed with his jaw.

It was strong and sharp like his cheekbones, and I loved the way it tightened when I said something he found unsatisfactory. I longed to put my hands on it, use my fingers to trace the angle of it. And I'd had fantasies about how his perfect jaw would move when he kissed me.

A little voice in the back of my head whispered I was forgetting something, but when he took a step closer, it drowned everything else out.

"I should go," I said and tried to back away instinctively. Only I was already against the counter, so when I banged into it and the cabinet beneath with a loud thump, Macalister went stiff.

Was that hurt that flashed through his eyes? No, it couldn't be, and it was gone too fast for me to examine it. I had flinched like he scared me, and although he did, it wasn't for the reasons he'd think. It wasn't because he'd accidentally killed his wife or gone to prison or tried to steal a woman away from his own son. And it wasn't because he was intimidating and ruthless and could ruin me.

It was that, despite all of it, I foolishly wanted him anyway. His deep voice was empty. "I'll walk you out."

I wished desperately I could have stayed put. What would have happened if I had? Was it crazy to think he was having similar thoughts to mine, and he'd stepped closer because he wanted to be near?

We marched wordlessly through the house toward the entryway, and as Macalister fished my jacket out of the closet, a soft *meow* drew my attention into the front sitting room. It was dark out, and the wood paneled room was cave-like, but I made out the black coil of fur on one of the couch cushions. My feet carried me toward it.

Lucifer stretched one paw and then the other as I sat beside him and scratched behind his ears. Who was lonelier in this house and more starved for attention . . . the cat, or the backlit man holding my coat in the arched doorway, watching me like I was a puzzle he couldn't solve?

Macalister tossed my coat onto a side chair and moved swiftly toward the couch, only to shoo away the cat with an irked look. Lucifer hopped down with a protesting meow and scurried away, and I threw an accusing look upward.

"Rude."

"I agree," Macalister answered. "This is a priceless antique couch, and he knows he's not supposed to be on it."

It had been lingering in the back of my mind, but his bossy gesture finally broke it free. "You have to kiss her at the end of the night."

He was too controlled to let his entire body jolt with shock. Only the snap of his shoulders gave away his surprise. "Excuse me?"

I swallowed hard, even though my mouth had gone dry. "Your dinner with Evangeline. People might think it's business or you're just friends. You need to kiss her so there isn't any doubt."

Macalister Hale wasn't known for public displays of affection. In fact, in all the years they'd been married, had I ever seen him kiss his wife? I couldn't recall even a picture. Maybe he didn't know how.

God, please don't let that be true.

He stared at me now, his eyes glittering in the dark with an unclear emotion. Displeasure? He did not like being told what to do.

My body was tight with apprehension, and I treaded carefully. "I prepared her already, so she knows it's coming."

His tone was ice. "Did you?"

"She's nervous. She hasn't kissed anyone since her husband, but I told her it would be okay. I mean, I assume it's been awhile for you, but you probably haven't forgotten." The weight of his stare was crushing, and I could barely meet his eyes.

"No." He said it like he was wielding a scalpel and cutting me slowly piece by piece. "I have not forgotten."

As he gathered strength, all my power seemed to slide his direction and my voice became a ghost. "How will you do it?"

"Kiss her?" When I nodded, the cold draft of him flipped on its side and turned to heat. The corner of his sexy mouth lifted in a sinister smile. "I'm not sure yet. The way I do it depends on the woman. How I kiss her will be entirely different, for example, than the way I would kiss you."

I pulled all the air I could find into my lungs in an audible sweep, and my reaction was unmistakable. Victory claimed him and pushed into his expression, but he was controlled as he sat beside me on the couch.

It was the opposite for me as my insides began to fly apart. He was so close, the side of one of his powerful legs pressed against me, and I had to fight the couch to keep from falling into him.

Excited panic gripped me. "What are you doing?"

Shadows played across his face, highlighting his authoritarian look. "Demonstrating."

I turned into a statue as he dragged his cold fingertips across my cheek and threaded his hand into my hair. Static played in my ears and hummed through my body. I was imagining this. There was no other explanation. Like I did with shooting, I'd visualized this moment so many times I'd made it real.

My lips parted, although I wasn't sure if it was to gasp, or say something, or maybe I'd done it subconsciously to welcome his kiss. Or perhaps I was under his power now, and he'd silently commanded it. My eyes fluttered closed as he leaned in and the hand at the back of my head prevented my escape.

His fingers had been cold, but his mouth was hot when it pressed to mine.

And that was all the kiss was at first, just the gentle meeting of our mouths.

But my heart pounded, blood roared through my system, and my breathing went so shallow, I grew lightheaded. Macalister's kiss was like being connected to a power source. The electricity of him raced along my nerve ends and lit me up.

I didn't realize that was only the first wave until his lips slowly teased mine apart and his tongue slipped inside my mouth.

A noise of satisfaction drifted from the back of my throat, and it was all the encouragement he needed to deepen his kiss. His tongue was lush and oh-so-soft as it slid across mine, making a muscle between my legs clench against the ache he caused. His lips controlled. They dominated and took, and I gave in willingly.

I struggled for air while enduring his greedy kiss, which grew more overwhelming with each second. The temperature around us skyrocketed, threatening to incinerate me. Even in my hottest dreams, those kisses weren't half as good as the one he was delivering now. How was I going to come out the other side of it and not be singed?

The desire between us swirled like water circling a drain, pulling me deeper and faster into him with each pass. It was terrifying and fucking thrilling. He wasn't impervious either. His breath had gone ragged, and his other hand slipped behind me, his palm pressed against my back.

My fingers, which had longed to touch, finally got their wish, and I cupped his jaw, my fingertips sanding over his skin along his cheekbones—

Abruptly, Macalister's hand came off the nape of my neck and wrapped around my wrist like a shackle, pulling my touch away from his face before I'd had my fill. Whatever restraint he'd had on himself seemed to break down and dissolve. His mouth turned wild and aggressive as he forced me down onto my back, pinning my wrist to the couch cushion beside my head.

He'd moved us so quickly, it wasn't until I felt the pressure of his knee between my legs that I realized he was on top of me, one leg sandwiched between my thighs. White-hot pleasure burst through me, causing goosebumps to dot my skin, despite the growing heat in the room and the way we were both sweating.

It was awkward on the little couch, and he was huge, but he made it work.

And there was something about the way his strong hand held me down that was dangerous. Powerfully seductive and erotic. His thumb pressed against my palm and dug in, and although I still had one hand free, I felt dominated. Locked in beneath him, completely at his mercy.

It was *exactly* where I wanted to be.

He subtly moved his knee again, rubbing against me and bringing on a new wave of pleasure. His mouth was incessant, alternating between slow and languid kisses to passionate and demanding ones. Thoughts swirled in my mind until they were a bleary mess. All that mattered was that Macalister was now kissing me and that he continued to kiss me forever.

I moaned my satisfaction, and the hand wrapped around my wrist tightened, his thumb pressing into the center of my palm so hard, it bordered on uncomfortable. But I loved it. I set my free hand flat against his chest and enjoyed the hurried beat pounding inside. More proof he was human after all.

But while I was pliant and warm beneath him, the muscles in his frame grew rigid and cold. Something had happened. Maybe he didn't like how I'd discovered a heart lived inside him. When his mouth slowed and began to retreat from mine, I wanted to whine in protest.

The connection of our kiss wasn't just broken, it was severed. He turned and stared at my delicate wrist in his hold, gazing at it with pure confusion, like he hadn't realized he was pinning me down until that very moment.

It made my heart stumble. Had I done that? Made him lose some of the careful control he always placed on himself?

I was flushed and throbbing painfully at the center of my legs as he pulled away and moved to sit as far away from me at the other end of the couch as possible. He stared off, his unfocused eyes seeing nothing and his chest rising and falling rapidly, and he looked . . . drained. As if kissing me had taken everything out of him.

I awkwardly pulled myself up and back to a sitting position. Christ, my legs were shaking. With the heat of him gone, I was instantly freezing and crossed my arms over my chest. This house was a museum with overly enthusiastic air conditioning.

Was he going to say something?

Was I supposed to?

Macalister's posture improved until his back was straight, and he ran a hand over his hair, smoothing the wayward strands back into their perfect place. By the time he turned his head to look at me, his professional veneer was back in place.

Like our kiss hadn't affected him at all.

"That was," I said between still-uneven breaths, "a bit much. I don't recommend you do that tomorrow."

"I agree," he said quietly. "It was far too much."

He was up on his feet before I could process how he meant it. He strode to my coat that had been cast aside, picked it up, and held it open for me.

It was clear he wanted to help me put it on and hurry me along, but when I didn't move, he added, "It's time for you to go."

I clenched my fists as I shot to my feet. What the fuck was this? He just kissed the hell out of me, and now he was throwing me out? I sneered. "Well, there's that awesome Hale charm you're famous for."

That infuriatingly sexy muscle along his jaw flexed.

I ripped my coat out of his hands and pushed one arm through a sleeve as I marched toward the front door. I heard his footsteps and knew he was following, but I wasn't naïve. It was gentlemanly habit, not to chase after me and apologize for being an asshole—

"Sophia."

I hesitated on the landing at the top of the front steps, the chilly spring wind pricking at my heated face. He gazed at me with an unreadable expression.

"You were correct, it had been awhile for me." A slow, arrogant smile spread across the lips he'd used to turn my world upside down just a minute ago. "Thank you for the practice."

SIX

MACALISTER

RELIEF AND DREAD WERE FELT IN EQUAL MEASURE OVER WHAT had transpired on the antique couch in my front parlor. Marist had made me doubt my skills, and now my reputation was tarnished, but my evening with Sophia proved I was still capable of seducing a woman. I was confident if I hadn't stopped us, soon after she'd have begged me to take her to bed.

My trepidation came from the strong desire I'd had to continue the foolishness, and the worry it may not have been much longer before I'd been the one begging, demanding she join me upstairs and stay the night.

It was where I was now, lying in the dark, staring at the shadows the chandelier cast across my bedroom's ceiling. The cat had grown bold over the last few nights. Tonight, it attempted to curl up beside my feet, but I moved them beneath the covers, forcing the animal to the far side of my bed. If it were that desperate for companionship, I'd begrudgingly allow it to be near, but up against me was too much.

The kiss I'd given Sophia had only been to satisfy a curiosity. The signals she'd sent me over the last few days were confusing, and I was out of practice with reading women. I was an observant man, though. I'd catalogued all the times she'd glanced my direction at the office when she thought I wasn't looking. And, of course, there was the way she reacted whenever I touched her.

Like I burned her, and she wanted to burn.

She is too young for you.

I wasn't convinced I even enjoyed her company. She didn't know her place, talked to me as if I were a friend, and at times it seemed she'd go to great lengths just to annoy me. I wanted to reprimand. To correct her behavior. Instead, I clenched my jaw and held my tongue.

It'd given me a headache every night this week.

Now, it had become a pattern. I took a pain reliever, lay in my bed, and struggled not to think about her while I waited for the sleep I knew was unlikely to come. Two years of meditation had sustained me through the most challenging time of my life, but it did not induce so much as drowsiness.

Nothing could quiet my mind.

Since I despised wasted time, I threw off the covers, pulled on a pair of athletic shorts, and stepped into my running shoes. I needed to get at least four hours of sleep to be able to function tomorrow, and the treadmill was the only surefire way to make that happen.

While I ran, I used the time to comb through social media feeds on my phone. I'd been out of the loop but was determined to make it seem like I'd never left, that I'd been at every party and fundraiser. I filled myself in with the backstories of the important players in Cape Hill, studying captions and snapshots of the events others had deemed noteworthy over the last two years.

It was distressing how often I drifted back to Sophia's Instagram page.

She had a feed that would have impressed Alice and

pleased the brand managers at HBHC. All the images had the same tonal quality and consistency, making an eye-catching grid. Sophia's brand was clear and executed with precision. She was the refined socialite, invited to everything and friends with everyone.

She glowed in each picture, even the ones that were candid and she wasn't smiling. She'd posted one this afternoon of her sitting in a restaurant booth, a thoughtful look on her face and a half-eaten bowl of pasta on the table in front of her. Had she asked Evangeline to take this for her, or the waiter afterward?

For some unknown reason, my thumb moved to touch her face, and a white heart blinked on the screen. A frustrated sigh punched from my lungs. She had over a million followers, so it was unlikely she'd notice I'd liked her picture. It was just twelve hours old and had already amassed fourteen hundred comments.

Most were heart emojis or single words like *beautiful*, but one of them caught my attention.

Maybe lay off the carbs.

"Fuck you," I said into the silence of my empty gym.

That person didn't know what the hell they were talking about. I dumped my phone into the holder, ramped up the speed on the treadmill, and stared across the way to the mirror, finding my expression furious. I was covered in sweat and had a sneer on my lips, my feet pounding against the belt and my arms swinging to keep up with the ambitious speed I'd set.

I looked very much like the monster I could be.

The comment became a splinter buried beneath my skin and continued to bother me. I appreciated the way Sophia looked. She had high, full breasts, a narrow waist, and hips that flared. Everything was proportional in her perfectly feminine hourglass, and I found her more appealing than the emaciated look some retailers pushed with their advertising.

The remainder of my run was spent considering how much money it would take to track down the commenter, inform them they were wrong, and extract their apology. Whatever the figure, I could easily afford it. I had to let that knowledge satisfy me instead of acting on it.

Once I was physically exhausted, I shut down the machine, toweled off, and retrieved my phone. I continued to scroll through Sophia's older posts as I made my way up the two flights of stairs and turned in to my bedroom.

My feet slowed to a stop at the picture of her in a pink dress, her arm linked with a black man wearing a tuxedo. There was no need to look at the date to confirm when it was taken. I recognized the sunny background as the gardens on the south lawn of my estate, and furthermore—I was there the day the image had been captured.

It was Royce and Marist's wedding.

I'd either forgotten or never cared enough to remember that Sophia had been the bridesmaid paired with Tate. The photo had been taken as they'd paraded up the aisle at the ceremony's conclusion, and both were beaming a wide smile—although hers outshone his.

I'd been so blinded by my obsession that day, it was hard to recall anything outside of it. This picture was proof I had missed how stunning Sophia had looked. Together with Tate, they made a handsome couple.

Curiosity needled at me once more about why they hadn't dated. She came from a good family, was well-educated, attractive, not to mention she was a former Olympian, meaning she had excellent drive and focus. Perhaps that was his issue. He found her intimidating.

Well, I did not.

She was challenging, but I enjoyed a challenge.

I scowled at myself as I dropped my phone on the charger

and tried not to stumble on tired legs as I pushed toward my shower. The goal was to get it hot, but not hot enough that it'd put me to sleep. I'd rested on the shower bench and woken to freezing water running on me more times than I cared to admit.

Was Sophia seeing someone? There was no evidence of a man in her life on her feed.

I pressed my fingers to the center of my forehead like I could push the question away. All these inappropriate thoughts about her had to stop. They were merely the product of a curious mind weak with exhaustion.

She was helping me restore my reputation, and any kind of relationship, especially a sexual one, would be counterproductive. The last thing I needed right now was to pursue another woman drastically younger than I was. I should be focused on Evangeline, not Sophia. No matter how tempting the girl and her dazzling smile were.

You can't have her.

That, unfortunately, only made me want her more.

As I'd instructed, Sophia wore the blue dress.

When she strolled into the meeting carrying a tray of coffee cups and leaned over to set it on the center of the table, Mr. Parsons lost all sense of subtlety. His gaze washed down the length of her body and lingered on the sculpture of her legs.

A territorial urge, not unlike jealousy, flickered inside me.

It was unsettling. The whole point of her wearing that dress was to make the men look. Why was I now displeased that they had?

Her attempt to ignore me was valiant, but as the day dragged on, I decided I wouldn't allow it. After the meeting concluded, I found reasons to call her into my office. As my assistant, she'd been given the desk just outside my door, and she appeared aggravated each time I'd summoned her.

Did she understand we were playing a game? And if she had, did she realize how terribly unbalanced her forces were in comparison to mine? She was playing against a master. I'd gravely underestimated her talent when we'd shot our round of skeet, and I was eagerly anticipating the moment when our roles would reverse.

I was seated behind my desk, and my tone was unassuming. "That dress looks even better in person."

Sophia paused awkwardly at my unexpected compliment. "Thank you."

She resumed the menial task I'd assigned her of filling my office with the items that had been stored while I was away. She arranged a collection of awards I'd received during my tenure as CEO on the bookshelf, wiping away her fingerprints from the glass when she had the arrangement as she wanted it.

"You liked my Instagram post from yesterday."

My pulse went out of rhythm, then settled back into its steady tempo. "Yes."

"Why?"

There was a myriad of truthful reasons I could have given her, but I went with a lie. "It was a successful meeting with Mrs. Gabbard."

The way she held my gaze announced she did not believe me.

Or . . . perhaps it was something else? She angled her head as if contemplating. "What are you planning to wear tonight?"

I lifted an eyebrow before dropping my gaze to the black, three-piece cashmere suit I wore.

She frowned and abandoned her task, moving toward me. "Stand up."

Her order caused me to tick my jaw, but I found myself

rising from my seat. Was there something wrong with the fit? I'd lost some weight and muscle tone during my time away but had been working diligently to get it back. "This is one of my finest suits."

Sophia held one arm across her stomach and used it to support her other elbow, resting her fingertips against her lips as she studied me critically. I didn't retreat when she reached out and tugged at the knot of my tie, but my body went on alert. As I did last night, I wrapped my hand around her wrist and pulled it away, holding it aside.

"I didn't give you permission to touch me."

Her crystal blue eyes flooded with surprise at my abrupt action and curt tone, but like me, she didn't retreat. Both our gazes slid to my fingers trapping her wrist, and her voice wavered. "You didn't ask permission to touch me last night."

That was easily justified.

"I didn't need to because I already had it." A smug smile warmed my lips. "Tell me I'm wrong."

Her pink lips parted as she sipped in air. It forced me to consider kissing her again. I wanted to examine if her mouth would be as soft and inviting as it had been last night, and if she'd sigh the same way when I slicked my tongue across hers.

She didn't deny what I'd challenged her with. All she did was lower her hand to her side, dragging mine down along with hers since I couldn't seem to pry my fingers loose of her. She stood in perfect submission, allowing me to touch her, and as I watched the bob of her throat in a thick swallow, the desire to kiss her exploded inside me.

This . . . was not part of the plan.

Who exactly was holding the power between us now? I jerked my hand away, finally free of her strange witchcraft.

She blinked rapidly, as if bringing herself out of a trance. "Lose the tie and the vest."

I grimaced. "You seem to be operating under the mistaken impression you can tell me what to do."

Fire blossomed in her eyes. "Did you tell me how to dress today?" She shifted her weight to one side and put a hand on her hip, flaunting her sexy figure. "I wore this for you," she said, "so you'll do this for me."

War broke out in my mind, the two sides battling over her statement. Irritation took offense to her order, but on the other side of the battlefield, excitement was very pleased at her phrasing.

I wore this for you.

Logic became the mediator. I was no longer an expert in what women wanted, so listening to her advice was the sensible thing to do. I kept my gaze locked on her as I grabbed the neck of my tie and slipped the knot free, unthreading the silk from my collar. The patterned tie was discarded on my desktop.

My jacket had to be removed before the vest, and as I tugged one sleeve of it off, the atmosphere in my office began to turn. I wasn't taking off anything of substance, but it didn't lessen the impact. The fact remained I was stripping off clothes under her direction and watchful gaze.

I hung the coat on the back of my office chair, plucking away an errant silver strand of my hair that had been shed on one of the shoulders.

Sophia's pupils dilated. Her cheeks flushed pink, and her chest rose and fell quickly while I undid the buttons of my vest and took it off. She felt the same dark, sexual energy I did. It charged the air like an impending storm. All the conditions aligned to cause lightning.

I folded the vest and set it beside my tie on the desk. When I reached for the jacket—

"Open the top few buttons of your shirt."

She said it in a rush, perhaps hoping I wouldn't pick up

on the excitement lacing her words. It was flattering and enjoyable that I had this effect. Her eyes fervently followed my fingers as I undid my collar, then released the button below it.

I didn't want my question to be solely about my shirt, and I loaded the word with seduction. "More?"

Her chest halted as she held her breath tight in her body. Oh, yes. She wanted more.

It took her a century to answer. "Uh, put the jacket back on."

I did.

A three-piece suit wasn't standard for me—some days I'd forgo a vest. But I believed every suit required a tie. This state of underdress left me feeling exposed and my armor incomplete. Yet Sophia gazed at me as if the years separating us and my past did not matter. She forgot where we were and succumbed to the emotion channeling through her for one brief moment.

Pure lust.

It coated her expression and heated her eyes, causing me to answer in kind.

I'm wearing this for you, I hoped my expression read.

"Good," she breathed. "You look good like that."

"Thank you."

She nodded, turned back toward the shelves she'd been arranging, and promptly ran into the end of the couch. Embarrassment held her shoulders tight to her ears, but she didn't glance back to see if I'd noticed. She was wise enough to know I had.

It was disappointing she wasn't treated to my victorious smile, but I let it go, knowing this wouldn't be her only opportunity to see it.

Marquee was a modern fine dining experience. The space was minimalist, and there was no color palate by design. The room and tables were white and the chairs black. Only the fresh flowers in the centerpieces gave the eye some relief from the restaurant's starkness.

The food was the focus here, as it should be. The head chef had received rave reviews in *The Boston Globe* and *Bon Appétit*, plus a James Beard Award. I stood in the sleek waiting area in front of the host's station and perused the accolades framed on the wall while I waited for my date's arrival.

Heels tapped out a hesitant pattern as they approached. "Mr. Hale?"

Evangeline Gabbard was a pretty brunette. She wore a long-sleeved black lace dress, nude colored heels, and deep red lipstick. Anxiety wove through her eyes, but I didn't yet know if the cause were the evening, or the man she was about to dine with. Perhaps it was a mixture of both.

"Macalister," I announced, doing my best not to sound cold.

"Evangeline." She took the handshake I offered and flashed a shy smile. "Sorry for the clammy hands. I'm a little nervous."

"There's no need to be," I scoffed.

Her fixed smile tried to mask the uncomfortable reaction she wanted to have, and my heartrate stumbled. The very first words out of my mouth had already been a misstep. I needed to correct.

I forced a light tone. "I am nervous enough for both of us."

She blinked her surprise and laughed softly. My lie had put her at ease.

There was no spark in our handshake. It was professional, ordinary, and forgettable. I gestured to the host we were ready to be seated.

"Please follow me," the man said.

We wound through the dining area to a table near the

center. Was this luck, or had Sophia requested this one specifically for maximum visibility? I pulled out Evangeline's chair, and once she was seated, I took the one across the wide table from her.

When she set her clutch on the table, I noted the wedding ring still decorating her left hand. She should have left that at home, because it made it harder to sell this as a date.

"The wine list, sir," the man said, handing me a leather-bound book. "Terrance is our director of wine and can make some excellent recommendations if you're interested."

I took it from him only to speed along his departure.

"Would you like some?" I asked her.

"Yes, please." She couldn't have sounded more grateful if she'd tried, like she was desperate for the alcohol to take the edge off. "Which do you prefer?" she asked. "Red or white?"

I held the book out for her. "Get whatever you'd like. I don't drink."

Her eyes widened, and her gaze went to the cover of the wine list as she took it from me. "Oh, you don't?"

She peered across the table like something was wrong with me, and irritation heated my blood. When I told people I didn't drink, they made incorrect assumptions. I didn't struggle with addiction—this was merely a choice I'd made years ago. The unasked question lurked in her eyes and it forced me to answer.

"I don't care for how it affects me."

Control was essential, and that was hard to maintain when I was inebriated.

She bit down on her bottom lip, unsure. "Would it bother you if I—"

"No," I answered easily. "I meant what I said. Order whatever you'd like."

Relief coasted through her, and I wanted to grimace. Was I that intolerable? Sophia hadn't needed a drop of alcohol to survive dinner with me earlier in the week.

As Evangeline leafed through the wine list, my gaze drifted around the room. The restaurant wasn't large, but it was fully booked, and there were a few faces I recognized. Those I didn't clearly recognized me. I'd felt the shift in the room as I'd entered.

A woman near the back of the restaurant pretended to be texting someone, but the awkward angle she held her phone told me she was taking a picture.

Excellent.

Once our orders had been taken, Evangeline looked to me to begin the conversation.

"I appreciate your willingness to meet with me," I started, "especially under such unorthodox circumstances. I don't usually send an assistant to arrange these kinds of things."

She picked up her water goblet and took a drink as she contemplated what I'd said. "Honestly, if you'd asked me, I'd have said no. It's nothing personal." She set her glass down, and her fingers lingered on the stem as she worked up the courage to say what she meant. "Okay, it would have been a little personal."

I went still.

"I always found you intimidating," she admitted. "But Sophia came to me with your offer, and I was getting pretty desperate."

Beneath the table, my fist clenched at the idea of this woman only agreeing to dinner out of desperation. Last time I checked, I was Macalister fucking Hale. I could buy this restaurant and everyone in it twice over, and that wouldn't even touch my credit limit.

My anger leashed my tongue, and that gave her time to continue speaking. She crossed her arms, leaned forward on the table, and her expression flooded with emotion.

"I can't tell you how much your help means to me. My husband's foundation is everything." Her voice was quiet and somber. "It's all I have left of his legacy."

"My offer," I repeated.

Trepidation pricked up my spine. I'd been careless. In my distraction with Sophia, I hadn't gotten clarification on what exactly had been discussed during her lunch meeting with Evangeline. Sophia had mentioned there were finance issues, so I had assumed money. But judging by the emotion painting Evangeline's face, either I'd agreed to give up a lot of money . . .

Or something far more valuable.

"After John passed," she said, "I didn't have the strength to pay attention. Some people tried to help out, and I'd like to think they had good intentions, but the foundation is a mess. It's been mismanaged to the brink of collapse."

"You need me to look at your books."

I'd said it as a statement, but she mistook it for a question. "Oh, good heavens, no. Your slot in the auction is more than enough help. I'm not going to bother you for anything else."

Dread wormed through my system, but I wouldn't allow it to show. "I'm afraid you'll have to elaborate. Sophia failed to mention anything to me about an auction."

Evangeline froze, panic swamping her expression. "She didn't?"

I disliked having to repeat myself, especially when it was clear I'd been heard.

It took her a moment to compose her thoughts. "Well, every year, the Gabbard Foundation hosts a fundraiser over Memorial Day weekend. It's our biggest drive, where we take in eighty percent of our annual donations."

"I've been in the past," I said. "You host them at the marina clubhouse."

"Yes. Last year, we tried something new, and it was a huge

success." She picked up her glass of wine and took a sip, as if gathering courage, and it made my blood pressure rise.

I was impatient and frustrated with the delay. "An auction."

"A bachelor auction."

SEVEN

MACALISTER

A SWARM OF ANGRY BEES FILLED MY HEAD, MAKING THOUGHTS difficult, and my tone reflected it. "And Sophia volunteered my son Vance for it?"

I already knew this was not the case. Evangeline had said *your slot in the auction*, but I couldn't wrap my head around the ludicrous concept.

"No," she said, the panic in her voice now matching the emotion on her face. "She said you would be willing to participate. Is that not true? It's one dinner, just for fun, and for a good cause."

Fury corded in my body, twisting until I was rigid. I couldn't fathom why Sophia had put me in this position, and I hated the words as I had to say them. "I don't believe many women will be interested in paying for the privilege of an evening with me."

Putting myself up for auction was degrading enough, but I would not tolerate the embarrassment if no one were to bid. I'd be pitted against much younger men, none of whom had my notorious past, and my competitive nature was screaming this was a game I shouldn't play.

How could I possibly win?

The brunette across the table delivered an awkward look, and although it seemed impossible, my uneasiness found a new low to sink to.

"There's more?" I snapped.

"We talked about that. Sophia said instead of an evening, you'd make it an experience." She pasted on a smile like a broker trying to upsell me an unnecessary product. "Your dinner will be during the Food and Wine Classic in Aspen. The winning bidder gets an all-expense paid trip included."

I wasn't sure if I was going to fire Sophia or offer her a raise.

And I needed to find out if she played chess, because the woman had a head for strategy. Offering the dinner as a packaged trip not only ensured I'd land bids and avoid embarrassment, but it announced my plans to attend the festival, and word of it should travel to DuBois.

But Sophia had made this decision without my consent or approval, and my lack of knowledge about it left me looking foolish. I chewed out the words. "My assistant needs to work on her communication skills."

"Are you backing out?" Evangeline abruptly looked like she was going to cry, and alarms blared inside me. Making a woman cry during my first public evening out would be disastrous. Worse than if I'd just stayed isolated at home.

"No," I answered quickly.

She was too distraught to hear it. "Because we've had such a hard time finding volunteers this year, and when Sophia came to me with your offer . . ." She gazed at me with watery eyes, and there was pureness behind them I couldn't ignore. "You could singlehandedly save us."

She saw me not as a monster, but as a savior. My mind didn't approve the words, but they burst from my lips regardless. "I'll do it."

The smile that spread on her face was pleasant enough, but

I didn't like it as much as Sophia's. Evangeline's hand darted across the table, and she placed it on top of mine, her warm fingers touching my cold ones. It took all my strength not to move. Not only had she not asked if she could touch me, but her hand covering mine felt like dominance, even as it was meant as a friendly gesture.

Her words carried weight. "Thank you."

"Of course." I slowly slid my hand out from beneath hers, breaking the connection. "I'm happy to do it," I lied.

The last trace of anxiety she'd had about me evaporated in that instant, and her shoulders relaxed.

I stuck to the script Sophia had told me to, asking about the foundation. Mr. Gabbard's brother had served two tours in Afghanistan and came home with PTSD. He was fortunate to be able to provide his brother the help he needed, but during the road to recovery, he'd met other soldiers who didn't.

The Gabbards started their foundation and worked on the project together, although the bulk of the work was handled by her. He hadn't yet retired from HBHC. I pretended to know which department he'd worked in, but some of my better people moved around, and I'd been away when he'd passed.

At least I was pleased the charity I'd been talked into donating to was something worthwhile. It lessened the sting of being blindsided by the situation.

We ate our meal, and she talked, skillfully avoiding any topic that might force us to address my past, until she ordered a second glass of wine.

"This might be the best thing I've ever tasted," she said beneath her smile. She held out the large glass of white wine to me, her fingers wrapped on the bell. "Do you want to try it?"

"No, thank you. I only drink once a year, and then it's scotch."

Confusion splashed across her. "Once a year?"

Frustration directed inward. Why had I offered up this

information? "Yes," I said reluctantly. "The anniversary of the day Julia passed." I had to clarify. "My first wife."

"Oh," she said so softly, I didn't so much hear it as feel it. Shared pain and understanding filled her expression. This was the thing we had most in common—the tragic and sudden loss of a spouse.

"Why scotch?"

"It was her favorite, which she discovered on our honeymoon in Scotland." I didn't talk about private things, but I felt disarmed and unbalanced. This was Sophia's doing—the underdressed suit and the offer she'd made on my behalf which planted the addictive idea I could be a hero. "Scotch makes me feel close to Julia again."

Once more, Evangeline looked like she was going to cry, but she blinked back her tears. "That's . . ." she searched for the word, "romantic."

I hadn't been accused of being romantic in quite some time, because that part of my heart had died along with Julia. It made sense to me that the love of my life would take most of my ability to love with her when she left.

The way I'd felt for Alice, or even Marist, was a fraction of what I'd once been capable of.

"Does it get easier?" Evangeline's ache was palpable, and the noise of the people dining around us faded.

She looked to me to have answers, and for once in my life, I didn't want to be the expert. Since the conversation was no longer under my control, I gave in. "Part of you is gone. Over time, you'll adjust. You'll learn to live with this"—I struggled to say the word—"*hurt* that exists in its place. So, to answer you question, yes. It may get easier, but you know it will not be easy."

Even now, seventeen years later, there were days that were challenging. Particularly when I saw her reflection in my sons.

The way Evangeline peered into me suggested I was

entirely too vulnerable. I straightened in my chair. "That was my experience. Yours may be different."

"All of my friends are pushing me to get out there, and I . . . can't. I know it's been a year now and I'm still young, but John was it for me. He was the love of my life. How am I supposed to move on?"

I grew angry on her behalf. "They're not pressuring you because they're concerned about your happiness. They do it because seeing you in grief makes them uncomfortable, and they'd prefer you stop doing it. Ignore them. Don't think about moving on—only think about moving forward."

Her head angled, and she looked at me like I'd just torn away a mask and revealed a different person beneath.

Perhaps I had.

"You're not at all what I expected," she said. "The way people talk about you, Macalister, I wasn't sure I'd make it past the first course."

Three years ago, I would have been pleased with her statement. Often, it was practical to be intimidating, and, in fact, I enjoyed it. But it served no purpose tonight, and I certainly couldn't use intimidation to *make friends,* which Sophia had said was a vital step in her plan.

"Yes, well, much has changed for me in the last few years. I appreciate the opportunity to change your opinion of me." Hopefully, she could help set the record straight with her friends and explain how Macalister Hale was on the road to redeeming his evil ways.

"If you wanted to do this again sometime," she said, "I'd be okay with it. It helps both of us, right?"

"It does."

Two dates would be required for people to believe we were dating. Plus, getting a woman to go out with me once could be chalked up as luck—twice would prove skill.

I paid for the bill and was pleased when she didn't attempt to argue with me about it. I was traditional and had always held the opinion that women were the fairer sex. If she were willing to spend time with a man, the least he could do was pay for the evening.

As we made our way out of the dining room, every pair of eyes watched us go. Did it make Evangeline nervous? When we reached the atrium, she was pale and her eyes were wide.

"Is everything all right?" I asked. She had texted her driver from the table that she was preparing to leave, so it was unlikely the issue lay there.

"I'm just thinking about what happens next," she whispered as she retrieved her long black coat from the coat check. I took it from the staff member and held the coat out to help her put it on. It forced me to recall last night and how Sophia had ripped her coat from my hands, her anger denying me the opportunity to touch her again.

But Evangeline was distracted, too nervous about our impending kiss to notice or care. She turned away from me, slipped her arms into the sleeves, and held still as I brought the neck of the coat up onto her shoulders. I didn't let my hands linger there, but that brief touch was enough to reveal she was trembling.

"Thank you," she said.

She didn't wait for me to respond. Her feet carried her briskly across the marble floor and out the revolving door, leaving me no choice but to chase after her to say our goodbyes.

It was cool outside tonight, and the cars in the street were dotted with rain, gleaming in the streetlamps. We were protected under the lit awning of the restaurant as a black town car pulled up to the curb, which was obviously hers, but she felt compelled to say it anyway.

"That's me."

I lowered my voice so only she'd hear it over the sound of cars passing by on rainy asphalt. "We don't have to."

It would be better for me if we did, but I had no desire to kiss a woman who looked like she was about to be physically ill.

She shook her head, trying to be strong. "I said I would."

I went to her car and pulled open the backseat door for her, the closest equivalent to a doorstep kiss. The tremble in her grew until it was pronounced. She was terrified at the thought of my kiss.

Sophia's voice echoed in my head. *How will you do it?*

I stood on the sidewalk and had one hand on the top of the open car door and carefully set my other on Evangeline's waist, if only to keep the woman from vibrating apart. "It's all right."

Her eyes were wild and unfocused. "I haven't kissed anyone since John."

"I understand."

And I did. Perhaps this felt like cheating, and she couldn't bear to betray him. Or maybe since he was the love of her life, she didn't want to feel anyone else's lips against hers ever again. What right did I have to take that from her? I'd kissed a woman in love with another man before, and it wasn't a mistake I wanted to repeat.

I leaned forward, hearing her sharp intake of breath, and brushed my lips on her cheek, just outside the corner of her mouth. When I drew back, she was a statue of disbelief.

"Goodnight, Evangeline," I said, releasing her and stepping back.

Unable to speak, she simply nodded and faded into the back seat of her car. As it pulled away, I removed my phone from my pocket and angrily punched the screen with my finger.

I didn't give Sophia a greeting when she answered. All I did was bark out my order in an arctic tone before hanging up. "You will be waiting for me in the foyer when I arrive home."

EIGHT

SOPHIA

AT THE RATE I WAS GOING, MY PHONE BATTERY WASN'T GOING TO survive the night. I slid off the stool pulled up to the breakfast bar in the kitchen, snatched up the spare power cord my mom usually used to charge her phone, and plugged in.

I'd been texting Penelope all night for updates and used the time in between her messages to watch social media. As far as I could tell, no one had posted anything yet about Macalister's 'date.' He was still inside Marquee with Evangeline, so presumably it was going well.

My mother appeared in the doorway and trekked across our huge kitchen to the fridge. She had on a pair of black Nike leggings and matching hoodie, and she looked every bit the role of wealthy soccer mom.

Except I'd never played soccer.

Even if I'd wanted to, there wasn't time. During the height of my Olympic run, I'd trained five times a week, sometimes going through a thousand rounds per day, and the shooting range was a twenty-minute drive from Cape Hill. There's been competitions on the weekends and the travel that went along with them.

And there'd also been my mother's fight with breast cancer.

She was tougher than a lot of people gave her credit for. She'd survived a double mastectomy, kicked cancer's ass, and had come out the other side stronger. Her reconstructed and upgraded breasts helped complete a body few fifty-year-old women could have.

She looked fan-*fucking*-tastic.

But as strong as she was, Colette Alby still had her weak moments too, and I wasn't sure if I could ever get past them. Maybe I just needed a few more years.

My father would disagree. She could do nothing wrong in his eyes, and he always took her side. He'd say I needed to move out of the house and try living on my own. He'd use every opportunity to get rid of me.

It wasn't like I was attached to my parents or the house I'd grown up in; it was more that moving out didn't make sense. Why should I leave the nest where it was warm and comfortable and rent free? I lived in the far end of the house, the in-law suite, and rarely saw my parents unless we crossed paths in the kitchen or the Wi-Fi went down.

It was just us three here in this big ol' mansion.

Colette and Stephen Alby only had one child, and my father was heartbroken that I'd been a girl. The Alby family line that had come to America on the Mayflower would officially die when I married. Even if I kept my maiden name—which I wouldn't—I'd never pass the Alby surname on to my children.

Cape Hill was steeped in tradition. Sometimes I wondered if the biggest one was every family had some form of dysfunction.

"You're addicted to that thing," my mother said, gesturing to the phone in my hand.

I shrugged. "I'm working."

She brushed her light brown hair back out of her eyes and

poured herself a glass of water from the pitcher in the refrigerator that had lemon slices floating on the surface. As she set the pitcher down, her gaze zeroed in on me. "I don't think Macalister Hale is paying you to play on Instagram."

"I'm watching for notifications about him."

She didn't like my new 'job.' And my dad? Oh, he *hated* it. I'd been treated to a long lecture about Macalister being his biggest client and how this was going to cause problems for him when I eventually screwed up and got fired. I'd told him it was too late, a done deal. It'd reflect worse on Stephen Alby if he was the reason Macalister's newly hired assistant quit and left him in the lurch.

"I know you don't want to hear it—" she started.

"I really don't."

"But this job is beneath you. You have a degree from Columbia, for Chrissake."

I didn't look at her as she chastised me. Nothing I said was going to change her mind, so why bother? I'd done everything they'd ever asked of me, and it still wasn't enough.

So, I stopped.

I'd watched Marist, with her green hair flying in the face of all the Cape Hill conservatives as our newly appointed queen, and found myself strangely inspired. I'd figured out what *I* wanted, and now I was going after it.

I doled out the platitude to my mother in an indifferent voice. "Everyone has to start somewhere."

Just imagine how fast I could climb in HBHC's ranks if I became invaluable to the owner of the company. I'd be a brand manager by thirty, maybe even the director of marketing by forty. Plus, there was the nice five-million-dollar bonus if everything worked out.

"Your father and I have talked about it some more, and we think you should try to find a replacement for Macalister. That way, you can quit, and he won't be upset with any of us."

More specifically, with my dad. I lifted my gaze from my screen and glared at her. "I just started, and I don't *want* to quit."

"And I don't want you working for a man who killed at least one of his wives, Sophia."

My breath caught. "What? I thought his first wife died in an equestrian accident."

She took a drink of her water but held my gaze as she did it. "That's how he said it happened, but you know, I never saw Julia ride without her helmet. And after what he did to Alice, a lot of us have been talking. Is it possible he had something to do with Julia's death too?" She said it in a patronizing tone. "Or could he really just be that unlucky?"

He'd told me he held himself responsible for both of his wives' deaths, but he hadn't meant it literally. It was because he thought he was cursed.

Right?

I shook my head like it could rattle the question away. "It was an accident."

My mom frowned, and an emotion washed over her. It was something so rarely seen from her, it took me a moment to place. Was that honest-to-God concern?

"That man has a temper, and I don't want you to end up on the wrong side of it."

I opened my mouth to tell her she was overreacting, but my phone vibrated with a text. My stomach flip-flopped at the words.

Penelope: He kissed her & she just left.

Three dots blinked to tell me more was coming, but I didn't get a chance to read her next comment. The screen went black as my phone rang, and I tensed at the name displayed.

"Hello?"

Macalister sounded fucking *pissed*. "You will be waiting for me in the foyer when I arrive home."

It was followed by chilly silence, and by the time I could form a response, it was too late. He'd hung up on me.

"Who was that?" my mom asked.

My mouth went as dry as a desert. "Macalister." Shit. I'd have to change out of these clothes and back into the teal dress. "I have to go."

"Go where?" She glanced at the clock on the microwave. "It's ten o'clock."

"It's an emergency," I said.

It wasn't a lie. I knew he'd be upset when he found out what I'd signed him up for, but I hadn't expected him to be this level of angry. It made worry puddle in my stomach. At least he hadn't fired me over the phone. Meeting him at his house would give me a chance to plead my case.

Unless his legendary temper prevented him from listening.

Maybe I wasn't going to get a word in. He'd spend twenty minutes berating me until there was hardly anything left then cut me loose. His plan might be to send me home in tears, as he was known to do when he was CEO.

I slipped my phone into the back pocket of my jeans and hurried toward my bedroom. I'd spent years toughening up my skin from all the online haters. Whatever Macalister threw at me, I was pretty sure I could take it.

The Hale house was silent. There were no ticking grandfather clocks or fires going in the fireplaces. Macalister had told me he didn't like to see his staff unless they'd been summoned. Even the cat—what was his name? Lucifer. He wasn't sitting defiantly on the couch in the front room like last time.

The cavernous space of the grand entryway was empty except for me. Its vaulted ceilings and ornate chandelier which was so old it probably predated electricity and had been wired since, exaggerated the feel of loneliness. This house had held generations of families, but now it was a mausoleum.

After parking my Jaguar beside the sprawling garage, I'd dashed through the light rain to the front door and hurried to punch in my access code. I wiped the damp from my face as I stepped inside, pulled off my coat, and hung both it and my purse in the closet. It'd only taken me twenty minutes to change and get here. With the rain, the typical thirty-minute drive home from Boston might take Macalister's driver longer.

I took my phone from my purse and sat on the second step of the staircase, putting my arms around myself for warmth. Not only did this house feel like a tomb, it was as cold as one too.

There were several messages I'd missed from Penelope during my drive over. She'd wanted my approval on the best picture before posting it to Instagram, but when I'd gone radio-silent, she'd gotten anxious and made the call without me. Of the three images she'd sent, there was a clear winner, and she'd picked the correct one.

The caption she'd used was innocent. *Look who I caught kissing in the rain.* She hadn't tagged Macalister in the post, but the hashtags she had used would help put it on the right people's radar, and I amplified the signal by reposting it.

Penelope's side hustle was photography, and she'd gotten a seat at the window in the coffee place next door to Marquee. She'd patiently waited two hours to grab that picture, and she hadn't disappointed.

But I didn't know how to feel about the image. Wasn't I supposed to be happy? This was my plan, and he'd executed it just as I'd asked him to. But a spike of jealousy stabbed into my chest while my gaze traced his fingers on Evangeline's waist, his mouth pressed against her skin.

Penelope's timing must have been a fraction off. She'd missed the actual moment of their kiss, but the image was close enough. People discussing business did not say their goodbye this way.

As the notifications began to roll in, I could feel the buzz down in Cape Hill like a current. *Look at that Macalister Hale,* they were saying. *Already out prowling for another wife to kill off.*

Headlights glanced through the front windows, and a car rumbled up the circle drive, making me shoot to my feet and leave my heart behind on the stairs. A figure in black moved up the steps outside, the security system chirped its response, and the front door burst open.

My lungs constricted until I couldn't breathe.

If the rain had touched Macalister, I couldn't tell. It was more likely the raindrops were too frightened to dare fall on him, because the only gleam in his hair were the faint strands of silver. He was still dressed how I'd styled him this afternoon in the gorgeous black suit and fitted white shirt. The undone buttons at his neck relaxed the look, giving him just enough ease to not seem stuffy.

He shut the door behind him with a bang that made me flinch, but my gaze didn't break from his. His dark, furious eyes were like gravity. He was sexiest when he was displeased with me, but the outraged expression he wore now was so hot, my knees softened.

And then he lifted a hand and pointed one long, sharp finger at the couch in the front room, shouting his order without saying a word. I wasn't sure he would have been able to. The muscles across his jaw looked strained to their breaking point.

My heart raced along at a faster clip than my feet could

match, but I reached the couch and sat obediently on the edge of it, trying not to think about how he'd kissed me in this exact spot last night. A sane person would have been terrified in this situation, but I was obviously broken because I went giddy with excitement.

It made me reckless. "How was your date?"

Macalister's heavy footsteps slapped against the hardwood floor as he strode into the room and stood over me. "You committed me to that auction without my approval."

I swallowed a breath. "Yeah, because if I had asked you, you would have said no. But this is good for you. It got me to close the deal with her, and—"

Color rose in his neck. "I understand your reasons. My issue is the lack of communication, which will end right now, Sophia."

He brushed back the sides of his suit coat and put his hands on his hips. It was an assertive, confrontational posture, but all it did for me was flaunt his trim waist and powerful frame. It hinted at the curves of muscle packed beneath his expensive clothes.

"I will not be kept in the dark," he said, "and made out to be a fool. Do you understand me?" His tone was absolute. "Tell me what you're planning."

I knew what he meant, but I sidestepped answering it. "You're going to throw a party for Damon Lynch."

It somewhat derailed Macalister's anger. "Excuse me?"

"You'll say it's for his sixtieth birthday, but it'll really be a fundraiser for his campaign." I put my hands together in my lap, trying not to worry loose a hangnail. "Then you'll sponsor a new show so it can open at the Boston Opera Theatre."

He stared at me like I was speaking utter nonsense. "An *opera*?"

"Yes, because Mr. Scoffield's daughter, Erika, was an opera

major and still needs her big break."

His gaze jerked away from mine and fell to my hands in my lap, disdain painting his expression. "Stop fidgeting." When I froze at his command, his voice turned patronizing. "But please, continue. I'd like to hear more of these incredible ideas of yours to waste my money."

I let his accusation roll right off me. "Vance won the Cape Hill regatta the past three years because your family has one of the fastest ships in the marina. There's nothing Elijah Powell wants more in life than that stupid trophy."

Fire flashed in Macalister's cold eyes. "Vance wins because he's an outstanding sailor."

"Great," I said. "Then it won't make a difference to him if you lend your boat to Powell for the race." We both knew it was bullshit and that boat was a clear advantage. Even if Powell raced with it and lost, the gesture should still count. "That one doesn't cost you anything," I added.

"It will cost me," he abruptly sounded unsure, "with Vance."

My chest lifted when I pulled in a heavy breath. I didn't know where any of the Hale men stood with each other. Vance had an affair with Macalister's wife, and Macalister had tried to steal Royce's. They were the richest family in New England, and certainly the most fucked up.

"You could try explaining it to him," I said cautiously.

Judging by the look on Macalister's face, that wasn't fucking likely. "Anything else?"

"I want you to get Mitch Vanderburgh's son Jason a job at HBHC. He came out last year, and his dad kicked him out of the house. Totally cut him off, all because he's gay."

His gaze narrowed, although I wasn't sure if it was with confusion or dislike about what I'd said. "You explained the idea is for me to make friends, but this sounds counterproductive. Mitch won't want his son working for us."

"No, he won't, but that guy's a fucking asshole."

Jason was a good guy, and I'd watched him wrestle with the decision to announce who he was. It took a lot of courage, yet the reward he'd been given was to be shunned by his family.

"You're not doing it," I said, "to make friends with Mitch. There are a ton of closeted people here, and you have a chance to make a statement. You show them how a decent human being should be about this, and maybe Cape Hill will follow your lead."

Because at the end of the day, money was power, and Macalister had more of it than anyone else. Tragic history and sordid past aside, he was still the de facto king.

Macalister considered it.

"He is an asshole," he said in quiet agreement, like that settled it and Jason was as good as hired. His eyes hardened and pierced deep inside me. "There's a rather important name that appears to be missing from this charm offensive you've drafted."

My pulse quickened. Our primary focus was the HBHC board of directors, and I hadn't mentioned Liam Shaunessy yet. "I'm still working on that one."

"I see." He let out a tight breath, perhaps relieved I wasn't going to make him play nice with a man he utterly despised. His broad shoulders rolled back. "Now you'll tell me the rest of it."

My blood froze in my veins. "No."

His eyebrow arrowed up into a perfect upside-down V. He was a man who'd grown up never hearing that word, and something like eagerness ringed his blue eyes. We were quite the pair. I enjoyed seeing him displeased, and he thrilled in how I denied him.

"No?" he repeated. "You're not in a position to tell me no."

Did he have any idea how hot his stern voice made me? I licked my lips but stayed quiet, and the tension between us contracted until the large room felt microscopic.

His order wasn't playful or cute; it was as harsh and cold as a Nor'easter. *"Tell me."*

"I'll tell you anything . . . except for that," I whispered.

Frustration teemed in his eyes, and for a moment, he looked like he was considering either throwing a tantrum, or me out into the rain. But instead he lifted his chin with a smugness that was arrogant and sexy, and delivered the evilest smile I'd ever witnessed. "You'll tell me anything? All right. What happened between you and Tate?"

I reacted on instinct, bolting to my feet and my gaze flying toward the door. I wanted to run. But if I did, my bluff would be called, and Macalister would fire me. He'd put up with a lot from me already—more than I had expected him to. And I'd come into this knowing that in order to achieve my goals, I'd likely have to sacrifice something.

Pride wasn't that valuable to me, anyway.

A sigh seeped from my chest. "We slept together last year. It didn't," I struggled with how to put it, "really go that great."

He sobered and seemed surprised. "The sex was bad?"

"Like, *everything* was bad." My face had to be a million shades of red because it was on fire. "Tate's girlfriend had just broken up with him, and we ran into each other at some stupid party. He was kind of drunk, and maybe I was too." I wasn't, but I wanted to save what little face I could. "He was single and lonely, so when I saw the opportunity, I took it."

It was strange how he looked at me. There wasn't judgment, only curiosity. "You seduced him."

"Yeah," I answered, my voice clipped. "I mean, it didn't take much. He was horny, and he didn't really care who he was with that night."

"But you cared." There was a gravel in Macalister's voice that made goosebumps pebble on my forearms.

I tugged the corner of my mouth into a sad smile. "Yeah,

I cared a lot." I used nervous fingers to brush my hair back behind an ear. "So, anyway, the sex was awful. Like I said, he'd been drinking, and I'd wanted that moment for so long, I had all these expectations that were totally unrealistic. But it was just so awkward." I winced as I remembered our fumbling frustration, followed by Tate falling asleep on me. "In the morning, he was hungover and miserable, which meant he wasn't exactly subtle about how much of a mistake he thought he'd made with me."

I fiddled with the pleating on the side of my dress while my gaze drifted down to Macalister's black dress shoes.

"That was really hard," I said, "and I didn't handle it well. I gave him this big speech, like a fucking idiot, about how much I loved him. I'd thought if I just laid it all out there, he'd—"

"Fall in love with you." Macalister turned to stone.

I nodded. He understood somehow.

There was a long hesitation before he finally broke the painful silence stretched between us.

"Perhaps," uncertainty hazed his eyes, "you can take some comfort in the fact you did not give him this speech on his wedding day."

Confusion nearly made a laugh climb out of me, but it died when the meaning of his statement slammed into me.

Holy shit.

He'd done the same thing? Confessed everything to Marist out of hopes she'd fall for him?

One of my hands went to my mouth, covering the worst of my gasp. "You didn't."

"Oh, I did." He grimaced. "It was . . . poorly received."

That had to be an enormous understatement, and I couldn't stop the short sound—too joyless to be a laugh—that it punched from my lungs. I remembered the morning of her wedding when he'd blown into her room like a storm and demanded a moment alone with the bride. After he'd left her, Marist had been as white as her dress.

"Does it help," I asked, "to know that she's happy?" Because knowing that Tate would rather be alone than with me had been crushing.

"Yes," he answered simply. "It makes it easier."

Either he'd crept closer during our conversation or I'd drifted mindlessly toward him, because only a foot separated me from Macalister now, and I peered up at him with unasked questions crowding my eyes.

Was he over her?

Did he want to move on?

Had he spent every available minute today thinking about what I tasted like, as I'd done with him?

His gaze traced over my face so slowly, he had to be studying and cataloguing every inch with his icy eyes. It was hypnotic, and I sighed softly as he pushed closer. This time I didn't try to run from him. The room was stifling, filled completely by him, but I didn't mind.

His voice was velvet as he tipped his head down, his lips drawing near. "You don't have to tell me your secret tonight. Just give me the name."

It was like being ripped from a cozy hot tub in the dead of winter, the way he took me from my dreamy spell to the harsh reality. He'd tried to use his power to manipulate the secret from me, and Christ, it'd nearly worked. I stumbled backward, eager to put distance between myself and the heat he could generate in a single look.

"No," I snapped.

Gone was the seduction from a moment ago, replaced by the cold, irritated demeanor he'd had when he first arrived home. "I suggest you save us both the time and stop fighting what's inevitable. This isn't a battle you're going to win."

I groaned my frustration, balled my hands into fists, and lifted my gaze to the ceiling.

He said it as a dark warning. "Don't you roll your eyes at me, young lady."

Excuse me. *Young lady?*

His eyes went enormously wide, having surprised himself. This wasn't something he'd meant to say.

I gaped at him and loaded my voice with as much sarcasm as I possessed. "Oh, I'm so sorry . . . *Daddy.*"

The word echoed in the room like a gunshot.

It charged the air with a violent, sexual energy that strangled us both to a stop. My 'daddy' response had been without thought, but now that word was out there, never able to be unsaid. It clung to our skin like a stain that'd never wash off.

My heart tottered and crashed clumsily against the walls inside my chest like a baby just learning how to walk, but he seemed to be faring better. Macalister smoothed a hand over his hair, grabbed the sides of his coat to adjust how it sat on his shoulders, and gave me a firm look.

"You are behaving like a child, so I will punish you as one." He lowered himself to sit on the couch, his posture straight and his hard stare burning a hole through me. "Down in my lap," he demanded. "Across my knee."

NINE

SOPHIA

MACALISTER CREATED STATIC IN MY BRAIN AND STEAM IN MY BODY. I was boneless and had to stay absolutely still. If I moved, I'd collapse into a puddle at his feet. This concept of me bending over his knee was ridiculous. Insane, really.

It was so fucking inappropriate, I wanted to throw myself immediately into his lap. But it was a bluff; it had to be.

"You're not serious," I scoffed.

Yet he looked deadly serious as he growled, "Get over here and find out."

He had command over my body, and it was disorienting when my feet moved, bringing me to the couch where he waited impatiently. I didn't have to think about how to get into the position. He wrapped a hand around my forearm and jerked me down. My palms flew out, catching myself on the cushion beside his legs.

He touched me like he had every right, positioning my body over him so my stomach was pressed against his thighs, which were like granite. The man was as addicted to his treadmill as I was to my phone.

"Hands behind your back."

Shivers rolled in waves down my bare legs as I stared at the damask pattern of the upholstery. My mind was disconnected, like he'd pulled it out and plugged in a new operating system that was controlled by him. That would explain why I followed his order, laying my cheek against the couch cushion and twisting my arms behind me.

His hand was ice as it clamped down on my wrists, and although his grip wasn't rough, I felt the squeeze of him all over. It forced the air from my lungs, made my heart beat frantically and my stomach rattle.

Like last night, the lights weren't on in this room, so the only source of lighting came from the chandelier in the entryway. It was better this way with the moody shadows heightening the experience. What was happening didn't belong in a brightly lit room.

I didn't know what he was going to do, exactly, but the waiting? Each second dragged along my skin, creating tension in my center until it began to ache. I snagged my bottom lip between my teeth to keep quiet. If I spoke, he might come to his senses, realize how I was provocatively draped over him, and put a stop to this nonsense.

My breathing was shallow, but his was deep, and although I couldn't see him, I pictured his gaze sliding over me. It evaluated every place on my body he had access to, and which spot would be best to dole out his punishment.

"Are you scared?" There was a teasing lilt to his voice.

I swallowed thickly and shook my head, unable to answer.

"This trembling is, what? Excitement?" He sounded disappointed, and dear God, it tripled the ache inside me. I imagined how hard his jaw was set and the muscles there I wanted to run my tongue along the length of. Down his neck and back up the other side.

Macalister shifted slightly beneath me, his legs spreading

and adjusting his position, as if readying himself. My breasts flattened against the top of his thigh.

"Your actions yesterday were unacceptable, Sophia. To reinforce that point, you require a firm hand."

His grip on my wrists tightened a degree, but this wasn't what he meant.

It was preemptive, because his actions were going to cause me to jolt, and he wanted me to stay in place. He didn't spank me, though. The bottom of my dress was lifted, exposing the swell of my bottom and my black lace underwear that was covering it. I flinched as cool air wafted over the backs of my newly bare thighs, the sensation causing me to pinch my knees together.

He inhaled sharply. Had the sight of me sparked unexpected pleasure? It may have been the sexiest thing I'd ever heard.

His fingertips trailed over the lace. Was he tracing the patterns? No. His fingers slipped under the edge and tugged—

"Oh, my God," I whispered.

The word was sharp and corrective. "Quiet."

It meant I had to hold my breath as he eased the sides of my panties inward, wedging them uncomfortably between my cheeks like a thong and exposing more of my skin to him.

Every inch of me was now combustible. I was going to burst into flames, which would consume him, his antique couch, and likely raze the entire mansion. That was how much heat he was generating. Beneath his strict grasp, I clenched my fists and dug my fingernails into my palms.

I'd never been spanked before. Not by my family, and certainly not by a lover.

Macalister fell into neither of those categories currently, but that wasn't surprising. He wasn't a man who could be labeled or categorized. He was unique. An enigma.

The first smack of his hand against my backside physically

felt like nothing. It made a staccato slap of skin striking skin, but it sounded far worse than it was. There was no discomfort or much of a sensation, really, yet my body's desire to respond was enormous. I'd wanted it to hurt, to burn, to take my breath away.

He spanked me a second time, this one on the other side, but he maintained the same level of energy, so the blow fell harmlessly, and disappointingly, across my skin. I craved more. It was like an itch I couldn't quite reach. Scratching the skin close to it gave some satisfaction but didn't do the job.

I wiggled under his grip, my hipbones grinding against his thighs, and he hissed, "Stay still."

The first pair of spankings he'd given me were a test, which I'd passed, because his second set were quick, hard, and no fucking joke. My eyes went wide at the sting that lingered like a band of heat across my bottom, and then I hazed as he pressed his palm against my enflamed skin, massaging in a slow circle.

My head spun with how turned on his touch made me. Pleasure simmered inside my center, building with each circuit of his hand smoothing over my skin. And he wasn't immune to the effects of delivering this spanking either. There was a bulge thickening beneath the fly of his suit pants, impressively firm against my belly.

He'd told me to be quiet, but it was beyond my control, and the words came from me like a long, soft sigh. "This doesn't feel like punishment."

He said it as a challenge. "It doesn't?"

Before I could process the question, he struck me so hard, my cheek reverberated with the impact and I inhaled sharply through clenched teeth. Okay, that one was legit, and I—

"*Fuck*," I groaned, my eyes fluttering closed.

Macalister's fingers pressed against the damp center of my panties, rubbing gently against my clit, and the pleasure it produced was white-hot. It curled my toes inside my shoes, and I melted across his lap, threatening to liquify and drip down his legs.

"Watch your language."

It was shockingly natural the way we fell into our roles. I was the disobedient little girl who craved attention, and he was the disapproving dominant, determined to teach me a lesson.

I wanted it to sound snarky, but his fingers twitched, and more pleasure jolted through me, so my retort was breathless. "Sorry, Daddy."

His hand cracked across my ass. "Do not call me that."

I bit down on my tongue, but the inappropriate chant continued in my head. *Daddy, daddy, daddy . . .*

God, his fucking fingers. They teased without mercy.

I squirmed against his hold, not wanting to break free but enjoying his restraint. And when I writhed in his lap, it made me rub against his erection, and the faintest grunt of pleasure escaped his lips.

Strain filled his voice, so his order verged on a plea. "You will hold still as I've asked you to."

"I can be good," I whispered. With the thin lace, it was like nothing stood between his touch, and he pressed harder on my swollen clit, causing sparks behind my eyelids. "I can be *so* good . . ."

Whatever had been holding him back broke down. He came unleashed, overwhelmed with desire. He let go of my wrists so he could curl the fingers of both his hands into the waistband of my underwear and peel the fabric down until it was gone, hung on the backs of my knees.

No longer inhibited by the lace, Macalister slid two fingers across my most intimate part and discovered exactly how powerful an effect he held over me. I was wet. So wet, it had to be shocking to him, but all he issued was a hushed sigh. My hands moved mindlessly, seeking whatever part of this gorgeous yet cold man I could find. One latched onto his leg, and the other followed the line of buttons on his shirt upward, searching for skin to connect with.

The gravel in his voice did nothing to hide his lust. "I suspect this also doesn't feel like punishment."

The pads of his fingers strummed over my clit. I quickly shook my head and dug my nails into the suit fabric covering his thigh. His strokes pulled a whimper from the back of my throat.

But abruptly, his touch was gone.

He was harsh and wicked. "And now? Is this punishment?"

Oh, my God. Yes. The absence of his touch after he'd built it up wasn't just cruel—it was torture. But it was one I was far too familiar with.

Perhaps it was hard for him too, because he didn't stay away for long. Only a series of deep breaths, long enough for me to mourn his absence and revel in his return. His fingers kneaded and probed . . .

And again, he suddenly went still. The muscles in the legs beneath me hardened.

"What—?" I'd never heard him sound so uncertain.

My desire was a thick fog and slowed my response time. It took me a full two seconds before I understood what had caught him off guard, and more blood rushed to my face. "Uh . . ." I pinched my eyes closed tightly. "I have a VCH piercing."

"Which means?"

My pulse roared like a jet engine, so loud I wasn't sure if my faltering voice could be heard over it. It probably didn't help that I spoke like I was dying. "It stands for vertical clitoral hood."

He took in a lengthy breath. "Stand up and show me."

It was impossible to hear any emotion in his tone, so I

couldn't tell if he was interested or horrified by this new development. I'd gotten the piercing last year during Kelly Sumner's bachelorette party in Vegas. I'd heard it could increase stimulation, and I loved the way it looked. But leave it to me to find the one guy who might not find this sexy.

I was still shaking in response to his touch, plus my panties were caught around my knees, so it was difficult to push off the couch, but somehow, I managed. I stepped out of my underwear and left it behind on the floor, teetering on my unstable legs as I stood in front of him.

He was sexy as fuck as he sat back against his couch and crossed his thick arms, his Cartier watch peeking out from behind a sleeve cuff. His hair was dark in the low light, and his angular face and expression were darker still. The look in his penetrating eyes was carnal. Macalister was a wolf watching its next meal from the shadows, planning exactly when to strike.

Anxiety twisted me tightly, and the heated blood flowing through my system left me jittery and quivering, but I placed my sweaty palms over the tops of my thighs, pressing my skirt against my legs, and slowly began to drag them up.

It was terrifying and exhilarating, this idea of showing off my body to him and the jewelry I wore that no one else knew about. A fantasy of mine come to life. I was a member of his royal court, submitting myself to the king for his evaluation. Up my dress went, all the way to my waist, baring my nakedness to him. And I was starkly naked. I liked a clean look and had shaved bare just this morning.

His scrutinizing gaze focused between my legs, and it was so intense, I felt it like a caress, as if his hands were gliding between my thighs. But his eyebrows tugged together, creating a crease between them, and his attention rose to my face.

"Well? I'm waiting," he said impatiently.

Oh, God. Because he couldn't really see the piercing like

this. I pinned the bottom half of my dress to my hips with my wrists, and reached my fingers down, peeling myself open.

It was vulgar. Pornographic.

But the way his shoulders lifted as he sat forward? That was obscene and erotic. Excitement spiraled inside my stomach. His eyes zeroed in on the small set of pink gems decorating my skin, one stacked over the other, just above my clit.

"Do you like it?" I breathed.

His expression was unreadable, and he didn't answer me. But he licked his lips, and my entire body shuddered. The lewd thoughts in his mind began to seep out at the edges of his expression, and I let out a slight sigh of relief.

"It's new," I whispered. "You're the first person to see it."

Oh, this, he definitely liked. The corner of his mouth tugged upward, not quite a smile, but he was pleased. I knew a thousand secrets, but this was the first one I'd only shared with him.

I dropped my skirt, covering myself, and his scowl that followed was epic.

"You wore that dress for me today," he sat against the couch and slung an arm across the back of it, "but now I think you'll wear nothing."

I went weightless, yet also as heavy as the grand piano that sat in the corner. I didn't say no, because I didn't want to—and I wasn't capable. That was the only thing that scared me about him. He could make me do almost anything.

But the question burst from my lips. "Why?"

He tilted his head, curious. "Because I want to see everything." When I didn't move, he added, "I haven't seen a naked woman in years, Sophia, and I have no doubt you will be an exceptionally beautiful one."

Electricity crackled across my arms, and goosebumps rose from my skin. There was something satisfying in knowing I'd be his first, not only after prison, but after *her*. The first woman he'd chosen to pay attention to in the post-Marist era of his life.

The room wasn't warm or constricting anymore as I reached behind my back, caught the zipper pull of my dress, and eased it down. The back of the dress peeled apart, it slipped from my shoulders, and the whole garment tumbled from my body, leaving me dressed only in a black bra.

He'd been doing that thing he often did, where his hand was in a loose fist and his thumb ran back and forth over the knuckles, but when my dress was a puddle at my feet, his thumb stopped moving. I held his gaze as I arched my back, reached behind myself, and undid the hooks of my bra.

Macalister's eyes hooded, the lids suddenly too heavy to stay all the way up.

I didn't have a body like statuesque Alice did, and I wasn't as slender as Marist. No amount of diet and exercise could overcome my genes, and I was never going to have thigh-gap or a perfectly flat stomach. But I was healthy and fairly happy with how I looked, even in a bikini. The advantage to my curves meant I had breasts. Big, full ones that made other girls envious.

The summer before my senior year at Columbia, Carrie Jensen had asked if I would send her a topless picture to use as an example for her plastic surgeon. Since pictures were forever and I didn't trust a soul in Cape Hill, I went with her to the consult instead.

Her new tits were nice, but they weren't as good as mine.

Macalister's gaze moved like a glacier over me, taking in every inch of my bare skin, lingering on my nipples that had pebbled from either the cold or his attention.

"Turn."

I shivered with enjoyment at how his voice had lost its power. Staring at me was undoing him. He'd said it as an order, but it came out as a request, and I obliged him. I turned in place, treating him to a full three-sixty view of my body, and when I came back around, the unadulterated lust in his eyes made my heart skip.

Fuck, he looked at me like I was everything he'd ever wanted and couldn't have.

"Oh, Sophia," he said, "the things I'd do to that *fucking* perfect body of yours if I were a younger man."

It was so rare that he swore, the curse word carried more weight. The impact of it disrupted my mind, and the truth spilled free. "I don't want you to be a younger man."

His eyes turned stormy. "Don't say things like that to me."

"Why not?" It was true, and I suspected he knew it.

He glared at me with his strict eyes and his sexy mouth pressed into a scowl, and it was scorching. Sweat threatened on the back of my neck.

"Because," he seethed irritation, "just look at the state you've put me in."

To emphasize his point, he smoothed a palm down the front of his pants, attempting to tame the erection bulging from behind his zipper.

My shoulders lifted as I inhaled deeply, and I flicked my gaze to his. "I can take care of that."

Desire swirled like dust motes in the air, and it was intoxicating. Macalister stared at me with a mixture of emotions, but they blurred together, and I couldn't pick a single one out. His gaze was inescapable, though. It was quicksand, and I stayed absolutely still, knowing it'd suck me in faster if I tried to fight it.

His unspoken words suspended between us. *We can't.*

The battle waged inside his head over the sensible thing versus what he wanted to do. His banker's mind considered the pros and the cons, and when he arrived at the decision, he tossed it aside and gave me a stern look.

I can take care of that, I'd said.

His hand went to his belt, and he began to undo it. "Yes," his tone was absolute, "you will."

TEN

SOPHIA

WAS THIS ANOTHER FANTASY I'D VISUALIZED ENOUGH TIMES that it had now become real? My heart lodged in my throat as Macalister sat on his tufted couch and used both hands to slide the end of his belt free, then worked to undo the button and zipper beneath. Like everything else he did, he moved efficiently, and it took him no time to complete his task.

My body forgot how to work. I didn't blink or breathe as he fisted himself and stroked down his length.

Holy mother of God, he was *huge*.

His enormous ego had to be at least partially backed up by big dick energy.

"Breathe," he reminded.

I filled my lungs with air as I took in the erotic scene playing out in front of me. His gaze meandered over my naked body, drinking me in as his hand pumped leisurely along, pleasuring himself.

He used a finger from his free hand to point at me, and that demanding finger turned upside-down and curled back toward him. Once, then twice. He was beckoning me to come closer, and I had no choice in the matter. An unseen force propelled me forward.

"Stop."

His sharp word could make the world stop turning, I was sure of it. I froze, one knee buried in the couch beside him, on my way to straddling his lap.

He peered up at me with his trademark disapproval. "What do you think you're doing?"

I blinked, stunned. "I thought we were going to—"

"No, you are mistaken," he said. "You haven't earned the full privilege of my cock." He set his cold hand on my hip and pushed me back. "On your knees. Your mouth will be adequate."

"Adequate?" I asked, dumbfounded.

"Yes." He was indifferent to my shock, and his fingers dug in as he guided me down onto my knees in front of him. "I will show you how I like it."

And then I was kneeling between his spread legs, my hand on one of his knees. Was he fucking serious? I used the most condescending tone I possessed. "I already know how to give a fucking blowjob."

Macalister scooped a hand behind my head, his fingers twisting into the strands of hair at the nape of my neck. "Excellent." He jerked me forward, thrusting my face into his crotch. "Then, demonstrate."

I wished I didn't like his bossy way, but—oh, how I did. His forceful tone, his arrogant demeanor, his critical eyes . . . it all worked for me. I'd spent a lifetime getting attention from everyone but the people I desperately wanted it from.

He was the first to reciprocate.

So, while I loved Macalister's disapproving looks, I hungered to please him. I wanted him to find satisfaction, to be as consumed with me as I was becoming with him.

He made a tight noise of pleasure when I latched a hand around the base of him and prepared to take him inside my mouth. Despite his best efforts, he couldn't hide how badly he wanted this. His pupils were large and dark, and his chest rose and fell with his stilted breath.

I closed my eyes, opened my mouth, and slid down on him.

The legs I was nestled between tensed, and he exhaled loudly, his gasp punching the silence. His hand was still on the back of my head, but there wasn't any pressure or guidance there. His other reached out and grasped the corded edge of the couch cushion beside us.

Macalister's cock was thick and hard, and when I closed my lips around him and sucked, he pulsed against my tongue. The sensation was vocalized in a pleasure-filled sigh, and warmth flooded down my limbs.

Would he moan?

Oh, my God, could I make him curse?

The idea thrilled me. I swirled my tongue around the fat head of him and was rewarded with a louder, deeper sigh. Heat buzzed through my body. Every reaction I caused in him gave me one in return.

It wasn't all that comfortable kneeling on the hard floor with bare knees, and although his suit pants were undone, the tails of his dress shirt kept getting in my way. It was Macalister's first blowjob in years, and I wanted to rock his world, so I backed off and fisted the top of his pants.

Our gazes met, and he understood what I wanted. He lifted, helping me pull his pants and underwear down over his hips, and then he sat forward on the edge of the couch, pushing his clothes down to his ankles. I was going to resume what I'd been doing, but he seized my face in his hands and crushed his lips to mine.

He'd said my mouth would be adequate, and it was clear he meant to use it in every way.

His kiss obliterated.

It could level buildings and decimate cities and win wars. I gasped into his hot mouth. When his tongue stroked against mine, I felt it between my legs. And as our kiss deepened, his hands moved, slipping down my neck and over my shoulders. His fingers flowed down my arms then inched their way onto my back.

I'd thought his kiss last night was the best of my life, but he topped it easily with this one. I was naked, held in his suit-clad arms while his lips were fused to mine, and his hands skated up and down my back. He trailed the hollow of my spine with the sides of his thumbs, and the way he touched me . . . it was reverence.

Like I was some priceless thing he'd chased after for so long and couldn't believe was finally his.

I wanted to touch him the same way, but when I put my palm on his chest, buttons reminded me of the barrier in my way. I picked at the first one, clumsy and fumbling, struggling with my urgency.

Perhaps he wanted my touch even more, because Macalister broke the kiss. He delivered his piercing stare while he effortlessly undid the buttons and opened his shirt, revealing the beautiful landscape of his chest.

There was a faint scattering of dark hair across his upper body, and a line of it that led my gaze downward. He was toned and sculpted, looking like he spent more time in the gym than in an office, which up until recently had probably been true. Damn, he was way too good-looking to be fifty-five.

I placed my hand on the center of his chest and gently pushed, urging him back, and as he slumped into the couch, I trailed my fingers down over his skin and the faint notches of muscles they discovered.

Lust filled my bloodstream like a drug, and Macalister peered at me with anticipation brimming in his eyes as I took hold of his cock, resettled myself on my knees, and went down on him again.

His knees were spread wide, but his halfway-off pants were still sort of in my way. Once I tucked my legs beneath them, I had complete access. I looked up the long, bare slope of his body while I sawed my mouth side to side, inching as far down as I could go.

He'd promised he'd tell me how he liked it, but I must have been doing a satisfactory job, because he gave no notes. Macalister's lips parted and his face twisted with pleasure, which sometimes was so strong it looked a little like agony. I pumped my mouth on him, alternating between short, quick strokes and long, deep ones where I could tease with my tongue.

There was a quiet thud as he tossed his head, and it banged against the back of the couch. His chest heaved when I squeezed my hands along the part of him I couldn't take inside my mouth. My fingers were wet with my saliva and the drops of arousal that had leaked out of him.

It was so fucking hot.

Hotter still when his hand went back to gripping the edge of the couch, and his knuckles went white.

I slid my fists and lips over him faster, and faster, and—

"Slow." He was hoarse with lust. "Make it last."

I paused my mouth, resting his tip against my smiling lips, using my tight fingers to stroke from the base to the head at a measured pace.

"Yes," he whispered, looking down at me with a hunger I felt in my bones. He was short of breath, making it come out between two pants for air. "That feels incredible."

My smile widened to a full grin. Seeing him like this? That felt incredible too, like a secret he was sharing only with me. His fingertips brushed across my cheekbone, and his hand slowly curled behind my head.

This time, he *was* intent on directing. He'd given up control to me long enough. His other hand abandoned its grip on the cushion so he could gather my long blonde hair up into a loose ponytail, and he held it out of our way. It gave him an unobstructed view as he disappeared beneath my rounded lips and slowly reappeared, glossy and wet.

He gently pushed and pulled me, establishing a slow, steady tempo to seesaw in my mouth. The deep breaths he took carved dark hollows beneath his cheekbones, making him look powerful and commanding. I heaved my hands up and down outside of my lips, twisting and squeezing and wringing pleasure from him with each pass.

The pace he demanded began to build, both in speed and urgency, like a switch had been flipped inside him and now he was desperate for release. His hands tensed in my hair, some of the strands pulling awkwardly to the point of pain, and my jaw ached with discomfort. But it was worth it, because his sighs had grown too loud, too full of satisfaction.

They were moans, the kind that welled up from deep in his chest and the back of his throat.

I moaned softly too, thinking about what was happening, how I was naked between Macalister's large thighs, my head bobbing furiously as I went down on him and brought him closer to ecstasy.

"I want to finish," he gasped, "in your mouth."

He didn't phrase it as a question, but he was asking for consent. If I didn't like this idea, all I had to do was pull away. Of course, I wasn't going to. I wasn't just enjoying it. I wanted to please him, to push him over the edge and make him lose control. And he sounded oh-so-close.

It took only a few more pumps before it happened. The muscles in his legs strained, and he jerked, his breath cutting off. One of his hands let go of my hair, making it spill like a curtain around my face, but I could still see well enough to watch his head tip back to the ceiling. He threw his forearm over his eyes, his entire body shuddering.

"*Fuck,*" he groaned.

I nearly came myself, hearing my favorite word draw from his lips and to know I was the cause.

He spurted in rhythmic jerks, filling my mouth, and I swallowed as quickly as possible, keeping my lips fixed tight around him. Not that I could go anywhere. His hand cupped the back of my head and held me in place as his climax rolled through. When the pleasure began to ebb, he eventually released me. The flick of my tongue as I made my retreat caused him to flinch, still overly sensitive from the orgasm.

I sat back on my heels and gazed up at him sprawled across the couch. He looked devastatingly gorgeous laid out like this. As if I'd drained most of the power from him, but each ragged breath he took worked to restore it. His Adam's apple bobbed as he swallowed hard, and he finally lifted his head and set his intense, focused gaze on me.

He'd found his release, but he stared back at me like he wasn't yet satisfied. Macalister was still famished, and the pleasure he wanted to consume now would be mine.

But trepidation flooded my stomach, and years of anxiety weighed me down. I craved attention, but only when it was for the right reasons. Foreplay for me was nice and all, but it was an exercise in frustration. With sex, I was able to just enjoy without feeling the pressure to achieve. Because everyone knew women didn't come every time they had sex, so it seemed normal to guys when I didn't.

But foreplay?

I'd never had an orgasm from someone going down on me. Or using their fingers.

In fact, I'd never come in front of anyone else. I could do it myself, but only in the darkness of my room, alone in my bed.

Macalister leaned forward, his face close to mine and his woodsy aftershave faintly noticeable, grabbed the sides of his pants, and pulled them back up. He tucked himself away, zipped up and buttoned, then refastened his belt, moving with practiced hands. The mood in the room was still sexually charged, but it morphed into one that was taut with tension.

"Stand up," he commanded.

I wasn't trying to defy him, but my body wouldn't cooperate. All I could do was stare at his feet. I sensed his confusion, even without looking at him. A breath passed between us, and he climbed to his feet, standing beside me before holding out a hand to help me up.

I took it, only for him to haul me upright and into his embrace. His fingers were cold, but his body was hot, and when my breasts flattened to his bare chest, desire licked at me. It burned in his eyes as well, but I only caught a glimpse before he buried his mouth in the crook of my neck.

His stubble scraped across my sensitive skin as he feasted on my neck, sucking and nibbling. I was pliant in his arms, growing weaker with every kiss. And then he leaned down, just enough so he could course a hand between my thighs and drag it upward, pulling a moan from my throat.

God, that felt good. Just the brush of his hand over me gave a warm flash of pleasure.

His voice was wrapped in seduction, slinking through the cloudy desire in my head. "Give me the name," he whispered, "and I'll let you come."

The laugh that burst from me was unstoppable. He might as well have said he'd let me sprout wings and fly away, so I didn't bother to rein in my sarcastic reaction. "No, thanks."

He went wooden, his eyes turning hard. "Why do you find that amusing? You don't think I can bring you to orgasm?"

"Nope," I said without hesitation.

It was like I'd just spit on his mother's grave. Macalister's eyebrow lifted sharply, and his posture straightened. "I'm good at nearly everything I do, but there are two things I truly excel at." His expression dripped with arrogance. "Banking is the *other* one."

I rolled my eyes for the second time tonight. "Awesome."

"I am not exaggerating."

There was something about me that made people want to confess their secrets, like I was human truth serum, but I wondered if he was the same for me. I'd already revealed things to him I hadn't told anyone else, so what difference did it make if I did some more?

"Maybe you are great, but your talent would be wasted on me."

His brain hit a wall while going sixty miles an hour. "What the hell does that mean?"

I sighed. "I don't have orgasms."

Horror washed down his handsome face, and his arms tightened like steel bars around me. "Ever?"

My heartbeat was frantic, fluttering in my chest. "Not with other people."

Macalister was at a total loss, unable to process. His gaze drifted down to my lips, and it went unfocused as he considered my statement. Abruptly, his eyes sharpened, and his attention snapped back to mine. "But you can orgasm? You have before?"

"Yeah." It was weird to be shy about this, given what we'd just done, but it felt like I was admitting I was abnormal, and I didn't want to see judgement from him.

The last thing I expected was to see him smile. It widened until it spread all the way to his eyes and consumed his face. It was the first genuine grin I'd ever seen from him, and it was breathtaking.

"You'll allow me to be the first, then," he said.

To prevent discussion, he bent and swept my legs out from beneath me, scooping me up into his arms.

Was he aware this was also a first? No man had ever picked me up and carried me before, and it was hardwired into my brain to respond to the swoon-worthy gesture. I blinked up at him with my mouth hanging open in surprise, but he wasn't looking at me. His gaze surveyed the space, searching for something, and when it was located, he strode deeper into the room.

Our destination was the tan, single-armed chaise lounge in front of the fireplace, and he deposited me there before righting himself and moving to the mantel. I sat up and banded an arm across my chest to hold in my warmth while watching him turn the key to activate the gas. The fire in the fireplace burst to life, its orange-blue flames dancing over the realistic ceramic logs.

Had he done it to light the dark room, or to keep me warm?

With that task completed, Macalister turned and faced me, and I had the strangest sensation he was visualizing his next move the same way I did before each shot in skeet. It made my already racing pulse skip faster and my breathing go shallow.

"You seem certain," he said, "that I won't be able to bring you to orgasm. Why don't we strike a deal?"

He crossed his arms over his chest and leaned back against the side of the fireplace, and although his shirt was still unbuttoned and his posture attempted to be casual, I was smart enough not to fall for it. For one thing, Macalister Hale wasn't casual. Another was that I was naked, and he was dressed, plus there was his positioning, since he was standing while I was perched on the lounge. He had the upper hand in every way, all the power.

I hesitated. "What kind of deal?"

The fire was already putting out warmth, and it cast flickering light over his face. It made him look sinister and provocative. "An orgasm for the name."

Had he forgotten how our last bet had worked out for him? I smiled, thinking about how bad the hit would be to his massive ego when he lost to me a second time. I was competitive, always playing to win. "There'd have to be rules, though."

He nodded. "Of course, such as a time limit to complete my task. Should we say an hour?"

I jolted and my eyes widened. "You think it'll take you an hour?"

Annoyance glanced through him. "No, I think it'll take me less than fifteen minutes."

I stared at him hard. "Then make it fifteen minutes."

Amusement tugged at his smile. "No, you misunderstand. Just because I *can* do it in fifteen minutes doesn't mean I will. I'd prefer to take my time with you."

Well, fuck if that didn't turn me on, just a little—but he didn't need to know that. "It's late," I said. "Aren't you tired?"

He paused, hesitant to reveal it but then accepted it. "I suffer from insomnia, so, yes. But I am always tired. I would rather give you pleasure for the next hour than spend it on the treadmill, working myself to the point of exhaustion."

It was impossible not to picture him running, beads of sweat darting erratically down his amazing chest. I swallowed thickly. "What do I get if I win?"

Some of Macalister's looks were easy to read, and this was one of them. There was no doubt in his mind I'd lose, and he was only humoring me with his answer. "Then I won't ask again."

He was entirely too smug, and his confidence reminded me not to underestimate him. He'd done that with me, and I'd made him look bad. It was smart to be cautious.

I'd gotten close to orgasm once with a partner. I'd been tipsy and high, and my boyfriend at the time had gone down on me long enough to make me wonder if he was going to get me there. Macalister had been married twice, so it stood to reason he wasn't clueless about sex. His personality was persistent and methodical. Given a full hour, he might be able to do it with his tongue.

"You can only use your hands," I said, throwing his carefully selected word back in his face. "That should be *adequate*."

I expected him to push back, but all he did was tilt his head. "All right. To clarify, no oral sex." He pushed away from the wall, and as he moved closer, shadow fell across his face. "But I am allowed to use my mouth elsewhere. Agreed?"

There was a worried voice in the back of my head that I promptly silenced. "Fine."

He gave a conquering smile as he sat on the lounge beside me. "Do you think you've hindered me, Sophia?" He skimmed his knuckles across my cheek, and his eyes, which never seemed to miss a thing, swept down over my face, zeroing in on my mouth. "You may think you've taken away my only weapon, but I have so many more." He leaned in and whispered it against my lips. "Eleven twenty-two."

I was already succumbing to his magnetic pull. "What?"

"My hour starts now."

ELEVEN

MACALISTER

Sophia was visibly nervous. Anxiety tensed her shoulders and kept her posture stiff, which I found fascinating. I was the one beneath the clock, but if her apprehension was over losing to me, then it wasn't misplaced.

This was easily the smartest wager I'd ever made.

If I won, not only would she tell me who she wanted named in DuBois's book, but I'd get to be the first man to give her an orgasm, and I loved nothing better in this world than being a woman's source of pleasure. In the unlikely event I lost, I'd get an hour of almost total rein over her body.

And what a body she had. The mouth that went with it was another story.

I despised the way she'd taunted when she called me Daddy, but what was more troubling was my own reaction to it. A warped and twisted delight lingered even after her fetishized word had dissipated.

It had pushed me beyond sense, and the spanking I'd delivered escalated far beyond what I had intended. The desire to discipline and correct had been my original goal, and then abandoned at the wayside the very moment my cock had grown hard.

My selfish needs had taken command, and I'd been weak enough to let them.

Sophia had alleviated much of the ache she'd created tonight, and thankfully, now I was back under control, my mind firmly in charge. I was displeased I'd let myself get into this situation, but happier now with the turn of events.

I'd allow myself to indulge, as long as I remembered this was all there'd be. One night of indiscretion was easy to write off, but it could not happen again.

She sighed when I brushed my lips against hers and softened further when I kissed her in earnest. The meeting of our mouths worked to dispel her anxiety one layer at a time, like fingers unlacing a corset. Each slow stroke of my tongue freed her more.

Yet kissing her was . . . worrisome.

After Julia, I viewed kissing as a tool. It was an act to be performed by the man and experienced by the woman, and I typically used it to deepen my level of seduction. Kissing was the most effective way to establish who was in control.

But whenever my mouth was on Sophia's, I hadn't a clue who was leading our kiss, or who between us was in charge. It was disorienting, leaving me unbalanced. Kissing was supposed to be a device. A checkpoint to pass on the way toward a sexual encounter. But with her, it had *feeling*—it had its own version of pleasure.

I kissed her with no motive or agenda, other than I enjoyed the way she kissed me back. I surrendered to the experience, rather than be the one driving it. Thankfully, my competitive nature, which had been lurking in the back of my mind, cleared its throat to remind me of my responsibility.

I used my body and my kiss to drive her down onto her back, and her golden hair fanned around her on the lounge's cushion. She looked so young and untouched, staring up at me with her big eyes. Why did she stay, when she seemingly knew every awful thing about me? She'd sought me out when she should have run the other way.

I didn't apologize for the things I'd done, not even the terrible ones. For most of my life, I'd been incapable of admitting a mistake, and now it was too late. I didn't see the point. If you broke a glass, an apology would not put it back together.

I balanced over her on my arms, and her warm hands distracted me from my thoughts when they dove inside my open shirt, roaming over my chest. A teasing look filled her face. "You realize you've already wasted ten minutes kissing me."

Irritation at what she'd implied clamped my teeth together. "I did not find the last ten minutes *wasteful*, Sophia."

Her brow furrowed in dismay. "I didn't mean it like—"

The statement died as I sat back from her, peeled off my suit coat, and tossed it aside. I trapped her under my gaze as I went to work undoing my cufflinks, dropping them one by one to the floor with a quiet *ping*, each followed by a short skitter.

Then I set a foot on the floor and rose onto the knee of my other leg, halfway off the chaise lounge as I stripped off my shirt and discarded it. The way her gaze traced over my bare chest and down my arms caused pride to warm inside me. I'd done the best I could under the circumstances for the last two years and had hoped for admiration from her, but she gave me something far better in return.

She stared at me with unfiltered lust.

I savored it until her gaze settled on the silver watch on my wrist.

The clock is ticking, Macalister.

The firelight cast flickers of orange and yellow across her nude body, and I leaned over her, setting a hand beside her head for support. It left my other hand free to begin. My touch had an enormous effect on her, and I would use that to its fullest advantage tonight. I trailed my fingertips down the column of her neck and watched how her chest lifted in a deep breath.

Her lips parted when my palm smoothed over her shoulder and down her arm. I teased with my caress, sliding my hand over the flat expanse of her stomach, carving a path down her body as if I were brushing away all the others who'd tried and failed what I was going to accomplish tonight.

When I reached her knee and began to move back up, I appreciated the way her legs subtly parted for me, and I rewarded her action by brushing my thumb along the inside of her thigh. Up I went, sliding over her smooth skin, inching toward the slit between her legs. Her eyelids fluttered closed in anticipation.

I veered my hand away at the last moment, continuing its journey upward, and I enjoyed how her eyes burst open in surprise. She'd thought I'd slide my fingers over her clit or perhaps push two deep inside her, and while this was eventually my plan, it was the endgame. There were several moves I had yet to make.

Seduction was a multistep process and began with her mind. Once I had her turned on, I still had to prime her body. The more work and preparation I put in, the greater the reward would be. When she arched up off the cushion into my touch, it signaled she was ready for more. I tilted down and planted my lips against the pulse point on her neck just below her ear, sucking until her hands tightened their grip on my arms.

Sophia smelled like an orchard, sunny and fruity, and it lulled me to want to stay right where I was, nestled against her throat with my hand on her waist, but time was my opponent. I was confident in my abilities but would need to leave a few extra minutes in case she really did have difficulty achieving orgasm and it wasn't just lazy, inept partners.

I loved a challenge, and this one had been tailor-made for me.

She moaned faintly when I skated my fingertips over her breast, teasing her nipple with a featherlight touch. Her arms were dotted with goosebumps, and her chest rose and fell rapidly as I closed my fingers on the bud, pinching and testing her response. I didn't use much pressure, as I planned to do that with my mouth, but it was enough to bring her knees together, and a wicked smile spread across my lips.

She'd done that to squeeze against and prolong the pleasure my touch had given her.

"Spread your legs," I ordered.

I inhaled sharply when she did it without hesitation. She didn't have an inkling of how satisfying that was. I craved control, and her instant response to my dominance was a drug. I had to be careful not to become addicted.

Now that there was room for me, I shifted on the lounge and knelt between her parted legs, cupping both her breasts in my hands. They were soft and warm and full—likely the best I'd ever seen. If I'd had more time, I would have lavished them with attention, but tonight I had to be efficient and deliberate.

I bent down and closed my lips over a nipple, sucking her into my mouth.

This was the loudest moan I'd heard from her so far, and it shot straight to my groin. It was frustrating how physical desire was already reawakening in my body. I'd never been slow to recover, but for once, I didn't want to. How could I trust myself not to take her to bed, when she constantly worked me up, and I hadn't had sex in three agonizing years?

Because you can't. You shouldn't even be doing this.

I captured her nipple between my teeth and bit down hard.

"Oh," she gasped as she jolted, trying to squirm away, but I soothed the tender skin with the flat of my tongue.

"Did that hurt?" I mumbled against the curve of her breast.

"A little," she whispered.

"Can you handle it?"

She went stiff beneath me. "What?"

I nuzzled into her cleavage, rubbing the stubble on my chin against her skin. "Is that an acceptable amount of pain? I ask because your brain releases endorphins to counteract and dull pain." I moved to focus on her other breast. "These are the same endorphins that can produce euphoria."

Her swallow was so hard, it was audible, and she dragged in a heavy breath. "You wanted it to hurt, because you think it'll help?"

"Precisely." I used the tip of my tongue to spin a circle over her pebbled skin. "To make sure it triggers the release, I'll need to do it again." Several more times, if she was willing. I latched onto her nipple, sucked until my cheeks hollowed, and then released her from my mouth with a soft *pop*.

She licked her lips and blinked slowly, her eyes cloudy with desire. "Yeah," she whispered. "I can handle it."

Eagerness raced through my bloodstream, and I went to work. Her startled gasps mixed with whimpers as I toyed with her, doing my best to walk the fine line between discomfort and true pain. I wasn't interested in hurting her, and I didn't get off on tears or agony, but I understood how lower valleys lead to higher peaks.

I nipped at the top of her breast with perhaps too much force, because Sophia's whimper changed its pitch, and my heart thudded like it was made of stone. "Too much?"

Her gaze darted away from mine, and every muscle in me went to full alert.

"Should I stop?" I asked with concern.

"No." Her head turned back so she could look at me, and she threaded her hands into my hair. Why did she look embarrassed? "It kind of hurts but . . . I like it. It feels good."

My heart restarted at twice its usual speed, and inside my

pants, my demanding cock twitched. *No,* I said to myself in the strictest voice possible. There were thousands of other women in this world who made more sense for me than Sophia Alby. I had to finish tonight, and tomorrow I'd go find that woman.

They probably wouldn't beat me in skeet or respond as perfectly to my dominance, but they wouldn't destroy the last bit of reputation I had left. If I had to choose between my desire or my name, I'd choose my legacy.

No matter how much I wanted what I couldn't have.

I snagged her skin between my teeth and coursed a hand down her stomach. She'd said the pain felt good, but the time had come to make her feel very, *very* good.

My fingers found her just as wet as she'd been after I'd spanked her, but her reaction was dramatically bigger this time. When I touched her, her back arched and she bowed up off the upholstery, letting loose a gasp that was filled with stunned pleasure.

"That feels good, doesn't it?" My tone was dark and pleased.

"Yes," she said breathlessly. Her hand slid down my forearm so she could wrap her fingers around my wrist, but not to stop me. She'd done it to ground herself to me, to know exactly what I was doing to her. How I was touching her.

I pressed the pads of my fingers against her swollen clit and rubbed them steadily back and forth, gradually increasing my speed. Her breath came and went in stuttering bursts, the beautifully erotic sound of it ringing in my ears. I planted a final kiss at the center of her chest then straightened so I was upright, sitting back on my legs folded beneath me.

She was perfectly bare and pink, even down to the two sparkling gems at either end of her piercing jewelry. I'd never cared for piercings in general, and so I had assumed one in such an intimate place would have been a turn-off, but I'd been incorrect.

I wanted to touch, and my tongue craved to trace over it.

I adjusted my hand so my fingers and palm lay across her lower abdomen and swiped my thumb over the metal barbell struck through the skin right above her clit. Sophia moaned, just loud enough to be heard over the pop and hiss of the fire in the fireplace, and more pressure built beneath my fly, pushing against my zipper.

My body needed to stop. My pants had come off once tonight, and that was already one time too many.

While my thumb teased and massaged, I ran the palm of my other hand up and down her legs. I wanted her to feel my presence everywhere, so I'd become inescapable, inevitable. I'd already hooked her. Now I had to focus on reeling her in, and then she would be mine.

Mine? I frowned. I didn't want her to be mine.

Liar.

My hand swept up the inside of her thigh, and I relished the way her legs had begun to quiver. Could I make them tremble harder before she came? My voice was strict. "Open your eyes."

She wasn't allowed to think about someone else during this. I was the one in charge of her this evening, which included everything—even her thoughts. Her unfocused blue eyes blinked open and stared up at me, drunk off the sensations I was giving her, but she was able to watch as I pushed my index finger into my mouth, all the way to the knuckle.

It was unnecessary. She was incredibly aroused and her body cooperative, but this act of me wetting my finger in preparation was another way to flex my power over her. It demonstrated that I'd do all I could to deliver the best experience possible.

Sophia watched me intently as I withdrew, my skin damp with my saliva. I turned my palm up to the ceiling and eased that long finger inside her hot, tight body.

Her mouth rounded into a silent *oh*, but then she voiced it. It spilled from her lips, soaked in enjoyment. "Oh, God."

My hands worked in tantum, my thumb from my left rubbing slow circles as my right index finger stroked in and out. Almost immediately, her hips began to move to match my unhurried tempo.

She bit her bottom lip and threw her head back, trying to stifle her moan, but it made me hunger to hear her. Communication was key. I increased my speed and pressure, causing the muscles inside her to clamp down on my finger.

A victorious smile swept across my face. I hadn't gone after her G-spot yet, and she was already halfway to ecstasy. She clawed at my arms like a mindless, needy thing, and the situation in my pants graduated from a nuisance to a full-blown irritation. I was hard and throbbing uncomfortably but pushed it aside. This wasn't about me right now.

It was a slick glide as I sawed my finger into her cunt, and I reveled possessing her this way.

"I like how my finger looks inside you," I said. "I imagine it'll look even better with two."

She bucked as I pushed my middle finger in alongside the first, and a groan of heat rolled out of her. The girl's eyes were wild, frenzied with lust and need, and I thrust my fingers deeper, watching for a telltale signal. Would she cry out? Or would Sophia go utterly silent, her eyes rolling back in her head, as I located the spot that had eluded everyone else before me?

It didn't take long. The cadence of her uneven breath shifted, and she jammed her hands into her silky hair. Her eyes slammed shut, but I allowed it when she whined the word, begging me.

"Macalister."

My name in her broken voice was fire, raging a million times hotter than the one burning in my fireplace.

When I thrust my fingers faster, hammering the spot, her hands weren't able to stay still any more than her body was. She slapped her palms against the cushion beneath her, her fingers splayed out, and she used her arms for leverage to help lift her hips, meeting my rapid pace.

I flicked my thumb back and forth, watching the barbell slide side to side as I manipulated her clit, using the rest of my hand to keep contact with her. It had grown challenging with how much she was writhing, but I was up to the task.

Air choked off in her lungs, and I saw the realization take hold in her eyes. I was going to win. Her body wanted that outcome. It was clamoring for it, and I'd done all within my power to make sure her mind couldn't stop me.

"Wait," she said with dread.

"Why?" I didn't hesitate. "Because you don't want to lose?"

"Yes," she admitted. She couldn't control herself when she was under my command, and she kept moving, encouraging me to do the same. Whimpers of pleasure seeped from her as she reluctantly neared the threshold. Her legs shook with such force, they looked powerless.

"Give it to me," I demanded.

My dark order shoved her over the edge, and Sophia cried out as her orgasm gripped her. *My* orgasm, I corrected in my head. She contracted both inside and out, pulsing on my fingers as she collapsed onto the lounge, flinching and jerking with aftershocks. It made her perfect breasts undulate and her hands curl into tight fists. I took it all in, this viciously sexy scene that she'd never shown anyone else before.

It was our secret now.

I withdrew my hands from her and crawled over her body, settling my hips to hers and bringing our bare chests together. My cock was aching for satisfaction, but it would have to settle for my hand later. There was other satisfaction I needed.

I planted my lips on hers. To the victor went the spoils, and I took my fill while she continued recovering, one deep breath at a time, although I had the suspicion my kiss delayed it. I held her captive beneath my lips.

When our kiss finally ended, fear and wonder mixed together in her eyes. She was stunned I'd done as I said I would, and perhaps she was grateful, but her trepidation was growing over what had to happen next.

It was hard not to sound smug. "The name."

Panic flooded through her expression, and then it shuttered. She slid out from under me, retreating. "There are two."

I raised an eyebrow. "Are you asking for double-or-nothing?"

Because a second orgasm would be even easier to pull from her, but it'd take its toll on me. I was already thinking of ways to justify carrying her upstairs. Excuses that would permit me to discover how her piercing felt against my tongue.

"No," she answered. "I'm only giving you one name."

She tried to fold herself away from me, and I didn't care for it. I scooped her up into my arms and pulled her into my lap, using the tip of my nose to draw a line up the side of her neck. Either the product she used in her hair or her perfume was the source of her apple scent.

"All right," I said in a persuasive hush, right beside her ear. "Tell me."

The orgasm had left her body, but the tremble remained. It wasn't a shiver. The fire was warm, and I was holding her, which left me to believe this was stress. Was she worried once I had the name, I'd go after this person with surgical precision until I'd uncovered every last secret?

She wasn't wrong.

Her eyes closed, unable to look at me. "The name," she said, "is Sophia Alby."

TWELVE

MACALISTER

MY EYES WERE BURNING WITH EXHAUSTION, AND I KEPT MY GAZE directed out the conference room window to the sunlight while the men prattled on about the mortgage forecasts the lending team had presented. I had never fallen asleep during a meeting because doing so would be disastrous. My subordinates had lost enough respect for me; they didn't need to lose any more.

I spent far too much time thinking about Sophia and didn't realize the meeting had concluded until the room was nearly empty and a hand was on my shoulder.

"Dad?"

I looked up into the face that was so similar to his mother's, sometimes I hated it. A constant reminder of what I'd had and was stolen from me. Royce's eyes were mine, though, and concern lurked in them now.

"I'm fine," I said in my usual gruff tone and stood from my seat.

My son didn't believe me. His arms crossed over his chest, and he gave me a hard look. It wasn't as severe as the one I had mastered, but it did its job well enough.

"It's nothing," I added as I grabbed my iPad off the table

and brushed past him, heading for the exit. "I didn't sleep well last night."

It wasn't technically true. Once I'd climbed into bed and the infernal cat stopped rubbing its face against my hand to encourage me to pet him, I'd quickly fallen asleep and slept soundly. But while I'd gotten quality, there hadn't been nearly enough quantity.

As soon as Sophia had dropped her name, she'd leapt from my arms and pulled on her clothes, refusing to elaborate. It wasn't part of the deal, she'd protested. I'd been bested by her *again*, more or less. She'd given me the one name I'd spent the evening trying to convince myself I wasn't interested in.

Not fifteen minutes after she'd left, I'd pleasured myself in the shower, fantasizing all the ways I'd have her if I allowed it.

Royce followed me out into the hall, past the pictures of the different branches our family company had planted across the globe. "Take the afternoon," he said. "Go get some rest."

He didn't say it with force, but I couldn't tolerate it regardless. I halted and turned to face him. There weren't tired lines etched at the corner of his eyes, and when he rubbed his fingers at his temple, I noted the flash of his cufflinks. Ares, the god of war—a gift from Marist.

It was difficult to tolerate how he had everything he wanted. His youth, his wife's love, his high position within the company I'd done more for than any other Hale. In my desire to win at all costs, I'd lost practically everything.

Even people to desperately pin my failure on.

I kept my voice low so as not to disturb our employees in the offices nearby. "You do not tell me what to do."

Royce's shoulders lifted as he assumed a confrontational posture but matched my hushed voice. "You were an embarrassment in there." He motioned back toward the conference room. "Go home, Dad. We didn't fall apart while you were gone for two years. I think we can handle one fucking afternoon."

When I didn't move, he closed his eyes and pinched the bridge of his nose, which was a mannerism he'd unwittingly picked up from me.

"I'm asking," he said. "Please."

The word didn't come easily to him, and I could respect that. We were both aware of the hierarchy at HBHC and how far he'd risen, and I appreciated that he chose not to flex his power or throw it in my face, especially since when the roles were reversed, I'd done it to him.

I was a sore loser, yet my son was gracious in his victory.

"You've made your point," I said, conceding. I was tired and no good to anyone. "You'll call if anything comes across your desk that needs my input."

He relaxed a degree. "Yeah, of course."

I gave a short nod as a goodbye and resumed my journey toward my office, but felt his gaze at my back. Despite everything I'd done, he still cared enough about me to worry, proving he was a better man than I'd given him credit for. It gave me a sliver of hope we'd find a way to repair some of the damage I'd done.

Sophia was at her desk, hunched over her computer for once instead of her phone, but when my shadow fell over her, she lifted her gaze to mine and kept her face blank.

"My office," I barked. "Now."

As expected, she did exactly as asked and shut the door behind us. However, alarm made her tense when I strode to one of the couches and sat, pointing to the other across from me.

There was an edge of panic she tried to keep out of her voice. "Are you firing me?"

"No." I watched her scurry toward the couch. "We need to discuss last night."

"Oh." She wore a red top and a black and white houndstooth

skirt, which rode up a little as she crossed her long legs. Her expression was guarded. "Which speech am I getting?"

"Excuse me?"

Her eyes were dull and resigned. "I have a lot of work to do, so let's save us both some time. Is this the 'you're a great girl, and last night was fun, but it didn't mean anything' speech? Or the 'it was a mistake and it can't happen again' one?"

It was stunning how quickly she upended my thoughts. I had spent the ride in this morning carefully crafting the specific language to use to minimize how upset she'd likely become when I told her I was putting a stop to this. Yet she didn't seem upset at all.

"It wasn't a mistake," I clarified, "but you're correct. It cannot happen again."

"Okay," she said plainly, the matter settled. "Is there anything else?"

Her dismissive attitude was a knife in my gut. I should have been pleased to have it over with so painlessly. It was a better outcome than I could have hoped for. But the idea that she had no qualms about walking away from me after what we'd done—what we'd *shared*—last night . . .

It rankled.

No, worse. I despised it.

"Don't misunderstand," I tried to keep my tone even and not seethe, "this isn't what I want, but it's necessary. You are too young, and if anyone were to find out, it'd destroy us both."

"I get it." She uncrossed her legs and smoothed her palms down her skirt before rising to her feet. "It would be bad if anyone knew." She stared at me with electricity in her eyes and a cruel smile on her lips. "It's really a shame," she deadpanned, "that neither of us is any good at keeping secrets."

My tired mind failed me with a response, and by the time I'd drummed one up, she was halfway out the door.

It vexed me the way Sophia pretended nothing had happened between us. Perhaps she was proving her point. I knew nothing about any of the secrets she held, or why she wanted the focus of DuBois's book to be partly on her.

It was staggering the way she could compartmentalize her emotions, but it made sense. To compete at the Olympic level, she'd learned to turn off everything that had the potential to distract from her goal.

I was downright jealous of her ability.

Arrangements were made as we'd discussed. On Monday, I had dinner with Damon Lynch and offered to host an event for him and his campaign at my estate in July, which he graciously accepted. On Tuesday afternoon, I went to the Boston Opera Theatre to speak with the theatre director and came back to the office $200,000 poorer, but a guarantee that my grant would be used to produce a show casting Scoffield's daughter Erika in a role, even if it were a minor one.

On Wednesday, I went to human resources and put someone on hiring Jason Vanderburgh, whatever position would be a good fit for both him and my company.

And on Thursday, Sophia came into the office wearing slacks.

I saw right through her attempt to test my limits. We were playing a different form of chess, and my next move was easy to execute. All it took was one phone call.

Friday morning, I was already in my office when she arrived, waltzing in to deliver my coffee, and for once I was pleased to see she was wearing pants. I gestured to the large, flat white box tied with a silver bow resting on the table in the sitting area.

"That came for you."

She nearly spilled my coffee as I took the cup from her.

"What is it?" She eyed it warily, like it might explode if she touched it.

I feigned indifference. "Go find out."

She trudged to the table and picked at the ribbon, tugging slowly until the knot slipped free and she pulled the satin away. The lid was lifted, and she hesitated, her gaze lingering on the designer logo stamped on the sticker holding the tissue paper closed.

It was unclear if her question was for me or rhetorical. "What is this?"

The tissue rustled as she opened and pushed it aside, and then the lid she'd been holding on to crinkled under the sudden pressure of her hand. She didn't seem aware. Her free hand leaned down to touch the fabric of the midnight blue dress as if she weren't sure it was real.

Once confirmed, she stroked her fingers over it lovingly and gave the smile I hadn't realized I'd missed seeing until this moment.

"I took the liberty of purchasing you a new dress, as you seem to have run out of options in your wardrobe."

Her focus drifted my direction, like she'd just remembered I was still in the room. She peered at me with confusion and perhaps a grain of distrust. "You bought this?"

"I approved the purchase, yes." It hadn't been difficult to track down a stylist yesterday, explain what I needed, and have it delivered by six a.m. the following morning. Money solved all problems.

She plucked at the price tag still attached and gave an amused look. "This dress is twelve grand."

"I'm aware of how much it costs." This was a nonissue as far as I was concerned. I would pay an additional twelve thousand dollars to see her in it. "You will wear this dress today," I said. "For *me*."

Her breath caught, and color warmed across her cheekbones.

When she didn't move, I added, "Now, Sophia. You may use my private washroom to change."

It was powerfully satisfying when she scooped up the box and carried it into the attached restroom without a word of disagreement, and I may have detected a spring in her step as she went.

There were marketing proposals to look over, but I found it difficult to focus as I sat at my desk and listened to the rustling coming from behind the washroom door. It was inevitable that I pictured her standing beside the sink in only her bra and panties as she stepped into the dress and pulled it on. The fabric would glide over her curves as I wished my hands could.

I scowled at my thoughts.

When the door opened, she turned off the light, stepped back into my office, and my heart forgot how to complete its one and only task.

The blue dress was sleeveless but professional, its design understated. It was long, stopping several inches below her knees, and the length misled my eye into believing her legs were even longer. Like the sweater dress she'd worn the day she approached me, this one clung to her curves.

Her waist looked impossibly narrow and as if it were begging me to put my hands on it.

"What do you think?" she asked innocently and turned in a circle, and I leashed the groan that threatened to reveal my thoughts. It wasn't just how good her feminine figure looked in the dress; it was all that went with it. I'd chosen the garment. Purchased it. Demanded she wear it.

Her brilliant smile announced she was happy to, and heat

slicked down my spine, spreading out until it enveloped the rest of me. My voice was tight, choked with desire and the need to disguise it. "It looks fine."

I'd overcompensated, and she didn't believe a word of it. Sophia strutted toward me, gathering her hair in her hand, and when she reached me, she turned her back, presenting the tag still dangling from a ribbon pinned to the neckline.

In chess, I always plotted two moves ahead, but Sophia Alby made that impossible. She blinded me and it was difficult to trust my own instincts. I should have anticipated this, and perhaps I had on some level, but I was not prepared for how eager my fingers were to skate across the skin at the nape of her neck and undo the clasp of the pin.

I dropped the tag onto my desk and allowed myself a moment of weakness. I'd paid for this dress, after all.

She sucked in a sharp breath as my hands closed on her waist, preventing her from escaping, although it became evident escape wasn't on her mind. As I moved into her space, she melted back into me, my chest becoming a wall for her to lean against.

Thoughts scattered and disappeared, such as logic and propriety and sense, making room in my mind for an unfamiliar feeling of longing. Without my consent, my head dipped, and I pressed my lips to the base of her neck, just at the edge of the dress.

Her shiver moved through her frame, and I experienced it with her, my body translating it into pleasure.

"Thank you," she swallowed thickly, "for the dress."

"You're welcome." I released her while I still could and stepped back, savoring how she seemed to sway in my absence.

The back section of the Cape Hill Yacht Clubhouse was a ballroom with a soaring pitched ceiling, supported by arches that dropped columns to the sides of the room and didn't detract from the view at the back. Out the windows and beyond the veranda, the Cape was dotted with piers and boats, and then the water swept out deeper into the Atlantic.

I was pleased for Evangeline. The event appeared to be well attended, and the space was crowded, full with the finest families the town had to offer. It was loud with conversation and laughter, aided by liquor and drugs, some of which weren't likely procured by prescription.

The Shaunessys were here in the crowd somewhere.

I knew because posters displaying the bachelors and their bios had been posted in the front lounge where I currently stood, and Liam's pissant son Richard was featured on one of them.

If that snot-nosed kid brought in more money than I did, I'd go down the pier to my yacht, *Checkmate*, sail away, and never return.

"They're getting ready to start," a female voice said from behind me. "Did you mingle at all?"

The gentlemen had been encouraged to be friendly and work the room to give potential bidders a taste, and since I viewed this as a competition, I'd done my best. I'd made small talk as Sophia had coached me, chuckled at things I did not find amusing, and forced myself to smile.

I turned to face my assistant. "Yes, of course."

She was still wearing the dress I'd given her, and my pleasure at her doing so hadn't waned all day. The smile that warmed my face now was the first genuine one I'd had all evening.

There was a glass of champagne in one of her hands and her phone in the other, but as she gazed at me, a frown crossed her expression. She thrust the glass to me to hold, and I took it to free up her hand, which she immediately used to reach toward my chest. I stayed motionless as she dug her fingers into the breast pocket of my suit coat and fixed the white pocket square. It was an innocuous gesture, and yet my body thrilled at her touch.

I said it low, so no one would hear it. "You didn't ask permission to touch me."

Her eyes sparkled with amusement. "Tell me I didn't have it."

You are letting this become a problem.

I forced my gaze off her and on to the poster with my picture and bio, gesturing toward it. "Where did you get that?"

"The picture?" She glanced at the signage. "I took it during the sales meeting last week." Her posture stiffened, realizing I might not approve. "Um, is that okay?"

The image she'd captured was through the glass windows of the conference room, and she must have cropped and edited it, so I filled the frame and was the only focus. I was seated at the head of the table, my gaze turned up at whomever was presenting at the other end of the room. My hair was peppered with gray, more at the temples, but I didn't dislike how it looked. I appeared distinguished and thoughtful and unassuming.

I exuded a quiet power with that look. Confident, but not pretentious or intimidating.

It wasn't the brand I had strived for once, but now? This image sold a promise of the new Macalister Hale, older and wiser and worthy, and I was determined to deliver.

Sophia was on edge, waiting for my approval, and her voice faltered. "I think you look great."

It was unclear if she meant in the picture or in general, but either way was good. "I agree," I said. "I also appreciate that it didn't require me to sit for a photographer."

Unlike the rest of the bachelors, who obviously had. Their pictures reminded me of yearbook head shots. It made mine more visually interesting, drawing the eye, and I would take every advantage afforded me.

She shook her head when I tried to pass her glass of champagne back to her. "Keep it."

"No, I don't—"

She lifted a hand like it was beyond her control. "I know, but you look better holding it." She grinned. "The thirsty bitches are going to start a bidding war over you."

Either she'd already had a glass or two, or she felt comfortable enough around me to say such a teasing thing, but her statement made me feel . . . good. It left me at a loss at how to respond, but then the music faded in the ballroom, and the announcer asked the gentlemen participating in the auction to report to the captain's room.

I started to move past her, but Sophia's hand gently grasped my arm and made me hesitate. "Hey," she said in a hush. "You don't need it, but good luck, Macalister."

There was a rush inside me, a sensation similar to falling unexpectedly. It was both frightening and exhilarating at the same time. My voice wasn't as steady as usual, but hopefully she'd hear the weight I put behind it. "Thank you."

We parted, her going into the ballroom to join her friends and me taking the long way around the building to avoid the crowd. The gift shop and offices were closed and dark. I walked past them, planning to cut through the restaurant which was also closed due to the event, but there were pictures lining the hallway, and I paused at one of them, recognizing the face.

It was last year's regatta winner, likely taken moments after he'd crossed the finish line. Vance's brown hair was wild in the wind, and the bright sunlight bounced off the hull of his boat and made the water around him a vivid blue.

He was smiling ear to ear. Happy.

My heart felt heavy, sinking in my chest. I hadn't seen him

look like that in years. Was it my absence and, with it, the lack of the enormous pressure I put on him that made this possible?

There were voices in the restaurant, both male, laughing and speaking far too loudly for the topic they were discussing.

"Come on, man," one of them joked. "They should have used his mugshot for his picture."

"Like it'd matter." The second voice was bitter. "Macalister makes more money in a year than we'll make our whole goddamn lives. And, hey, you know what likes money? Pussy."

"Uh, speak for yourself, dick. I'm already making mid-six, and I've *never* had a problem getting pussy."

Chair legs squealed across the floor like they'd risen from their seats. "You are so full of shit, Lynch."

This had to be Duncan Lynch and not his father Damon. The voice was too young, and Duncan was one of the bachelors participating, not to mention, as a board member, the older Lynch made far more than six figures a year.

"You never had a problem getting pussy?" the other man continued. "Then I've got two words for you—Sophia Alby."

My muscles solidified upon hearing her name, turning me into stone.

Duncan scoffed. "Okay, that was all her. I tried a couple times, but she always looked at me like I had a disease. I got tired of how she acted like she was better than me."

With what little evidence I had, I concluded Sophia's assessment had been correct. She was far better than Duncan Lynch.

The other man's tone was teasing but contained an edge of meanness. They were striving to be friendly, but not friends. "Was that before or after Madeline gave you the clap?"

Duncan didn't miss a beat. "Just so you know, I heard she got it from your dad."

"That's funny. I heard she got it from *yours*."

Both men laughed like venereal diseases were hilarious. I

pressed my fingertips to my forehead and rubbed the crease I felt developing there. During my tenure, most of the board members had trouble staying faithful to their wives, and Damon Lynch was no exception. But I assumed he'd taken precautions during his indiscretions, and now he was running for Congress on a 'family first' platform.

"I saw her," the other man said, "so I know she's here. What are the chances she'll bid on me?"

"Who? Sophia?" Duncan paused. "None, bro. She's only into dark meat."

Anger flared inside me on both her behalf and Tate's. Cape Hill wasn't welcoming to anyone deemed 'new money,' and was even worse regarding race. It was shameful the number of times a member of the Isaacs family had been told they were in the wrong place when attending social events. I couldn't tolerate Duncan's statement, and the heat melted the stone from my body. My large feet fell silently on the carpet as I made my approach, readying to confront them.

"She just needs a little convincing," the other man said.

"She's not the prom queen anymore, and you're still so desperate to fuck her."

"Because it's gonna happen." His tone turned dark and twisted, making the air around me cold. "I know how to be persuasive."

"Yeah, good luck with that, dick. Girls watch their drinks. She, or maybe one of her friends, will catch you."

It was the second time Duncan had used the derogatory term, and awareness took hold. He wasn't insulting the other man; he was merely using his name. Ice climbed over my skin, and my jaw set so hard, it ached. I'd never heard anyone address Richard Shaunessy as Dick before, but I'd never paid much attention either.

I stepped into the empty restaurant, lit by the security

lights and red emergency exit signs, and spotted the two men standing beside the empty bar.

No, not men. They wore suits and each held an alcoholic drink in hand, but these were boys, posturing to outdo one another. Richard surveyed Duncan critically, watching as his acquaintance used a credit card to push white powder into lines on the glossy counter.

Neither noticed me lurking in the shadows.

"Stop calling me that," Richard said. "It's not my name, and if you want to keep being an asshole, I'll take my coke somewhere else."

Fury washed down me in waves, each more rage-inducing than the last. The audacity of them to do this out in the open, where anyone could walk by, was staggering. Had Duncan forgotten his father's political ambitions, or did he not care how his actions had the potential to derail the campaign?

It was further proof of how entitled and impervious this younger generation of Cape Hill had become. Like Marist's beloved Greek myths, my generation were the gods who'd created the monsters populating the mortal world.

However, it was the comment about persuading Sophia that broke my grip on my control. I wasn't proud of the techniques I'd employed to try to win Marist's affection, but the idea of drugging another person—especially Sophia—turned my stomach.

Seduction was a game a man should enjoy playing, and there was no victory in bedding a woman who couldn't surrender willingly. Richard Shaunessy was a fucking coward, just like his father.

I cleared my throat, startling both men, and when their gazes spied me in the low light, they nearly pissed themselves.

"Mr. Hale," Duncan said in a rush, dropping the credit card to the counter like he suddenly didn't know where it had come from, and turned his back to the bar. Richard followed suit, both men looking extra pale in the security light as they tried unsuccessfully to hide what they'd been doing.

"Duncan," I acknowledged with a look so severe, the boy's gaze went to the floor. I turned my attention to the other one, and his name tasted vile on my tongue. "Richard."

Their fear permeated the space like a dense fog, and I breathed it in like the Minotaur devouring the sacrificial mortals sent to him in the Labyrinth. Time suspended painfully for them, and I enjoyed it.

"Clean that mess up," I snarled, jabbing a finger toward the bar, "and I don't mean with your noses."

"Yes, sir," they said at the same time, whirling to hastily scoop the powder up into their hands. It was disposed of in the nearby trashcan, and then they stood, shoulder to shoulder with their heads tipped down, insolent children awaiting punishment.

"They've called for us to gather in the captain's room," I said, "and I believe we've kept Mrs. Gabbard waiting long enough. Let's go."

Relief released their muscles, and the two boys eagerly started for the back exit.

"Oh, Richard, one more thing." I relished the way he halted and braced himself at my voice. "You'll steer clear of Sophia. If you go near her, I'll make sure you, and your entire fucking family, regret it. Do you understand me, son?" At my sides, my hands tensed into angry fists. "She is *mine*."

THIRTEEN

MACALISTER

AN ALARM CLANGED IN MY HEAD, LOUDER THAN THE BELL ON
Wall Street. The comment had come from me without warning
and left far too much open to interpretation.

"My assistant," I clarified quickly.

Richard gave a petrified bob of his head and followed
Duncan, who'd already scrambled out the door.

It gave me a moment of respite, and I set Sophia's glass of
champagne down on one of the tables nearby, then used both
hands to scrub my face. I was still jittery with outrage, but I had
to get hold of myself. That slip had been exceptionally sloppy.

There was a mirror behind the bar, and I glanced at it. My
hair was askew and my expression furious, and this absolutely
would not do. I closed my eyes, drew in a deep breath, and
forced myself to hold it for three seconds. As I exhaled, I let
go of the anger. I was in control. I rolled my shoulders back,
smoothed a palm over my hair, and touched the pocket square
Sophia had straightened.

She'd told me I didn't need luck.

I snatched up the champagne and strode from the room,
determined to find out if she was right.

The captain's room was a much smaller event space beside the main one and invested fully in the nautical theme. The widows were round and reminiscent of portholes, and oars had been mounted to the wall in a crisscross pattern to create a focal wall, which all the men had gathered under.

Evangeline brightened when she saw me. "I was beginning to think you weren't coming."

I wanted to pointedly tell her I was a man of my word, but Sophia's voice echoed in my head, warning me to be charming and not rude. "I was held up. I apologize for the delay." My gaze swept over her. "You look nice."

It was true. She wore a sherbet colored tailored dress, and the color was flattering against her skin. Surprise darted through her eyes, like she believed I was incapable of providing a compliment. "Why, thank you." She leaned closer and set a hand on my arm. "As do you."

"Thank you." My smile was practiced and efficient. Her gesture was friendly and mirrored Sophia's from earlier, but her touch didn't affect me the same. I didn't care for it, but why was that? Evangeline was a beautiful woman. Was it because she was in love with someone else?

That hadn't stopped me in the past, but perhaps I'd learned my lesson.

Or perhaps I was only interested in what I shouldn't be.

Evangeline finished greeting the other men before disappearing out the door to start the auction. I drank a sip of the warm champagne I was holding since my mouth was dry, and not because Sophia's lips had touched the glass. The bubbling wine was no longer cold, and it was too sweet, but it gave me something to do while waiting.

When my name was announced, I emerged from the holding area, climbed the set of steps up onto the temporary stage, and squinted against the bright light. The crowd had been jovial up to this point, with some of the women catcalling the bachelors when they appeared.

It was deathly silent as I went to my mark. No one dared move in the ballroom. All eyes were on me.

The auctioneer was a woman in her fifties who stood behind the podium set to the side, and once it was clear I was ready, she reminded the crowd of my resume, and that this auction was special. It wasn't just dinner with Macalister Hale, it included an all-expense paid trip to Aspen and a VIP ticket to the weekend-long festival.

"We'll start the bidding at one thousand," she said. "Do I hear one thousand?"

Each second of silence tightened my chest until it became a challenge to breathe.

A hand shot up, off to the side.

"One thousand, thank you very much. Do I hear two?"

The stage lights made it difficult to see, but the orange-pink dress came into focus. Evangeline. I smiled appreciatively.

"Two. Yes, thank you to the lady in the blue to my right."

My attention swung to the other side of the stage and landed on Ainsley Bellinger, who worked in the mobile banking department of HBHC. She was my age or a few years younger, but it was impossible to tell with some women. She took care of herself; that much was clear. She was direct at the office, which I admired, but I had heard grumblings from the men working beneath her.

My biggest qualm was I found her personality to be like so many others—tedious.

"How about three?" the auctioneer asked. "Can I get three?"

Evangeline's hand went up.

But Ainsley's did at four thousand.

The shift in the room was subtle, like a gate that had been slowly cranked open and now was acceptable to pass through.

The unsure women were satisfied I was now safe, and when the auctioneer called for five, several hands went up.

After that, it was too fast for me to pick them out of the crowd, but my hurried heartbeat slowed to a leisure pace. Royce was better at putting people at ease than I was, so I slid a hand into my pocket and tried to mimic the casual stance I'd often seen him assume. The auctioneer's sing-song voice rolled on as the bids continued to climb.

Five thousand.

Ten.

Each bid was a declaration from the people of Cape Hill that the story of Macalister Hale didn't have to end on a rooftop balcony.

Bids began to slow as we reached twenty.

"Twenty-two is the bid, do I hear twenty-three?" The woman pointed at Evangeline. "Yes, thank you. Now we're at twenty-three, going on to twenty-four."

Ainsley's hand waved, and the people around her tittered with excitement.

All the other bids had dried up, and the collective gaze in the room turned back to Evangeline, wondering what she'd do.

Her bidding war helped build the narrative that she wasn't having financial difficulties. That she'd moved on and we were seeing each other. It prompted Sophia's words to come back to me. Perhaps when she told me I didn't need luck, she'd meant it literally.

She'd planted Evangeline as a ringer.

If it was win at all costs, this was what I should have done, rather than rely solely on my money and looks. I'd been distracted and unfocused, still finding my footing after my long absence, and I was grateful Sophia had taken care of this for me.

Evangeline's manicured nails glinted as she lifted her hand, accepting the bid at twenty-five thousand. People murmured their surprise. When the auctioneer asked for twenty-six, the room held its breath.

Ainsley shook her head, signaling she was out, and I was pleased. I did not want to spend an evening with her, let alone a roundtrip flight on my jet. My gaze turned back to Evangeline—

"One hundred thousand dollars," a woman called out from the back of the room.

There were gasps, followed by applause, and the damn lights blocked my view beyond the first few rows of people. The crowd split, parting to make way for her, and the shadow of the woman ambled toward the stage.

No.

My body went rigid, my face frozen, and my mind blank when Vivian Shaunessy stepped into view.

Sound distorted in my ears as the auctioneer accepted the bid and called for another, but I didn't pay any attention to it. It took all my focus to maintain a look that didn't reveal the turmoil inside me.

Vivian was still married to Liam, and her outlandish bid invited more scandal to my doorstep. Sophia knew about Liam's affair with my wife, but I was unsure about the rest of Cape Hill.

"Sold!" The woman's voice rang through the speakers and punched into my chest.

My body took over the perfunctory tasks, moving me down the stage steps to where Vivian was waiting. I stood painstakingly still as she met with the administrative manager at a side table. I was powerless as Vivian signed a form on a clipboard, produced her checkbook, and scribbled out all those zeros on her check.

As she tore it free, the sound of it twisted my insides.

The deed done, her nervous gaze lifted to mine.

She was a slight thing, pretty and elegant and almost birdlike, and her timid demeanor matched her exterior. Her eyes darted around with anxiety, struggling to keep her gaze on me. Some of my anger dispelled, making way for intense curiosity. She looked terrified, so why had she done it?

I gestured toward the back doors. "Let's discuss this outside."

The covered porch was empty of people. The auction continued inside, but it was muffled enough that we could hold a conversation. The water below lapped softly at the docks, and the air was warm and breezy, ruffling Vivian's dark brown hair.

She said it like the words caused her pain. "Did you know? I don't mean to speak ill of the dead, but Alice and Liam—"

I straightened. "Yes. I was aware."

She was relieved not to have to break the news of my wife's adultery. If I was honest with myself, I should have seen it coming. It wasn't long into our marriage before she began to stray, and we'd come to an understanding. Divorce wasn't something that happened in the Hale family, so I released her to pursue other partners, provided she was discreet, and as the years went by, she'd grown more brazen in who she became involved with, desperate for my attention.

Alice was hollow. It was one of the things that had originally attracted me to her. I'd thought I could fill her up and mold her as I wanted, and it had worked in the beginning. But when her appetite grew beyond me and I was no longer enough for her, we were finished. She craved newness, consumed it relentlessly, but never could find satisfaction.

"I don't want to go to Aspen with you," Vivian said.

Suspicion coiled in my stomach. "Is that so? You paid a lot of money to do just that."

There was fierce woman hiding inside her shell, and she came forth. "No. I paid a lot of my *husband's* money. I wanted to embarrass him like he did me, and I thought it was fitting that I'd use you to do it."

The coil untwisted inside my body, dispelling some of the

tension. What she'd done unexpectedly pleased me. *Hell hath no fury like a woman scorned*, they said.

As if on cue, Liam charged through the doors, barreling at her with anger coating his face.

"Vivian, what the—" When he spotted me at her side, he pulled up short. "Macalister."

"Hello, Liam." I peered down at him and was grateful for my height. I was taller than most men, placing me at a physical advantage, and I used it now. "I was just thanking your wife for her generosity. What an enormous amount of money you've donated."

He stared at my chest, refusing to meet my gaze, and he looked like I'd just put a fist in his stomach.

Over his shoulder, I watched as Sophia slipped out and stood near the side of the building, and although her focus didn't appear to be on us, I was certain it was. I settled the full weight of my intense gaze back on him.

"You made a mistake when you slept with Alice," he shrank back, but I kept my tone even, "and your wife has just paid for it, so I suggest you thank her."

Disbelief finally drew his gaze up to mine, and when he saw I was entirely serious, he turned hesitantly toward her. "Thank you."

It was humiliating for him, and it gave me a modicum of satisfaction. I rolled my shoulders back. "I consider this matter settled between us."

He couldn't believe it. "Really?"

"Yes. I am striving to be a better man these days." I couldn't stop the pointed directive from coming forward, though. "But you will remember how forgiving I was if you're ever asked to vouch for my character."

Liam nodded quickly. "Of course."

He took his wife's hand, anxious to be gone from my sight

before I changed my mind, and it wasn't long before Sophia moved in, filling the space at my side.

"That was unexpected." It wasn't clear if she meant the results of the auction or the abrupt forgiveness I'd given a man I despised. She asked it in a hush. "You all right?"

Strangely, I was. It felt good not to have the burden. "I'm fine."

She accompanied me as I walked to the edge of the porch, and I rested my hands on the railing, looking out over the water. For a long moment, the two of us lingered there in enjoyable silence, admiring how the moon looked as it hung over the ocean.

"I assume you encouraged both Evangeline and Ainsley to bid."

"Yeah. I did." She gave me a guilty smile. "But you want to know something interesting?" Electricity sparked in her eyes. "I told them you'd cover fifteen K. So, that last ten grand they bid? It was all them."

She had an infectious smile, and that saying was appropriate. I was becoming infected by Sophia. I'd never been quick to smile, but it kept happening when she was around.

"Thank you for your help tonight," I said.

My appreciation landed on her and she nodded, perhaps unsure of what to say.

"What's next in this plan of yours?" I asked.

She looked up at me with mischief in her eyes, and it was enticing. "I start telling you Cape Hill's secrets."

Instead of reading blogs about the stock market during my run tonight, I used that time to evaluate what I wanted and how I would achieve it. Once the decision had been made, I increased the treadmill to the highest speed I could sprint and told myself if I could complete a quarter-mile while maintaining that pace, I'd allow myself to have Sophia.

I set a new personal record.

And although I was gasping for breath when it was over, I was pleased with both my victories.

After my shower, Lucifer sat on the edge of my bed and meowed angrily, displeased we were behind the schedule he liked to keep. I did not like being summoned, and I glared at him as I made my way toward the bed. "All right, I'm coming."

I'd barely lain down before he was beside me, turning in a circle to find the right spot to settle into, where he'd be irritatingly pressed to my side.

My phone buzzed with a text message.

Sophia: You up?

Me: Yes.

Sophia: Just left a party where everyone was talking about you.

Me: In a positive light?

Sophia: Oh, yeah. Everyone loves a bad boy who's secretly a good man.

FOURTEEN

SOPHIA

Damon Lynch's fundraising party was masquerading as his sixtieth birthday celebration and devouring my life. I didn't have to plan every detail, as Macalister had authorized a budget, told me to hire a team of coordinators, and Mr. Lynch's team said they'd send someone from the campaign to help, but I still had to run point on all of it.

I enjoyed this kind of work, but the pressure was intense. It was beyond important to me that I do a good job. If the party was a success, it was further proof to Macalister that I was a valuable asset and, oh, how I desperately wanted to please him. If I wasn't thinking about the party, my thoughts were on the man in the office next door.

I'd gone down on him.

He'd given me an orgasm.

And now he wanted to pretend none of that had happened. Well, fine. I'd play his game, and I'd freaking beat him at it. Macalister could say whatever he wanted, but Monday morning after the auction, there was another white box on the table in his office waiting for me.

This dress was black with an asymmetrical neckline and

a skirt that was shorter than the last one he'd given me, ending just above my knees. I didn't have to change today, he'd explained.

"Tomorrow will be fine." His voice was exacting, and electricity sparked down my legs. I liked how he gave me orders and disguised them as casual statements. It was better this way too. I was already wearing a silk blouse and a skirt, and tomorrow I could wear the right shoes and accessories with it.

After his gift had been opened and discussed, Macalister joined me on the couches, his coffee in hand, and I began to spill the first of my secrets. I started small. Things like how Janice in accounting didn't get invited to parties anymore because stuff always went missing after she'd left. I worked my way up to telling him that Jared Nasbaum's wife was having an affair with her personal trainer, as was Jared, and occasionally the three of them fucked each other at the same time.

Macalister's eyebrow arched, and I pretended I didn't find it sexy. "Does that make you uncomfortable?" I asked. "Knowing your head of credit financing sometimes sleeps with men?"

"No," he said, his gaze tracing the HBHC logo on his mug. "The only news to me is they've moved on. It used to be their nanny."

I grinned. "Really. I hadn't heard that."

He was quite the gossip, and it was surprising the things he knew. Nothing recent, of course, but like me, he'd collected a file on everyone in his head. Everyone, it seemed, but me. I hadn't been on his radar before, but what about now?

"I've decided you'll go with me to Aspen," he said. "I have a vacation home there, and you'll stay in one of the guest rooms." To put a period on the end of his declaration, he set his coffee down with a loud thud, like a gavel banging his final verdict.

Inside me, there were fireworks, but I tried to remain calm. Anyone who was *anyone* in Cape Hill went to Aspen during

Thanksgiving weekend, and I'd heard rumors of how amaz-ing the Hale house was, but I'd never been. "You're not taking Evangeline?"

His expression gave nothing away. "She's planning to meet me there."

"Mr. Lynch's party is the week after," I said. "Are you sure it wouldn't be better if I stayed in the office?"

I don't know why I said it. I wanted to go with him, if for nothing else but to be there when he met with DuBois the first time.

Macalister shot me a look that reduced me to a puddle. "I trust you can multi-task, Sophia. I need you in Aspen with me."

As soon as his words were out in the room, it became vola-tile. They lingered in the air, dangerous and exciting. His eyes went wide then narrowed in displeasure, although it seemed like it was with himself.

"I think," he continued, "we can both agree this first im-pression with DuBois will be everything."

"Yes," I said softly.

His icy blue eyes cut right to my heart. "I cannot overpre-pare, so you will travel with me, and we will use every available moment to practice for it."

He was waiting impatiently on my approval, and how could I say no to him? "Okay."

A faint smile lurked in his eyes, but then they turned seri-ous. "I must ask a personal question." He hesitated for a single breath. "Have you been tested for sexually transmitted diseas-es recently?"

My brain slammed into a wall. "What?"

"Last weekend, I overheard a conversation I found dis-tressing. You and I have had sexual contact, so I need to know this answer."

My face heated until it was on fire, both with embarrassment but also irritation. Macalister and I had fooled around, but it wasn't like we'd had sex. Plus . . . was he implying I was careless and had caught an STD? "I, uh, haven't been tested, but I've always used condoms."

"Is that your only form of birth control?"

In my disorientation, I forgot this was none of his fucking business. "No, I'm also on the pill."

His face didn't change. It remained cold and detached. "For my peace of mind, you'll take the afternoon to complete that testing, and bring me the results."

My jaw dropped. "Are you serious?"

He looked irritated he had to answer me. "Yes."

I couldn't catch my breath and floundered for something to say.

"Have I upset you?" His gaze sharpened, studying me.

It took all of my willpower to force a natural look on my face. "Nope." I was an adult, and this was an adult thing to do, right? "I'll take care of it."

"Good. That will be all, then."

His dismissal made my blood boil, and I launched to my feet, eager to get the fuck out of his office. He was an emotional rollercoaster. One second I was on an exhilarating high, and the next he sent my stomach crashing to the ground.

On Tuesday, I wore the black dress with the asymmetrical neckline as I marched into his office, carrying the test results from the lab. Macalister was already seated at his desk, watching coverage of the markets on the television mounted to the opposite wall, the sound barely audible. I flung the paper down in front of him.

"Clean bill of health," I said pointedly.

He picked up the paper and scanned the results then cast it aside with indifference. I was a heartbeat away from letting loose a groan of frustration, but then he opened a folder and lifted the top sheet, thrusting it toward me.

"As you can see, the same for me as well."

I took the paper and glanced at the text with surprise. Sure enough, his results were negative and the date at the top was from yesterday. "You went and got tested?"

"My doctor comes to me, but yes." He finally set his full attention on me, and the gravity of it threatened to crush the world. "It's important we both feel safe in the event things were to escalate between us again."

I reached a hand behind me to grab on to the bookshelf and stabilize myself. What the fuck had he just implied? I wasn't sure what kind of look I was giving him, but maybe it was confusion, because Macalister's gaze swept slowly down my body, and as it slid back up, it was scorching hot, leaving no doubt what he'd meant.

In the aftermath of it, I was flushed and aching.

"Would you like to keep that?" He was amused.

Keep what?

His gaze went to the sheet of paper in my hand, his test results I'd accidentally crinkled in surprise. I dropped it to the desk and smoothed my hand over my hip, like I was wiping away the radioactivity of what his test results meant.

My voice was breathless. "No, thanks."

"All right." He motioned toward the table. "That came for you."

Yet another white box. I bit my lip, excited to see what else he'd bought and also anxious about it. "Macalister, you can't keep doing this."

Oh, fuck that sexy jaw. When I tried to tell him what to do, it set, the muscle tightening and flexing. "Why is that?"

"Because people will start to ask questions, like my parents. They'll wonder why my boss keeps giving me expensive gifts, and isn't this, like, exactly the kind of rumor you're trying to avoid?"

He rose from his chair, used the remote to mute the television behind me, and gave me a hard, evaluating look. My mouth went dry and my knees weak. Whatever he was considering, it was big, and . . . yeah. I was already into it.

"I won't mince my words." He leaned over the desk and set his hands on it, like a businessman entering serious negotiations. "I enjoy having a say over what you wear each day. This was the vehicle to do that with. If you don't like it, I can suggest another."

My heart galloped along, nearly coming out of my chest. "Okay."

"You give me control."

The word was like a flash grenade, a silent, beautiful explosion that was blinding. All I could do was stand still and experience it.

It took me forever to find the word. "How?"

"Once you're dressed, you'll send me a picture every morning for my approval."

I swallowed a gulp of air. This command wasn't sexual, and yet I reacted to it as if it were. A muscle deep between my legs clenched. There was something about the way he said the word *approval*. It was an arrow piercing my center, lodged inside me, and I wasn't sure I wanted to pull it back out.

He'd been the businessman, but his expression shifted into one of power and seduction. "Does that interest you?"

I knew agreeing to this was a gateway drug. I'd want more, even when it was wrong and bad for me, but it'd be too late. He was a pusher, and I'd become addicted, a junkie for Macalister's dominance and control.

I knew all of it, and I still didn't care. He'd asked if this interested me, and my body screamed its resounding consent.

I whispered it because there was so much meaning

crowding to get out, I could barely squeeze the word along with it. "Yes."

His shoulders lifted as he drew in a deep breath, filling his lungs with air and expanding his already broad chest. Was this how he looked after closing a billion-dollar merger? Like he'd finished conquering the world?

Macalister pushed off the desk and made his steady, methodical approach, and he seemed ten fucking feet tall as he closed in. He came to stand just inches away from me, far too close to be considered professional. His intoxicating cologne was faintly noticeable, and his warm breath wafted down across the skin my neckline bared.

His gaze moved over me in a slow sweep, like he was taking in every detail and committing all of it to memory. The thorough way he examined me felt no different than if he'd used his hands to do it, and goosebumps pebbled on my arms.

My breath hung when he reached out and plucked something from the fabric covering my shoulder. It was a piece of lint too small to see in his fingers, or just an excuse to touch me, but I wasn't going to complain. As he moved away, his fingertips grazed down my arm.

He spoke softly, but it was deceptive. Power swelled behind his words. "The weekends too, Sophia. Every day, I want to see what you've chosen to wear for me."

I exhaled and shuddered.

"You're shaking," he said, pretending to be surprised, but it was an act. He knew *exactly* what he was doing to me. "Are you nervous about this arrangement?"

"No," I admitted in a rush. "I'm excited."

He smiled darkly, his eyes thrilled. "Good. I am too." Our gazes held for so long, I worried I'd burst from the tension, but he turned abruptly and motioned toward the box. "You'll start tomorrow by wearing this."

The dress was silver-gray, with bishop sleeves that went to my elbows, and deep V that plunged down so low, I wouldn't be able to wear a regular bra with it. I glanced at him then back to the dress, unsure. Did he realize how much cleavage I'd be showing at the office?

I thought about his schedule. He had three hours blocked off tomorrow to discuss the rollout of a programming update, so yeah. He totally knew.

Normally, I despised waking up early, but handing control over to Macalister suddenly made it easy. Each morning since I'd agreed to his offer, I was eager to select the perfect look, snap a picture, and text it to him.

I imagined him standing in his enormous closet, his crisp dress shirt not buttoned yet and a swatch of his bare chest visible, his sleeve cuffs unpinned as he paused to glance at his phone. He'd scrutinize the image then thumb out the word that set my blood on fire.

Approved.

It was a word I longed to hear in any of its forms. Accepted. Chosen. *Yes.*

In reality, he was probably already dressed and on his way to the office by the time my text came through, but it was more fun to imagine the scenario my way. And after a week of texting, I got my first note.

Macalister: Your hair will be worn up.

So, I twisted it back into a bun, put on longer earrings, and sent an update.

Macalister: Approved.

It was unreal the effect that word had on me.

We fell in sync with each other. I delivered his morning coffee and went over his schedule with him, making adjustments as needed, and then I'd take what few minutes I had with him to go over salacious details. Who needed to go to rehab, who was caught with questionable porn on their phone, which guy was rumored to be sleeping with his stepdaughter. The last one didn't sit all that well with him, but it probably hit too close to what he'd tried to do with Marist.

The day before we were set to leave for Aspen, my desk was a mess, and Macalister gave me some serious side-eye about it before heading into his office after lunch. I sighed once he'd closed the door. I had too much on my plate right now to be tidy, but his irritation ate at me.

I was reorganizing the stack of things still needing my attention when my phone rang. Why was Natasha calling me? Usually we just texted. She worked for a busy literary agency in New York, which meant she never had time to talk.

"Hello?"

"Hey, girl," she said. "I've got some bad news."

It was apparently bad enough to warrant a call, so I braced myself. "What's wrong?"

"I just got off the phone with my boss. James DuBois's mother died this morning."

All the air went out of the room. "Oh, shit."

"Yeah. I know you were hoping to meet up with him in Aspen, but that's off his schedule now. Thought I'd give you a heads-up."

My mind raced with panic. Everything Macalister and I had been working toward, and now our plans were scrapped. What the hell was I going to do?

"You still there?" Natasha asked.

"Yeah, sorry." I stared blankly off into the distance. "Thanks for letting me know."

"Sure thing. I gotta run. My next client is—"

"Wait!" The idea formed, taking shape quickly. "I need a

favor, please."

After hanging up, I was instantly out of my seat and marched into Macalister's office, hurrying to close the door behind me. He raised his critical gaze to me and the now-closed door, and suspicion cast over his face.

"Yes?" He did nothing to hide his irritation.

I'd learned quickly in this job he did not like to be disturbed, but this was important.

"DuBois's not going to Aspen," I blurted. "His mother passed away this morning."

Macalister's shoulders stiffened as the news settled over him, then fell a touch as he leaned back in his chair, his gaze breaking away from me.

Even though he wasn't disappointed with me, it was still hard to see.

"I have an idea," I said. "We get someone from Lynch's campaign to reach out and invite DuBois to the party at your house next week."

The invite couldn't come from Macalister. It needed to look like he had no idea the book was in the works and he was a man striving for redemption with no ulterior motive.

He considered the option. "If DuBois *is* considering writing the book, then he'll accept this invitation. It would be too good of an opportunity for him to pass up."

"Right."

Macalister was traditional, but that didn't mean he couldn't adapt. He nodded, which I understood as his acceptance of this new plan. "I'll tell Damon this afternoon. Perhaps Kristin is a fan of his work."

"Fucking doubtful," I said. "The only thing Mrs. Lynch reads is the labels on her prescription bottles."

He scowled dark enough that he didn't need to speak the words to scold. He didn't like cuss words, especially in the office setting, but he'd tolerate them from others. Not me, though. I was held to a higher standard. And although I was supposed to be his partner, I'd given him control over one aspect of my life, and now it was bleeding into other areas.

"Whether or not she is a fan is irrelevant," he said. "We only need a reason to push the invitation." His gaze returned to his computer, like his personal life was sorted and now he'd focus on HBHC. "Cancel our Aspen plans."

I shook my head. "You still have to go." His head snapped my direction so he could level a glare at me, but I did my best to stand tall. "You have plans with Evangeline, and the place will be crawling with celebrity photographers."

His icy scowl was epic, and I shivered. I watched the thoughts in his mind play out through his beautiful eyes.

"You know I'm right," I added softly. "You have to go and charm everyone."

Just not Evangeline, a voice in my mind pleaded.

He swiped his palm down his tie, turning his gaze out the window, as if he couldn't look at me as he gave in. "Fine. We'll go."

It hurt to have to say it. "Macalister, I think I need to stay here. I still have so much to do for the event."

Anger simmered in his expression. "It sounds as if you are saying I gave you more responsibility than you can handle."

"No." Panic tinted my voice. "I totally can handle it, but it's, like, *incredibly* important to me that this event be the best possible. I want people to be floored, for it to be all they talk about for the next month."

It wasn't just to impress Macalister either, although that was part of it. I wanted to be seen and acknowledged by Cape Hill. Show my parents and Tate and the other people who didn't care about me what they were missing out on.

The mood in the room had been tense, but the passion

in my voice broke through, and Macalister's lips parted with pleasant surprise. "If that's the case, then it's difficult to argue with you. I very much understand the desire to strive for excellence," his gaze turned intense, "and how it can consume you."

How did he do that? He could layer innuendo into nearly any phrase and make my insides melt. I swallowed thickly. "I need to stay, no matter how badly I wanted to go with you."

It was terrifying to say the truth with him, but it was a calculated risk, and it paid off when he inhaled a deep breath. "I was looking forward to it as well."

Desire cinched around me, making everything tight and locking me in place, but his admission lit me up inside. Warmth bloomed over my skin as I stood and endured the onslaught of his gaze.

It whispered things to me. Made promises and threats and guarantees that this thing between us would come to a head. Try as he might to resist, we were doomed.

Macalister and I were inevitable.

He paused and looked unsure, which was so rare, it was strangely beautiful to see. "Tell me the other name."

The connection between us crumbled and disintegrated, and I sighed with hurt. I'd thought we were forging something, but he was just drawing closer to get my guard down. "I'll tell you . . . soon."

"When?" he demanded.

The words were bitter in my mouth. "When you're ready to hear it."

He said nothing else as I hurried from his office.

FIFTEEN

MACALISTER

DAMON LYNCH'S BIRTHDAY WAS A BLACK-TIE AFFAIR, AND IT WAS good to see the grounds bustling with people. It'd been three years since Royce and Marist's wedding, the last big event hosted here, and I was anxious to create a new memory of the Hale estate for the people of Cape Hill.

I stood in my entryway, wearing my tuxedo and a hostile look as I watched the valets outside laugh and joke around with each other. I wasn't paying them to have a good time and act like unprofessional idiots. Guests would start arriving soon, and first impressions were everything.

Especially tonight.

Movement at the top of the stairs caught my attention, and I glanced up, expecting it to be Lucifer—although the cat often hid when there was commotion in the house. Instead, it was a different gorgeous creature in black.

Sophia had been here at the house all day, although I'd barely seen her. She'd arrived early this morning, wearing minimal makeup and yoga pants, just as the rental furniture trucks were parking down by the stables.

I wanted to tell her I hated what she was wearing, but it

would have been a complete lie. The stretchy fabric clung to her shapely legs and tight backside, and every lustful thought I'd had about her over the past three weeks set upon me with a furious crash.

She had information I needed, yet she withheld. I needed her in Aspen with me, yet she stayed behind. And the desire to give her a hundred different orgasms in a hundred different ways was threatening to swallow me whole.

I *needed*.

And I was going to take.

Spending the weekend pretending to care about anything other than what she was doing at any moment solidified my decision. Once she gave me everything she'd been holding back, I'd do the same in return. It was a game, and I always won, no matter the cost.

When I put my mind to something, I was unstoppable. As she'd told me that day in the penthouse restaurant, she had a way of getting what she wanted—had she realized the same was true for me?

Late in the afternoon, Sophia had disappeared into one of the guest rooms with two women, likely a hair and make-up team, and twenty minutes ago the duo had departed the house. She'd remained upstairs, changing into her gown, and I relished the idea of her being undressed under my roof for a second time.

Perhaps I'd make that a rule at some point. If we were alone in my house, I'd require she be naked. I wanted access to her body at all times, nothing hidden from me.

The black dress she wore was strapless and fit her as if it had been painted on, all the way down below her hips, before flaring out to the floor. The outer layer was sheer lace, and as she moved down the stairs, it trailed behind her like a dark veil. Her blonde hair was twisted back and pinned up off her shoulders, except for the carefully placed strands softly curling to frame her face.

Her makeup was dramatic and sultry.

She didn't look twenty-six. She looked . . . *timeless.*

Once again, my ridiculous heart forgot how to function. Sophia descended gracefully to the bottom of the steps, fixing me with her gaze, and I was struck by the idea that the sight of me in my tuxedo was somehow having the same effect on her as she held over me. Her chest rose and fell with her hurried, uneven breath.

Her voice was hushed. "Does this meet your approval?"

Since she hadn't sent me a picture. Perhaps she wanted to show it to me in person and knew she could return to the room upstairs and adjust if something weren't to my liking.

"No," I said. She hadn't met my approval. "You've exceeded it."

The dark eye-makeup made her blue eyes deeper, and they melted at my words. It was dangerous the way she made me feel. All-powerful and mighty, as if I didn't need to control every inch of my world because she gave me hers.

"You look great, by the way," she said. "Are you ready?"

"Of course." I kept my tone light, so she'd know I wasn't serious. "You are the one behind schedule. I thought I was going to have to come fetch you."

I watched her reaction carefully, enjoying how she blushed at the idea. "It's your cat's fault. He's needy," she said with a shy smile. "But he's looking much better."

"Yes, he is," I agreed. When Sophia blinked in surprise, I paused. "What?"

She grinned. "I thought the 'animal' was Royce's."

I gave her a hard look. "I don't like what you're implying."

But she just laughed, and the bright sound was music that didn't play in this house when I had lived in it. I'd forgotten how nice it could be, the sound echoing in the spacious room.

"It's the most shocking thing I've ever heard," she teased. "Macalister Hale owns a cat."

"Sophia."

She was undeterred and pressed her hands to her chest dramatically. "I hope no one finds out. It's just simply *scandalous*."

When she pushed me, my instinct was to shove back. I reached out and seized her hand, not in affection, but in domination. At my touch, her eyes went enormously wide. Her gaze dropped to my fingers wrapped around her wrist then slowly returned to mine with heat pooled in her blue irises.

"What are you doing?" she whispered.

"Correcting your behavior." I matched her low voice. "I would do more, if I had the time."

Her red lips parted, and I focused on them, studying the heart shape as she struggled to find her breath.

But the sound of a car pulling up in the drive and the valet supervisor's voice telling his men to line up brought reality back upon us. I tore my hand away, the feel of her warmth still lingering.

I straightened and turned toward the door, and by the time the first guest had climbed the front steps, Sophia was gone, off to ensure everything was being carried out to our mutual satisfaction.

Damon and Kristin Lynch were the second guests to arrive. They looked perfectly styled for the event, conservative and safe for mass appeal. They displayed the correct amount of gratitude to me for hosting the party, which I appreciated.

"Duncan will be along shortly," Kristin said, as if I cared whether their son attended. It would be important to the Lynches, though. Damon's campaign touted that his family was the bedrock keeping him strong and supporting him every step of the way. He'd need to reinforce that with family pictures tonight.

Which reminded me of the issue I'd witnessed at the charity event weeks ago.

"Damon, a word." I motioned toward the sitting room.

He followed me without hesitation, and I waited until we were out of his wife's earshot.

"I'd prefer your son not bring any drugs onto my property."

He let out a heavy sigh, which confirmed my suspicions. If he didn't know, he would have balked. Instead, he was resigned. "Who told you?" He gave me a look of disdain. "The Alby girl?"

"No," I growled. "I caught him and Liam's son at the bachelor auction with cocaine. He wasn't subtle either. Anyone could have walked by." I lifted my chest and glowered at him. He was the frontrunner by a considerable margin. "This race is yours to lose, and Duncan's issue is a liability."

I needed Damon to win, because it could catapult Vance's career. Being a part of a congressional staff would open doors and allow him to ascend much faster.

Also, now that Vance was part of the campaign team, Damon had to win. Losing wasn't something the Hales did.

He sat down on the couch, right in the center. I tried not to think about how I'd sat in that same place more than a month ago and guided Sophia to wrap her mouth around my cock. Jesus, I spent enough time thinking about it already.

I pushed the image from my mind as his head sank into his hands.

"Do you need help?" I asked, striving for gentle tone. "Or can you handle it?"

I didn't mean it as a threat. I wanted it to be another friendly gesture, for him to view me as someone to rely on.

"No," he answered quietly. "I'll take care of it."

"Good."

He lifted his head and peered up at me, his eyes cloudy. "Can I give you some advice? Your assistant . . . Just be careful. Duncan tells me she's famous for spreading lies."

I raised an eyebrow, irritated. "As I understand it, she's not too keen on your son either."

"No." He stood and looked away, lost in thought. "They've never been friends."

There was a note of sadness in his voice that could not be ignored. It whispered of things unsaid, and I went still as the thought struck me.

Duncan Lynch.

He was the other name Sophia refused to tell me.

But . . . why? What had he done that Sophia was desperate to reveal, and yet so reluctant to tell me?

Voices sounded in the entryway, meaning I had more guests to greet, so I released Damon to go down to the gardens and encourage people to open their pocketbooks and donate to his campaign.

Evangeline was waiting for me, wearing a sapphire blue strapless dress, paired with an elaborate necklace and earrings, that I found to be too much. If she were Sophia, I'd have asked her to pare back and take the necklace off.

But, as I was painfully aware, she wasn't Sophia.

I enjoyed my conversations with Evangeline. She was an intelligent woman with a pretty face and more compassion than I'd ever have. She took a chance on me, and I was grateful for her partnership. Yet there was no spark between us. She didn't challenge or irritate me, didn't declare she hated me as both my wives had once done, before I'd worn them down and convinced them to fall in love with me.

I'd had a weekend with Evangeline under my roof in Aspen, and not so much as an inkling to seduce her. We played our roles, smiling for cameras while we'd sampled chefs' signature dishes, and privately vented to each other about the tedium of it. We'd discovered a comfortable ease with one another.

We'd never be anything more than friends.

But we *were* friends. If nothing else came out of my campaign for redemption, at least she was a genuine and honest person, exceptionally rare in Cape Hill, and had become someone I respected.

And I hoped one day my friend would be able to find a love again like the one she'd had.

"Your smile is getting better," she whispered when we embraced in brief hug. "I kind of believe it's real."

"It is real." This party was necessary, but I despised frivolous small talk. With her, it was easier. She did most of the talking, and I stood at her side, participating only when required. "I'm pleased you could come. You make me look good."

She grinned knowingly.

The door swung open, and three people spilled into the entryway, all sharing the Hale name. Marist was in a deep purple dress, and both of my sons in tuxedos, and rather than go to her, my gaze drifted to Vance.

He looked more like me than Royce did, although his hair was a lighter shade of brown. He had his mother's smile, which he used as a weapon. It made women forget to breathe and looked excellent on promotional material, evidenced by the Cape Hill Yacht Club's website and membership brochure.

It had been years since I'd seen it in person, leaving me to wonder if I ever would again. Vance could barely hold my gaze, and it could be caused by a variety of reasons. He had guilt about his affair with Alice, but perhaps he felt shame both at what I'd done to her and tried to do with Marist. How I'd spent most of my sons' lives pushing them to be better, sometimes to their breaking point, and even pitting them against one another.

"It's good to see you," I said to the group. "Thank you for coming."

I was treated to awkward nods, but Evangeline unwittingly made it worse when she spoke. "Macalister, I'd forgotten what a beautiful family you have."

Perhaps she was thinking I wasn't alone, that at least I had my sons after my wife's death. She meant well, not understanding that my desire for control had forced my family to crumble inside my dominating grip.

Royce was masterful at ignoring tension and delivered an easy smile. "It's my wife. She makes the rest of us look good."

Evangeline chuckled as she glanced at me. "He sounds just like you."

Royce didn't bother to hide his grimace at the comparison.

"Yes, well," I lifted my chin and addressed my family, "Damon is already outside, so don't let us keep you from the party."

They understood what I meant, how there was work waiting for them. I'd done an enormous amount of damage to the Hale name, and their help was needed to restore it. The event had to be a success. We would remind Cape Hill which family was American royalty.

Once they disappeared down the hall toward the back of the house, more guests arrived. Some were still intimidated by me and some were curious, and a few had the audacity to look down their judgmental noses, but I forced a tight smile and greeted them as friends.

Tonight, I couldn't be ruthless. I was to be the benevolent king.

I'd set a schedule with Sophia that I would only receive guests until seven-thirty, and then I would move outside and join the party. Those who arrived late would be guided by staff, and I'd be updated on arrivals periodically throughout the

186 | N I K K I   S L O A N E

evening. I checked my watch, and frustration crawled along my back and made my neck hot.

DuBois hadn't made his appearance, and it would be much easier to control the conversation if our introduction was made this way. He was set to attend, though. He'd accepted Damon's invitation and RSVPed to Sophia.

There were only a few minutes left when I caught a glimpse of him at the back of the receiving line, and the tightness in my chest released.

He wore a single button tuxedo jacket, white shirt, and a black bow tie, and while it fit him well enough, it wasn't tailored. A rental. A smile peeled back my lips. He was just a visitor to my world, an observer. I would do everything in my power to make sure he saw what I wanted him to see.

"Good evening," I said and offered my hand when he approached. "Macalister Hale."

He was my age, with short, sandy brown hair and a tough, rugged face that morphed into a charming one when he smiled. His hometown of New Orleans rang through in his accent. "It's nice to meet you, sir. James DuBois."

He took my handshake, and I respected his firm grip. He was several inches shorter than I was, but his frame was stocky and compact, as if he spent more time pounding weights than a keyboard. The picture of him on his books' dust jackets didn't do him justice. They didn't reveal how cunning his eyes were.

"DuBois?" I repeated for effect and pretended to consider where I'd heard it before. "The author?"

He gave a rueful grin. "Guilty as charged, I'm afraid."

"This is Evangeline Gabbard," I said. We'd discussed it and began using the label for each other in Aspen, but the lie felt unnatural. "My girlfriend."

They exchanged pleasantries before his focus shifted back to me. "Thank you for the invitation."

"Of course. Welcome to my home."

He turned his gaze up and scanned the surrounding area. "And what a home you have. I didn't need directions. I just followed the line of Bentleys."

His good ol' boy routine likely worked on a lot of people, but I wasn't susceptible. He expected to be underestimated, but his gaze was too sharp and observant. It was exactly like mine.

"Thank you," I said. "It's been in my family for six generations."

"I'd love a tour sometime." He blinked as if he had stunned himself, and embarrassment crept down his expression. "Forgive me, I've forgotten my manners. You have more important things to do than show some stranger around your house."

I didn't hesitate. "How long are you staying in Cape Hill?"

This time, his surprise was real. "After the fourth."

Perfect. "Do you shoot skeet?" Independence Day was Tuesday, so the office would be closed. "I'm hosting a holiday game of it here on the grounds. I'd be happy to give you a tour afterward."

He was quite pleased with this offer, likely thinking he'd have an entire afternoon to mine me—his unsuspecting target— for information. "I can't say I've been before," he said, "but I'm a quick learner. Are you sure, though? I'd hate to impose."

"No, of course. You'd be doing us a favor. We're currently a man short." I gave him a grateful look. "I'll have my assistant find you and work out the details. Her name is Sophia."

The sun was low, and the gardens were mostly in shadow. The lights strung overhead were already on, casting a warm glow on the lawn and illuminating the rose bushes that lined the edges of the space. While the setup for the party was similar to the events I'd hosted in the past, there was a distinctly different energy tonight.

Excitement hung in the air, and it felt like I was on the cusp of reaching a new level. Smiles and laughter seemed to come quicker to the guests as they mingled around the tables and temporary dance floor.

I made the requisite rounds with Evangeline on my arm, keeping my razor-sharp tongue quiet whenever it craved to lash out and cut someone down to an appropriate size. I smiled so frequently I'd begun to worry I came off looking maniacal.

The red, white, and blue décor served both Damon's campaign theme and the upcoming holiday, even down to the enormous birthday cake and the sparklers decorating it. After I introduced him, he gave a speech full of promises and patriotism, and when it was over, Kristin led the crowd in song.

The liquor was flowing, so I assumed the money into his campaign was as well.

When dinner and dessert were finished, the sun had set, and people moved to the dance floor. Evangeline was off in deep conversation with some of her friends, and I sat at an empty table, surveying the crowd.

It was an upbeat song, but Marist and Royce were out on the floor, swaying slowly, completely oblivious to the fast-moving dancers around them. For the first time, I saw my son and his green-haired wife as they were meant to be—two people in love, who didn't care what anyone else thought. It almost made me smile, but my muscles were taxed from overuse.

Sophia was out there too, snapping selfies and pictures with her friends, and it was impossible not to follow her with my gaze, which I'd done most of the night. Some guy—probably from Damon's staff—had been annoyingly hovering around her all evening like an eager puppy, and his lack of subtly made me groan.

This boy had no skill or finesse. Couldn't he see she was so far out of his league that he was embarrassing himself? I wanted to pull him aside and inform him to stop leering at her.

She'd worn that gorgeous dress *for me.*

The fast song ended, and the next one was slow, the female singer crooning about love and longing. My pulse increased as the boy leaned much too close to whisper in her ear, and she reluctantly nodded. My breathing went shallow as they strolled out onto the hardwood tiles and he set his hands on her narrow waist.

No.

The word was wrapped in barbed wire as it tumbled through my brain. I'd lived silently with jealousy for so long, it didn't make sense why I wasn't any better at dealing with it. Every slow circle they turned as they danced together, his hands inched downward, and my blood pressure climbed toward the sky.

She gave a tight smile, grabbed his hands, and dragged them back to her waist. He shrugged playfully with a laugh. I couldn't hear what he'd said to her but didn't need to. *"Can't blame a guy for trying."*

Oh, did I fucking blame him. There'd been no seduction or effort on his part, and she was a woman who deserved all of that. I tightened my jaw so furiously, it should have cracked my teeth. Guys like him were the reason Sophia's sex life hadn't included orgasms. This young generation had no patience or work ethic.

As I'd already demonstrated to her, I had it in spades.

I lasted until the song was finishing, before rising from my seat and stalking across the dance floor. "Excuse me," I said to the boy, "I need my assistant."

It was satisfying the way she instantly abandoned him and

gave me her full attention. "What's up?"

I didn't answer. I turned and strode away, expecting her to follow, which she did. When we were a safe distance away, I finally spoke. It came out more forceful than I'd meant it to. "Take a walk with me."

She pulled to a stop. "I can't."

Displeasure fired through my veins. "What do you mean, you can't?"

My irritation grew worse as she dropped her gaze to the screen of her phone. "It's time."

I stared at her dubiously. Time? There was nothing left on the schedule as far as—

"Ladies and gentlemen," the announcer's voice boomed on top of the music coming from the speakers, "your host requests your presence on the dance floor. We need everyone to help take part in a special celebration tonight."

I hadn't been privy to her plans and didn't care for surprises, but Sophia looked ready to burst. Her brilliant smile covered her face, and her eyes were wild with excitement, and it was so beautiful it was downright incapacitating.

"Come on," she whispered in a thrilled hurry.

Four hundred of Cape Hill's elite gathered in the available space, anxious and as intrigued as I was. Staff had assembled in stations around plastic crates at the edges of the garden and began handing out white squares approximately the size of record albums to the guests.

Sophia grabbed one and passed it to me then grabbed another for herself.

"What you are receiving right now," the announcer said, "is a sky lantern. Once you have one, please unfurl and hold it by the edges of the ring. Someone will be by momentarily to help you light it."

The paper was delicate like silk, and when I grasped the

ring, the balloon unfolded, falling to the grass. Thin wooden dowels crossed an X over the ring, and at the center, there was a tan square the size of a matchbox.

The music faded to the background so the announcer could be heard clearly. "While you wait, please know these lanterns are one hundred percent biodegradable, made from paper, bamboo, and wax. I'm told the wind will carry them out over the Cape, but the fire department is also monitoring the launch in case there are any issues."

A man in a staff uniform came to Sophia, carrying a small butane torch, and lit the tan block of wax at the center of her lantern. As soon as it began to burn, he leaned down to grab the paper and expertly flipped the ring over before handing it back to her. The white balloon glowed yellowy-orange and expanded as it began to fill with hot air.

The announcer surveyed the crowd from the podium. "We've all seen fireworks, but Mr. Hale wanted a display that you, his honored guests, could each be a part of. When everyone is ready, we'll start the countdown and release the lanterns together."

The man with the torch repeated the same process for my lantern as he'd done with Sophia's before moving on to assist another guest. I watched the staff with torches work as quickly as possible to ensure everyone was ready for launch, and the balloon in my grasp was already gently tugging to lift off.

I glanced at Sophia. "How long will these be in the air?"

"The wax burns for ten minutes, and once it goes out, it floats back down. When we tested, it was like twenty minutes tops."

"All right," the announcer said. "I've been given the signal. Since it's Damon's sixtieth birthday, we'll count down from sixty."

"What?" Sophia angrily muttered under her breath, voicing

the same thought I'd had.

"I'm just kidding, folks!" There were humorous and appreciative groans from the crowd. "And here we go. In three . . . two . . . one. Release!"

I let go, and as if it were attached to a string, my lantern went straight up. Sophia's rose faster than mine, and mine quicker than some of the people around me, as ours had more hot air inside. The night sky instantly became a rising sea of four hundred flickering, glowing lanterns, floating among the stars, and the crowd gasped in awe.

I nearly did as well.

It wasn't a word I'd used before, but nothing else would suffice. No other word did it justice.

Magic.

Magic she'd created, and as I looked around at my guests, their heads lifted and their mouths hung open with astonishment, I lost the ability to breathe. I'd done fireworks before. Loud, colorful shows to impress people, but they were quickly forgotten. This silent display was a once-in-a-lifetime memory. People rushed to pull out their phones so they could take pictures and video, and pride swelled inside me.

From this moment on, when Cape Hill thought of me, perhaps this memory Sophia had offered, would be the first thing that came to their minds, and not my troubled past.

I turned my head and set my gaze on her, ignoring that she may have been taking video and I was now interrupting. The urge to explain to her how pleased she'd made me was too strong to suppress, and I was desperate to do it in a place where I could express myself freely.

"Talk a walk with me." My voice was thick with desire.

"Now?" she whispered.

"Yes. Right now."

I wouldn't accept any other answer, but thankfully, she gave me the one I needed.

"All right."

SIXTEEN

MACALISTER

GUESTS WERE MURMURING TO EACH OTHER IN WONDERMENT AS I
led Sophia to the edge of the garden and the mouth of the hedge
maze. Everyone was too busy staring at the surreal landscape
in the sky to notice us, and even if they did, it was likely they'd
think nothing of it. Just a business discussion between an employer and his assistant.

There was a security guard stationed at the entrance of the
maze, an unfortunate necessity after Royce's wedding. That
evening, guests had ducked behind the velvet rope drawn
across it to signify it was off-limits, and one woman had
emerged at the end of the reception drunk and soaking wet,
announcing she'd had the brilliant idea to cool off in the water
fountain at the maze's center.

"No one comes in," I said to the man standing watch, who
nodded back his understanding.

I moved at a fast clip, my shoes crunching on the pebbled
path, and Sophia did her best to keep up as we disappeared
between the eight-foot-tall walls of evergreen, but quickly
lagged behind.

"Wait," she said as I turned the corner. "This dress isn't

made for your long strides."

No, I thought. *It was made to drive me crazy.*

I slowed my pace, and we wove through the passageways lit only by the subdued ground lighting. The maze had been planted by my mother and as it had grown, so had the required maintenance, but it was worth it. I shared my mother's love for games, and as she'd passed away when I was young, this was my greatest connection to her.

We bypassed the turns that would lead us toward the statues or decorative urns placed at dead ends. I could solve this maze with my eyes closed and knew all its secrets, but Sophia didn't, and she stuck close to my side, letting me guide her.

Rocks skittered with her steps, and when she took a corner too sharply, her ankle unexpectedly went under her, and as she stumbled, I was there with a steady hand. Although my grasp on her arm only seemed to make her more unstable, and pleasure snaked its way through my system. I loved how responsive she was to me.

We made the final turn, and the hedges parted, revealing the circular space and the round, tall fountain bubbling in the true center of the maze. Each of its tiers were lit in amber light, making the falling waterdrops shine and sparkle.

Had she made it to the center before? She looked around, taking it all in, before lifting her gaze to the sky, where the lanterns continued to float and slowly drift out toward the sea.

"Did you like it?" Her shoulders were tight, like her whole life hinged on my answer.

I couldn't overstate it. "Yes. It was spectacular."

Out came her breath in a rush of relief, and she pressed a hand to her stomach. "You have no idea how anxious I was all day. The wind shifted this afternoon, and they were telling me it was too risky to launch, but then it changed again when the sun went down."

It hadn't been an easy feat to pull off, but she'd executed it flawlessly and given me all the credit. Just like the bachelor auction, if she'd told me beforehand, I would have said no.

My voice was uneven as we stood side by side, watching the lanterns go like slow moving fireflies. "The sound people made when the lanterns went up . . . I'll remember it the rest of my life, Sophia."

She went still, like she worried if she moved, she might not be able to hold herself back any longer.

The music from the sound system was quieter here, but I could hear Chris Isaak singing that he didn't want to fall in love. He accused the girl of playing a wicked game, and without thought, I took Sophia's hand. Her eyes widened as I drew our joined hands up and slipped my other one around her back.

I didn't ask her with words if she wanted to dance with me. Instead, I used my body to lead her through a simple pattern, moving to match the tempo of the love song wafting in the air. Her hand was small and warm in mine, and I brushed my thumb over her skin just above the back of her dress, causing her lips to part and an inaudible sigh to tumble out.

I'd planned seduction for her, but with our private dance to the sultry music and the lanterns glowing overhead, we crossed into a territory that was fraught with danger.

This was romance.

It was one of the few areas of my life where I had no expertise, and I hadn't practiced it in more than two decades. Alice was practical and had no need for romance, and I'd been smart enough not to try to woo Marist—my attack on her had been a combination of strategy and brute force.

Everything about Sophia put me off-balance.

While the lust inside me wanted her beneath me, I couldn't stop the craving to have her beside me after our partnership ended.

Typically, I enjoyed dancing and how it put me in control, but this dance was far more satisfying than anything I'd had before. She moved when I did, and she turned beneath my hand when I guided her through it, the hem of her dress dusting across the stone-filled path. She was trembling when she came back into my arms and stared up at me with big eyes, the reflection of the lanterns faintly noticeable in her pupils.

I was in command of our dance but had no illusions that I was in control. My feet slowed us to a stop, my hand on her back urged her forward, and I dropped my head, capturing her lips with mine.

A jolt of surprise went through her, but she softened into my kiss, molding her body to my frame like she wanted every inch of contact I was willing to provide. The fabric of her dress crushed against the ribbed front of my tuxedo shirt, and the heat of her breasts soaked through into my skin.

It was foolish to be doing this. However unlikely it'd be that someone would wander in and catch the two of us in such a passionate moment, it wasn't impossible, and the consequences would be catastrophic. Warnings beat like angry drums in my head, but I ignored them. Her soft mouth was too enticing, and no matter how strong I was, I could not resist its pull.

She whimpered with pleasure when I teased her lips apart and slipped my tongue inside. The slow, lush slide caused sparks to cascade down my spine and race toward my groin. She tasted sweet, from either the champagne or the cake, or perhaps that was simply the flavor of her lips.

I let go of her hand, freeing it so I could cup the back of her neck and angle her head to give me further access to her mouth. And once she was released, she plunged that hand inside my tuxedo jacket and slipped it around my back, deepening our embrace.

It wasn't a kiss I was used to delivering.

There was no reason or goal or benefit that could be quantified on paper as to why I kissed her, but the need to possess her was crushing. I was desperate to show her how powerful her effect was on me, and how it rivaled the power I held over her.

She was breathless, and her pulse roared, pounding in the spot on her neck beneath her ear, and I moved my mouth until I could cover it with my lips, sucking gently. Sophia wilted in my arms, and for a moment, I recklessly considered laying her down on the bench beneath the fountain and taking her right there.

Luckily, common sense won out.

I didn't want a dangerous, quick fuck with her, and additionally—I had plans. I would extract both orgasms and information from her, and it was unlikely I'd be able to do either right now. When I had her under my control, neither of our focuses should be split with worry over being caught.

I lifted my lips until they brushed over the shell of her ear. "I know the other name."

She didn't believe me, and her smile tinted her voice. "Do you?"

"Yes." I drew back enough so I could gauge her reaction. "Duncan Lynch."

Like the first of the lanterns in the sky, the warmth of her flickered out and went cold, her expression turning hard and distant. "No."

When I'd landed on the name, I'd expected she'd either reluctantly admit it or adamantly deny it to overcompensate, but . . . what was this? She shut down and stepped back out of my arms, eyeing me like she'd drawn a line in the sand and I'd just put one foot across it.

It left me with no choice but to surge forward with my assumption. "Why? What did he do?"

Bitterness stained her eyes. "Duncan? He didn't *do*

anything." She said it like perhaps he should have, though.

Sophia had backed away from me, and I didn't like her retreat. I grasped her waist and blocked her from putting space between us. On some level, I knew it was unreasonable to be demanding answers from her, especially after all she'd done tonight, but I was impatient and frustrated I couldn't have her in any of the ways I wanted.

"Does Duncan's secret have something to do with drugs?" I guessed.

She shook her head in anger and spat the words like bullets. "I said it's not Duncan."

"Then, *tell me*." My order was curt, and Sophia cracked under the weight of it.

It was one thing to see her intimidated. The twisted part of me enjoyed when people cowered in fear, but when her beautiful face flooded with panic, it poured the same emotion into my stomach. Her eyes went glassy and wet, and she blinked rapidly to keep back the sudden tears.

"Don't," she whispered. "We can't have this conversation right now. We don't have the time, and I *can't*. I don't have the strength needed to tell it to you tonight." Her long lashes fluttered as a single tear escaped, but it was quickly wiped away. "Please, Macalister," she pleaded. "Don't ruin this night."

But I'd destroyed the magic between us, and I was certain I already had, so I stayed silent.

Her gaze moved away from me, and she sucked in a calming breath. "We need to get back before anyone notices we're missing."

I didn't want to leave things so undone with her, but she had a point.

Reluctantly, we returned to the narrow hedges, and the walk back through the maze was slower, my feet heavier to move. The awkwardness I'd created between us flooded down the passageways, choking my breath, and I despised the sensation.

My eyebrows pulled together before we made the final turn that would make us visible to the rest of the world and lead us out past the walls of evergreen. "It's my nature to push," I said quietly. "I am relentless with myself, and it often affects the way I treat other people."

Her face contorted, not understanding what I was trying to say.

I let out a breath. "I'm sorry. Usually, I am a patient man, but you . . . disrupt me."

It was as if I'd just confessed I hated money. Sophia turned to stone at my admission. "Was that an apology?"

Discomfort settled in my chest. "It was. Did I not do it properly?"

"No, it's—I didn't think you apologized very often."

My unease faded, and I lifted the corner of my mouth in a pleased smile. "I don't." She understood it was difficult for me to admit a mistake and appreciated that I'd been willing to do so. My apology was sincere.

"Thank you," she answered.

It cleared enough of the tension suspended between us, and we pressed forward, emerging from the entrance of the maze undetected by the partygoers. Although it didn't last long. We'd put a professional amount of space between us before Damon signaled to me and began to make his approach. He was grinning ear to ear with a million-dollar smile.

"Macalister, wow." He held out his hand, and I took it, letting him give me a hearty shake. "Thank you. This whole evening has been incredible, and I don't know how I'm ever going to repay you."

"All I ask is that you win in November." I tried to match his smile, so he'd interpret the statement as friendly, even though I was dead serious. "As for your gratitude, I can't take the credit." I turned and tossed a hand toward the beautiful woman standing to my left. "It's Sophia's. She suggested the event to me and planned the entire evening."

In the past, I wouldn't have said such a thing. As CEO, I was responsible for my subordinates' failures whether I was directly involved or not, so this meant I was allowed to take credit for their successes as well.

It was my money, after all.

But my time away had changed me, even as I'd struggled not to let it in. My selfish thinking had contributed to my downfall, and I was determined to be a better man. Plus, Sophia had worked hard to make this event a success and exceeded my expectations when I'd given her zero support or guidance. She was due all the appreciation.

And yet, all Damon Lynch did was stand there and stare at her dubiously.

My annoyance flared, and I glared at him while issuing the command. "So, perhaps you should thank her."

"Yeah, of course." He returned to life and gave her a quick smile. "Thank you."

"You're welcome," she mumbled back, but it felt perfunctory. She'd given it without thought, as a conditioned, polite response.

Not that Damon noticed or cared. His gaze was already back on me, the girl forgotten, and I set my teeth in displeasure as disappointment sank her shoulders. As soon as he began rattling off all the donations he'd garnered at the party, she turned and strolled away, abandoning us.

I'd once been as selfish as Lynch, unaware of anyone who didn't have something I needed or wanted, and Sophia had been invisible to me. And, yes, there were things I wanted and needed from her now, but I was sure I'd always be aware of her regardless of what happened.

Etiquette dictated that Damon Lynch provide me with some sort of gift as a show of appreciation for the party I'd thrown for him, and Monday morning I sent an email instructing him to send it to Sophia. I would have told him in person, but with the holiday tomorrow, office attendance was poor. Most executives chose to extend their weekend through today.

"Good morning," Sophia said as she delivered my coffee, setting it beside my keyboard in the spot I preferred. "*People* magazine reached out to me last night and asked for the rights to publish one of my pictures."

She had lit the internet on fire with the party. Twitter, Instagram, and Facebook were flooded with pictures from Saturday night.

"Which one?" I asked.

Her smile was coy. "The one of you."

Electricity crackled between us.

When I'd turned to her after the lantern launch and demanded she join me on a walk, I'd thought she'd been shooting video. I hadn't realized she'd snapped a picture instead. She'd captured me in my tuxedo, my face turned up toward the sky and a smile on my lips, surrounded by the glowing lanterns.

She'd cropped and edited it so the composition and focus were exactly right.

All the pictures taken of me during my fifty-five years, and Sophia had now shot the best two.

I'd forgotten what I looked like with a real smile, but she'd trapped it and posted it for the world to see, even flattering me with her caption.

My boss is better than yours.

The endless comments from strangers of #silverfox were nice, but I'd obsessed over her line all weekend. Did she mean it strictly as an employer, or as I hoped she did—that I was the one she allowed to be in charge and responsible for her?

She'd continued to send me morning pictures for my approval, and today she wore a white sleeveless dress with a high collar and her hair pulled back in a bun. She was polished, but her youthful blue eyes and tan skin kept her from looking too severe.

I feigned indifference. "What did you tell *People*?"

"I said I'd check with you first."

I turned my full attention to her. "I appreciate that and, yes, it's fine. You must know I'm pleased with the picture." I'd used it to update my profile image on all my social media.

"I got lucky," she said.

I narrowed my eyes. "Don't do that." When confusion played across her face, I continued, "Don't pretend you're not competent. You are good at what you do, Sophia. Own it."

She gave a lopsided grin, as I'd caught her in a harmless lie. "Yeah, okay. I was hoping I'd get a smile out of you."

"You did," I agreed. She prepared to leave and return to her desk, which meant it was time to strike. I motioned toward the sitting area. "By the way, that came for you this morning."

Surprise darted through her expression, and she turned her gaze toward the table, expecting another large white box and a silver bow.

"Macalister, we talked about . . ."

Her words petered out when she spotted the smaller, glossy black box tied with a sinful red ribbon. Her shoulders lifted with her deep breath.

She offered it hesitantly, smart enough to know it wasn't likely. "Shoes?"

I pushed back in my chair, stood, and steeled my expression, not wanting to give anything anyway. She'd surprised me with the lanterns, and it was only fair that I do the same to her. "Open it and find out."

She walked to the couch opposite me, sat down, and carefully pulled the box into her lap. I could sense her curiosity, practically taste her interest, as she slid the ribbon off the corner and lifted the lid. She stared at the contents, not understanding what she was looking at, and then the lid was replaced in a rush.

I found it comical the way she furtively glanced around, checking to see if anyone had seen inside the box. Had she forgotten we were alone in my office?

"Oh, shit," she gasped. "Is this what I think it is?"

"Language," I corrected with an amused tone. "That depends on what you think it is." It was clear she knew, but I wanted to make her say it out loud.

Her cheeks tinged red. "I think it's—uh—a vibrator."

"Oh," I said plainly. "Then, yes. You are correct."

SEVENTEEN

SOPHIA

ALL THE MOISTURE EVAPORATED FROM MY BODY AS I'D STARED inside the box in my lap. The interior was lined with black velvet, but it wasn't jewelry. The shape was what had thrown me at first. Most of the wand vibrator was black, but the long stem descending from the head had a slight bow to it, narrowing in the center before curving out at the bottom, which was covered in chrome plating.

I slammed the lid shut and flushed, instantly sweating even though the office was always frigid.

Macalister had bought me a vibrator, and from the looks of it, a *very* expensive one.

I was strung so tight I could barely squeeze the question out. "Why did you get this for me?"

He looked so fucking powerful in his charcoal gray suit and black tie, standing behind his desk with his arms crossed and a dark, intense look in his eyes. It was thrilling. "You deserve a reward."

I sipped in air, although it had gone thin in the room. The box on my lap was burning, but my hands itched to lift the lid and look a second time. Just to make sure it was still in there, I told myself. Not because I was curious or excited.

He tilted his head, giving me an exacting stare. "You've had one orgasm in front of me. I'd like to see more."

Holy shit.

My mind went blank. "How many more?"

His smile was sinister. "Until you feel comfortable having them in my presence."

Um, holy shit.

My brain was stuck on repeat, and my gaze dropped to the box, not sure what else to do. If I kept looking at Macalister, I'd spontaneously combust and ruin all his nice office furniture.

It was just a statement from him, but it rang as an order in my ears. "Open it."

I licked my dry lips and lifted the lid—

Sure enough, the beautiful sex toy was still cushioned inside. My fingers trembled as I touched it and discovered the silicone sheathing was silky soft.

Macalister's voice was wicked. "What do you think?"

It seemed strange to describe it this way, but the sleek design was attractive. "It's," I stumbled over the word, "sexy."

He made a sound of approval. "Yes. It is."

He uncrossed one arm so he could pick up the coffee I'd brought him and take a sip, but his eyes stayed on me, and I couldn't help but feel like he was drinking me in at the same time. Each swallow was a throb deep between my legs.

The cup was set back down. "I'll need you to stay late tonight."

I'd figured as much since tomorrow was the big day with DuBois, but it was hard to focus on anything right now because there was a goddamn vibrator on my lap. All I could manage was a dull nod.

"Excellent," he said then pointed to the built-ins beneath the television. "That cabinet is empty and has an outlet. You'll plug that in now, so it will be fully charged for later."

I jolted. "Later?"

He got that look he always did when I repeated his words back to him. Mild irritation but delight too. Confusion and surprise were some of the tools he used to exert power over me. "Yes." It was both a promise and a threat. "*Later.*"

It was apparent he meant for me to complete this task right now, under his supervision, so I swallowed a breath and pulled the wand free of its casing. Then I lifted the panel imprinted with a fancy logo and pulled out the charging block and cord.

The vibrator had a nice weight to it, and the curvy design wasn't just for aesthetics. It gave the wand balance. My legs wobbled as I stood and sauntered over to the cabinet, putting my back to Macalister. The cabinet was on the floor, but rather than squat, I bent over to open it. My dress wasn't excessively short, but it rode up and flashed him a considerable amount of the backs of my thighs.

Did he like that?

Would he scold me for being too provocative or unladylike? I kind of wanted him to.

Once the cord was plugged in and attached to the bottom of the wand, a red light began to blink, and I closed the cabinet door, concealing it from view. But then Macalister was beside me, the box in his hands.

"This goes in there too."

I tucked the black box in the cabinet, and when I straightened, he was already moving back to his desk.

"That will be all for now, Sophia. I have a product launch call with Europe to sit on and won't be available until after lunch."

Meaning we wouldn't be having our typical morning meeting. I nodded at my dismissal and shuffled out of his office in a daze.

The Lynch event was over, but I still had plenty of work to do. There were calls to return and emails to answer and invoices to authorize payment on. The opera premiere was in two weeks and, as the major donor, Macalister would be the honored guest. I called his head of staff at the house to make sure his tuxedo would be dry-cleaned in time.

I tried to keep my mind on work, but the black device charging in the office next door kept stealing my focus. What did he have planned for me? Thinking about it made my blood run like lava through my veins, my body needy and craving satisfaction.

I was painfully turned on, and this state of being where I was hanging on edge persisted throughout the day. He'd done it deliberately, I was sure. The vibrator's proximity made it easy to whisper seducing thoughts to me, even when he was locked away in meetings.

By late afternoon, the office was nearly empty. The people who'd come in today began to duck out early to get a head start on their Fourth of July celebrations, and at four-fifty, I said good night to Mr. O'Leary. He was officially the last person left on this floor besides Macalister and me.

At five sharp, my desk phone chimed, and Macalister's voice rang through the speaker. "Sophia."

Pleasure fired through my body with how he'd said my name. It was a summons in his domineering voice, and I was eager to comply, nearly tripping over my feet as I stood and hurried to his closed office door.

I didn't waste time knocking.

He was seated behind his desk as usual, but I could instantly tell something was different. Where was his laptop, or the spare mouse and keyboard he used in here? In fact, his whole freaking desktop was bare.

He'd cleared it off to make room for something, and my pulse quickened as I considered that *something* would be me.

Macalister doled it out casually. "Lock the door."

I rotated the dial on the knob until it clicked, and the sound reverberated through my body. When I turned to face him, tingles washed down my skin and my mouth dropped open.

His desktop wasn't empty anymore. The black vibrator lay on top of it, his fist wrapped around the base, and the sight of it liquified me. I traced each tendon in his strong hand with my gaze and struggled to keep my breathing under control.

"Come here." His voice was rough but controlled.

I put one foot in front of the other and moved under his direction. He let go of the vibrator, leaving it on the desk, rolled his chair back, and stared up at me with his steel-colored eyes that were full of restraint.

"What are you wearing under your dress?" he asked.

Words were hard. Showing him would be easier. I grabbed the fabric covering my hips and shimmied it up until he could see the plain nude thong I wore. His eyes turned hazy, and when he grasped the band covering my hip, I jumped. His fingers were freezing.

His gaze flicked up to mine. "Take this off."

I sucked in a breath and swallowed it down.

The door was locked and the office floor empty, but it didn't matter. It still felt like we were breaking rules and sneaking around, which added to the whole experience. It was bright outside, and sunlight streamed through his windows, so it was like the whole world could see me with my lifted skirt, showing my boss what I had on underneath.

"What if I don't?" I asked breathlessly. "Would you spank me for not obeying?"

Up went his eyebrow in displeasure, and I had to bite my lip to hold in my eager moan. I shivered in enjoyment when he gave me a hard, cold look. "You are not the one in control. I'll be dictating how this will happen, do you understand?"

"Yes, *Daddy*," I said.

He moved so abruptly, it didn't register until he was standing, his hand clenched on my arm and squeezing so hard it drained the insolence right out of me.

"No," he seethed. "I do not care for that. Say it again, and I'll make you regret it."

My mouth dropped open. He liked to push, but he didn't like to *be* pushed . . . not on someone else's terms.

To reinforce his point, his hand came off my arm and latched on to the bun at the back of my head, twisting the pins painfully as he tilted my head back and his mouth crashed down on mine. His kiss was ruthless and cruel, his teeth sharp and merciless.

I moaned my approval, drinking up his aggression.

He released me with a shove, his eyes furious and hot, and then he wiped his mouth with the back of his hand. Oh, fuck me, it was so erotic, my hands dug under my skirt and clawed the scrap of fabric down, pushing it past my knees.

Macalister raked a hand through his hair, and as the strands fell back in place, so did his calm, collected demeanor. He lowered back into his chair and curled his lip to speak the order. "On the desk. Show me your cunt."

The word was the same as a hard slap against my ass. I didn't hate it . . . but it got my attention.

As I sat on the edge of the desk, my thong fell past my ankles and onto the floor. It was forgotten as I pinned my gaze to his, and I was anxious to watch his reaction as I spread my legs. Except my skirt was down, teasing him with shadows, and his expression filled with impatience.

"I'm waiting."

I grabbed the front of my skirt and pulled it up to my waist, leaving nothing to the imagination. He'd seen it before, anyway.

His nostrils flared as he stared at me, and lust descended on the room. It filled every inch and crevice, made it so it was all I could taste, became all I could think about. The desk was no longer cold against my bare skin or uncomfortable as the edge dug into the back of my thighs. All I desired was his touch, and it felt like I'd burst if I didn't get it right this instant.

But Macalister didn't touch me.

His hot gaze slid over the most intimate, secret part of my body, caressing my pink jeweled piercing, before moving up to peer into my face. His eyes were lidded, and his chest moved quickly, but otherwise he maintained his cool exterior.

"Do whatever you need to," he commanded, "to make yourself comfortable, and when you're ready, pick my gift up, turn it on, and make yourself come."

I exhaled loudly, disappointment snaking across my exposed skin. "You're just going to watch?"

His smug smile was irritatingly sexy. "Show me how you follow my commands, and I'll give you more." The desire in his office was so thick, I was drowning in it, and even he seemed to struggle now against the current. "I'll give you *so much more*, Sophia."

He'd told me on Saturday that I had disrupted him, but did he know he did the same to me? Everything blurred and spun around him. Down was up. I couldn't get the rest of the world to notice me, but Macalister didn't miss a detail now.

I lay back on the desktop and propped myself up on my elbows, wanting to keep looking at him as he stared back at me. His cheekbones were so high and sharp, and his pale blue eyes intense. God, he was gorgeous. There were brand guidelines out there somewhere for "Cutthroat Billionaire Executive" and he adhered to them flawlessly.

He was a classic man with discerning tastes, and I was happy to be a flavor he currently enjoyed.

I picked up the vibrator beside me and pressed the button on its handle, making it spring to life. It was quiet but powerful, and I hesitantly set the head of it between my legs.

Just the whisper of contact against my clit, and I collapsed onto my back, banging loudly onto the desk. "Fuck."

I'd wanted to watch him as I did it, but I'd spent the whole goddamn day turned on. It'd take next to nothing to make me come, and seeing him shift in his chair was already too much. He'd leaned an elbow on the armrest and rested his chin against his hand, one finger crooked over his lips like he was considering a tempting offer.

The sensation of the vibrations was so good, it felt like agony. I kept having to pull it off for a few seconds to catch my breath, before starting again. Sparks danced down my legs, making me flinch with pleasure as I stared at the ceiling.

Part of me wanted someone to walk in on us right now. They'd discover the chief shareholder and owner of Hale Banking and Holding sitting at his desk, supervising his young assistant while she got herself off with a vibrator.

The scandal would be *decadent*.

"Are you close already?" He asked it like he already knew the answer.

I whimpered. "It feels so good." The wand was easy to hold, like it had been designed with self-use in mind, unlike my generic one at home. Sometimes I got a cramp holding it. "Whatever you paid for this—it was worth it."

He chuckled. "I'm glad you're enjoying it. I am too." His voice wasn't cold or strict anymore; now it was filled with smoke and heat. "You're so fucking sexy."

"Language," I whispered with shock, pretending to scold him. But I drew the pulsing head of the wand away from my clit to stop the orgasm his words nearly brought on.

"Did you think about this all day?" he asked.

"Yes." The buzzing toy was truth serum. He could ask me anything, and I'd tell it to him, no matter how embarrassing or dark the secret was.

"I did too. I wondered if you'll make the same sounds as you did last time. Or will your moans be different than when I had my fingers inside you?"

"Fuck," I gasped again, squirming away from the wand. I both did and didn't want to come. Last time I hadn't believed it was possible, and it'd been dark in the room. There was no-where to hide this time. He'd see everything.

Macalister stood and stepped between my parted legs, looming over me, and adjusted the cuffs of his shirt beneath his suit jacket sleeves. The way he moved was practiced and graceful and deliberate.

"Why do you keep doing that," he asked, "pulling it away?" He leaned over, using his body to pin the vibrator back against me. "I've already shown you this is a battle you can't win."

I groaned with pleasure as the vibrator crushed against me. I wanted to submit completely but was also afraid. What if he saw something he didn't like? Or what if he got what he want-ed then cast me aside?

Or . . . what if this was all just a game to him? He hadn't gotten Marist. Was I her replacement, the consolation prize he was settling for?

His gaze was vicious in its pursuit, determined to see down into the depths of my mind and discover what I was thinking, and I turned my head away, unable to look.

"I don't know if I can," I panted for air, "with you watching me."

"You can," he said. "And you will. I'm going to make you do it a hundred different times if needed."

Desire flashed through my center. I liked Macalister's plan a lot.

"But right now?" His tone was firm, teeming with arrogance. "I'm going to bring you to orgasm with my tongue."

I groaned and jerked at the idea, my entire body shuddering in acute pleasure. But instead of dropping to his knees as I expected, he clamped his hand down on top of mine, so we were gripping the vibrator together. And then he directed me to push it harder against my sensitive clit, making my piercing rattle.

I arched off the desk as the orgasm gathered like a storm, and Macalister shoved his free hand beneath my neck, scooped me up into his kiss. Lightning cracked across my chest, and flames licked at my legs. The swell of pleasure built, and built, and *fucking built* . . .

He forced my lips open, and the sliver of his tongue glancing against my own sealed my fate.

A panicked moan ripped from my throat and was gasped into his mouth as I came. Heat blasted up my spine, setting my nerve endings on tingling fire, and I contracted with each pulse of ecstasy as the waves rolled through my body. I had to push the wand away, overly sensitive and overwhelmed, and he allowed it, taking the vibrator from me, turning it off, and setting it aside.

I was still shuddering as he lowered me back onto his desk, my head nearly off the back of it, and I slammed my eyes shut. It was too much, too sexy, the way he examined me in my vulnerable state of post-orgasm recovery. He'd said he was going to bring me to orgasm with his tongue . . . and he had. There'd obviously been some mechanical assistance, but when he'd licked into my mouth, that was what had sent me over the edge.

That connection was the last tumbler clicking into place and unlocked my pleasure.

I wasn't sure how long I lay on his desk, but once my breathing slowed to a languishing pace, he helped me up onto my trembling legs, lowered my skirt, and folded his arms around me in a reassuring embrace. Or perhaps it was to trap me. Either was possible with him.

His heartbeat was steady, an insistent, reliable drum marching along, while mine was still erratic. There'd been heat in him, but it cooled slowly, layer by layer. I wanted to stay like this longer, but he searched my face, and his eyes went cautious. "I would like to continue, but . . . there is business I don't believe we can put off any longer."

Tomorrow might be Macalister's only opportunity to speak with DuBois, which meant I was out of time. I nodded slowly and turned my gaze toward the couches. I was still weak, and no way was I standing through this conversation. "I need to—"

"Yes," he said, releasing me and gesturing for us to sit. When I reached for my discarded underwear, he stopped me. "No. You can put that back on when we're done here."

My heart skipped and tumbled at his order, and I straightened slowly before moving toward the sitting area, my head still foggy and in the clouds. But reality was coming. I sensed it like I was falling and the ground swelled up to meet me.

"Would you like something to drink?" he asked.

I wanted to smile at his offer because I'd spent the last month bringing him coffee, and I liked the idea of telling him to fetch me some—but my nerves were jagged fragments. I sat on the gray couch, and my voice went small. "Water would be nice."

He retrieved a bottle from his mini fridge, unscrewed the cap, and handed it to me. With that done, his focus went to the couches, and I could see the consideration as it played out in his eyes. He wasn't sure if he should sit beside me like a friend, or a safe distance across from me like a colleague.

It was disappointing when he moved to the opposite couch after what we'd just done, but not surprising.

I took a sip of the water and replaced the cap, turning it slowly and stalling. I'd never told anyone what I was about to. Plus, I hadn't a clue how he was going to react, other than he'd look at me differently after this was over, and that scared the hell out of me.

Macalister settled into his seat, subtly prompting me it was time for me to begin.

"You were close, but it's not Duncan Lynch," I said, pinning my reluctant gaze on him. "It's his father."

EIGHTEEN

MACALISTER

SOPHIA SAT PERFECTLY STILL ON THE EDGE OF THE COUCH IN her white dress, her back straight, knees together, and ankles crossed like a lady should, but the water bottle in her hand was shaking. I didn't care for seeing her in visible distress. I'd hoped the orgasm she'd just had would help relax her, and it was meant to strengthen the trust between us.

Damon Lynch.

I hesitated as the name rolled through my mind. Damon was no saint, but neither were any of the men who sat on HBHC's board, myself included. In fact, the residents of Cape Hill each had their share of secrets and dark deeds. Money was power, and power corrupted, making the people here believe they were untouchable. I hadn't realized how twisted and un-controlled our little hamlet had become, but Sophia's daily briefings had clarified it for me.

We lived in a den of lies, full of betrayal and debauchery and crimes.

"What has he done?" I asked.

"For starters, he's a hypocrite." Fire ringed her eyes. "He touts all that 'family first' bullshit, but you have to know he'll fuck anything that moves if it looks at him twice."

Her coarse language was, unfortunately, appropriate. Damon's only requirement with a sexual partner seemed to be that she could fog a mirror. "Yes, I'm aware he often strays in his marriage."

"It doesn't matter if they're married, or in a relationship, or if the girl is too young for him. He flashes his smile, and the panties drop almost as fast as he abandons the woman the morning after."

A chill swept along my frame, followed by a rush of possessive anger. Had he touched her? I steeled my voice. "You've slept with him?"

She looked like she was going to be ill. "What? *No.*" She shook her head, trying to cast off the horrible thought, but it did nothing to remove her frown. "Let me back up." She drew in a deep breath. "My parents were tough on me. They had big expectations because I was their only child."

I raised an eyebrow, both at her abrupt switch in topic and what she'd said. "I can certainly respect their desire to see their daughter achieve. I held both of my sons to a high standard."

"Yeah. Do you know how jealous my dad is of you? Not just your money, but what you just said right there. *Sons.*" Bitterness smeared over her expression. "Imagine you only had daughters. No one to carry on the Hale name."

I didn't patronize her and pretend she was wrong. She knew how traditional my values were, and they echoed through our town. Plus, Hales were more than just their bloodlines—HBHC was our family namesake.

"I hoped for a girl when Julia was pregnant with Vance. I wanted one of each." I scowled at myself. Why had I told her that? "Familial names carry a lot of weight, and yes, it's rarely fair, but that is how it's been for generations."

"No, it's not fair," she agreed. "My dad didn't keep his feelings about me hidden either. I was a constant disappointment."

How was that possible? She went to an Ivy League school. She was the homecoming queen and prom queen. Everyone loved her, including countless strangers on Instagram. Also, "You went to the Olympics."

She gave a joyless laugh. "Did I bring home a medal?"

I digested her statement, and it forced me to reflect on my actions. I'd pushed Royce and Vance relentlessly. Nothing was ever good enough to satisfy me. So, it applied to me as much as it did to Stephen and Colette Alby. "I was unaware your parents are fools. They have to be, if they're not proud of you."

Her shoulders snapped back in surprise, and her pretty face softened.

"Thank you." She held my gaze for a long moment before it went unfocused and shifted away. "Things weren't that bad until I was fourteen, when my mom got sick and almost died."

"Cancer." I remembered because, after her recovery, Colette became heavily involved with foundations and drives for research funding.

"Yeah. It started as pneumonia, but then she went into sepsis." Her gaze drifted down, landing on her knees. "It looked like it was the end, and she didn't want to take the secret to her grave." Her face was sarcastic, yet grim. "A true deathbed confession."

Cold realization leached from my bones. Puzzles intrigued me, and she'd given me more than enough pieces to solve it. "She had an affair with Damon."

Her eyes turned dull and glassy. "If one time counts as an affair, then, yeah. But one time was all it took."

Sophia wasn't Stephen Alby's daughter; she was Damon Lynch's.

Jesus, how had I not seen it? His million-dollar smile was the exact same as hers.

220 I NIKKI SLOANE

A thousand questions vied for attention in my mind, but I was smart enough to know when to stay quiet. Silence often prompted the other person to fill it, and now wasn't the time to push.

"My dad—Stephen," she clarified, "can't have children." Her voice filled with contempt. "Me not being able to carry the Alby name was hard enough. Imagine how thrilled he was to learn I didn't have Alby blood in my veins."

"And he didn't know?"

"Maybe he suspected on some level, but he couldn't accept it. He was just as shocked as I was that she'd been lying to us for the last fourteen years."

I sat forward, ignoring my posture, and rested my elbows on my knees, wanting to be closer. It was irrational, this desire to somehow protect her from such an awful betrayal that was twelve years in the past. "But he stayed with her."

"I'm sure he wanted to leave, but he didn't have a choice. What kind of man leaves a wife in her final days with cancer? And if he walked out and she did die . . . Fuck, I'd have *no* one." She unscrewed the water bottle and took a long drink then set it down on the table like she didn't know what to do with it anymore. "He loves her too. That's why he stayed when she got better. My dad may not want me, but he still wants her, even after she massively fucked up."

Her offhanded comment made me uncomfortable, like my suit was suddenly constricting. How could anyone not want her, when I *couldn't stop* myself from wanting her?

"After that," she said, "I decided I'd never be in the dark again. I'd learn every secret I could."

I respected that and directed my ire at a new target. "What about Damon? Does he know?"

She tilted her head up to the ceiling. Like an imbecile, I also glanced up, not sure what she was looking at, only to dimly realize she'd done it to blink back tears. My body went on alert. I never felt more powerless than when witnessing a woman cry.

"Yeah." She sniffled, composed herself, and used her anger to burn away her tears. "He fucking knows."

There was no scenario I could see that made this acceptable, and I sensed there wasn't one either.

"My dad scheduled a meeting with him. I think Damon thought it was going to be a sales pitch from my dad's firm. Instead, I ambushed him with, 'Surprise! I'm your daughter.'" Her smile was pained and didn't reach her eyes. "He told me I was fourteen years too late. I was Stephen's daughter now, not his."

I inhaled a sharp breath, stunned at the cruelty, then anger bubbled to the surface. "He can say whatever he wants, but he cannot argue with biology."

Sophia nodded, but it was only to appease me. "I was such an idiot. I thought maybe if I just got him to see me, he'd come around. You want to guess how I got into shooting skeet?"

There was a brick in my stomach, sinking me down. "I don't need to guess," I said quietly. "I know Damon's an excellent shot. He's nearly as good as I am."

This drew a fraction of a real smile across her lips, and I enjoyed seeing it. "He's better than you, Macalister."

"Perhaps," I begrudgingly admitted. "You didn't see me at my best last time."

"You were too busy giving me those helpful tips."

I deserved that. "I will be better tomorrow." The conversation lulled for a weighty moment. "That's where you left it with him? He's not going to acknowledge you're his daughter?"

She pressed her lips together. "I have two fathers, yet neither one wants to claim me."

Displeasure slid down my back, wrapping around my chest, and intensified with my next thought. "Duncan doesn't know he's your half-brother." It explained why she'd treated him like he was diseased. "Does Kristin know?"

She stared at me like I was missing something obvious. "Macalister, no one knows. Just the people involved . . . and now you."

Normally, I would have relished knowing such a secret, but there wasn't any satisfaction here. Sophia had become important to me, and my disappointment in Damon was beyond limit.

"Had I known any of this," I said, "I wouldn't have hosted that event."

Her gaze ran away guilty. "I know. It's why I couldn't tell you."

"I wouldn't have spent a penny on a man who shirks his responsibility and abandons his own daughter. Especially when it's you, Sophia. I wouldn't have let him step a foot in my home."

Anger swelled, an unstoppable force, as I recalled the callous way he'd treated her once I'd explained she'd been the one to organize the entire event. I had the terrible suspicion she'd done it for him, another attempt to impress the father who refused to acknowledge her.

I rose abruptly and pulled my phone out of my interior coat pocket. "This is unacceptable."

She leapt to her feet, and her warm hands closed around mine, stopping me. "What are you doing?"

I didn't want to like how her touch felt, but it happened, regardless. "I'm going to explain to Damon I want this corrected."

"You can't, and also, how? He doesn't work for HBHC anymore."

"He still sits on the board."

She said it quietly, as if she were trying to soften the blow. "But you don't."

Frustration curled its irritating fingers in my stomach, twisting. Would I be able to talk Royce into this? Unlikely. My relationship with the board was tenuous at best, and Damon had been my closest ally.

He'd worried about me learning the truth, and it was why he'd warned me about Sophia. *"Duncan says she's famous for spreading lies."*

She wanted to spread the truth, though.

Her hand stayed on mine, even as I lowered my phone, and her expression was defeated. "You can't convince him to do the right thing. Believe me, I tried."

"I don't understand why you have stayed quiet. He doesn't deserve your silence."

Her eyes filled with shame. "No, he doesn't. That's why he pays for it."

She'd told me once she didn't need money, and now I understood. I pulled my hands from her grasp and ignored the way she looked bereft. "I see."

"Don't you dare judge me," her tone was defiant, "for taking the only thing he's willing to give."

I pocketed my phone as I considered her statement. Why shouldn't she take his hush money? I would do the same, if I were in her position. "You make an excellent point. But have you considered what this will do if it gets out? I seem to recall you said your goal wasn't to destroy anyone."

I don't know what compelled me to do it, but I stepped closer and placed my hand against her cheek, forcing her gaze upon me. Her breathing went short and shallow, and her pupils dilated.

"I don't want to destroy him," she said. "I gave him plenty of chances to admit the truth. He only loves his picture-perfect family, which doesn't include me. He wakes up every day and makes the choice that I'm not good enough."

I wasn't any good at tenderness, but I wasn't in control anymore. I brushed my thumb over her smooth skin and watched her pink lips part, like she was preparing for my impending kiss.

"You are good enough," I said. "More than *good enough.*"

As soon as the words had left my mouth, she rose and closed whatever space was left between us. Her lush lips pressed sweetly to mine, and her kiss disrupted. It was the first time she'd initiated, and I wasn't certain I should allow it. I preferred when our power dynamic was clearly defined, and I was the one in charge.

She did too, didn't she?

I groaned as her hands pushed inside my suit coat, sliding over my chest. It was much too enjoyable. Her needy fingers clutched at my shirt, holding me still as she explored my mouth with her tongue. My instinctual reaction was to pull away and correct this behavior before it escalated.

You are too old to fuck her on your office couch, and you can't do it properly there, either.

I eased her back, and her eyes blinked open in surprise, finding my fixed expression. "Thank you for telling me." Her face froze. She was confused and disappointed, but I ignored it and pushed forward, needing to get her back on track. "I'm glad you enjoyed my gift. You'll take it home, and you'll think of me every night while you use it."

She swallowed so loudly I heard the click of her throat.

"Yes?" I asked.

"Yes," she whispered.

"Excellent."

James DuBois was a terrible shot, and I was glad for it. I'd made him partner with Damon, and they were currently in last place. I'd taken Sophia as my partner, and we were well ahead of the rest of the pack.

"That is quite a sight," DuBois remarked the first time he'd watched her annihilate both targets within a quarter of a second. He eyed her with admiration and respect, and unwarranted pride filled me. She was my partner.

Mine.

As predicted, I'd done better today, but when I missed my second target, Sophia whispered to me under her breath, "Watch your flinch."

I nodded, and then turned my gaze across the playing field until it located Damon. There was a small part of me that wished to be ignorant about who her real father was. To a much lesser extent, this impacted my family. I'd expected Vance to ride Damon's coattails.

If DuBois's book came out before the election, it'd put his entire campaign in jeopardy, and the timing wouldn't leave any room to recover. It'd be more damaging to come out after he'd been elected. The scandal was a huge, dark cloud coming for him.

It frustrated me immensely that he hadn't gotten out in front of it. What, exactly, was his plan? Did he assume he'd pay her off until one of them died? I'd thought he was smart. Something this volatile couldn't exist indefinitely in the shadows. It was going to come out and destroy both his career and his family.

That was, if I told DuBois and if he published it.

The rest of our shooting party didn't concern themselves much with the outsider in our group. The writer was unassuming and friendly, letting everyone else do the talking while he quietly observed, taking stock. He was grateful to let Sophia offer him pointers, and I watched from my seat on the lawn as she pulled the butt of the shotgun firmly against his shoulder.

Nearby, her true father waited impatiently for her to finish, and for the fiftieth time today, I welled the anger down to stay quiet. I couldn't be reckless and brash or allow myself to be a slave to my emotions. I could lie in wait as she'd done and strike when the time was right.

It was hot in the sun today, a perfect July day with little wind and low humidity, but a bead of sweat trickled down the valley of my spine. I was glad when the match ended, so most of my guests would leave, and I could begin working toward my goals with DuBois in earnest, inside the air conditioning of my home.

"You were right," Sophia said as she zipped closed her shotgun bag and slipped on a regular pair of sunglasses. "You were better today."

It was surprising that I was more pleased about impressing her than with winning. Although we had done that, and easily. She'd only missed one bird out of the seventy-five rounds she'd shot. She hadn't been distracted by Damon's presence, but then again, she'd had twelve years of practice pretending he was little more than a stranger.

"Good luck," she said in a hushed voice, lifting her chin toward DuBois. "But you don't need it."

I gave her a confident smile. "No, I don't."

Sophia ushered the rest of the guests toward the line of waiting carts, but I motioned to DuBois, signaling for him to come to me. "Shall I give you the tour?"

He gave a disarming smile.

We rode together in a golf cart up the winding path that would lead us to the back of the house.

"That was some party the other night," he drawled.

"Did you enjoy it?"

"Very much. You must be close friends with Mr. Lynch to put on such a thing."

Sophia had told me to use every opportunity to be vulnerable, which I dreaded, but I understood its necessity. Also, I would make an effort to tell the truth, as long as I could put the right spin on it. I'd spent my life trying to achieve excellence, and now I had to show the struggle behind it.

"Damon and I were close when I was CEO, and he was supportive in the aftermath of my second wife's death, so, yes. You could say that."

DuBois had been looking at the grounds as we traveled along the path, but his gaze turned to me and sharpened. He hadn't expected me to be quite so forthcoming.

"Supportive how, if you don't mind me asking?"

"He understood I'm human and that I'd made a terrible mistake, but that it does not have to define me." It wasn't hard to fill my voice with contrition. In the months after I'd come home, I'd learned how to feel things again, and my remorse was genuine. "It's what I do now that determines what kind of man I truly am."

It was why I now hated Damon Lynch. As Sophia had said, he could have corrected his mistake, and chose every day not to.

"Well," DuBois gave me a mischievous grin, "you're a fascinating one, at least. Not what I was expecting, and I'm a generally curious person, but I haven't quite figured you out yet."

"I am private," I admitted. "My name and fortune make that necessary."

"Oh, I'm sure they do." The cart eased to a stop, and we climbed out. "But to hear people tell it, you've changed since you've returned to Cape Hill."

"Yes." I gave him a direct look but kept my tone simple. "Losing nearly everything can have that effect."

I went up the marble staircase and onto the patio, hearing his footsteps as he followed.

"I imagine so," he commented. "If it's of any consolation,

I've only heard good things."

Inside, I smiled, but I kept my expression fixed. "That is good to know. I have much to atone for, besides my wife's death."

I held open the door to the conservatory for him, but he paused at the threshold, staring up at me with surprise. "Oh?"

"I suspect I don't have to tell a man as observant as you that the money and influence in this town can have a powerful effect on its residents. The people here are in a class of their own. Infallible and untouchable, and when accountability is removed, so are their inhibitions." I did my best to affect a resigned tone. "I thought I was above reproach, and I've strived to do better, but this is how the rest of Cape Hill lives."

DuBois stepped into the room, likely for no other reason than it was letting the air conditioning out. He scanned the space, which during Alice's time here had been filled with plants and potted trees, but my housing staff had begun to scale back. It was more living space than greenhouse now.

"I've only been here a few days, but I find it intriguing—the history and culture of this place," he mused while examining one of the African violets on the windowsill.

"Intriguing enough to write a book about it?"

He turned and gave a knowing smile. "Perhaps."

The room was flooded with light and all the things we knew but weren't saying. It was a different kind of negotiation than I typically participated in, but the rules were still the same. We both wanted something from the other, and neither of us needed to walk away from the table unsatisfied.

"If I were writing a book," he sounded casual, "would you be interested in being a part of it?"

I feigned surprise and dismay. "As a subject?"

He ticked his head, playing up his 'golly, gee, shucks' persona. "As a consultant. I'm an outsider. It'd be good to have the point of view from the inside of Cape Hill, and who better than the man who rules over it?"

I saw through his attempt to flatter but pretended it'd worked. I paused as if considering. "I may be open to the idea."

NINETEEN

SOPHIA

TEN DAYS IN A ROW OF USING THE VIBRATOR MACALISTER HAD given to me, and I worried I was going to burn my clit off. He had a habit of asking me about it right as I delivered his morning coffee, I think in hopes of making me spill. Did he want me to, so he could punish me?

He hadn't touched me since I'd confessed the truth.

But in my nightly fantasies? Oh, yeah. He couldn't keep his domineering hands off my body. Was he ever going to let that become reality?

He had given me very little detail on his discussion with DuBois either, other than to say it went well.

On Friday, there'd been a major dustup with the German branch and government regulations, so he'd gone with Royce to Berlin, and they hadn't come back until late the following Thursday.

Which meant I wouldn't see him until the premiere at the opera house tonight. At least, not in person. I'd still been texting him pictures for approval, and his second day in Germany I'd asked for a picture in return. I didn't get to see him in the office, after all.

The picture came back five minutes later. It looked like he was standing in the lobby bathroom of an upscale hotel, wearing his steely blue suit with a gold and blue striped tie. The picture was slightly off center, and he was caught staring at the screen of his phone, a look of concentration on his face.

I laughed. Was this the first bathroom selfie he'd ever taken? I imagined him standing awkwardly in front of the mirror, fumbling with his phone and being unhappy with the results. Had he taken several, and this was the best of the bunch? It was classic dad, but it didn't matter. His sheer hotness made up for it.

> Macalister: I wore this for you.

> Me: I approve.

God, did I approve.

He sent me pictures every day after that.

It made me bold. Plus, I hadn't seen him in a week, and ten days of orgasms while thinking about him had me conditioned. A Pavlovian response to drool at the thought of him.

This morning as I dressed for work, I'd put on a pair of white panties that were so thin and sheer, I looked naked—other than the white lace detail at the edges. I stood in front of my full-length mirror in the black dress he'd given me, one hand lifting the hem of my skirt and flashing him. The faintest cleft was visible between my thighs.

> Me: I wore this for you.

Three dots appeared, then disappeared.

They blinked again, longer this time, before vanishing, and I grinned. My racy picture had put the great Macalister Hale at a loss for words. It came a few minutes later.

> Macalister: I approve.

It was followed by an image of him lying shirtless on his back in his bed, his hair askew, and the shadow of his arm across his chest as he held the phone out overhead. It was so he could get Lucifer in the frame. The black cat was asleep, under Macalister's arm and snuggled to his chest.

Macalister: I had no choice in wearing this.

I laughed but also my brain fried, wires crossing and shorting out, throwing off sparks. He was gorgeous, as was the cat, and the two of them together was overload.

Me: He missed you.

There was staff at the Hale house that took care of Lucifer, but the cat had made it clear to whom he thought he belonged to, now that Macalister had warmed up to his pet. I understood how the cat felt. I'd gotten Macalister to like me when he hadn't wanted to, and now . . . I belonged to him.

Me: I missed you too.

As soon as I sent the message, I wished for it back. We had such a strange relationship, where him giving me a vibrator and making me come on his desk was safer than me admitting feelings for him. I didn't know if he was interested in me in any capacity outside of sex. We were attracted to each other and both enjoyed him having control, but where did our boundaries stop?

We couldn't date. For one thing, he already had a girlfriend, as far as Cape Hill knew. Evangeline would be accompanying her 'boyfriend' in the box seats this evening, and I'd be watching from my seat down on the floor.

Another issue was our dramatic age difference. People would assume I was a gold-digger determined to get her claws in him, and he was only after me as a hot piece of ass. And perhaps that was true, that he was only interested because I was some pretty young thing who'd sucked his cock and did what he told me to . . . but it didn't *feel* true.

Macalister and I had a lot in common. He knew more about me than anyone else in the world.

And he'd told me I was more than enough.

Those damned dots blinked and disappeared. Once again, he was having difficulty composing a response. I started to write a follow-up to downplay it, but the dots returned, cycling through until his message was delivered.

> Macalister: I am surprised. Your aim is usually impeccable.

I slowed and stared dubiously at the screen. Was this why he'd hesitated? So he could make a joke? I furiously punched my thumbs on the screen, tapping out my question, but before I could send it, his next message rolled through.

> Macalister: I missed you as well. Looking forward to seeing you tonight.

I nearly dropped the phone in my excitement.

Opulent gold leaf work decorated the arches of the cathedral ceiling in the lobby of the Boston Opera Theatre. The red damask wallpaper was full of old-world drama. Black carpet with matching gold scrolls covered the marble staircase that led up to the balcony, and overhead, a three-tiered crystal chandelier hung, looking as old and beautiful as Boston itself.

I hadn't been to the theatre in years, and not since they'd restored it to its original grandeur, but growing up, I had adored musicals. The revitalized space took my breath away. It was perfect at setting the mood too. The best shows could take you to a different world, and this lobby was the holding area to start that transition. I already felt like I was somewhere new and surreal.

The cavernous room was full, with most guests enjoying a cocktail before heading inside to find their seats. I went to the bar, ordered a glass of white wine, and snapped a few pics for Instagram while waiting for Macalister and Evangeline to arrive.

There weren't many faces I recognized as I surveyed the crowd. I had a few friends who'd take any excuse to dress up and try to make the society pages, but it wasn't likely there were many photographers here at an opera premiere hoping to catch a glimpse of celebrities.

Wait . . . was that Richard Shaunessy?

He was the last person I would have expected to like the opera, but then Blythe Andrews appeared at his side, carrying two drinks, and passed one to him. That made sense. She'd been a big theatre freak in high school and tried to make it in New York for a time, but it hadn't worked out. I hadn't heard they were dating yet, which meant this was probably their first time.

She was way too pretty and nice for him, but I smiled to myself. I bet she knew what she was doing. She'd wrangled a date out of him to this black-tie opera premiere because she wanted to go . . . not because she wanted to spend time with cokehead Richard.

"Sophia," came a deep, familiar voice from behind me. *Looking forward to seeing you tonight.*

I wanted to shiver but commanded my shoulders not to move. Macalister had told me there was nothing between him and Evangeline, but I still had to mentally prepare myself for a long night of them looking like a couple.

He'd always looked good in a tux. It was the same classic

one he usually wore with a black bowtie and white shirt with pleats and a line of black buttons down the front. His ice-colored eyes skated down my body from head to toe, taking in my dress. He'd seen it earlier—I'd texted him a picture of the one-shoulder dress that was such a soft pink, in certain lighting it looked white. It had an oversized bow on the shoulder, one large loop of it dropping down over my front. The skirt was A-line and had a slit all the way to my hip, but it was unlikely anyone would catch the band of white lace on my underwear there.

I'd already shown it to the one person I wanted to see.

I felt amazing in this dress, and a big part of it was the way Macalister was looking at me. Which he shouldn't be, even as it made me dizzy and my heart beat faster. "Where's Evangeline?"

"She messaged when I was on my way to pick her up. She's ill."

"Oh, no. She's not coming?"

His eyes didn't reveal whatever he was thinking. "No. You will take her place and join me in the box."

A thrill flashed through me, and I clutched my wine tighter, hoping my eagerness didn't show. The boxes were on the same level as the balcony, meaning the people inside were often visible to much of the audience. I dropped my voice and glanced around. "You think that's okay?"

He gave a pointed stare. "I won't sit by myself."

He was right; it would look strange to see him there all alone. I swallowed thickly, keeping an even tone while my insides raced with excitement. "All right."

The theatre itself was just as beautiful as the lobby had been. Gold filigree and ornate plasterwork decorated the arch over the black stage. The rich red curtain was trimmed in gold fringe and draped closed across the stage.

The box was its own separate balcony, and the two

armchairs in it were wide, with low backs and the cushions covered in plush red velvet. The chairs angled toward the front, and as I took the seat to Macalister's left, I felt like I was on stage. Rather than sing to the audience from the balcony like Eva Perón, I looked down at the playbill in my hand.

"What language is this opera in?" Macalister asked as he unbuttoned his tuxedo jacket and lowered in his chair.

"English. It's a modern opera that premiered in Chicago, and they've been trying to bring it here for a while. Your grant made that possible."

There was an edge of relief in his eyes. He was glad it'd be in a language he understood. "I wasn't aware opera could be in English. I thought those were musicals."

I shrugged. "I thought so too, but no."

When we went quiet, I plucked up my wine and took a sip. I was so fucking nervous, I thought I'd explode, and it was stupid. How many mornings had we been alone in his office discussing secrets? Sure, we'd sat across from each other, rather than together, and we'd been wearing business clothes rather than black-tie, but . . .

And—oh, yeah—we'd kissed a bunch of times and he'd seen me naked and brought me to orgasm.

This isn't a date. No matter how much it feels like one.

I wanted the show to start so it'd distract from this uncomfortable longing. I pressed my lips to my wineglass and stole a glance at him, only to discover he was staring at me, the open playbill in his lap ignored.

"What's wrong?" I whispered.

His forehead wrinkled with confusion. "Nothing."

"Then why are you looking at me?"

His jaw clenched, only long enough to give me a sexy flash of it. "I enjoy looking at you. Have I not made that clear?"

My skin went hot as sparks coasted down me. "Oh."

I wanted to tell him it was the same for me, but the lights dimmed, the orchestra began, and the curtain lifted, silencing us.

The production was completely different than what I had expected. The only opera I'd ever seen were the flashes of it in movies. A fixed stage with overly made-up women in big gowns standing in the center and belting out high notes in Italian.

Villain opened with a sparse stage and a chorus of young women in contemporary clothes. The music and story were dark and twisted, about a woman sold by her father into marriage to a terrifying rival. Hellbent on getting her revenge, she seduced her new husband and convinced him they should kill her father but fell in love with her husband in the process.

The set design was amazing. I wanted to take a million pictures and post them on Instagram, and slave over the images. The way they could paint the scene with just a few key pieces blew me away, and I was riveted. Macalister was too. At the intermission, he admitted he was enjoying it.

It was sexy too. The scene of the woman's seduction was provocative and made my breathing go shallow. The chemistry between the leads was sizzling.

Perhaps it was in my nature to always fall for the bad guy, who I believed was secretly good, because during the climactic end sequence, the husband was wounded badly, and the wife's emotional song as he lay dying cut my heart in two. I was right there beside her, asking for the devil to spare his life and let him live.

Tears trickled down my face, but I didn't move to wipe them away, not wanting to call attention to them. My hand was tense on my armrest, itching to move, but I refrained.

Macalister's cold fingers were abruptly on mine, pulling my hand down between our chairs.

I flinched in surprise, causing a tear to shake loose from

my cheek and drip down my neck. We were alone in the box, and no one could see what he'd done, nor could they see how I turned my hand beneath his and laced our fingers together.

At first, I thought he'd done it solely to comfort me, and I had to take air into my body in controlled sips. But my mind was distracted by the woman on stage singing about how the love of her life was dying, and my heart broke further.

Macalister had probably held the love of his life in his arms while she was dying.

Had he taken my hand to find comfort with me as well?

I tightened my grip, and he answered in kind.

A cold, fluttery panic slipped inside me, squeezing until I couldn't breathe. I was already dumb enough that I'd developed feelings for him and gotten too attached. I could not be stupid enough to fall in love with Macalister.

He'd been married twice before. He'd killed his last wife—possibly the first one too, if my mother's friends were to be believed. He was sure he was cursed.

All of that, yet I didn't want the show playing out on the stage to end. I swore in my head as the actors gathered and sang the final grand reprise. No matter how beautiful or powerful it was, it wasn't going to last forever, and I wanted this moment to. The world needed to stop turning so it was just me and him together, our hands linked in this real connection, and I worried that once it was severed, we'd never get it back.

While the rest of the theatre watched the stage, I turned to look at him with my face still wet with tears and glimpsed a sight I never thought I'd witness. Macalister with his guard down. He was stripped bare of his bravado, becoming just a man who struggled to hide all he was feeling.

He was devastatingly handsome, but even more so when he was human and stared back at me like he had the same worry. He didn't want to fall in love with me.

The audience below was already on their feet at the final note, clapping and whistling their praise, and when the curtain fell, we were out of time. The tension went out of his fingers as he drew away, our hands parting, and I choked back the noise of loss that threatened to escape.

When I'd read the name Oksana Markovic as the composer in my playbill earlier, I'd expected an older Russian woman with a hard look in her eyes, but holy shit, this woman was young and stunning. She'd come out with her husband from Chicago for opening night, and when she learned I was Macalister Hale's assistant, she asked if I could introduce her, so she could thank him for making this possible.

I'd done that, and now he was somewhere in the crowded lobby, which was hosting the afterparty. Cast members still in costume floated around with the guests and celebrated their success. Erika Scoffield had come over to me early on, taking pictures and chatting before moving on to work the room and visit with other donors. She'd played the lead's sister, and had been great in it, but I couldn't help but wonder . . . Did she know how she'd gotten the role?

Her father did. He'd thanked Macalister soon after she'd landed the part, so I'd bet she did.

My hand still tingled from where Macalister had taken hold of me, like part of him hadn't left. God, I was in trouble. My head swam with thoughts of him, even when there wasn't a vibrator between my legs.

As I left the bathroom, I forced myself to take small, even steps so as not to run back to him, but my slow stroll had a distinct disadvantage. It allowed Richard Shaunessy to step into my path.

"Sophia." He looked at me like a prize he'd discovered at the bottom of a cereal box.

"Richard," I answered politely.

He walked toward me as he spoke, radiating frantic energy. His eyes were overly bright and his smile too wide, so I was pretty sure he'd just finished doing a few lines in the bathroom.

"Some show, huh?" He invaded my space, forcing me to take a step back. "I thought this was going to be fucking awful when Blythe dragged me along, but it was actually kind of good." His gaze dipped down, lingering over my dress like he wanted to get inside it.

He moved closer, and again I put distance between us. "Speaking of Blythe, where is she?"

"I dunno." He made half an effort to glance around. "Probably talking to Erika or some shit. They're, like, inseparable."

"Oh, yeah." That made sense. They were both into theatre. "Wasn't she great?"

Richard took another step, bringing him so close it pushed all the air around us away. "Not as great as that dress you're wearing."

At first, I'd thought he was just high and dumb, too excitable to pick up on my signs that I didn't like his proximity, but I was wrong. He understood exactly what he was doing, how he was pushing me deeper down the hallway and separating me from the pack of people.

Shit, there was nothing worse than an overly confident, entitled man. He thought I owed him my body and my attention. How many times were we going to have this conversation?

At least once more, apparently. I sighed. "Thanks, but can you—like—*not*?"

"Not what?" He faked innocence, but his smile was playful. "Not tell you that you're even hotter than when we were in high school?" He gave up being subtle on his approach, driving me backward in the empty hall. "Not tell you I've got a penthouse with huge windows and bay views, and I want to fuck you against them?"

I stepped to the side, but my attempt to outmaneuver him didn't work. He hooked an arm around my waist and pulled me stumbling into his arms.

Macalister's voice was loud in my head, and I echoed his angry words. "I didn't give you permission to touch me."

Richard let out a short laugh, either not believing I was serious, or not thinking this was a big deal. "Come on," he whined, "don't be like that. Why can't we have some fun together?"

"Because I'm not interested, Richard, and if you don't—"

His expression soured. "What's the problem? My dick might not be black, but I promise it's still big enough to get you off."

Holy fuck, he went there.

"Wow," I said. "What a racist thing to say." A cruel, joyless smile spread across my face like wildfire and burned a million degrees hotter than one. "And about your dick size—that's not what I've heard." He went stiff, but his eyes flooded with doubt, and I wanted to destroy it. "You know women talk to each other, right? Like Julie Sheehan, and Francine Clarke . . . and Marist Hale."

Marist had never said as much to me, but it was an educated guess. She'd gone to prom with Richard as "friends," and he'd bragged how she'd come on to him in the limo, but him—being the gentleman he clearly was—turned her down. There was a lingering awkwardness between them ever since, too strong to be a simple rejection from either side.

Plus, Royce hated him.

The fear that spilled across Richard's face told me I'd hit my mark, and my evil smile widened. But hyperawareness pricked like needles on my skin. I sensed Macalister's arctic

gaze on me before I recognized it. He stood at entrance to the
wide hallway, one hand on his hip and the other hung at his
side, clenched tightly in a fist.

I tried to imagine what this looked like to him. Richard's
arm was still around my waist and I was smiling at him, and
Macalister was probably too far away to read the viciousness
in my eyes or the tension in my body. We'd look extremely
friendly, or worse, like two people having an intimate, romantic moment.

The blood red wallpaper lining the hallway exaggerated his furious expression, and it was so scary, it literally sent
Richard running. I didn't know he could move that fast, but he
was a tuxedoed blur as he let go of me and disappeared down
the hallway.

Heat gripped me like a vise, constricting tighter with each
deliberate step Macalister took toward me, his eyes teeming
with fire. He glared at me like a teenager who'd wrecked her
daddy's favorite car and then laughed about it.

"What was that?" he demanded.

"It was nothing."

His glare was a vat of liquid nitrogen poured all over me.
"It did not look like nothing."

My mouth went dry, and my heart banged violently inside
my chest. Was he jealous? Of mediocre Richard Shaunessy?

"You don't speak with that boy ever again," he decreed.

Maybe I was reading too much into it. Alice had cheated
on Macalister with Richard's dad, so perhaps Macalister was
upset about 'who' he thought I'd been flirting with, and not
that I'd been supposedly flirting at all.

I was still worked up from my encounter, and although the
two men had barely anything in common, I was once again facing an arrogant, entitled guy at the pinnacle of privilege, one
who believed everything in the world belonged to him.

He'd given me an order I'd be happy to follow, but I pushed back. "You don't own me."

Whoa. I'd never seen Macalister's eyebrow arch so high.

His cold fingers latched on to my arm, just above the elbow, letting me feel his dominance, and I went weak at his touch. He saw it all, how I softened and swallowed a deep breath, melting beneath his hand.

You don't own me, I'd told him.

"Oh, yes, I fucking do," he growled.

TWENTY

SOPHIA

POWER CASCADED OFF MACALISTER IN WAVES SO ROUGH, THEY crashed over me and nearly knocked me down.

"Let me prove it to you," he said. "Come with me."

He let go of my elbow, but the faint burn of cold still kissed the spot, like snow trapped against skin by a sleeve. I followed him submissively as he turned around and stalked back into the party, quickly locating the theatre director and interrupting the man mid-conversation.

"My assistant would like to see the costume room," he declared.

The man hesitated. "Of course. We can set up a tour tomorrow morning before rehearsals."

Macalister said nothing, his expression fixed in stone.

Realization dawned on the director, and his voice was full of apprehension. "You mean now?" He glanced away, considering what to do. Macalister had donated nearly a quarter of a million dollars, and if the director refused him, that would likely never happen again. A tight smile was squeezed out. "I'll take you myself. This way."

We followed the man, who Macalister clearly made nervous,

to the back of the theatre then up two ancient flights of stairs, climbing high into the attic. He fumbled with the knob on the old door, pushed it open, and flipped on the lights.

The room was essentially a warehouse. Long industrial bulbs hung sparsely from the exposed ceiling, lighting the green linoleum flooring below. There were rows of clothing racks, each garment hanging inside a clear zippered bag with a picture of an actor in costume tacked to the front.

"Thank you," Macalister said. "We will find our own way back."

Dismay visibly went through the man. He did not want to leave us alone in here, probably assuming we'd planned to play dress-up and potentially damage the expensive costumes. But he didn't want to piss off such a powerful donor either.

"She only wants to look," Macalister said casually. "You have my word we won't touch anything."

The man's shoulders relaxed. "Oh." He brightened and turned his focus to me. "Would you like me to pull any particular pieces?"

"No," Macalister answered. "Sophia and I also have business to discuss, which needs to be done privately." His sharp look politely announced, 'fuck off.' "Please don't let us keep you from your patrons."

The man hesitated a moment longer then decided it was beyond his control. "If you could turn off the lights and shut the door when you're done, I'd appreciate it."

Macalister gave a dismissive nod. "Of course."

The director left us at the threshold of the door, and the creak of his footsteps on the stairs gradually diminished until it couldn't be heard anymore.

Macalister's head turned to the room, wordlessly commanding me to go inside, and I carried out his order immediately. He stepped in after me, pulling the door closed with a soft thud, and the tension between us drew taut.

"How did you know about this place?" I asked.

"He gave me a tour before I wrote the check."

We were utterly alone in this room full of costumes. Slips of clothes that allowed people to become a completely different person, and as I stared at him, standing in the shadows between two tall racks, I wanted to be someone else.

I wanted to be the woman he'd fall in love with and break the curse.

In this seclusion, Macalister was safe to look at me however he wanted, and my heart pounded like fists against the side of a cage trying to break free. He was its captor, and he knew it.

He stated it like it was an unarguable law. "I own you."

It was the truth, but it was hard to surrender. I'd given him everything else. Shouldn't I hold on to this last thing and use it to bargain for his heart? I dug deep inside myself, gathering all the strength I had not to give in, and lifted my chin in defiance.

I couldn't say the word, but I hoped my expression told him *no*.

Rather than look irritated or frustrated, a slow, pleased smile crawled along his lips. I'd challenged him as best I could, and he was excited I'd given him the opportunity to prove me wrong.

It was sexy and terrifying when he charged toward me, and I turned and fled, running as fast as I could in my heels and dress through the maze of towering racks of clothes. It would only be a matter of time before he caught me, and I ran with no intention of escaping, anyway. At the end of the row, I turned blindly to my right and dashed past shelves full of shoes and hats in plastic bins.

At the edge of the room, the wall was lined with cabinets, a seamstress station, and a bare dress form. There was a large mirror, and I caught a glimpse of myself running, my soft pink dress billowing around my legs, and Macalister behind me.

He probably could have caught me sooner, but either he was enjoying the chase too much or was waiting to pounce until he had me exactly where he wanted. He grasped me by the elbow and jerked me to a stop, spinning me around so I crashed into his chest, and I let out a grunt of surprise.

I'd worn my hair up at his request, and so the back of my neck was bare, and his palm slid up to hold me there, steadying me as he dropped his mouth to mine. His untamed kiss brought on delirium. It buzzed through my core, radiating outward.

But he abruptly tore his lips away, like a possessive child throwing a fit and taking their toys back. "Say it."

Possession was nine tenths of the law, and I felt utterly possessed. "I'm yours."

His eyes widened. It wasn't clear exactly how he'd wanted me to say it, if I was supposed to repeat it word for word, but I'd gone with the full truth.

He had one arm along my back and the other wrapped on my waist, and as soon as my words registered, I was lifted into his arms, just enough so my feet no longer touched the floor. I was carried to the empty wall that had been partitioned out in sections, this one for long garments, and he jammed me in the corner, ducking his head slightly so not to hit the hangar bar.

I was set down on my feet, my back wedged between the wall and the wooden partition, and his mouth was hot on my neck. His breathing came and went in a rush, but I wasn't sure whether carrying me had caused it, or if it was how I'd surrendered.

His voice was dark and rough, filling my ear. "Only I'm allowed to touch you."

I gasped as his hand moved, sliding over my hip and down until he found the slit in my skirt and slipped through it. He unapologetically stroked his fingers over the crotch of the white panties I'd worn for him, making me shudder.

My hands moved mindlessly, pushing inside his jacket, sliding over his shirt and beneath the braces he always wore with his tuxedo. Because he was old-fashioned and classic and sexy as fuck. But he wasn't a gentleman right now with his harsh hand up my skirt as he rubbed me through my underwear, and I loved it. Blood roared in my ears so loudly, I had to focus on what he was saying.

"This isn't how I planned to do it." His tone was seductive as his lips brushed over the shell of my ear. "It will be quick, Sophia. Probably too fast for you to achieve an orgasm, but you'll enjoy it, and then you will come home with me and I'll take the time to do it properly."

His fingers worked their way down the front of my panties, finding my clit, and I moaned, clutching at him. Holy shit, it felt good. I slumped back against the corner, my eyes falling closed.

"I need release," he whispered into my neck. "So, you will consider this a taste. It's only a fraction of what I'm capable of."

Lava flowed through me, melting my bones, flooding between my thighs. The desire increased exponentially when he took a knee in front of me, pulled down my panties so I could step out of them, and pocketed the lacy underwear.

I stared down at him in his perfect tuxedo, his silver-threaded hair, and piercing eyes, and tried not to pass out. Macalister on his knees, even if only for a moment, was such a huge turn-on. It was nearly fatal.

Not that I needed any more help getting turned on. Electricity shattered across my body and throbbed in my center as an insistent need.

He rose back to his full height, our gazes connected the whole way, and when he claimed my lips, I sighed and slipped my arms around his neck. His hands were between us at his waist, working quickly to undo the inside buttons that fastened the braces to his trousers.

It wasn't until he had his pants undone that my lust-laden mind started to assemble the thought of what he intended.

I was so eager it came out in a squeak. "Are you going to fuck me?"

"Yes." He flashed a look like I was interrupting him. "I just explained this." But then his hurried movements slowed with hesitation. "You may tell me no."

If I didn't want something, he didn't need to give me permission to say so, but I appreciated what he meant. Perhaps he was worried I was so far under his spell that I didn't realize saying no was an option.

"Why the fuck would I say no?" I cried.

"Language," he said, a little serious and a lot teasing, and resumed his task of getting his dick out while his mouth latched on to mine.

He was mostly hard, and with two rough jerks of his own fist, he was as ready as I was. Probably more—it hadn't been three years since I'd had sex. But he moved with determination and restraint. Urgent but not desperate.

Macalister widened his stance to prevent his undone pants from slipping too far down his legs, and then his hands were in my skirt, pushing it up enough so the split parted and he had full access. The cool air brushed over my exposed, vulnerable skin, heightening anticipation.

He didn't ask me to, but I picked one leg up and hooked it behind his back, and when the bare tip of him brushed against my piercing, we both exhaled in a rush. *So close.* Even just that light caress caused fireworks to shoot down my supporting leg, and I wobbled.

Fuck, was I going to be able to stand?

I tightened my arms around his neck, and one of his hands slid under my ass, helping to support me. The bottom half of his shirt had been unbuttoned and parted out of our way, and he ringed his fingers around the base of his cock, steadying as he lined himself up.

There was a long, suspended moment where neither of us moved. A final beat to consider what we were doing and recognize there was no going back after this. I couldn't breathe as I stared up into his pale eyes. They seemed bottomless, endless. I could study them for a hundred years and still not learn every secret.

But we didn't have a hundred years. He'd told me this taste had to be quick.

"Oh," I gasped as he found the angle he needed and began to ease himself inside. My body was tight and not entirely prepared for something so large, but it felt uncomfortably good. I whimpered at his slow, metered intrusion, making a soft sound of pleasure mixed with surprise.

His jaw was straining, and it was clear he was holding himself back when he wanted to drive and take. Deeper he pushed, stretching inside, and I let out breath through clenched teeth. He was . . . a lot. More than I'd ever had, in every way possible.

"Shit, you're huge," I groaned, clenching a fist of his soft hair in one hand and the back of his jacket collar in the other.

Macalister gave a sound of satisfaction under his breath. He'd liked hearing that, and it wasn't bullshit. He was splitting me down the middle as he impaled me, advancing relentlessly until we were connected in the most basic way.

He held still and let me adjust to his size, but he didn't kiss me. He seemed intent on studying my response to him, and it was nice this way. I got to see his eyes haze as he slowly retreated, and his mouth part to pull in a ragged breath when he advanced again, this time faster.

"All right?" he whispered in a strained voice.

I nodded, not completely understanding what he was asking.

His gaze flicked up to the wooden pole mounted overhead. "Grab the bar."

As soon as I did, his hands scooped up under my legs and he lifted me completely, pressing my back against the wall. The shift in weight and the change in angle allowed him to slip deeper inside me, and we both groaned, our sounds of pleasure mingling with each other's.

Our foreheads pressed together, and he stared unblinking as he made his first actual thrust.

"Oh, God," I cried. My toes pushed into points, and then his teeth brushed against my bottom lip, gently snagging it.

It made it difficult to discern which I liked better. His cock was fire and pleasure, but his mouth was bliss. I whined with need into his mouth as he established his tempo. I locked my ankles behind his back, the wool of his tuxedo jacket soft against my legs, and I listened to the steady thump of my body against the wall as he drove his hips into me.

Could anyone hear us in here? There wasn't a lock on the door, and I imagined what it'd look like if someone came in and discovered Macalister holding me in his arms, his pants to his knees and the backs of his bare legs visible beneath his jacket.

His back blocked the view, but the way he moved and the enjoyment twisting on my face would reveal exactly what we were doing.

The room was temperature controlled, but it was hot up here in the attic, and we both began to sweat. His temples were damp, and I felt the sticky cling of the lining of my dress to my back. My makeup was probably melting too, but it was worth it.

The push of his body inside mine was *intense*.

His nearly silent sounds grew louder and blurred into moans as he picked up the pace.

My arm trembled from the exertion of holding on to the bar to help distribute my weight, and I could tell his muscles were beginning to fatigue, but he was too focused to notice. The composed man I knew was fading away, replaced by this raw, need-driven male with a singular desire.

He rutted into me, thrust after thrust, slamming my body carelessly into the wall as he closed in on his goal. This was for him, for his enjoyment, his satisfaction. His aggressive, rough way was erotic. It doused me with more heat, and although I wasn't close to coming, he'd been absolutely right. I wasn't just enjoying it—I loved it.

Who'd have thought the best sex of my life would be when Macalister Hale screwed me against a wall?

The urgency of his punishing thrusts changed, becoming dire. The rough edges of his five o'clock shadow chafed against my cheek as he buried his mouth in the crook of my neck and bit down. It was like he was punishing me for how good I made him feel. And even though he pumped himself into me like I was nothing more than a hard, quick fuck, he didn't let me think that.

"I own you." He kissed away the discomfort from the spot he'd bitten. "So, you tell me," he said between two mind-numbing thrusts, "I can finish inside you."

I'd never had sex without a condom before, and holy shit, it felt good. What would it feel like when he came? "Yes," I panted. "Oh, please, do it."

He grunted like an animal, and the sound of this civilized man doing it caused me to quiver. It was savage. Brutal. *Necessary.*

He came in a hot rush, spilling his seed inside my body, pulse after pulse of it. My internal muscles clenched on him like I could siphon off some of the ecstasy he was experiencing.

Macalister's jerky movements came to a stop, and he held me, pinned to the wall with his cock still inside me, our sweaty bodies beginning to cool. His mouth moved across my cheek, searching mindlessly for my lips until he found them, and then delivered a slow, thorough kiss. It wasn't what I'd expected. I'd assumed after sex he'd snap back almost instantly to his calm and collected state as he had after I'd gone down on him, but this version was out of sorts.

He seemed undone.

It was . . . sweet. His tentative, unsure manner reminded me of my first kiss years ago. How it seemed to have gone well for both of us, and we were thrilled, but then had no fucking idea what to do after we'd pulled it off.

He lowered one of my legs, letting me find my footing, and did the other, gradually retreating. It was suddenly too hard to look at him, because I worried I might blurt out something ridiculous and ruin the moment. Instead, I stared at the quick rise and fall of his chest and blinked rapidly, trying to get the emotions swirling inside me under control.

I could feel gravity's impact on the results of his orgasm, and while the physical sensation was kind of strange, the thought of it was insanely hot. Maybe I was blushing, or had an odd expression on my face, because Macalister grasped my chin with his thumb and forefinger and forced my head up.

"Look at me," he commanded. "What are you thinking about?"

I swallowed hard, but the answer came because I wanted to do whatever he told me. "That you're the first guy to come inside me." My voice was breathless, nervous. "I liked it. And I liked that it was you."

His fingertips skated over my skin, brushing back the loose wisps of hair off my forehead. His tenderness was startling. "I understand why people tell you their secrets." His eyes were the color of ice, but they were warm and inviting right now. "You have this power where you make it feel safe. We become the only two people in the world with no one else to tell. When

I'm with you, everything outside of that ceases to exist."

I gasped. It was the most romantic thing anyone had ever said to me.

But his face froze and then his expression shuttered. Up went his shields, and he backed away, leaving me with only the wall for support as he pulled up his pants and hurried to dress.

I'd run earlier, and now I was the one chasing him. I launched forward, seized his head in my hands, and jerked him down into a blistering kiss.

We'd both been in love before, and I wondered if it was the same for him when he fell as it had been for me. It wasn't a sudden, abrupt drop. The realization of it could be, sure. But the actual act happened through a collection of moments. Kisses, and words, and gestures, all building toward the awakening where you could no longer deny what had happened.

This was one of those moments, and I needed him to know that. I channeled all the passion I felt into my kiss, arching up to meet his mouth and reward him for letting his guard down. Everything else in the world stopped for me too when I was with him.

It was frightening being in charge, so when Macalister's hands grabbed my waist and he took command of the kiss, I sighed in relief. I sensed it was the same for him. We had our roles, and there was comfort in their structure.

"We need to get back," he said with deep reluctance.

"Yeah." But it was still hard to part ways.

It took him a lot longer to get his clothes in order than for me. While he refastened the buttons of his braces, I walked to the mirror and stared at the repercussions of letting him take me against the wall.

I was flushed, and a faint sheen of sweat clung to my skin. My hair wasn't too bad, and I thought he'd done his best to avoid touching it, but I ran my fingertips beneath my eyes to

clean up the smudged makeup. My lipstick was gone, completely kissed off, and there was a faint red mark on the side of my
neck. Hopefully, people would assume I'd recently scratched it
and it was a temporary irritation, and not my boss's bite mark.

There was a box of tissues at the sewing station, and I
grabbed one in a hurry, using it to clean up between my legs,
and dropped it in the trash before he made his way over to me.

He was put back together, other than the sweat-darkened
temples of his hair, but there was a lightness to him now, as
if some of the ice trapping him had thawed. His hand disappeared into his pocket and produced a flash of white lace.

"Would you like these back?" When I nodded, he added, "Ask me."

He enjoyed playing games, and I did too. "May I have my
underwear, please?"

"No." He was smug as he tucked them back in his pocket.
"Perhaps you can earn them back tonight."

Anticipation crackled through my limbs like lightning.

We both knew it was better to reemerge at the party separately, and I disappeared into the bathroom while Macalister
went straight in, mentioning he was going to the bar to get us
both a glass of water.

*When I'm with you, everything outside of that ceas-
es to exist.*

It replayed continuously in my head during the remainder
of the party. It was an endless loop during the long, silent car
ride to his house, where we sat in the back seat that was filled
with delicious tension. We were both working on our phones
but occasionally stole glances at each other. I still felt him between my legs in a pleasurable soreness and was eager for more.

God, I was going to burst out of my skin as we arrived at
the Hale estate and exited the car. I stared up at the stone
house, lit warmly from the outside, but the windows were dark

and secretive. My mouth was dry when we wordlessly climbed the steps and went inside.

Would we go straight to his bedroom, or would he start us off in the front room?

Neither.

Macalister gave me an authoritarian look and pointed to the door that led to the dining room. We were in his palace now and disobeying his orders would be treasonous.

Breath halted in my lungs as I pushed open the door and stepped inside.

I'd thought he'd been answering emails during the drive, and perhaps he had been, but at some point, he'd contacted his staff and instructed them to prepare the room.

Two candelabras evenly spaced on the long dining table, and one on a side buffet, were all that lit the enormous room. White tapers flickered in each of their five arms, but the wax had barely begun to drip, so they hadn't been burning long. They must have been lit as we'd passed the front gate.

The Hale dining room was deadly formal, and even in my fancy pink gown, I felt subconsciously underdressed. The walls were paneled in rich wood, and the elaborate chandelier seemed to have a billion crystals in it, every facet glinting in the flickering candlelight.

The table was only set for one, the seat to the right of the head chair. The white plate contained a slice of a decadent look-ing dessert. Chocolate torte? The ganache on top was glossy and flawless, decorated with a single raspberry and gold flakes, and between the layers of chocolate cake was a sinfully red jam.

I was instantly hungry looking at the sexy dessert, but there was only one fork and napkin set beside it. I couldn't imagine he intended to share with me, and when I glanced at him, his expression didn't reveal whatever he was plotting.

But he was definitely plotting something.

"I've decided you'll be naked for the remainder of the evening." He announced it the same way he told me he wanted another cup of coffee. "I need to go upstairs for a minute. When I return, you will be sitting," he motioned toward the dessert, "in that seat." The candlelight made him look wicked and sinister. "And you will be waiting for me in the nude."

All the moisture evaporated from my body as he turned and walked out the door.

TWENTY-ONE

SOPHIA

MY DRESS WAS FOLDED AS NEATLY AS POSSIBLE, AND I PLACED IT on the cushion of the seat beside me, my shoes tucked beneath the chair. I was stark naked and fucking freezing as I sat in front of the dessert, my arms crossed over my chest to hold in my warmth.

Thankfully, I didn't have to wait long.

The door behind me creaked open, and I straightened in my seat, turning to glance at Macalister over my shoulder. He was still in his tuxedo, and I wasn't sure which was more appealing to look at, him or the slice of rich chocolate cake. He looked pleased I'd done as told as he strolled confidently to the ornate chair at the head of the table.

"Eat," he commanded after he undid the button of his jacket and sat, his intense gaze feasting on all my bare skin.

Instinctively, I picked up the fork and prepared to use it but paused with a thought. "Aren't you having any?"

His eyes were electric, connected to the sexual current flowing through the intimately lit room. "I would like to watch as you enjoy this."

I gulped down a breath, speared my fork into the cake, and

pushed the first bite into my mouth. The raspberry and chocolate combination was one I loved, with just the right amount of sweetness. It was rich and exquisite.

And—oh—how he stared at me, like I was the sexiest thing ever. His gaze traced the lines of my body, flowing over my breasts and the hardened points of my nipples. It made my heart flutter, and if I weren't already freezing, it would have caused goosebumps.

"Do you like it?" he asked.

"Oh, my God, it's so good."

It was arousing and sensual, this act of him observing me as I devoured the dessert in slow, savoring bites. It was the mirror image of the sex we'd had, reversed so I was the one receiving the most pleasure, but he got enjoyment out of watching me experience it.

There was only one bite left. "Do you want some?"

He sat in the chair beside me, his elbow on the armrest and his thumb brushing methodically over his knuckles, like he was eager to get to the next part but trying not to show it. "Finish."

I put the fork in my mouth, closed my lips around it, and pulled it out oh-so-slowly with my hooded gaze holding his. His nostrils flared, and his jaw clenched, not with dissatisfaction, but with desire.

The tines of the fork *ting*ed as I set it down on the plate and nudged it away, showing him I was finished. The whole thing had been provocative and seductive, and I was humming with lust. He'd given me my amuse-bouche, and now dessert, but I wanted the promised meal.

Macalister stood, set one hand on the tabletop, and leaned over until he could dip a finger into the leftover chocolate ganache smudged on the plate. I watched with anticipation as he swirled it around and collected a dollop onto the pad of his finger. He straightened and focused on me, and the power of his exacting stare flooded every inch of the room, even where the candlelight couldn't reach.

His clean hand went to the back of my head, gripping my hair and pins holding it in place, and tugged backward, angling my face up toward the ceiling. It was so he could smear the chocolate across my lips, and then chase it with his mouth.

My knees pinched together as he tasted me, kissing and licking until every trace of it was gone, either consumed by him or melted away beneath his fiery kiss. And it was exactly how I felt—consumed. The thought made me go boneless. I was owned by him, but also revered.

"I've decided I'll eat after all," he commented. "Get on the table."

My stomach flipped over with excitement, and more lust flooded my bloodstream, so much of it that I became a jittery mess. It made it hard to move, but I stood, moved the plate out of my way, and climbed up on my hands and knees. I'd barely gotten up before Macalister's strong hands guided me to sit on my bottom, my knees pointed toward his chair and my bare feet dangling over the edge.

Once I was how he wanted, he stepped up to the edge of the table and used his hips to urge my knees apart and make space for him. His expression was firm, but not cold. He looked elegant and refined in his tuxedo, a man determined to get what he wanted, and I was naked before him as an offering.

His hand dipped into his jacket. "This came for you."

My entire body solidified as he produced the tiny black leather box and held it out flat on his palm. *Holy shit.* My eyes went so wide it was painful. I had to be hallucinating, because there was absolutely no way he was presenting me with a ring.

The corner of his sexy mouth lifted in a cunning smile. "No, Sophia. You won't wear this on your finger." His eyes turned serious and commanding. "But you will wear it for me."

My hand was trembling as I took the box and popped it open. The box had promised jewelry, and that was what he'd given me. The curved barbell was white gold, ending at one end with a ball and a large, brilliant diamond set in prongs at the other. I nearly dropped the box in surprise.

"This is fourteen gauge," he said. "If that's not correct, I also have one in sixteen."

He was the type of man who could buy whatever he wanted and in multiple sizes, including diamond VCH jewelry. "Fourteen is right," I whispered.

"Excellent. Do you like it?"

I nodded, still floored. He was giving me expensive jewelry that I'd wear intimately. He was the only person who knew about it, and it was like he was celebrating our shared secret. "It's beautiful," I said. "Thank you."

He set his palms on my knees, resting them there as I stared at the sparkling gems, mesmerized.

"This comes with conditions." Light and shadows danced over his expression, exaggerating his sexy and ominous appeal. "The first being that you wear this for me, and no one else. I am the only man who sees it."

My pulse jumped. He wanted me to be exclusive to him, and that was easy enough to agree to. "Okay."

"The second is that when you wear it, you belong to me. I own you and your body, Sophia. This means I can have you whenever and however and," his gaze crept downward, "*wherever* I want."

Oh, my God. Heat blasted through me in an explosion of volcanic proportions. I didn't care what I was signing up for, I'd do it. I was adventurous, and I'd take whatever order he gave. His conditions made me frenzied and needy and eager to sign this contract.

"Yes," I croaked. Macalister began to smile, but it froze

when I tacked on, "Wait."

I stared up at him, my lips pressed together.

"Speak," he ordered.

"I want the same. I'm the only woman you get to own."

He blinked away his surprise, like this was a request I shouldn't have to make. "Yes, of course."

He'd told me the world ceased to exist around me, but he was still a man and capable of flowery words and promises that meant nothing. His sons weren't exactly known for their honesty, either. But as I searched Macalister's eyes, they contained conviction, and if he wanted to own me, I'd make sure it was a full-time job.

"Okay, then," I breathed. "Yes."

This time, I didn't stop him as he pulled his lips back into a satisfied smile. He plucked the barbell from its perch, closed the box with a snap, and set it beside me on the table. His gaze swept down the length of my body before returning to my face, and his expression shifted to one of determination. "Lie back."

My pulse skipped along, and nerves trembled in my belly. He was going to change out my piercing right now, and holy fuck, my insides turned to liquid, rushing toward my center. The table was smooth and cold against my back, and I brought my feet up to rest flat on the edge.

His cool fingertips pressed to the inside of my thigh and nudged my knee to the side so he had more light and more room to work in. There was a faint *clink* as the diamond barbell was set aside for a moment, and he leaned in, using both hands to peel me apart. I pressed my lips together as he grasped both ends of my existing jewelry. The silver barbell had pink rhinestones encased in a ball at both ends, but they were internally threaded, so he might not know how it came out.

"The bottom one unscrews," I whispered.

I lifted my head to spot his expression etched with

concentration. It was a delicate area, and he was mindful, not wanting to hurt me as he began to twist. A tiny moan drifted from my throat as his fingers brushed over me, and it gave him pause. His gaze flew up to check in with me.

But I made it clear he hadn't done anything wrong. It was merely a side effect of his touch.

His fingers resumed moving, and then they were gone, screwing the barbell back together in his hands. It was stored in the black leather box, which was then pocketed, and the diamond one was picked up.

It wasn't as easy to put the new one in as it'd been to take the other out, but after a few attempts, he'd pushed the stem through to the other side of my piercing and began screwing on the silver ball at the bottom. When it was done, he stepped back, one hand resting on my propped-up knee, and admired his work.

Macalister sighed contently, the sound filling the dining room and causing a bolt of pleasure to course through me. I looked down, and the sparkling diamond winked back at me. It looked so, so good.

"I love it," I said, suddenly bashful.

He didn't respond with words, but he didn't need to. There was no doubt in my mind he loved the way it looked and all the conditions that went with it. The glaciers of his eyes heated with desire.

That was the only warning I got of his plan before he began to act. He dropped down into his seat and pulled it up to the table, then slid his arms under my legs. He wrapped his hands around my thighs and jerked me closer, my bare skin squealing across the table as I was dragged along it. It was so he could lean down and cover my new jewelry with his mouth.

"Fuck," I said in a startled moan, arching my back.

A sound of disapproval at my profanity came from him,

immediately followed by a sound of enjoyment, and the hands around my thighs squeezed, his fingers digging in. There was a tug of suction against my clit, and white-hot heat shot down my legs.

I'd always enjoyed it when a guy went down on me, but every sensation was multiplied a thousand times over because this was Macalister. The slow slide of the tip of his tongue over my clit made moans leak from my mouth. His sharp flicks caused gasps and jolts.

I peered at him in his tuxedo, his handsome face deep between my legs, and loved how his eyes were closed as if he were savoring me. He opened his mouth for a moment, so I caught a glimpse of his fluttering pink tongue as it played with the diamond, and the vision seared into my brain. It was beyond sexy.

It was mindless the way I writhed on the table beneath his hot, wicked mouth. He varied his speed and technique, finding new ways to pull sighs and deep, throaty moans from me. His hands strayed from my legs, roaming up to fondle and grip my breasts.

His tongue worked me over, massaging and caressing, and he seemed to enjoy exploring and playing with my piercing, tracing down one side and back up the other. My legs were shaking, and the trembling moved along my body, sweeping across my stomach.

"Oh, my God," I gasped.

I'd dreamed about this. I'd visualized grabbing onto his salt and pepper hair as he tormented and teased with his incredible mouth, using it to do what no other man had before. In my fantasizes, I came so fast.

Had visualizing been the trick I needed? Intense waves of pleasure built inside me, and my climax didn't seem like a distant idea. Or perhaps it was the fantasies paired with the nightly vibrator sessions that had been the key. I was training my body to associate orgasms with Macalister.

His hands on my breasts kneaded, sliding over my distended nipples, plucking and pinching, making me whine with need. *Fuck*, his tongue. I closed my eyes and saw sparks behind my eyelids. My heart raced, and I panted through the bliss he was giving me.

"That feels so good," I said in a rush, breaking the quiet surrounding us. I closed a hand on top of his on my breast, wanting to touch him as he touched me.

He lifted his mouth off me, turning his head so he could drop a kiss on the inside of my thigh. "Does it feel good enough to bring you to orgasm?"

I hesitated. "Maybe."

He stared up at me over the slope of my nude body, and he *smirked*.

I wasn't one hundred percent sure if it could happen, but him? Oh, he was. He looked powerful and arrogant.

"We're not leaving this room until you do." He planted a kiss on the inside of my other thigh. "But there's no reason to feel pressure. It will happen, and I can do this all night." He went back to my center, his lips brushing against my bare pussy as he spoke in a seductive hush. "I'm happy to do it, Sophia."

His tongue lapped at me, and my eyes threatened to roll back in my head. His mouth would get me there eventually. I just wasn't sure if it would be with his tongue, or his words, or the two working together.

Tension twisted in my core, rising like mercury in a thermometer.

It climbed higher as time dragged on, nearly slowing to a stop. Or maybe it raced forward and was hours. Time seemed to have abandoned us here in this dark room while a hungry man feasted on me. I squirmed and shifted, rubbing my body against his soft, unrelenting mouth. I was desperate for release.

He'd made it a rule, and I'd do whatever I could to obey.

My chest heaved, and I lifted my head to look at him better over it. Oh, God. His gaze was fixed on mine. His eyes were resolute.

He paused just long enough to ask it. "Do you want to come?"

"Yes," I pleaded in a whisper.

Macalister's chair gave a quiet groan as he sat up straight. His fingers came down in an abrupt slap, right across my swollen clit, and I yelped with surprise. It hadn't really hurt, but it'd startled the hell out of me.

His tone was dark and firm. "Do you want to come?"

I didn't understand this game. "Yes."

This time when he struck me, it was aggressive and with purpose. The first slap had been to get my attention, but this one was meant to punish. His jaw flexed and his expression hinted at his frustration.

He said it like I should know better, every word weighted and measured. *"Do you want to come?"*

Anticipation knotted in my belly. He kept asking the same question, and if I repeated my answer, his sharp, stinging fingers would follow. Was . . . was I supposed to say no? I glanced futilely around the room, like the answer was somehow hidden in the shadows.

"Macalister," I whimpered. "Please . . ."

Triumph flashed through his eyes. "There is the word I was looking for."

He dove down, his mouth a flurry of activity, and I bucked from the sudden pleasure. It was acute. He licked away the sting from his slaps, and as the pain went away, intense satisfaction moved into its place.

"Please," I moaned, out of my mind with need and giving him the word he wanted again. I thought I'd needed to come before, but the craving was so urgent, I was panicking I'd die if it didn't happen.

The room had been quiet until now, but I thrashed, my back banging against the table, causing the candelabra to jump, the flames to flicker, and wax to splatter on the tabletop. One of my feet came off the edge, and my leg draped over his back, trying to hook him. The hands on my body were everywhere. Smoothing over my breasts, my stomach, my legs as he searched for every inch of touchable skin within his reach.

And when his palms slowed to a stop, bracing my waist, he nuzzled into me, his head furiously rocking side to side. There was something primal about it. Like a predator with its prey locked in its jaws, shaking its victim to death before consuming it.

I threw my head back and arched my neck, my eyes slamming shut, and cried out as the force of the orgasm descended upon me. It was brutal and unforgiving. My hands clenched in his hair, holding him in place as pleasure wracked through me, sending fire searing through my bloodstream.

He didn't stop. Every flick of his tongue made me contract, prolonging my orgasm, and he sighed long and deep when tension went out of my fingers in his hair. The grip of my climax loosened and faded, and after it was gone, I lay on the tabletop like a woman devoured.

Macalister's hair was messy as he sat back and wiped a hand over his face, revealing a dark, victorious smile beneath.

"That was the second time I've brought you to orgasm." His tone was powerful and smug. "Once is luck, but twice is skill."

I was still breathless. "You've made me come more than twice." I was honest in the aftermath. "Dozens of times while I was thinking about you."

It didn't take him long to do the math. He was a banker, after all. He understood that I'd fantasized about him a lot longer than he'd instructed me to, and he liked hearing it. Satisfaction flashed through his expression.

"I've made you come twice too, you know," I teased.

He stood, only long enough to scoop me up and sit back down in his chair with me in his arms. "More than twice," he conceded.

A thrill glanced down my spine and warmed my chest. "How many times?"

His hands were in my hair, fishing out the pins and dropping them to the tabletop in a neat stack, working until my hair tumbled free. "More than I'm comfortable admitting."

I grinned, running my fingers through it to shake out the kinks. "Dirty old man."

Up went his eyebrow, and tension corded the body holding me. His tone was frigid. "Yes, well, let me remind you that this *old man* has accrued the expertise in the places your former lovers were sorely lacking."

I frowned. "I was kidding. And, yeah, you're a lot older than me, but so what?" I slipped my hands around his face, cradling his jaw, and stared into his guarded eyes. Had I not made this clear? "I'm into it, Macalister."

I was *so* into him.

But he looked skeptical, like it was too good to possibly be true.

"You don't believe me?" I searched his face, and my hands bristled against the rough edges of his jaw that hadn't seen a razor in at least sixteen hours. "Just ask Marist who I've always said was the hottest of the Hale men."

I didn't want to bring her up and invite him to think about her, but I needed to prove my point.

His skepticism increased, but I saw the faint hope that was buried inside. "You think I'm more attractive than my sons?"

I laughed softly. "Are you serious? Yeah. *Fuck, yeah.* And that was a while ago," I threaded my hand through his hair, running the silver strands through my fingers lovingly, "even before you had this."

His shoulders lifted with an enormous breath, and he didn't bother to hide the impact my statement made on him, how I found his gray hair appealing. He did try to deflect, though, and his voice was uneven. "Your generation overuses that word."

"Fuck?" I shrugged. "But it's the *best* word." He clenched his jaw at my casual use, and I smiled. "Is that what we're going to do soon? Are you going to *fuck* me right here on your dining room table?"

"No," he said, his hands clamping roughly on my waist. "I've brought you to orgasm with my fingers and my mouth." He leaned in, nipping at my throat before kissing the hurt away. "We'll go upstairs, you'll climb into my bed, and then I'll make you come with my *fucking* cock."

TWENTY-TWO

MACALISTER

THERE HADN'T BEEN A WOMAN IN MY BED SINCE THE NIGHT MARIST had forced me to watch her, demonstrating what she'd said I'd never have, and I was anxious to wipe that memory away.

Sophia stiffened in my arms at the order I'd just issued.

"You want me to walk through your house naked?"

"I'll be the only one to see it. My staff is discreet."

I gathered her things, carried them for her, and marveled at her perfectly nude body as she lifted her chin and climbed the grand staircase, her hips swaying with each step, taunting me. A man my age didn't deserve to bed a woman like her, with a body like that, but I justified it by telling myself I could give her pleasure no one else could.

She was shivering as she strolled into my room, padding on her bare feet to stand beside one of the green chairs in the sitting area, and waited there for further instruction. Her arms crossed over her chest, her stunning breasts barely visible beneath the wavy curtain of her blonde hair.

It was dark in the room, but the drapes were open and the exterior lights on, and it caused a yellow glow to pour across my bed like a spotlight.

I set her clothes down on the low table between the chairs and moved to her, running my palms up and down her arms in an attempt to warm her. Her skin was smooth and soft, and I inhaled the apple smell of her, letting her invade as much of my senses as possible. She'd taken me in her body, and I wanted to do the same. Sex was infinitely more pleasurable to me when I was immersed in my partner.

Sophia's mouth yielded to mine when I took it, and there was that strange pull deep in my chest that had plagued me from the beginning. Why did I find kissing her so . . . satisfying? It felt like if this was all we had, the only way for us to connect, I could be content with it.

My body, however, protested angrily. The quick rendezvous in the costume room had been murder on my back and only a temporary fix. An emergency adjustment to relieve the pressure that had risen above the levels of safety and control. Now that it had been taken care of, I would have her the way I originally intended tonight, before I'd seen Richard Shaunessy's arm around her waist and I'd nearly snapped.

The fury of it sliced through my mind, and I wasn't sure if I was more upset with him or myself. I'd been careless and hadn't defined the rules with her. I hadn't made it clear I expected Sophia to be as invested in me as I was her, and I'd gotten a glimpse of what it would look like if I didn't make my claim.

She'd find a younger man to take my job, and I'd already suffered that once in the professional world. I would not allow it to happen again, and certainly not in the bedroom.

As I kept my mouth latched on to hers, my tongue deep in her mouth, I pulled off my tuxedo jacket and dropped it to the floor. When she realized what I was doing, her hands went to the tie at my neck, tugging to undo the knot, and the silk spilled free.

We worked as a team. While she undid the buttons of my

shirt, I unlatched my cuff links. I peeled off my braces and undid the button of my trousers, followed by the zipper. My movements were fueled with the urgency to be as naked as she was, to press my body against her warm skin and experience that completely.

Confidence came to me easily, but not tonight, which was odd. I'd already had her, knew exactly what it felt like to slide inside the wet heat of her body, and I was sure she wanted that again. But I could not ignore the anxious feeling drifting through me, and the idea that although it had been a long time since I'd had a woman in my bed, that wasn't the cause for this nervous sensation.

It was Sophia.

It was important to me I delivered on my promise to her.

When my clothes were a heap on the floor, I urged her toward the bed but was distracted when she closed a strong fist around me and stroked my cock from tip to base, sending fire and satisfaction radiating outward and a shudder wracking my body. It required me to inhale a deep breath through tight teeth. It felt good—

Much too good.

I grabbed her wrists and pulled them away, using my hold on her to force her down onto her back on my bed, so quickly that she bounced as she hit the mattress and her hair fanned out around her. She was angled across the corner, and I followed her down, pinning her hands to the sheets, and put one knee up on the bed while keeping my other foot flat on the floor.

Her shapely legs were parted around my waist, and the weight of my erection dropped heavily onto her belly. I canted my hips back just enough to slide my cock over the diamond I'd given her that signified my ownership, and a possessive growl threatened in my chest.

This girl was *mine.*

Was she aware her gift of submission had far more value to me than the material one I'd given her?

I released her hands, wanting her to use them. "Spread the lips of your cunt."

Her expression filled with disdain. "Whoa. Language."

I paused and let the evil grin spread across my face. "Have I offended you, little girl?"

Challenge flashed in her eyes, bright as the sun. "No, *Daddy.*"

The power that word held was obscene. It made me hot in ways that were wrong . . . but felt right. I wrapped a hand around her throat, using my thumb to turn her head to the side so I could lean in and speak directly into her ear. "Reach down and spread the lips of your *pussy*. Show me what I own."

Her eyes fluttered closed, and the quiver from her was pure lust.

I straightened and, rather than be a brat, she did as instructed. Her red polished nails gleamed as she stretched her pink skin wide, showing off the glittering diamond, and my gaze slid over it appreciatively. This woman wasn't shy, and it was incredibly attractive. As she held herself open for me, I gripped myself and traced the jewelry with the sensitive tip of my cock, soaking in her wetness.

Sophia made a soft mewling sound of need that reverberated up my back. She was ready, as was I, and there wasn't sense in waiting any longer. Tomorrow, I could tease her. We could spend hours on foreplay. I could discover all the secret places on her body that made her gasp.

But tonight, I'd show her what we were capable of.

I grasped her narrow waist in one hand and used my other to line myself up, and slowly began to ease inside. As I entered her, her blue eyes lidded and her mouth widened into a silent 'oh,' and her skin dented around my fingertips as my grip tightened. The urge to thrust was strong, but I enjoyed watching her response as I claimed her inch by inch.

Her snug heat enveloped me, and the sensation shortened my breath. My head swam with pleasure, and I leaned over, cupping handfuls of her full breasts. I pushed them together, running my tongue from one nipple to the other and back again as I buried my cock as deep inside as she could take me.

"Shit," she groaned, "is it bigger than last time?"

Her half-serious question pulled a short laugh from my throat. It was flattering to hear, and I dragged my parted lips along the curve of her neck, my hot breath rolling over her. "I can go as slow as you need, but you took all of me before."

Her arms wrapped around my back, and she sighed with enjoyment as I began to move my hips, starting with gentle, shallow thrusts. Her legs hooked behind my back, and I slid a hand beneath her, using it to encourage her to angle her hips and take me deeper.

She whimpered in pleasure, and pride expanded my chest.

I slipped my other hand beneath her head and trailed the edge of my tongue over her ear, letting her feel the weight of my body on top of hers, our chests flattened together. She trembled beneath me, and I brushed my lips against the pulse throbbing in her neck.

I knew the answer but asked it anyway to tease. "Still cold?"

She shook her head, and I withdrew from her, pulling back until the tip of me was barely inside, and then charged forward. The force of my thrust drove her into the mattress.

"Oh," she gasped in satisfaction, her back bowing.

I did it again, and again, sawing myself in and out of her, and she went breathless, her desperate pants ringing out and floating in my room. I'd fucked her with my mind earlier, and then my tongue, and now I used my whole body. She grew hotter and wetter, and I had to close my eyes and concentrate, blocking her out for a moment to re-center myself.

She was tight, choking me in the way a woman's body did to maximize her pleasure, and blood rushed like fire through my veins. My heart pounded, beating faster than my quickening thrusts.

Control yourself.

I ground my hips against her and blinked at the odd sensation, like a scratch against my abdomen just above where we were connected. What was—

I let out an amused breath. If I'd bought her a smaller diamond, perhaps I wouldn't feel the prongs of the setting as much, but I enjoyed the reminder of its existence. It did make me curious, though. I was the first man she'd been with since she'd gotten pierced.

"Do you like the way the jewelry feels?" I asked, rolling my hips for emphasis.

"Yes." She groaned it into my shoulder. "But I like the way you feel better."

I exhaled loudly and braced against the pleasure her words caused, but I jerked inside her. Warnings flashed through my mind. I needed to focus. It was embarrassing and unacceptable how close I'd already become.

The heat of her made sweat cling to my skin, and I stood up while keeping us connected, balancing my weight between my knee on the bed and my foot on the floor. She stared up at me with her face flushed and her lips swollen from my kisses, and my heart lurched. Jesus, she was beautiful.

"Thank you," she said, sandwiched between two moans.

Since I'd unknowingly said the compliment out loud.

I snared her hips in my hands and drove into her, making her breasts undulate with my steady, deep thrusts. Everything blurred in my vision outside of Sophia. The only sounds were her needy whimpers and the slick slide of my skin moving inside her. The air in the room had gone thick, making me struggle to take in enough breath to fill my lungs.

My mind went to war with my body, and the tingling heat building at the base of my spine was winning. I put my hands under the backs of her knees and pressed them toward her shoulders, opening her wider and allowing me to hit the spot I'd need to if I was going to give her an orgasm both inside and out, which was my intent.

My left hand smoothed up the back of her thigh until my thumb was against her clit, and as I rubbed, the diamond above moved and glistened.

"Oh, God. Oh, *fuck*." Her eyes went wide and then slammed shut under my power as her hands latched on to my forearms. The muscles of my back and legs were warm and tired from exertion, but I kept my unrelenting pace, beating my hips against her, determined to push her past the brink. My thumb swiped back and forth, going as fast as I could, trying to stay on her as she swiveled and bucked.

"Yes," I urged.

She was wild and gorgeous, spread open for me, and I enjoyed the view of my cock disappearing inside and emerging wet with her arousal. Pleasure snaked through me, desperate for release, but I shoved it aside. My body was only a tool for her satisfaction right now, and I would not stop until I had it.

Her face twisted with bliss, verged on being overwhelmed, and her chest heaved with strangled breaths. The moans swelled from her throat, building in intensity and volume, and her internal muscles clamped down.

"Don't stop." Her plea was urgent, and yet full of surprise. "Oh, my God, I'm so close."

Yes, my mind chanted.

A victorious grin spilled across my face when a cry burst from her, loud and deep. Her legs shook uncontrollably and so hard I had no choice but to stop and hold on to her to keep her from vibrating off the edge of the bed. It was better this way. I could feel each rhythmic pulse of her body as the orgasm gripped her.

I stared at this girl strewn across my bed with her hands clasped on my arms while she was in the throes of her climax, and I was overcome with the thought that seeing this once wouldn't be nearly enough. Maybe a hundred times wouldn't be. My hands looked so good on her, and my cock buried deep looked even better.

Dangerous.

That was what that idea was. Over time, she wouldn't be able to separate sex from her feelings, and she'd grow attached like Alice had. Or worse, I'd be the one to blur the lines, and that could not happen. I thought highly of myself but was smart enough to know I was no good for her.

Sophia's body went limp, relaxing into the mattress as she descended out of her euphoria and back to me. Her eyes blinked open, but they were foggy and unfocused, and then fluttered shut.

I didn't like the loss of our connection. I leaned over, placed my hands gently on the sides of her face, and held her head still so I could hover a breath away. "Open your eyes," I demanded. "Watch me."

She obeyed, and her blue eyes peered up into mine, sharpening into focus as I began to move, gradually building my pace back up until sparks crackled inside my body, threatening to ignite. I wanted her to see what she did to me. I liked watching her come apart, and so it stood to reason she'd feel the same.

We stared at each other with such intensity, it was as if nothing could make us look away. Blood roared in my ears, but the heat building inside me burned away all my fatigue. The raw need to find my end inside this girl and share myself with her was all that mattered.

A groan welled up from my chest, my muscles corded, and the pleasure became a force I could no longer hold back. It ruptured and broke free, flooding my limbs with electricity that was both scorching hot and ice cold in the same instance.

My gasp was loud and my movements erratic while my cock throbbed and filled her in blissful spurts, diminishing in intensity with each one.

I stilled, took in a preparing breath, and lowered my mouth to hers.

Her kiss was more powerful than I could ever hope to be. It wiped my mind clean of thoughts and doubt and whispered promises. It seduced and disarmed. And in my weakened state, I let it in, believing all it had to say.

We can find a way to make this work.

Our bodies cooled as I kept her trapped beneath me, my mouth roving against hers. I despised wasted time, but that wasn't happening when our lips were locked together. Time seemed to stop altogether, anyhow.

Eventually, I relented and withdrew, letting her up, but my gaze tracked her, watching carefully in case she was plotting her escape as she disappeared into the bathroom. I'd already told her she would stay the night with me, and I had meant it exactly as I'd said.

It would be nice to share my bed with someone instead of an overly affectionate and persistent cat who had decided he owned me, and it wasn't the other way around. I'd had the staff keep my door shut tonight and make sure Lucifer wasn't inside so Sophia and I wouldn't be treated to his scolding lecture of meows when we arrived.

She shut off the bathroom light as she emerged back into my bedroom, and her footsteps were quick as she went to the pile of clothes I'd left discarded on the floor. She plucked out my white shirt and had one arm in a sleeve before she abruptly stopped.

I'd told her she was to remain naked for the rest of the evening, and perhaps she was recalling that now. Or maybe she worried she hadn't asked permission. Her back was to me, and I admired how stunning she looked as she turned over her shoulder to speak.

"Do you mind if I . . .?"

"No." I didn't mind in the least, and it was a cliché for a reason. The possessive streak inside me responded eagerly to seeing her in my shirt. While she'd been gone, I'd gotten into bed, my back against the upholstered headboard and the sheets across my lap. My gaze went to the empty space beside me. "If you're cold, there is a blanket here."

She finished buttoning the bottom few buttons on the shirt, the sleeves far too long on her and the cuffs unfolded, but the way she looked was incredibly appealing. Her hair was tousled, her makeup softened and smudged, and she was—for lack of a better word—glowing.

I'd done that.

And after we had a few hours rest, I'd do it again, no matter how sore we both were in the morning.

"You sure you want me to stay?" She glanced away, hesitant. "You don't seem like the type of guy who wants to cuddle after."

I tilted my head to level a hard look at her. "Get in my bed, Sophia."

She moved swiftly, sliding in beneath the sheets and laying her head on the pillow, then stared up at me like I might change my mind at any moment and ask her to leave. It bothered me. All the careless boys she'd been with before had shaped her view of sex, including what happened afterward, and I was determined to change that.

"Will you sleep?" she asked softly.

"Yes." A faint smile crossed my lips. "You've successfully

worn me out."

I undid the clasp on my watch and slid it off my wrist, but she reached out and pulled it from my fingers. She studied the face then turned it over, reading the inscription on the back. "It's about time. Love, Julia."

An uncomfortable sensation banded across my chest as I took the watch from her and deposited it on my nightstand.

"A gift from my first wife. It was an inside joke," I explained, although I wasn't sure why. Perhaps it was the way she stared at me with questions hiding in her eyes. "Julia didn't like me very much when we first met. She thought I was quite arrogant."

Sophia feigned shock. "No."

I ignored her sarcasm and pressed on. "That didn't matter to me. I'd decided fairly quickly that I wanted her, and even though she'd tell me she hated me every day, I didn't give up."

Her eyes widened. "She said she hated you?"

"My competitive nature means I will use any means necessary to win. She claimed some of my tactics were . . . unfair."

Distrust filled her expression. "Like what?"

"She'd been dating someone else at first. When I'd offered him ten thousand dollars to walk away, he did."

Dismay ran visibly through her. "You paid her boyfriend to break up with her?"

"I did her a favor. If someone had made me the same offer, I would have refused. There was no amount of money that would have made me leave her, and certainly not ten grand. He was a fool not to see how priceless she was."

"Oh," she said, her outrage fading somewhat.

It'd taken Julia weeks to speak to me after that, but I'd stayed committed. The man she'd been with moved on quickly too, confirming my suspicion that their relationship hadn't been serious. It didn't exonerate me completely, but I had no regrets.

"It took her some time to forgive me. So, I bet her that if I could beat her in a game of trivia at the bar, she'd let me take her out." All these years later, the memory still caused a smile. "I'd rigged it, of course. I paid the host earlier to give me the questions." I'd done it for a solid month until she'd taken me up on my wager.

Faint amusement lit her eyes. "Scoundrel."

"I convinced her to date me, and a few months later, when she finally admitted she was in love with me, I didn't say it back. My first response was to tell her—"

"It's about time," she finished.

"Yes."

She smiled and mashed her pillow down so she could look at me better. "That's a nice story."

It was. "I've never told it before."

I was glad I'd shared it with her, and it appeared the same was true for her. Sophia's expression was soft and warm. "I don't really remember her," she said. "What was she like?"

We'd just slept together, and procedure dictated I not speak about past lovers. "You don't want me to talk about her."

She frowned. "I asked, didn't I?"

I shook my head to placate her. "She was a lot like you, actually. Not intimidated by me, even when she should have been. She enjoyed getting under my skin."

"I am intimidated by you," she grumbled. "I'm just good at pretending not to be."

I gave a knowing smile. "And also like you, she was well liked. Friends with everyone who met her."

I hadn't expected my statement to fall as flat as it did. Her gaze dropped from mine, staring vacantly at my chest.

"I'm not like that."

Was she thinking about the father who refused to acknowledge her? Her parents? Tate Isaacs, who slept with her then cruelly brushed her aside? I wanted her mind off them. "You have dozens of friends. Hundreds, even."

She lifted a shoulder. "Not really."

"Every event since you've been my assistant, I've watched as people gather around you."

"They don't count," she scoffed. "I mean, sure. I'm popular. But those people don't give a fuck about me."

"What about Marist?" I countered.

Sophia's lips pressed together. "We're not friends."

"You were in her wedding."

"Because I'm useful. If anything, she sees me as a frenemy and goes the whole 'keep you enemies closer' route."

What? How could that be?

I must have appeared confused because she continued. "If we were really friends, don't you think she would have told me the story about the time she almost died?"

I inhaled a deep breath. "She wasn't allowed to. I forbid it."

She hesitated. "Can I ask what happened?"

It was becoming easier to share secrets with her, but this one carried a heavy amount of shame. "When Alice learned of my infatuation, she saw Marist as a threat, and . . . she poisoned her. Had I not discovered Marist dying on my staircase, it's possible Alice would have succeeded."

Sophia sat upright in her surprise, turning to face me. "Wait, what?" I watched as she put the pieces together. "The allergic reaction Marist had before the wedding, the one that put her in the hospital."

"Yes."

"I don't understand. You stayed married to Alice, like nothing happened." Her eyes widened. "Why didn't Marist go to the cops?"

"Because the Hale family couldn't be involved in that kind

of scandal, and she understood that." The irony wasn't lost on me that had I done the right thing then, I would have avoided everything that came after, and it was possible I'd still be CEO and Alice would be alive. My legacy wouldn't have been dragged through the mud.

"But," I added, "it was not as if nothing happened. She was punished and banished from the house. Alice and I had been over for years before that incident, but that was the day she knew she had truly lost me." I swallowed a lump in my throat, wanting to justify what I'd done. "You need to understand, I aspired to sit on the board of the Federal Reserve, and I couldn't risk divorce. She had the ability to ruin me, and at the time, that was the only thing that mattered. My name was everything."

It still was now.

And it was likely hard for Sophia to hear. The name she had wasn't her own, and the one she deserved wouldn't be granted to her.

The judgement in her eyes was intolerable, worse than two years of wearing state-issued clothes and having every decision taken away, and although I didn't deserve it, I craved relief.

"Tell me the truth," she said softly. "It will be our secret." She leaned close and set her hand on my chest, the heat of her palm soaking through like it could melt the ice in my heart. "Did you mean to kill her?"

I stared into her eyes, wishing I had a confident answer, but since I didn't, I'd give her what I could—the truth. "I don't know. Everything on the balcony is hazy in my memory, and those final moments are . . . gone." I set my hand on top of hers, pressing it harder against my skin, like I was swearing it to her. "I hope I didn't. I want to believe I'm not a man capable of that."

She evaluated me with a critical gaze, and it stripped me

bare. There weren't any secrets left to hide from her.

"I don't think you are capable of that," she whispered. "At least, not anymore."

TWENTY-THREE

SOPHIA

MACALISTER WOKE ME IN THE MORNING BY ROLLING ME ONTO MY back, unbuttoning his shirt I was wearing, and then he went down on me. He brought me to orgasm with both his tongue and two fingers inside me, and when I was a quivering mess, his steely eyes filled with power.

"Up," he ordered. "On your knees and face the wall."

He didn't leave me time to catch my breath, but I scrambled to follow his command. I buried my knees in the mattress and stared at the headboard, tracing the nail head detail at the edge while he yanked the shirt down off my shoulders and tossed it away.

His damp mouth was hot on my neck as his chest, faintly dusted with hair, bushed over my back. Goosebumps lifted on my arms, and my nipples hardened into points while his hands roamed over my body. They closed on top of my hands, lacing his fingers through mine, and I surrendered to his direction. I moved under my master's power as he lifted our arms and slammed my hands to the wall just over the headboard, making me bend at the waist.

It was uttered sternly in my ear. "These stay here."

I shivered with anticipation. His dick was hard, jutting against my back, and he rubbed it provocatively over my ass. Teasing. Promising. He unlaced our hands and dragged his palms along my arms, his fingers trailing over my skin like he wanted to assess each goosebump he'd given me.

Up his hands moved to my shoulders, they smoothed down my back, gliding even slower, and I arched into his touch. The sensation of it pumped fog into my mind and steam into my body.

"Fuck me," I whispered.

The heat of him went away, and his tone was frosty domination. "You do not tell me what to do."

He had me addicted to him already, and I was jonesing for my next fix. It made me desperate and reckless, and I affected a patronizing voice. "Sorry, Daddy."

Fire cracked across my ass, the pain of it registering a split-second after the sound of his skin striking mine. Holy fuck, that spank was serious. I gnashed my teeth to hold in the groan.

Anger filled him, so hot I could sense it without even looking at him. Each of his words were deliberate. "Do not call me that."

Would he do it again if I did? Give me a matching red handprint on the other side? Excitement bubbled over. "Okay . . . Daddy."

It stole all my breath when he slapped the other cheek. Pinpricks tingled across my skin.

"*Enough.*"

I pressed my hands hard against the wall and turned over my shoulder to look at him. He stared at my ass like a man transfixed. He put a palm over the irritated skin and gripped a handful, clearly enjoying the way my red bottom looked in his hand. When his gaze lifted to me, he scowled, upset I'd caught him looking.

I swallowed so hard he must have heard it.

"Don't," he warned.

But his dick was hard and throbbing, and the fire in his eyes was beautiful, and I couldn't stop pushing him even if I'd wanted to. "Please, *Daddy*."

He grabbed the back of my neck with one hand and clamped down on my waist with the other, flattening his chest to my back. "You want to be punished, little girl, is that it?" he snarled. "I can accommodate."

He wasn't gentle or slow as he entered my body. I was impaled. His cock roughly split me in two as he pushed his way inside without regard or apology.

"Fuck," we groaned together in our pleasure.

My eyes pinched shut, and with my vision gone, it made space for him to completely take me over. He was deep inside my body and my mind, and if I wasn't careful, he'd force his way into my heart too.

His hands were rough and his hips rougher as he fucked me. His teeth latched on to the spot where my neck met my body, biting until it ached. I clenched down with the muscles inside me, squeezing every drop of enjoyment from him I could.

"You like this?" he taunted. Or perhaps he was asking for real. It was impossible to tell over the violent slap of his body against mine and his ragged breath heaving into my ear.

"Yes," I sobbed.

The electric charge of him sizzled through my system, overloading it. It grew more intense when his hand on my waist was shoved between my legs, touching us where we were connected. He found my clit and rubbed furious circles on it, and a tremble snaked up my legs.

Moans poured from me, growing shamefully loud. Would his staff hear them?

My arms were already shaking, fatigued from bracing myself to the wall against his aggressive, unforgiving thrusts. White flashes burst behind my closed eyelids. Oh, God. He was going to make me come again, and in this position, where his cock seemed to go on forever, I wondered if it might kill me.

Pain radiated down my scalp as he snatched a handful of my hair and jerked my head back onto his shoulder. His tone was sinister, sliding into my mind like a knife. "You like the way *Daddy* fucks you?"

Without warning, my climax slammed into me, causing my arms to buckle, and I collapsed forward, face-first into his pillow. But Macalister didn't stop. He followed my descent and drove into me, riding my orgasm and using it to propel him into his own. He clenched a hand on my ass as his shuddering gasp punched the air in the room, and he held on to me even after the pleasure waned, leaving us panting for breath.

"Jesus." He pulled out of me and moved to my side, gathering me up into his arms. "Are you all right?"

I stared up at him in my dreamy state, confused. It was easily the best sex I'd had in my life, so, yeah. I was more than all right. I reached up, wiping away the bead of sweat that had formed near his hairline. "Why wouldn't I be?"

His eyebrows pulled together. "That was rougher than I'd intended."

I said it like an apology. "I pushed you."

"You did." His gaze washed over my face, searching to see if I'd lied to him and he'd accidentally hurt me. He traced a fingertip over my forehead, brushing the hair back out of my eyes, and his tender gesture after such aggression was shocking.

"Are you mad at me?"

Surprise flitted through his expression. "No. I was worried you would be with me." His eyes went unfocused as he stared at my lips. "I have no business having sex like that."

I blinked, and then a grin widened on my face. "Oh, so you didn't like it?"

His attention snapped back to me. "That is not what I said."

I laughed softly. "It was fucking hot, and you know it."

He didn't argue with me. All he did was sigh and shoot me a fake, stern look. "Language."

And he grabbed my wrist, pinned it to the bed, and used his mouth to deliver a punishing kiss that left me unable to speak.

Before I left his house that morning, Macalister announced that going forward, I would ride to and from the office with him every day. It was wasteful for us to travel separately, and it'd give us more time to discuss work, he'd said. I was to park in one of the spaces of his garage and meet him in his foyer at seven a.m.

It didn't take long to realize his true motive, but I wasn't upset by it.

There was dinner for two waiting at his house when we arrived after work on Monday. We ate, and then he ordered me upstairs, and we'd barely made it inside his room before he'd had his hands up my skirt.

Although we didn't spend every night together, because sometimes we had different obligations, it became a pattern. I'd text him my outfit for approval in the morning, drive over to his house, and then ride with him to work. And at the end of the day, I'd come home with him to have dinner, and sex, and conversation where he seemed intent on learning everything about me.

And then I'd hurry home to fall asleep so I could repeat it all over the next day.

He was typically great at shutting off the part of him I saw behind closed doors, but occasionally he'd slip on the drive home. He'd lean too close, or his fingers would graze across my thigh, or he'd tell me in a seductive voice he had plans for us after dinner.

His driver had to know we were fucking. By this point, most of his household staff did.

But the people who worked directly for Macalister Hale were well paid and had signed ironclad NDAs, and they were either too smart or too intimidated to leak the faintest whiff of his personal life.

Very few secrets ever came out of the Hale house.

I'd told Macalister he should view getting people to like him as a game, and holy shit—did that work. He began to look for ways to help. On the first Friday of August, he went out to dinner with Evangeline and some of her friends, and by the end of the evening, he'd arranged an introduction with the head of admissions at Cape Hill Prep for one of the couples who was desperate to get their thirteen-year-old in. Besides money, Macalister had accrued a vast network, and now that his reputation was climbing, it was easy for him to connect people.

The man who owned me was becoming the hero I'd hoped he could be.

He lamented my "terrible" taste in Netflix shows, but was stunned and impressed by my excellent taste in porn. One evening after dinner he'd taken me downstairs to his home theatre and streamed his favorite for me to watch while he went down on me. I'd leaned back in the recliner, his head buried happily between my thighs, and gazed up at the mesmerizing couple fucking on the huge screen.

I came twice before he pulled me down to the floor and on top of him, making me fuck him the same way the girl on-screen did. The whole experience was hot, but getting to see what specifically turned him on made it that much hotter. I loved how filthy he was, and how obsessed he'd become with giving me orgasms.

Shit, he was *obsessed*. Like it wasn't a hobby but his one and only job.

A tiny voice in the back of my mind worried I was just a temporary fix. Something to be plugged into the hole of loneliness he felt, or a substitute for the woman he couldn't have, but I shook it off. Macalister was not a replacement for Tate, so I hoped it was the same for him.

"Dude, what is with you?" Penelope asked me, snapping her fingers in front of my face.

I turned my gaze away from Marist and shifted my focus back to my friend. We were at a fundraiser for the Boston Zoo, and for anyone else, Penelope's leopard print dress would have been a bit too on-the-nose. But on her it looked fabulous.

"Sorry." I smiled with embarrassment. "I got distracted. I like Marist's dress. Don't you?"

It was such a dark purple, it looked black until she moved. The boning lines of the corseted top were visible, and the skirt burst out into shimmering layers of tulle.

Penelope gave Marist a once-over glance, taking in the dress and the way it worked with her dark green hair. "I guess. She's weird."

I frowned. "We're all weird." I gave her a pointed look. "You did the foot thing with Dean Halbeck, remember?"

She nearly spit out the gin and tonic she was sipping. "Oh, my God! Don't bring that up." She tucked a strand of her maple syrup colored hair behind an ear. "And I didn't just mean now, you know. You've been totally MIA the last month." She leaned closer and dropped her voice low. "Who is he?"

I fought the desire to seek him out. He was here tonight, probably lingering beside Evangeline and pretending to listen to conversation he'd tell me later he found insipid. No one knew while he'd been escorting his "girlfriend" around the room, he'd secretly been sending text messages to his assistant he was fucking on the side.

Although I couldn't see him, I felt Macalister all over my body. Literally. He'd bought me expensive French lingerie, which I was currently wearing under my dress. With every step, I felt the straps from the garter belt pinned to my stockings and the delicate lace of my bra as it brushed over my nipples.

This was why I was distracted. I couldn't *not* think about Macalister.

There'd been other gifts too. A potted orchid appeared on my desk the day after he'd discovered an orchid picture was my phone's lock screen. When the zipper broke on my favorite handbag, a new one was delivered the following morning. The office kitchen suddenly stocked my favorite black vanilla teabags.

Before, he'd been a man who only thought about himself, but it couldn't be true now.

He spent a lot of time thinking about me.

Penelope stared expectantly, waiting for me to tell her who I was secretly seeing.

It wasn't really a lie, because I thought few people in Cape Hill did. "You don't know him." That wasn't enough to satisfy her, so I tacked on, "He works at HBHC."

Hopefully, she'd assume that was where we'd met. I didn't like lying, and I was eager to talk about my feelings for him with someone else, but I couldn't. Penelope was the first person to admit she was terrible at keeping secrets.

"Interesting," she said. "Does he work with Tate?"

I frowned at what she was implying, like I was dating someone he worked with to try to make him jealous. "No, and I told you, that's over."

"I know you said that, but are you sure?" She looked disappointed. "Because I think he's flirting with Emily Northcott right now."

"Is he?" I felt a strange sense of relief that I was only interested in this as information. There wasn't even a spark of jealousy. "I didn't realize she came."

Since Marist's sister had a three-year-old daughter, she didn't go to many of these things.

Penelope lifted a carefully manicured eyebrow. "I mean, if you want to get out of here, let's go. I'm ready."

She knew I'd been in love with him and was worried about me, and I appreciated it. I laughed lightly and shook my head. "No, it's totally fine. I'm over Tate. This new guy I'm seeing is a million times better." Her gaze drifted over my shoulder, but I was too excited to talk about it to recognize what this meant. "The sex, Penelope. Fuck, he's so amazing. I've had so many orgasms I think I'm getting dehydrated."

"Mr. Hale," she announced with a strained smile.

"Ms. Marino," Macalister answered, his voice right behind me.

My body locked up. How much of that had he heard? If I looked embarrassed, at least she'd assume it was because I'd revealed this in front of my boss. I turned to face him, my cheeks on fire. His expression gave nothing away. He was cold, indifferent stone, and I did my best to sound natural and helpful. "Did you need something?"

His gaze drifted down my body, and I'd swear he could see through my clothes to the lingerie he'd bought me, but then his attention turned back to Penelope. "Sophia tells me you're a photographer. Do you do portraits?"

My friend nearly collapsed in her surprise. She hadn't expected me to mention her to him. "Uh . . . yes, sir." She stumbled to get her words out. "I have before."

He looked pleased. "I need a new family portrait taken."

Penelope was dubious. "You want *me* to do it?"

He had, until that moment. Macalister didn't like repeating himself, and my friend was about to lose this opportunity, which she couldn't afford to. She had struggled to launch her business on the side this past year, and like me, still lived at home with her parents. Photographing the Hales would be huge for her.

"That's a great idea," I said. "Penelope's work is fantastic. When were you thinking?"

He turned his head toward me. "You'll have to coordinate schedules. A weekend would be easiest."

"Yeah." I nodded. "I'll take care of it."

"Excellent." He held my gaze for a fraction of a second too long, just enough time to create a moment, and then he walked away, the conversation over.

She watched him as he went, her stare unblinking. "Did that, like, happen? Did I just book a job with Macalister Hale?"

I smiled. I'd sort of done that for her, but I didn't say it. She was frozen, a nervous look plastered on her face, and it was . . . strange. "What's wrong?"

"Oh, my God," she whispered. "I'm going to fuck it up."

"What?"

Self-doubt seeped into her expression. "What if he doesn't like what I come up with?"

She was being silly. "You're awesome, and—hello? Have you seen the Hales? They're the most photogenic people on the planet."

I eased her doubt somewhat, but she shook her head, making her long brown hair sway. "I don't know how you do it. I couldn't spend every day with him." She lowered her voice. "He scares the crap out of me."

My voice was matter-of-fact, but my pulse quickened.

"He's not so bad. He grows on you after a while."

She didn't believe me, but it was the truth. He'd grown on me so much, I was pretty concerned I was falling for him.

During the limo ride to Macalister's house, he retrieved a bottle of water from the side bar, opened it, and passed it to me. Arrogance glittered in his eyes. "You mentioned to your friend you were becoming dehydrated."

"Oh, my God," I muttered, wanting to sink into the seat and disappear. "How much did you hear?"

He ignored my question. "Drink." I did, and when I lowered the bottle from my lips, a confident smile crept onto his face. "You said I'm a million times better than Tate, but you're actually fourteen billion short."

I snickered at how he flaunted his wealth. "You're so extra."

He paused. "Extra . . . what?"

Of course he wasn't familiar with the phrase. "It's a thing people say. It means you're too much. Like you're trying too hard."

"I don't try *too hard*." He hesitated, considering something, and his voice went quiet. "But I will admit I do try, Sophia."

Since the partition was up and the driver couldn't see us, Macalister was free to touch me however he wanted. His hand went to my knee, slipped beneath the hem of my dress, and moved up until it rested on the band of lace decorating the top of my thigh-high stocking I'd worn for him.

"You flattered me tonight." His fingertips traced the curves of the scalloped edge against my bare skin. "You flatter me every night when you're in my bed, and you should be aware I will do everything in my power to keep you there. I know this

| Nikki Sloane

arrangement we have isn't ideal, but it's unfortunately one of the few things I cannot control."

I was short of breath from both his touch and his words. "I know."

It was the most we'd ever said about our relationship. I thought we worried if we tried to define it, the other would back away, so we continued in our precarious situation as secret lovers and friends, unsure if it would develop into more. I didn't want to think about the future, because doing so was too fucking scary.

Macalister's legacy was everything to him. If he had to choose between me and his reputation, well . . . that would be one of the easiest decisions he'd ever have to make. The way I felt about him now, though, meant he'd have to make it eventually, and I wanted to put that off as long as possible.

Macalister lowered the corner of the business section of the *Globe* and eyed the half-eaten breakfast on my plate. "Did you not care for it?"

I took the final sip of my orange juice and picked up my phone. The egg-white and spinach omelet wasn't really my thing. "I'm more of a bacon and pancakes kind of girl."

He folded the newspaper and grumbled under his breath. "My nutritionist advised me to watch my sodium intake."

I smiled in commiseration with him. A big reason he looked so good at his age was because he took such great care of himself. My appreciative gaze slid down over his shirtless form as we sat at his kitchen table, and he did not miss the way I traced his biceps and sexy forearms.

It was a question he already knew the answer to. "What are

you looking at?"

"You," I said. "Looking all sexy while you read your . . ." I pointed at the business section.. "What's this thing called again?" I pretended I didn't know how to pronounce it. "Newspaper?"

The muscle along his jaw flexed, making him even sexier. His eyes sharpened. "Yes. I'm sure it's an unfamiliar media to your generation because it contains things like capital letters and punctuation."

I laughed and made a mental note that the next text I sent him needed to be one run-on sentence, all lower-case, and contain as many abbreviations as possible.

"Would you like my chef to prepare something else?"

I waved a hand. "No, thank you. I'm not hungry, and I'd have to get dressed."

Since I was once again wearing nothing but Macalister's white dress shirt from last night. I'd brought over a change of clothes so I wouldn't have to wear my cocktail dress home, but he preferred me naked, and I preferred not to freeze my ass off, so this had been our compromise.

The shirt smelled like him, and I loved having it wrapped around my body.

He finished his coffee and set his mug down. "I need a shower. Will you be joining me?"

I glanced at my screen. I had a bridal shower for Carrie Patterson at lunchtime, and the restaurant was in Boston. "I don't have a lot of time." I gave him an amused look. "Can you be quick?"

"I can be efficient," he revised for me. "And the vibrator is waterproof."

A laugh rose in my chest, but it gurgled to a stop when someone standing in the back of the kitchen cleared their throat. The man had his arms folded across his body and leaned against the doorframe with a disapproving look splashed across his face.

Macalister's tone was dark. "Royce."

TWENTY-FOUR

SOPHIA

THE ROOM BECAME A VACUUM WITHOUT AN OUNCE OF AIR. Macalister rose deliberately from his chair, probably wanting to reclaim a position of power, if only in stature, as he stared down at his son.

"I raised you better than this," he said coolly. "It's courtesy to call before showing up at someone's house."

Royce was impervious. "Just because I moved out doesn't mean this place stopped being my home." He sighed loudly. "I only came by to get something for the apartment. What you do is your own business, but if I'd known I was going to be interrupting an important discussion about shower sex and vibrators, I would have sent a text."

Oh, my God. I stared at the plate in front of me while trying not to melt off the chair and disappear beneath the table. But, thankfully, my immediate discomfort was short-lived. Royce straightened, turned, and walked out the door.

"Damn it," Macalister groaned. "Royce, wait."

But his son was already gone, forcing him to follow. His heavy, quick footsteps carried him out into the dining room, and as soon as I was sure they'd cleared the hallway, I bolted out of my seat, sprinting for the stairs.

I dashed up them, into Macalister's room, and dressed as quickly as possible while nerves rattled my stomach. It was unlikely Royce would tell anyone what he'd seen, other than his wife and maybe Vance, but dread made my hands shake. Macalister was downstairs right now, having to explain to his son what we were doing . . . and I was sure once he was forced to say it out loud, he'd see how ridiculous and dangerous being with me was to his reputation.

He was going to end it, right after I'd collected enough moments to fall for him. God, it was so unfair. Tears stung in my eyes, but I blinked them back. I'd lived for so long with a broken heart, the sensation should hold a familiar comfort.

I jerked my hair up into a loopy ponytail and bent down, putting my knees on the carpet as I collected up all the lingerie he'd peeled me out of last night, shoving fistfuls of silk and lace into my overnight bag.

My movements froze as his door creaked open, and when I took in the full, dark expression cast over Macalister's face, my heart sank to the floor.

Don't, I wanted to plead with him. *I'm not ready for this to be over.*

His voice was tight, like he had a fingertip's grasp on his control. "Did you collude with him?"

"What?"

He walked toward me, and since I was kneeling on the ground, it forced me to arch my neck to keep my gaze on him.

"I do not like repeating myself. Did you and Royce plan this?"

Plan *what?* "I . . . I don't understand."

"He all but admitted this was the outcome he hoped for. It's why he pushed for you to be my assistant. He believed I'd try to seduce you, and once I was successful, I'd forget all about her."

My mouth dropped open. Royce had invited me to shoot

skeet, knowing I'd beat his father, and hoped it'd be enough to put me on Macalister's radar. And if I became his new obsession, he might let go of the torch he carried for Marist.

I swallowed painfully, both wanting and not wanting to know the answer. "Have you?"

Anger colored his face, perhaps masking his hurt. "How can you ask me that?"

That's not an answer, my brain cried. And no denial was answer enough. I frowned and stared at his feet, desperate to compartmentalize like I did when I'd missed a target. Set it aside and focus. There was plenty of time to be disappointed about it later.

"Look at me," he ordered.

I lifted my gaze over his black lounge pants, which were slung deliciously low over his hips, working up across his broad chest, until I finally reached his pale eyes, finding them unguarded for once.

"I told you when I'm with you, everything else ceases to exist," he said. "So put your doubts about that away."

It felt like everything was coming apart. Emotion swirled inside me like a hurricane, powerful and destructive. This was it. If I didn't say it, I'd never get a chance to. "I have to tell you a secret."

Did he sense what was coming? He stopped breathing. "What is it?"

"I think I might be in love with you."

He blinked once, staring at me with a pained expression hung on his face.

Then he blinked a second time, coming back to life.

"No," he said finally, like it was just that simple.

What the fuck did he mean, no? "Macalister—"

"No," he repeated. At least he didn't run, nor did he get angry. He crouched down, meeting me at eye-level, and his face was—of all things—practical. "I won't allow it."

I was so stunned, it sucked all the power from my voice. "Are you serious?" When he didn't answer, a cruel laugh erupted from me. "You don't get to tell me how to feel."

"Don't I?" He set a hand on my cheek, not to dominate, but to soothe. "I own you."

The balls on this guy. I shot him a dirty look. "I gave you control over my body, not my heart."

He seemed amused. "Last time I checked, the heart is located inside the body."

I pushed his hand away as my frustration boiled over. "Don't be an asshole. You know what I meant."

He hardened. "I understand you're upset, but you're not in love with me, Sophia. This is an infatuation, and it will pass."

"An *infatuation*," I seethed.

He ignored the volcano of anger threatening in my voice and stood, looming over me. "And even if I were capable, I care enough about you not to fall in love."

"Because you're cursed," I spat out.

"Yes." He was so somber, it broke my heart. "And because I destroy everything I love."

My heart stumbled at his quiet admission. When he hesitantly offered his hand, I took it and let him haul me up to my feet and into his warm arms.

His eyes had a gravity I couldn't escape. "I enjoy our time together." He visibly struggled to get his words out. "You . . . make me happy, and I haven't been happy in a very long time."

You make me happy. It reverberated through me, heating the marrow of my bones.

Reluctance deepened his expression. "But I don't want to be the selfish man I was before, so I will be honest. I can give you many things, but it's unlikely I'll ever be able to offer you what you truly want or need." He swallowed an uncertain breath. "I need you to tell me that I am enough. That what we have right now is enough . . . for you."

I studied him critically, the way I would watch targets launch and how the wind would impact their trajectory, determining their likely arc. Macalister was convinced he wasn't capable of loving, but I could see our path, and I could prove him wrong. When I put my mind to it, I usually got my way, and I was determined to have him.

"It's enough," I agreed, "for now."

I'd had to sit quietly with the information bubbling under my skin during Macalister's marathon meeting with the IT department. It was the third one this month to discuss the software upgrade rollout, and it usually put him in a foul mood.

He walked past my desk without a word, not realizing I was following him into his office until he nearly shut the door on me. I could tell he was trying to sound polite, but his patience was thin. "What is it?"

"Natasha," I said then realized I had to clarify. "My friend who works for DuBois's agent, sent me a text. His publisher just announced preorders for the book."

He ushered me into his office and closed the door while I tapped my screen to forward the image to his phone. The cover was sharp and slick, with the title in a strong, bold font that stretched from one side to the other, and the subtitle beneath it smaller and italicized.

ABOVE REPROACH:
How the Powerful
Families of Cape Hill Reign

He stared at the screen for a long moment, his expression cryptic.

"This is good, right?" I asked. "It says 'families,' so it's definitely not all about the Hales."

He nodded and looked pleased, but not as happy as I expected. He was still concerned about how much mention his family was going to get.

"When will it publish?" he asked.

"October twenty-sixth." I smiled. It'd be tight, but that should be enough time for word to get out to voters how much of a 'family man' Damon Lynch really was.

"That's soon." His eyebrows pulled together, creating a crease between them. "I'd expected it to take him a while to write it."

"I think it did. He started doing research back in February, right after you got—" He never talked about prison and actively avoided the word, so I did the same. "Right after you came back."

"Yes," he said, sounding distant.

He was worried he hadn't had enough time to transform into the redeemed Macalister Hale, and I understood that. But we'd done everything we could in the time we'd had, and the rest was out of his hands.

"Are you nervous about what it's going to say?" I asked.

"No," he answered quickly. "Whatever it is, I'm confident I can handle it. I don't have any other choice." He set his phone down on his desk and gave me an evaluating look. "You'll join me at the marina on Saturday for lunch."

His abrupt shift in gears made it hard to keep up. "I can't. I have tickets with some friends to the Harvard football game."

"Cancel," he said.

I was dubious. "So I can have lunch with you?"

"Yes." His expression softened into one I rarely saw. He was anxious for me to agree to this. "Please. It's important."

Please was a word I heard less often from him than profanity, and it was unnerving. I felt off-balance.

"Okay," I said.

If he wanted to dine with me out in the open where all of Cape Hill could see, that certainly was important.

Seagulls called to each other and swooped overhead, darting between the boats tied to the docks, and I stared at the end of the pier with anxiety building a stone in my stomach, weighing me down. It made it impossible for me to move.

Macalister stood at the edge of the dock, discussing something with a man onboard one of the boats, but he must have sensed my eyes, because he turned toward me, and the bright sunlight glinted off his sunglasses. He wore khaki pants and a navy sweater, with the collar of a red check patterned shirt peeking out at his neck, and he looked effortlessly New Englander as he strolled down the pier.

He hadn't finished his approach before he spoke. "Is something wrong?"

"I thought we were dining in the clubhouse."

"No, I've arranged for us to have a private lunch onboard." His head tilted as he studied me. "Is this a problem?"

I pressed my lips together. "It might be." I watched the wind ruffle his hair. "I don't do so well on boats."

He straightened, and although I couldn't see his eyes behind his sunglasses, it was clear this was unexpected. "Do you usually get seasick?"

Two years ago, Marist had invited me to join her, along with her husband, brother-in-law, and Tate, on Vance's boat.

I'd spent much of the afternoon queasy and eager for it to be over. I hadn't set foot on a boat since.

"Not . . . every time," I answered.

He relaxed and gestured for me to come along with him. "You'll be fine. It's a beautiful day and supposed to be calm."

Macalister didn't wait for me to argue, and I trudged across the boarded walkway behind him, listening to the water crash against the pilings. It didn't sound calm, and we were in the Cape. It'd be worse out in open water.

At least this boat was bigger than Vance's.

Macalister stepped out of his shoes and pulled off his socks, tossing them one by one into the basket beside the gangway that led to a large, white sailboat. It had a teak deck and a sleek design that made it look fast, even when it was tied down. It bobbed in the water, and the gangway creaked with the rise and fall, making my stomach churn.

"I don't know if this is a good idea," I said.

He set a hand on the railing and leaned closer to me, just past the edge of what was a professional amount of space between employer and employee. "I'm sure you're tired of spending all of our time together at my house. I thought it'd be nice to get away for an afternoon on the water."

I drew in a deep breath. "Like a date?"

A faint smile teased his lips, and my knees softened.

The door to the main cabin was open, and I could see the woman inside, moving around in the sophisticated galley as she prepared her station. She was the chef who'd serve us lunch, and I had a vision of Macalister and me sitting on the luxurious couch inside the privacy of his sailing yacht, me sipping wine while he talked.

It was terribly romantic.

Macalister wasn't the wealthiest man in the world, but he was filthy rich. His money made him royalty, and his scandal ensured he was recognized nearly everywhere. It meant this was as close to a real date as we could get right now.

I had no choice but to take it. Plus, he'd said this lunch was important, and my heart skipped with the possibilities of what that could mean. Maybe he was going to admit he'd been wrong when he'd said this was just an infatuation.

It wasn't for me.

He knew my decision before I'd made it and eyed my sandals. "No shoes on deck."

Once I'd slipped them off, dropped them in the basket, and shuffled across the gangway, my feet were cold against the wood. It was October now, and although it was pleasant in the sun, summer was long gone, and sweater weather had officially begun.

I was introduced to Captain Ridley, who wasn't much older than I was, but the guy looked like he'd been born at sea with a steering wheel in hand. His white uniform was crisp and his expression stoic, but his handshake was friendly enough.

Was it strange for Macalister when he was aboard? Everyone here was an employee, and he owned the ship, but he wasn't the one in charge. We stood dutifully as the captain briefed us on safety procedures before Macalister pocketed his sunglasses, led me below deck, and gave me the tour.

The cabin was surprisingly full of light. Windows lined the walls, and several skylights overhead helped to brighten the space and keep it from feeling small. The navigation desk was immediately to my left, and beyond that were the tan leather couches with a table raised and folded out between them.

The galley spanned the entire length of the right side. Was that starboard? I'd never had much interest in sailing. The kitchen was well designed to maximize space and storage. I didn't realize there was a full gas stovetop until the woman lifted the counter and tucked it back out of her way.

I got the impression Macalister had gone over the menu with Hilde already because as soon as she was done greeting us and finished her setup, the short, compact woman went up to the cockpit to assist Captain Ridley with the castoff.

The engine beneath us rumbled quietly to life.

Macalister showed me the main cabin head and the crew quarters at the back of the ship, and then we moved forward to the master's quarters. It wasn't much more than a queen-sized bed. It had a charcoal gray stitched headboard, was surrounded by white oak cabinets, and the windows hugged both sides of the room, which meant we could watch as the nose of the ship headed out for sea.

The room was fucking sexy, and my pulse kicked. "How many women have you seduced in here?"

Desire lurked in his expression. "None. I purchased this vessel the week before I gave Royce his seat on the board."

It explained why the boat looked so new.

Macalister moved in and grabbed the handhold beside me, trapping me against the wall. His voice was low and hypnotic, matching the purr of his yacht's engine. "Do you *want* to be seduced?" His mouth brushed over mine, teasing a kiss. "Would you like me to fuck you in this bed?"

Heat rushed to the center of my legs, and his mouth continued to ghost over my lips, stealing my breath.

"I wonder if you can be quiet," he mused. "Or if I'll need to put my hand over your mouth to keep my crew from hearing all the times I make you come."

"Oh, my God. Let's find out," I said eagerly, sliding my hand across the front of his pants.

But he abruptly stepped back from my touch and smiled like the bastard he could be. "Yes, but we've barely left port." He straightened his shoulder and gestured toward the cabin. "We will take lunch first."

We'd been together long enough for me to know he did it on purpose. He lived to turn me on and then leave me hanging in a state of arousal, convinced it made my orgasms come quicker.

This time, it backfired on him. Once the engine was off and the sails were up, my stomach began to churn. I tried to push through. I hadn't had much for breakfast and that had been hours ago, so maybe all I needed was some food in my belly. As Hilde prepared our salads, I silently pleaded for her to hurry, and when he poured me a glass of wine, I eagerly took it.

But the longer we sailed, the worse the pitch and roll of the boat seemed to become and it made sure sex was the last thing on my mind. Once we were served, I scarfed down my salad, not even tasting it.

"Evangeline and I," he said, "have decided to end our relationship, but we will remain friends."

It was hard to focus what he was saying, because it was taking all my strength to hold it together. "Oh, yeah?"

"We've," he said it like he was contractually obligated, "*dated* for five months. That seemed like an acceptable amount of time to the both of us."

"Mm, hm." I pressed my lips together.

"You look displeased." He peered at me with confusion. "You don't agree?"

"No, I do." I forced out a tight smile, not wanting him to know I wasn't feeling well. "Will you really stay friends, or is that just the official line?"

He set his fork down and wiped his lips with his napkin. "I'd like to think we will. Does that bother you?"

He'd confessed to me a few weeks ago he hadn't kissed her on the lips the night of their first 'date.' There was no spark or chemistry between them, and he'd implied I was the cause of it. The fire between us was too powerful and consuming for him to be interested in anyone else.

"No," I said, "it doesn't bother me at all. I'm glad you've made a friend."

He gave a pleased smile.

As soon as it faded, I was anxious again. The food and wine did nothing to settle my stomach. If anything, they made it worse, and I tried not to watch Hilde over his shoulder as she worked to prepare our lobster risotto. She always had one hand steadying herself to the counter or a cabinet as she swayed with the sea, making it look natural.

But it was very unnatural to my inner ear, and I couldn't disguise it any longer.

"Hilde," Macalister's voice barely hid his alarm, "do we have ginger ale aboard?"

"No, sir, but we have some ginger candies. Should I—"

"Yes," he ordered.

She set down her spoon, retrieved a box from a cabinet, and brought it to the table. When she glanced at me, her attention moved on to Macalister. "Oh, she doesn't look well."

"No," he said, irritated, although it seemed to be with himself.

"We have Dramamine," she said to me. "Would you like some?"

"Yes, please." When she went to fetch it, I sighed and put my weary gaze on him. "Usually, the way that works is it knocks me out, and I sleep through my motion sickness."

He said nothing as she reappeared and handed me a packet.

"I think we have ginger tea too," she added. "I'll boil some water."

I tore the foil open and downed the tablets. Best case scenario, the drug would start working in thirty minutes.

He opened the box of candies, unwrapped the green wrapper, and as he passed it to me, the boat pitched dramatically, making our plates slide across the table. I stared at him with a pained expression. There wasn't enough ginger in the world to overcome thirty minutes of this, let alone an afternoon.

"Move over," he ordered, rising from his seat and moving to sit beside me. "Give me your hands."

I popped the white candy into my mouth, grimacing at the taste, and did as he asked. He grabbed my forearms, his hands a fist's length away from my wrists, and pressed his thumbs into the soft undersides. It was sort of uncomfortable, but I knew what he was doing. Acupressure.

"It wasn't supposed to be like this." Annoyance tinged his words. "The forecast said the wind wasn't arriving until tomorrow."

"To be early is to be on time," I said dimly, throwing his platitude from my first day back at him, but he wasn't amused. The nausea made me weak and destroyed whatever filter I had. "The great Macalister Hale can control a lot of things, but apparently not the weather."

The boat pitched again, and water sloshed violently against the hull.

He pressed harder into my pressure points. "Better?"

I wished, but I was miserable. He searched my face like he would determine my answer himself, regardless of whatever I said.

"I really don't want to throw up on your yacht."

He frowned. "I don't want that either." He stood and used his hold on me to pull me up with him. "You might benefit from fresh air and the horizon."

"I'd benefit more if I wasn't on this boat," I grumbled.

He helped me up the stairs, which was no easy feat with how the ocean rocked us side to side, and once we were above deck, I clung to him, not caring if this was appropriate or what his staff would think. The sea was the most dominating thing right now, and I'd become a slave to it.

Macalister sat us down on one of the sun pads mid-deck,

and when my head dropped onto his shoulder, he wrapped his arm reassuringly behind my back. His tone was quiet. He was trying to help, not boss me around. "Stare at the horizon."

I tried to focus on it.

Then I tried to compartmentalize and shut down the part of my brain that was registering the nausea, but that didn't work either. I wanted to enjoy sitting in the sun with him, nestled close while the waves cast seawater misting faintly over us . . .

But I couldn't.

My stomach lurched, and once the panic set in that he might watch me as I vomited, it had a snowball effect. My anxiety made me feel so much worse. "Macalister," I croaked.

"I know." He eased me down so I could lie across the lounge. "I'll tell the captain we need to turn back."

I watched him clamp a hand on the back of the lounger and ride the undulating deck, gingerly making his way toward the cockpit. God, I envied him for not feeling the effects, and I despised my equilibrium.

This was supposed to be our date, and my body had ruined what was going to be a—

Tingles crept up the back of my neck, which was my signal I'd crossed the point of no return. The contents of my stomach were about to come up, and now it was simply a race to keep it down long enough to make it to the side of the boat.

I scrambled up over the lounger, stumbling blindly toward the corded railing that skirted the perimeter of the deck. It was extra hard because the boat was turning and pitching so sharply I practically had to climb.

It leveled off just as I reached the side.

"*Sophia!*"

Macalister's horrified yell yanked my attention to him. I didn't understand what was wrong or why he looked so terrified, but seeing him like that made my heart stop.

It meant I didn't notice the boom as it swung across the ship until it was too late to get out of its way. The heavy pole that jutted out from the mast slammed into my shoulder, the force of it sending stars of pain through my body and knocking me off my feet.

I didn't scream as I fell. My voice was too stolen by surprise, so I was silent as I tumbled headfirst over the side and plunged deep into the darkness of the Atlantic.

TWENTY-FIVE

MACALISTER

AWARENESS SCUTTLED OVER MY SKIN LIKE AN ARMY OF INSECTS. I didn't believe in premonitions, but the sensation of danger descended on me so rapidly, I couldn't ignore it. I'd asked Captain Ridley to turn us back to port, but it meant we were making a run downwind. The ship heeled over nearly forty-five degrees unexpectedly, veering us off course.

It was the perfect setup for an accidental gybe—one of the most dangerous events to take place while sailing. If the wind hit the mainsail, it'd caused the boom to swing from one side of the boat to the other. The violent crash of it could rip straps, tear the sail, and damage the mast.

Or it could sweep someone clean off the deck.

The cockpit was lower than the midship and back aft so there was more than enough clearance for me and the captain, but as the wind shifted and began to fill the mainsail, Sophia abruptly stood. My reaction was slowed by fear as she moved directly into the path of danger.

"Sophia!"

She turned to look at me exactly when the boom came at her like a missile.

Ice froze in my blood as it slammed into her body, knocking her over so quickly, one moment she was there and the next she was gone. The splash of her in the water was the same as if it'd been thrown in my face, spurring me into action.

"Man overboard!" I yelled, loud enough for Hilde to hear below deck, and I dashed to the stern, scouring the water for Sophia. The ship was moving at a fast clip, currently sailing away from her, and with the rolling sea, it'd make it difficult to spot her.

I'd approved her black dress this morning because I foolishly liked how low the neckline was, and she'd pulled on a black cardigan to combat the autumn wind. Her clothes made her blend in with the water, and her blonde hair wasn't nearly as bright when it was wet. My heart beat furiously, and it intensified every second as I scanned the ocean and couldn't find her.

Fuck! Where are you?

Ridley was dropping the sails, powering up the engine, and trying to turn, all while shouting things at me, but his commands fell uselessly at my feet.

No.

I caught a flash of her floating in the distance, unmoving, and that was all I needed to see. I tore open a compartment, plunged a hand inside, and fisted an orange life preserver. Then it was three steps to the edge before I dove off the side.

The water smacked my face, and the briny, acrid taste of the ocean invaded my sinuses, but it was the chill of the water that grabbed me the most. It prickled and stabbed, and once I was submerged, my sweater became a heavy opponent, fighting to pull me down. But I looped an arm through the preserver and began to swim for her.

"Goddamnit," Ridley yelled after me, pissed that now he had two men overboard to contend with, but we could discuss this later once Sophia was safely back onboard.

As I swam, I pushed all thoughts from my mind except the singular goal of reaching her as quickly as possible. My pantlegs tangled and impeded as I kicked, but I pushed through, letting my strong body power me forward.

"Sophia," I cried as I spotted her over the crest of a wave.

She was facedown.

True horror flooded every cell that composed my body. I launched forward, latching a hand on her arm, and dragged her toward me.

"No," I said, turning her over and slinging back a lock of her hair out of her face. Her eyes were shut, and I leaned into her, trying to gauge if she was breathing . . .

But I heard nothing from her.

Only the sloshing of the water around us as we bobbed in the churning waves.

"Fucking, *no*," I ordered her, as if she could listen and obey.

The water was frigid, my sopping clothes exhausting, and it felt like the entire fucking world was against me as I struggled to get the bright orange life vest around her. The motor of the boat growled as it approached and then cut off before reaching us, so there was no danger of being struck by the propeller.

As soon as I finished buckling the strap around her waist and cinched it tight, there came the hum of the hydraulics as the swim platform lowered. I coughed to clear the saltwater from my lungs, clenched a hand around the strap at the top of her life preserver, and swam for the back of the yacht with Sophia in tow.

Hilde knelt on the platform, opened the compartment that housed the ladder, and swung it out, the end of it splashing down into the water and the handrails popping up to lock in place. The boat was riding the waves, and seawater sloshed over the swim deck, soaking Hilde's knees. I was now faced with the realization I was going to have to board the boat while it rocked and careened wildly. It'd be difficult under normal circumstances, but I was weighed down with drenched clothes and had an unconscious person to hold on to.

"I don't think she's breathing," I said to Hilde, refusing to acknowledge the meaning of my words.

"Captain," she shouted over her shoulder. We'd need all hands to help pull Sophia onboard.

Ridley hurried down the stairs, bracing one hand on the ladder handrail, and staggered his feet for stability as he reached down and grabbed the shoulder of the life vest. I pushed from beneath as best I could, and as he began to drag her from the water, Hilde was there to help him.

Sophia was hauled onto the deck and laid face-up, and as I latched a hand on the ladder and began to heave myself up, Hilde leaned over Sofia and put her ear to her mouth, while watching for signs that her chest was moving.

But it wasn't.

My bare feet slapped onto the platform, and when my shadow fell across Sofia, her lips taking on an unnatural blueish hue, Hilde looked up at me stricken with fear.

The word was in my voice, but it was so absolute, I barely recognized it. "Move."

Ridley bound up the stairs, hurrying to get to the helm and restart the engine while Hilde scurried out of my way and pulled up the ladder. I dropped hard to my knees at Sophia's side, dripping on her as I jerked open the life vest blocking me from what needed to be done. I put the heel of my palm at the center of her chest, crossed my other hand on top, and locked my arms in preparation.

"Thirty compressions, two breaths," I said, looking for confirmation.

Hilde nodded urgently. "Yes, sir."

It'd been years since I'd had CPR training, and never seen

it performed when it mattered, but I had a sharp mind and an excellent memory. I could do this, and it would work, because the alternative was incomprehensible.

I pushed hard, counting my rapid compressions under my breath and watched Sophia's body move beneath the deliberate thrusts of my hands. Saltwater ran into my eyes, stinging and burning, but I blinked, trying to alleviate the worst of it. My hands were forcing her heart to keep pumping blood, and the oxygen it carried with it, through her body and to her brain. I wasn't about to stop so I could wipe my eyes.

. . . twenty-eight . . . twenty-nine . . . thirty.

I tilted her head back to open her airway, pinched her nose, and lowered my mouth to cover hers. Her lips were cold as I forced air in. One breath—and another—and I sat back on my heels, struggling to catch my own.

"No, Sophia," I shouted.

This time when I started the compressions, I leaned into them. I put the full force of my upper body into the sharp movements, jolting her shoulders on each stroke. I could feel a crunch beneath my palm, and the sound it made was audible, ripping through me like a gunshot.

"Don't stop," Hilde barked.

For once, it didn't bother me to take an order from someone else.

I resumed what I had to do, blocking out the idea of the physical damage I was inflicting on this beautiful girl who'd said she was in love with me.

The thirtieth compression done, I pinched her nose and once again sealed my mouth over hers.

I'd been alone when I'd discovered Julia in the forest, her head bloody and awkwardly resting against a tree stump while her horse aimlessly grazed nearby. My wife had been breathing at the time, and those shallow breaths were what held back my desire to move her until the ambulance arrived. I'd worried about her spine, not knowing it was already too late. The bleed inside her skull would only build in pressure as time advanced, and three days later I was a widower and my sons were motherless.

And I'd been alone when I'd found Marist crawling up the stairs in her green dress, nearly too weak from the poison inside her to tell me she was dying.

Twice in my life, I'd been utterly powerless.

I did not have the strength to bear it a third time.

"Fucking *unacceptable*," I bellowed, loud enough for the world to hear me.

Failure wasn't a word I allowed in my vocabulary, and until this moment, neither was desperation. But I would take that word gladly now and let it have me, if I could avoid the first one. I heaved my hands against Sophia's chest, pushing her physically and pleading mentally to not let this be the end. There were plans I'd laid and things I did not want left unspoken between us.

The exertion of it took its toll.

The cold wind swept over my soaked skin, making me shiver, and my chest burned with fatigue, forcing my eyes to water. Or perhaps those were tears trying to form in the corners of my eyes, but it'd been two decades since I'd last experienced it, and the sensation was unfamiliar.

"Wait!" Hilde threw an arm across my chest, bringing me to a halt.

Sophia's lips parted, and her quiet, strangled attempt for breath sent a wave of emotion crashing into me that was so powerful, I let out a cry of relief.

Hilde shoved her hands under Sofia's drenched body, trying to turn her. "Get her on her side."

We rolled her carefully away from us into the

recovery position.

"You're okay," Hilde said over the steady drum of the engine, rubbing her palm in soothing circles on Sophia's back, while I simply knelt there, my hand gripping Sofia's shoulder. I couldn't make myself let go.

She coughed, and then retched with a pitiful sound, seawater expelling from her over the side of the boat. I'd told her I didn't want her to throw up on my yacht, yet now I was grateful for it. It meant she was alive.

"Oh, God," she croaked, lifting a shaky hand to wipe her mouth.

I exhaled loudly at her voice and squeezed her arm, saying it for my benefit as much as hers. "Sophia, it's all right."

She tried to sit up, but instead I shifted her into my arms and pressed my lips to her forehead. The whimper she gave tore me into shreds.

I went still. "Where are you hurt?"

Her throat was undoubtably raw from the ordeal, so it was hard to hear her gravelly voice. "It hurts everywhere."

The swells were big, and we were going fast enough to put air under the bow, and as it came crashing down, the three of us jostled on the platform. We couldn't stay here. Hilde had the same thought, and we exchanged a look.

"I can carry her," I announced.

It was a bitter knife sliding through me as I collected Sophia in my arms and stood, making her moan with pain. Her wet, black dress was molded to her body, and damp clumps of her hair flew erratically in the wind as I mounted the steps, struggling to get us both to the lounge area just beyond the cockpit.

I sat with her in my lap, her shivering in my arms, which likely didn't provide much warmth, but there was nowhere else I would allow her to be. Her head rested against my collarbone, and I held her as tightly as I could without causing additional pain. Hilde retrieved blankets from storage and cast them around my shoulders, pulling them around us to help block the wind.

Sophia's cold fingers crept up to my collar, and her fingertips rested against the side of my neck, like she desired a connection with me where nothing stood between us, and I closed my eyes as I endured the intense relief it brought on.

"I'm sorry," she started.

"No." There was no reason for her to apologize. She'd done nothing wrong.

But she continued. "I ruined our day."

I inhaled sharply. I was overwhelmed, unable to take any more, and so it burst from my lips as an urgent plea. "Stop talking."

She flinched, and I clenched my jaw. It was a response to protect my emotions, but I didn't mean it how it had sounded.

"Please," my voice was grave, "just let me hold you and listen to the sound of you breathing."

Her hand curled around my collar, her knuckles against my skin. It allowed her to hold on to me without breaking our connection.

She didn't speak again.

Not even when the marina came into view with an ambulance parked at the end of the dock.

TWENTY-SIX

MACALISTER

PORT COVE HOSPITAL'S EMERGENCY ROOM WASN'T BUSY, BUT THE few people seated in the chairs in the waiting area watched me more than the television playing nearby. Their thoughts were loud on their faces.

What is Macalister Hale doing here, and why is he wearing hospital scrubs?

One of the nurses had given them to me to stop my shivering. I preferred the cold, but even I had my limits, and the chill of the water wouldn't leave my bones. Or perhaps it was the memory of Sophia splayed out on my yacht's deck, looking very dead, and the realization that it was entirely my fault.

It hurts everywhere, she'd said.

I felt that now.

The EMT in the ambulance had tried to reassure me as we'd raced toward the hospital that what I'd done was right.

"Sometimes that cracking sound," he'd said to me, "is the cartilage around the sternum separating. It doesn't necessarily mean you broke anything." When it was clear I wasn't convinced, he added, "Remember, better to wake up with a cracked sternum or broken ribs than not wake up at all."

I leaned back in the uncomfortable hospital chair, letting my head rest against the wall. I didn't care what anyone else thought for once, or this disheveled state they were seeing me in. All my energy was depleted, my emotions wrecked, and I shut my eyes to rest for a long moment.

"Dad."

I jerked upright at the hand on my shoulder, and once my son came into focus, he stepped back and straightened. Vance was the last person I expected to see.

There was a bag slung over a shoulder, and he pulled the strap off, holding it out to me. "Change of clothes."

I stood and took it from him. "What are you doing here?"

"Lucas called and told me what happened." He meant Ridley. I'd forgotten they'd been friends in high school. My son paused, and quiet worry filled his voice. "Is she all right?"

Shame burned through me. "I was waiting for an update, but I'm not sure how long I've been out. She was conscious and talking in the ambulance."

Vance ticked his head. "Interesting. You didn't think I was asking about the *Checkmate*."

"The ship is fine," I snarled, "no thanks to its captain." Soon to be *former* captain.

He read my thoughts. "Accidental gybes are *accidents*. It's right there in the fucking name. He had no way of knowing she'd go—"

"If you came here to plead for your friend's job, then let me save you your breath."

He threw up his hands and walked backward. "Nope, I came to see how you were, but you're obviously fine."

I was not fine. She nearly died.

It hurts everywhere.

"Stop," I commanded.

Vance scowled, but he stayed where he was. He eyed me

cautiously as I approached, and then alarm filled his expression as I put a hand on his shoulder and pulled him to me.

He went wooden. "What are you doing?"

It'd been so long since I'd hugged him, he didn't trust or recognize it. I'd always pushed him and Royce away, believing I didn't need help, and still—he'd come despite that. I patted him on the back, wanting to say more, but couldn't bring myself to. "Thank you for the clothes."

When I pulled back, he stared at me like I'd just told him I wanted to give all my HBHC shares away. His eyes were incredibly wide. "You're freaking me out. Are you okay?"

"Today was . . . difficult." And it wasn't over either.

His expression softened, reminding me of his mother's sympathetic one. "Royce mentioned you and Sophia are . . . friends."

I understood what he meant. "Yes."

He opened his mouth to say more, but a woman in hospital attire approached. "Mr. Hale?"

Both of us turned, and she hesitated. Her gaze bounced from me to my son, unsure which of us to address.

She gave up trying to figure it out. "Come on back."

He turned to me and sounded unsteady. "Want me to come with you?"

I appreciated the offer. "No. Thank you."

He nodded. "If you get a chance, tell us how she's doing. I'm sure Marist will want to know too."

After he left, I told the woman I'd like to change first, and she led me to a private restroom.

"When you're finished," she said, "she's in room four. It's just down there." She pointed to the hallway leading away from the nurses' station, and then she left me to it.

When I emerged in the new clothes, I felt marginally more composed, but still not myself. I longed for my cold indifference, the emotionless state I typically operated in. It'd make the impending conversation easier.

"Come in," Sophia called when I knocked on the door.

She sat angled up on a bed that looked too much like a gurney to likely provide comfort. She had on a pale blue hospital gown, a thick white blanket pulled up and tucked beneath her arms. Her long hair was wavy and wild, her pale face devoid of any makeup, and although she was still beautiful, it made her look impossibly young.

When she saw me, her brilliant smile burst on her face, lighting up the entire room. I hadn't seen anyone ever look at me like that before, as if I were the center of their universe, and presented with this evidence, I couldn't deny it any longer.

Sophia Alby was absolutely in love with me.

Something deep inside me warmed and came alive, but I suspected it was merely my pride responding, enjoying her affection. At least, that's all I hoped it was.

"My hero," she said, both teasing and serious, her eyes going glassy with tears, but she blinked them back. She lifted an arm to reach out for me, but then slowed and grimaced, pressing her other hand to the center of her chest for support.

"Don't." I wasn't sure if I meant for her not to move, or for her not to label me a hero.

She waved her fingers to encourage. "Come here."

Although my desire to go to her was strong, I stayed in place and forced my gaze to sweep the narrow room. My hatred for hospitals ran deep. With the exceptions of the births of my sons, I always lost here. My parents. My wife. My chance with Marist.

And now I'd lose whatever it was I had with Sophia.

"I left a message with your parents," I said, pretending to study the signage about proper handwashing posted over the sink. "I couldn't reach them."

"They're in Fiji for their anniversary." She was impatient. "Macalister, please."

I set my attention on her, not able to avoid it any longer. "I think it's better if we maintain some distance right now."

Chagrin took hold in her. "And why's that? You didn't want distance when we were on the boat. You didn't have a problem with it in the ambulance."

She'd curled her hand around mine as we'd sped through the streets of Cape Hill and on to Port Cove. I'd allowed her to twine our hands together, wanting to maintain our connection just as fiercely as she did. Or perhaps more.

I raked my fingers through my hair, destroying the work I'd done in the restroom to make it lay flat. "I have gained some perspective since then."

"Yeah? Well, I don't care about your perspective right now. You saved my life, Macalister. Come here and let me thank you for it."

"I didn't save your life." I sighed with frustration. "It's not heroic for a man to rescue someone from a burning building when he's the one who started the fire."

She stared at me unblinking as she digested what I'd just said, before lifting her gaze to the ceiling. "Oh, my God, this is the curse thing?"

I swallowed thickly. "You stopped breathing. You nearly died."

She shook her head. "For such a smart man, you're being really fucking stupid."

Anger flooded through me, and I charged forward, not realizing she'd baited me until it was too late. It put me within striking distance, and she snagged my hand in hers.

Months ago, my touch had disabled her, but now I found myself in the opposite position. Her warm hand squeezed my fingers, and I felt lost. Adrift with nothing to hold on to but her.

"Listen to me," she pleaded. "You're not cursed."

I frowned and stared at the identification band wrapped around her wrist. "You shouldn't have been on the yacht. I pushed for that, even when you didn't want to."

"Oh, I wanted to, believe me." She peered up at me with longing. "If I hadn't gotten sick, tell me we wouldn't still be out there right now, in your bed, finding out if I could stay quiet."

She wasn't wrong, and I drew in a breath, letting it fill my lungs.

"Things happen," she said. "And sometimes those things can't be controlled, even by you." She let go of my hand, only so she could grab a fistful of my sweater covering my chest and pull me down to her, bringing our faces level. "I know you want to, but you can't control everything."

On some level, I understood what she was saying. I hadn't been able to force Marist to love me, or Alice to *stop* loving me. Even now, I couldn't control the feelings developing for Sophia, no matter how hard I fought against them.

She leaned forward and pressed her forehead to mine as her hand slipped behind the back of my neck. Her skin was as warm and soft as her voice. "Thank you for saving me."

It was unclear who initiated the kiss, but once my lips were on hers, I took command, and the emotions I'd struggled to keep at bay poured through me. She sank back in the bed, letting me taste her longing and her eagerness at the passion I finally permitted to flow between us.

I'd put my mouth on her earlier to bring her back to life, but this time it was more powerful. I kissed her as if I loved her. Slow, and deep, and I lingered when it was over.

I asked it in a hush against her lips. "Are you all right?"

"I'll be fine." She tried to kiss me again, but I held back.

"You'll 'be fine' implies that you are not."

She strived for a joking tone, but it was forced. "It's one rib, no big deal. I have, like, a bunch more."

"Jesus." I straightened, setting my hands on the railing at the side of her bed.

"It doesn't hurt that bad, and they gave me something for it. It really only bothers me when I move."

"And breathe," I added.

Her mouth skewed to one side. She looked like she wanted to shrug but stopped herself just in time. "I'm happy it hurts to breathe because that means I'm still alive, and that's thanks to you." She put her hand on top of one of mine. "Got to be honest, though. There's no fucking way you'll ever get me on your yacht again."

When I nodded, her eyebrows pulled together.

"What?" she demanded. "You're not going to scold me about my language?"

"No. It is appropriate today."

She made a sound of approval. "Yeah, I suppose that's true." Her blue eyes scoured over me and filled with worry. "Are *you* okay?"

I could only imagine what I looked like. My reflection in the mirror of the restroom when I'd changed showed me that exhaustion had set in. The brief amount of sleep I'd gotten in the waiting room had been uncomfortable and restless and done nothing to help.

"I could use a shower," I admitted.

"You and me both."

It came from me without considering the consequences. "Come home with me."

I watched excitement form in her eyes, but they slowly darkened with disappointment. "Thanks, but my aunt is driving up from Providence right now to help me. Not sure how I would explain I want to spend the night with my boss."

I felt both letdown and relief. I wanted her near, but

nurturing wasn't in my wheelhouse. "I understand."

Sophia tried to disguise her hope. "Will you stay until she gets here?"

Although I was tired and hated hospitals, I'd stay with her as long as possible. There wasn't anywhere else to be but here with her.

"Of course."

The belt on my treadmill began to make a noise I didn't like, a mechanical whine that grew in intensity at faster speeds. I made a note in my phone to text Elliot, the head of my household staff, about it later today. It was one in the morning, and if he received a text from me now, he'd assume it was urgent.

Since my phone was already in hand, I opened Instagram and went to Sophia's account. It'd been four days since I'd revived her on the deck of my yacht, and four days since I'd seen her in person. She'd sent me pictures, though. One of them included the horrific bruise on her arm from where the boom had struck her, but she promised it looked worse than it was.

I admired how tough she seemed to be. We spoke via text throughout the day, and she never complained. She was eager to come back to the office, and I was eager for that as well. Not only was her working remotely a challenge, but I missed her.

Her Instagram post had surpassed one hundred thousand likes.

She'd taken the image from her hospital bed. The foreground was her ID braceleted wrist on top of the covers, her feet two lumps beneath the blanket, and in the background, a man slightly out of focus. He sat on a chair, looking down at the floor as if deep in thought, with a hand on the back of his neck.

Her caption told the story of our working lunch gone wrong and how her boss had resuscitated her. She made me out to be the hero of Cape Hill.

I'd been hounded at the office incessantly to retell the story, though I didn't want to. My employees thought I was downplaying it to be humble, but the truth was I didn't enjoy thinking about it.

The image of the boom hitting her.

Her floating face-down in the water.

The way her rib had cracked beneath my hands. Did she think of me every time her chest ached? With every breath?

She wasn't in her post today, which was disappointing. I'd have to wait for new pictures of her in the morning. Her post this afternoon was a video from her bedroom. She panned the camera around, showing off the 'get well' flower arrangements dotting every available flat surface. There were flowers from her friends, from the rest of the executive assistants on our floor at HBHC, and even the owners of the gun range where she practiced. It'd be awhile before she could resume that activity.

Her 'favorite' gift, she'd declared, sat in the window seat. The large glass bowl was full of stones, moss, and succulents, and three green stems rose out of it, supporting the magenta orchids that bloomed from them.

I smiled in victory.

When the video looped back to the beginning, I closed the app and set my phone down, cranking up the speed on the treadmill, and ignored the troublesome sound. There were no flowers from Damon Lynch. No card, or phone call, or even a text message. I felt confident she would have told me if there had been.

His daughter had almost died, and he couldn't be fucking bothered to so much as reach out.

My feet pounded on the treadmill while thoughts did the

same in my mind. I wasn't one to second-guess myself, but the plan I had drafted wasn't responsive enough. I needed to revise and adapt.

My phone chirped with a text.

Sophia: You up?

Me: Yes.

When my phone rang, I punched the 'stop' button on the treadmill's console, but my breathing kept its quick tempo. She wouldn't call unless it was urgent.

"What's wrong?" was the greeting I gave her.

She sounded panicked. "Natasha sent me the page proofs of DuBois's book this morning, and I just finished reading it."

Everything went cold and still. This book could save or destroy me.

"Well?" I asked. "How bad is it?"

My stomach turned at her pause, but then she was there. "It's not bad for you, Macalister, or your family. I don't think there's anything in there that isn't already online."

I let out a tight breath, feeling like I'd just shrugged a hundred pounds of weight off my shoulders. "Then what is the issue?"

"He doesn't say Damon's my father." I could picture her stricken face on the other end of the phone. "He doesn't fucking mention me at all."

My quiet word filled my empty gym. "Oh."

"Oh?" she repeated with confusion. "You have to do something. Call DuBois and ask him why he—"

"It's late." I grabbed a towel from the stack and wiped my face. "We should talk about this in the morning."

The line went deathly silent, and I slowed my movements. Was she still there? The screen said we were still connected.

Her voice was colder than I would have thought she was capable of. "I just told you the thing I've been working on for the last five months didn't happen. Why the fuck are you so calm right now?"

"Sophia—"

"Because you got what you wanted," she said, answering her own question. "That's what matters to you." I opened my mouth to defend myself, but she gasped with realization. "Oh, my God. Tell me you didn't know."

I closed my eyes, wishing we could have done this as I'd originally planned.

My silence was all the answer she needed.

"How?" she cried. "How'd you know it wasn't in the book?"

I lifted my chest as if bracing for impact. "Because I didn't tell him."

TWENTY-SEVEN

MACALISTER

SOPHIA MADE A SOUND OF PAIN, AND IT WAS UTTERLY MY FAULT. Not only had I shocked her, but she'd moved as a result, and that jolt had hurt her fractured rib.

"What?" she shrieked.

I tossed my towel angrily into the bin. "I don't want to do this over the phone." It'd been years since I'd driven a car, but it'd be faster than waking my driver. "You'll give me ten minutes and I'll come to you."

"No, we're doing this *right* now. What the fuck, Macalister?"

I paced a circuit in the room. "I planned to discuss this with you."

"Yeah? When?" she demanded. "When the fucking book came out?"

"This past weekend, on my yacht." With everything that had happened, I'd pushed my plan back a week.

"Oh, I see," she snarled. "Were you going to do it before or after you'd fucked me?"

Hearing all the profanity and how upset she was caused it to bleed over onto me, and I gave her the brutal truth. "During."

I was a Hale, which meant it was win at all costs. I didn't

fight fair, and I knew she'd be more agreeable to my plan if she was intoxicated with pleasure. I would have fed it to her in pieces, information layered between orgasms.

"Oh, my God," she gasped in horror.

"DuBois's book is not the right vehicle," I reasoned. "And the timing is not ideal."

I could hear her heavy gasps for breath, and I had the terrible suspicion her face was wet with tears. I had to push the image from my mind and get through the rest of it. Once it was over, then I could assess how bad the damage was and what I'd need to do to address it.

"I know you wanted this," I said, "but I believe it's better if you wait."

She was so much smarter than people gave her credit for, and I admired how she drove straight to the heart of the matter. "Better for who? You?"

"Yes," I admitted. "If Damon is revealed in DuBois's book, it won't take him any time to deduce it came from me. I can't control it. He could decide that if he goes down, he's going to take the entire HBHC board with him." I pressed a hand to the wall and leaned against it. "That wouldn't just ruin me, Sophia. It'd hurt all of us, including Royce *and* Marist."

Since she'd been the last woman to be initiated by the board.

"And it'd be better for Vance," I continued, "and his political career, if Damon serves a term before it's announced what kind of man he really is."

She said nothing, but she was still there because her labored breath came through.

"You've known for years and not revealed it," I said. "I'm asking for two more."

Sweat sheened my skin from the run, and as I stood motionless in my gym, awaiting her response with my phone pressed to my ear, an icy chill crept over me. It was a warning of how horribly I'd mishandled the situation.

Sophia was detached, like her voice was no longer contained in her body. "Why even ask? It's done, and it's clear you don't give a damn about me. You did what was best for you." Venom coated each word. "I hope you're happy."

This time when the line went silent, I didn't need to look to see if we were still connected. She'd hung up on me.

My eyes burned from the lack of sleep.

All the calls I made went straight to voicemail, and the text messages unread. After an hour of failed attempts at communication, I considered driving over, but it was the middle of the night.

She was upset. It would be better to give her time to calm down, I told myself. I climbed into bed with the disgruntled cat, who spent five minutes heckling me with angry meows, and the next fifteen rubbing his cheeks against my fingers. I wished for sleep to come, and when it didn't, I crafted a course of action.

It wasn't surprising when my phone stayed silent in the morning. There were no pictures for me to approve. Whatever she put on today, she wasn't wearing it for me. So, I dressed in one of my favorite bespoke suits, a dark gray one paired with a simple black tie, stood before the mirror in my closet, and took a picture to text to her.

Me: I wore this for you.

It had been lonely in the car all week riding to the office without her. There was only silence instead of her laughing at the asinine things she'd read on her phone, which she often insisted on repeating to me. I didn't feel her gaze sliding appreciatively down my body when she thought I wasn't look-ing, which always stroked my ego.

And it no longer smelled like an apple orchard in the car.

When I came down the hallway after my morning meeting, I discovered a stranger sitting at Sophia's desk, and my eyes narrowed to slits. "Who the hell are you?"

The woman reminded me of frightened mouse, stammer-ing out her words. "Uh, I'm Rosa. They said you needed a new assistant, so I'm here until you hire someone. Talent Solutions sent me over."

Irritation filled me, but my exterior remained calm and aloof. "No."

She blinked her confusion. "No?"

"I have no need for a temp. My assistant will be back tomorrow."

Rosa had no idea what to do. She glanced around the office as if looking for help. "They said your assistant quit."

"Excuse me?" I froze.

Once again, she glanced around like she wished someone would swoop in and save her. "The woman who placed me, she said your assistant called this morning and quit."

Displeasure heated the marrow of my bones, some of it self-directed. I'd underestimated the level of anger Sophia held toward me.

"I see. Forward my calls to my cell," I said. "And reschedule today's meetings. I'll be out the rest of the day."

I'd planned to do this later, but she had forced my hand.

In sharp contrast to mine, the Alby home was only a de-cade old, even though the family helped found Cape Hill more than two centuries ago. As Stephen Alby's business had grown, so had his assets, and they'd upgraded to this rambling mess of a house. It had a turret and two separate entrances, leaving my driver guessing which one to pull up in front of.

He chose correctly, and a housekeeper asked me to wait in the living room as she checked to see if Sophia was taking visitors.

I perused picture frames on the bookcase, the Alby family in various locations across the globe, and my gaze landed on the one in London with Tower Bridge in the background. Sophia looked so much younger that this had to have been taken during the Olympics. Her smile was bright and wide as she stood beside her mother. Stephen stood on the other side of Colette, and I noted the pattern in the pictures.

It was as if Stephen refused to be near Sophia.

I didn't have time to dwell on the uncomfortable idea.

"Mr. Hale? She'll see you. Follow me, please."

Sophia's bedroom looked exactly as it had in the video last night, with one major exception. The window seat was bare, and the stunning orchids I'd given her were nowhere to be seen.

She sat upright on her bed, above the covers and pillows stacked behind her back, wearing jeans and a Columbia University zip-up sweatshirt. Her hair was back in a ponytail, and if she was wearing makeup, it was a minimal amount. While I preferred how she looked when she was done up and in a dress, her casual appearance still made my pulse quicken.

Her gaze narrowed as she spied me lurking in her doorway. She didn't ask me to come in, but when she turned off the television she was watching and gave me her full attention, it was enough of an invitation to propel me into her room and shut the door.

"I understand you're upset, but I will not allow you to quit."

She smirked, and if we were in any other situation, I would

have found it incredibly appealing. "You honestly think you still get to tell me what to do?"

"There's another woman sitting at your desk. Your point has been made."

"My point?" She let out an exasperated sigh. "You're a businessman, aren't you? I'm out. We had a deal, and you broke it."

"I altered it," I corrected. "Your goal was for me to put the spotlight on Damon, and I will uphold that. But we'll use my method and timetable."

Outrage dripped from her words. "And you just decided that without me."

My gaze moved off her and out the window to the shore in the distance. "I'd like to point out that you've made decisions without my knowledge."

"Are you fucking kidding?" Frustration clouded her expression. "I signed you up for a *bachelor auction*."

I turned and gave her a hard look. "You believed you knew what was best for me, and I feel the same about this."

"Except the decision I made for you could be undone. The one you made? It can't." She sneered. "Natasha said it's already with the printer."

I frowned and approached her bedside, causing her eyes to widen, and I didn't enjoy how she shirked back into the pillows. It reminded me of the retreat she'd made in my kitchen the first time I'd attempted to kiss her.

I softened my tone. "Don't misunderstand. This was not easy for me, and I did not make this decision lightly. I'm aware I should have told you sooner."

She looked dubious. "Was . . . that supposed to be an apology?"

I closed my eyes and pinched the bridge of my nose. I'd plotted this conversation in my head on the drive over, and I'd veered off course the moment I'd stepped inside the room.

"Yes." I pushed the words out. "I am sorry."

"You didn't tell me because you worried if I found out, I'd go directly to DuBois."

"Yes," I admitted.

I'd done what was necessary to ensure the outcome I wanted, but the amount of shame I felt about it was surprising. I'd known the moment she'd named Damon I couldn't reveal him. Not only for the damage it could cause me, my family, and my company, but because her strike against him needed to be tactical. Surgical.

"I have a plan," I said.

"Yeah? So did I."

I ignored her statement and reached inside my suit, withdrawing the folded piece of paper, and handed it to her. She unfolded the check, and there was no reaction as she stared at the seven figures. We'd agreed on five million, less the one hundred thousand for her salary, and although I hadn't read the book yet, I trusted her review that my name was safe.

She lifted her gaze defiantly to mine. "Fuck your plan and fuck your money."

The world slowed as she lifted the check and tore it cleanly in two. It was a staggering display of power, and my mouth fell open. Like no amount would satisfy her now, because she was beyond numbers. I was a fool not to realize Sophia was priceless.

"I gave you everything," she said, putting the two halves of the check together. "My body," she ripped them apart and stacked the pieces once more, "and my secrets." Every rip she made tore through me mentally. "And what did you give me in return?"

She tossed the ruined check at my face, and the torn scraps fluttered as they fell, five million dollars' worth of confetti to celebrate my betrayal.

"You kept this enormous secret from me. I told you I never wanted to be in the dark again, and *you* kept me there."

The impact of it all was so brutal, it knocked me back a step, but the words came instantly. "I'm sorry." My shoulders lifted as I took in a deep breath. "I will make it right."

"Your money can't solve this." To prove her point, she swiped a hand across her bedspread, casting off the torn pieces of my check that had landed there.

"No, but I have a plan, and if you would be reasonable for a moment—"

"I don't care, and I don't need you, Macalister."

Something inside me snapped at hearing she had no use for me, like she hadn't said she loved me or our time together was meaningless. It broke the leash on my urge to control.

"Don't be foolish," I warned. "If you go after Damon now, it could ruin you. People won't see you as the victim. They'll say he didn't know." She was young, but she knew how the world worked. "They'll spin you as the girl hellbent on destroying the career of a good man who made an unfortunate mistake a long, long time ago. Depending on how his people get him to respond, he could come out the other side looking even better."

She closed her eyes and shook her head, not wanting to hear it.

"Have you considered that?" I demanded. "Because I have. Don't let him beat you at your own game."

It punched a cruel laugh from her, which made her wince. "Everything's a game to you. Even me." Her eyes watered with bitter tears. "You couldn't get Marist to fall in love with you, so you tried with me instead."

Her accusation cut me in half. In the beginning, there may have been a sliver of truth to what she was saying, but now? I slipped my fingers across her cheek, cupping the side of her face. "Sophia, no."

She jerked away, gasping with pain from the sudden movement. "I didn't give you permission to touch me."

The dominant side of my personality was demanding I get control of this situation. My touch was a weapon against her, and I should use it. But instead, I withdrew, trying to respect her wishes, and stared at the scraps of paper littered around my feet.

"So, you got me to fall in love with you," she said, "but I wouldn't pat yourself on the back. Because now?"

Fire invaded her expression as she uttered the same sentence every woman I'd ever loved had said.

"I *hate* you."

Her statement flared through my mind, awakening a sleeping giant.

It spurred the armies inside to pick up their weapons and prepare for battle. This was a challenge she'd issued, and I would fucking rise to meet it.

I had stumbled greatly, but I was prepared to do everything to gain her trust back and give her what she desired.

"You don't hate me," I said. "I won't allow it."

"Oh, my God, get out." She scowled. "I don't want to see you again."

I shoved my hands in my pockets to keep them from balling into fists at her order. "If that's what you need right now, I'll leave, but this isn't over." I gave her the full force of my intensity to let her understand how serious I was. "I want you. I'm no longer afraid to admit I want you in every way. And once I've corrected my mistake . . . I will have you."

Fear hinted at the edges of her face, and I was sure I wasn't the cause. It was worry that she might want the very same thing.

She tried to sound strong, but it was more of a plea. "Get out."

I took in a deep breath, turned, and walked out her door, ready to get to work.

The same housekeeper was waiting for me in the foyer when I tried to leave.

"Mr. Hale, if you have a moment, Stephen would like a word. He's in his study."

It was likely Mrs. Alby had cut their vacation short because of Sophia's accident, which meant Stephen was now at home. I followed the woman down the hall and into a room that looked more library than home office, although he was seated behind the desk with his laptop.

At my entrance, he rose from his chair and moved toward me, his hand extended. "Macalister."

I took his offered handshake. "Stephen."

"My wife and I want to thank you for what you did for Sophia. I doubt there's anything Colette or I can do to ever repay you for saving her life, but if—"

"There is," I interrupted. "I need you to pull five million dollars' worth of my HBHC stock and place it in a trust."

He drew his shoulders back with surprise. His eyes were narrow set and his nose long, and I wondered how I never noticed how different he looked from Sophia. He wasn't an ugly man, but he could not compete with Damon Lynch's looks. That had to have been some factor in Colette's night of weakness twenty-six years ago.

I tried not to speculate. No one could truly understand a marriage unless they were inside it.

"Sure," he said, although he sounded anything but. "And who is the trust for?"

"Sophia."

I watched a range of emotions float through him. Surprise. Skepticism. Then, distrust. He was an intelligent man, and he wondered what reason I would have to give her such a large amount of money. My mind would have followed the same route if the roles were reversed.

His expression clouded over. "May I ask you a question, man to man?"

"You may."

"Have you slept with my daughter?"

At first, I respected his assertiveness. I was his biggest client, and this was a tough question to ask, likely to upset me. I appreciated people with backbone, and although she didn't have his genes, some of Sophia's fight undoubtably came from him.

But I worried he wasn't asking as a father who wanted to protect her honor. He was asking because he wanted to exploit me.

"No," I answered.

When faint disappointment materialized in his expression, it confirmed my suspicions. He'd be pleased if she traded the Alby name in for Hale.

"As I understand it," I continued, "she's not your daughter."

His eyes went so wide, they were impossibly white, and he gasped. "She told you?"

"I respect how you did not abandon her or her mother at such a difficult time, when a lesser man would have. That says a lot about your character."

He reeled with this information, not sure where to look or what to say.

"However," I darkened my tone, "so does the way you treated Sophia once you knew the truth. You're a fool. You let your hurt and your selfishness blind you from seeing what an incredible woman she became. I would have been proud to call her my daughter."

Stephen blinked, and his defenses went up. His eyes went down to slits. "Glass houses, Macalister," he snapped. "I don't think you should be commenting on what makes a good parent. Your sons barely speak to you."

He had a point, but I wouldn't concede it. "Let me know when the trust is set up."

I walked swiftly to the front door, and as I came down the steps, I pulled my phone from my pocket. I dialed the desk phone of my temporary assistant, hoping I hadn't scared her off.

"Macalister Hale's office, this is Rosa speaking," she answered.

"Go find Marist Hale in benefits and compensation. I'll be back in the office in forty-five minutes, and I want her waiting in my office when I arrive."

Saturday morning, I had just stepped out of the shower when there was a knock on my bedroom door. I wrapped a towel around my waist and moved swiftly toward it. "Yes?"

"It's Royce," came from behind it.

When I pulled the door open, his startled gaze took in my bare chest and damp hair, and he glanced at the screen of his phone. "Cutting it a bit close, aren't you?"

"What are you talking about?"

"The family portrait you insisted we do. The photographer should be here any minute."

I paused. "That's today?"

"Yeah. Vance and Marist are downstairs."

I scowled. Sophia had set this up and likely put it on the social calendar, not the office one, and I'd forgotten to check it. Rosa had only been working for me a day and a half and wasn't yet up to speed.

"You didn't know?" Royce asked.

"Sophia and I are having some communication issues at the moment," I said, leaving the door open as I headed for my closet.

"Marist told me." He sounded smug. "That's what you get for dipping your pen in the company ink."

"Watch it," I growled. "It wasn't like that." I needed to correct myself, because as far as I was concerned, we weren't over. "It *isn't* like that."

I pulled on underwear and a pair of suit pants before sticking my head out to glare at him, only to find him smiling.

"What?" I demanded.

"This is great." He pointed his finger to me, then him, then back again. "You fucking up and me getting to play the role of judgmental asshole. It's way more fun from this side."

I sighed, too tired to spar with him, and Stephen Alby's words rang in my ears. Royce was being a jerk, but at least he *was* talking to me. I moved to the bathroom to finish getting ready, and he stood in the doorway watching me.

"I came up here," he said, "to see what your plans were after this thing is over. I've got something to discuss with you."

I pulled up my calendar on my phone, which I should have done earlier, and scanned it. "This is all I have on my schedule for the day. What is it?" He gave me a cryptic look, which I found irritating. "Is it bad?"

"That depends on you." He straightened. "I'll see you down there."

As soon as he was gone, I opened Instagram to see if Sophia had posted anything new, but something was wrong.

Her account suddenly had no posts. Surely, she hadn't deleted her account.

No, she hadn't.

A quick Google search revealed she'd blocked me, and I raised an eyebrow in displeasure.

We took the Hale family portraits at the center of the maze, staged around the fountain. I sat on the bench while my sons flanked me on either side, and Marist in her maroon dress stood beside her husband.

Penelope Marino seemed shy and nervous when she greeted us, which didn't help the tension my family had with me, but once she began checking her light meter and taking test photos, she settled. Her directions were confident and surprisingly humorous, allowing her to catch natural smiles. She showed me a few in the display screen, and I was pleased with the results.

"Thank you for doing this," I announced to everyone when we finished.

My family stared at me like I'd spoken in a language they didn't understand, and perhaps that was true. Gratitude wasn't something I'd expressed much of in the past.

After Vance left and Marist went in the house to visit with Lucifer, Royce fell into step beside me, walking the grounds. It was a beautiful October day, and the leaves were brilliant colors in the forest beyond the maze.

"Why'd you want to take a portrait?" he asked.

"The spot at the top of the landing is empty. We've always hung a family portrait there."

His footsteps slowed. "I should probably warn you. It's going to be out of date in about seven months."

I stopped and turned to face him, finding his expression guarded. He was nervous, unsure of how I would take the news. "Marist is pregnant?"

"We were going to wait until she finished her Masters,

but . . . oops."

I studied him and saw the excitement he tried to hide from me, but it was unnecessary. I remembered that feeling well. The exhilaration over creating something unique and lasting with the woman you loved. "You were the same for your mother and me." I lifted the corner of my mouth, attempting a smile. "We meant to wait, but in hindsight, I'm glad we didn't."

My statement caught him off-guard, and he gave a subtle shake of his head, like he was trying to clear his disorientation. "We haven't told anyone yet, other than Vance. She's only nine weeks along."

It came from me without hesitation and in a warm voice. "Congratulations."

Royce drew in a heavy breath. "Are you all right?"

I'd tried to take his wife from him, and still he worried about me. For years, I'd thought he didn't deserve her, that I was the better man, and I'd been wrong. "Yes. I'm happy for you both."

"Okay, good." Relief lightened his shoulders, and he smiled. "You're going to be a grandfather."

I suddenly felt all fifty-five of my years, and what I needed to do came into perfect focus. "You'll move back into the house."

"What?"

I set my gaze squarely on him, seeing all the traces of his mother, and I wished to undo so many things, but all I could do was move forward. "I'm sorry I wasn't a better father to you and your brother, and I'm sorry for what I did—and tried to do—with Marist."

Unease flooded through him, and he took a step back like he needed to regroup and evaluate what angle this attack was coming from.

"I'm sorry," I continued, "that my presence has made you uncomfortable in your own home, but I can correct that." This was what Julia would have wanted. "The house is yours. I'll have my lawyers start the paperwork to transfer it to you, and I'll move out as soon as I find a place."

Royce stared at me as if I'd lost my mind. "You're giving me the house? You've lived here your whole life."

"You're starting a family, and it should be here. If my moving out makes that possible, I will be fine." I adjusted my sleeves and fiddled with a cufflink. "I'm not *giving* the house to you, though."

His thought was plain on his face. *Ah, there it is.* "What do you want for it?"

I paused. "Lucifer."

Now he was sure I'd gone mad. "You want my cat?"

"He's my cat now."

"What the fuck is happening?" He glanced around, perhaps looking for hidden cameras or to see if he was still connected to reality.

"I didn't want to, but I've grown quite attached to him." It'd been six months since the cat had come into my life, and now I couldn't imagine it being any other way.

Like Sophia.

"Talk it over with Marist," I added. "If Lucifer doesn't handle the move well like last time, I'll bring him back."

He blinked slowly, considering it. "She told me you were different, but I couldn't trust it." It was almost as if he was talking to himself. "I was sure it was more manipulation, but . . . you *are* different."

"I'm trying to be." Since we seemed to be talking so openly, I decided to risk it. "May I ask you something?"

He nodded, but his throat bobbed with a hard swallow. Whatever expression was on my face had him worried.

My breathing went shallow and my voice low. "Was Vance in love with Alice?" It was a question that had haunted me every day since the balcony. "I need to know if I accidentally killed the woman my son loved."

Royce exhaled loudly with surprise. "No." He shook his head. "He wasn't in love with her."

He looked at me with sad understanding, as if realizing I'd carried this fear for so long it'd begun to crush me. And now that the weight of it was gone, I became so light it was difficult to stay stable. The world threatened to hurl me off it.

"He cared about her," he said, "but I don't think he could love her. She was too in love with you." His shifted with unfamiliarity. "None of us are any good at this kind of thing, but you should talk to him. He's ashamed, and he wants to apologize . . . I'm just not sure he knows how."

"Since I'd never taught him." I'd only recently learned myself. "I'll talk to him."

"Okay, good."

He resumed walking, and I joined him, and it was . . . not unpleasant. For the first time in ages, the tension between us wasn't stifling.

"Can I ask you something?" he said. "Are you in love with Sophia?"

I pulled up short. "Why would you ask me that?"

"Because you're different, and I think that's her doing."

Resignation filled my voice. "I went away for two years."

"True. Except you didn't start changing until you'd been home for months. *That's* why I'm wondering if you're in love with her."

Tightness constricted my chest. "She told me she hates me."

"All right, I get it." Royce smiled widely. "If you didn't love her, you would have just said so." His eyes lit with amusement. "But you didn't answer my question either time I asked, did you?"

TWENTY-EIGHT

SOPHIA

MARIST'S DARK GREEN HAIR COLOR WAS FADING, AND I WONDERED if she'd waited to touch it up until after the family portraits.

"Penelope said the shoot went well," I told her.

I didn't mention that my friend had sent me some of the raw images to look at. Penelope had snapped some great pictures, but I preferred the ones of Macalister I'd taken without his knowledge. I had a few stolen away on my phone he didn't know about, like the morning before Royce had interrupted our breakfast.

"Yeah," Marist said. "She did great."

The marina clubhouse restaurant was busy for it being a Wednesday night. There were people waiting for tables, but one of the perks of being friends with a Hale meant you never needed reservations.

I was a little surprised and a lot suspicious when she'd called and asked if I wanted to grab dinner, but I'd said yes. Since quitting abruptly on Macalister, I'd been stuck at home, bored to tears. I was toying with the idea of going on a month-long solo vacation once I was feeling better because if I stayed in Cape Hill, I'd break down.

I couldn't be here when Damon Lynch won the election.

And I certainly couldn't bear to see Macalister Hale. Penelope's pictures of him smiling had been a dagger to my heart. How the fuck could he smile, when all I felt was this constant ache, both physically and metaphorically?

"So," Marist cut into her steak, "I have a secret to tell you."

My suspicion increased ten-fold. Royce had played match-maker with his father and me. Was he getting his wife to do it this time? I asked it with guarded interest. "Oh, yeah?"

She leaned forward to share it. "Royce knocked me up." Her eyes sparkled. "We've only told our families, and I know we're not super close, but . . . we're friends, right?"

I blinked through my surprise, feeling like an asshole for suspecting the worst of her, and gave the biggest smile I owned. "Oh, my God, congrats!"

"Thank you. I'm too excited to keep it to myself."

"That is exciting. When are you due?"

"May seventh." She took a sip of her water and turned bash-ful. "My hormones were being weird, so I went off the pill for a few months. Let this be a lesson to you. The 'pull out' method isn't super effective when he forgets to actually do it."

I laughed and immediately pressed my hand to my ster-num. It'd been eleven days since Macalister had broken my rib and six since he'd broken my heart, and neither was healing as fast as I wanted.

"Thanks for the tip," I said.

"You want kids?"

I picked up my vanilla vodka and Coke and took a big drink. I loved babies and always pictured myself as a mother someday. "Yeah. I'd like to have kids, but . . . I'm not even dating anyone."

She gave me a sly smile. "Aren't you?"

I wasn't naïve. Her husband was her best friend, and he told her everything. A dark expression filled my face, so she'd understand I didn't want to talk about it. "We weren't dating—we were fucking—and that's over."

"Oh." Her shoulders pulled back, and she glanced away. "I didn't know. Sorry."

"It's okay. Let's talk about something else." I scrambled for a topic that didn't involve Macalister. "Are you hoping for a boy or a girl?"

"He wants a boy, and I want a girl, which means it'll be a boy. Those Hale men always get their . . ." She gave me a pained smile as she caught herself.

"Don't paint the nursery blue just yet," I grumbled. "They don't always get what they want."

"I couldn't paint it, anyway. We haven't decided which room will be the nursery yet."

What was she talking about? Their apartment was big, but there were only three bedrooms in it, and one was being used as an office. My confusion was obvious.

Marist lifted a shoulder. "We're moving back into the house."

"With Macalister?" I shot her a skeptical look, one that asked her if that was a good idea.

"He offered to move out, but Royce and I talked about it, and we're willing to give it a try." She tossed a hand up. "He's putting the house in Royce's name, so we can throw him out if he does anything, but honestly, I don't think he will." She stared at me like this was somehow my doing. "He's changed."

My phone was on silent, but it vibrated on the tabletop, scooting along as it rang. I didn't recognize the number, but I was happy for the momentary escape from a discussion about Macalister.

"Sorry, one second," I said to Marist. I tapped the screen and pressed the phone to my ear. "Hello?"

"Hi," a male voice said. "Is this Sophia?"

I didn't recognize the caller, but he sounded young. "It is."

"Hey, this is Ian Holzman. We met at Damon Lynch's birthday party." This was the guy who'd hit on me all night and I'd been dumb enough to dance with. "I hope you don't mind that Vance gave me your number."

Oh, I fucking minded. I opened my mouth to unleash my fury, but he kept talking.

"I swear I'm not a stalker," he said. "It's just, I've been looking at your social media accounts, and I think you'd be a real help to the team. Damon's social media presence is good, but it could be better."

My fury was sidetracked. "Are you offering me a job?" Working for Damon?

"Uh . . . not exactly." He hesitated. "I'm not in charge of that, but I was hoping you'd be interested in, like, volunteering."

I closed my eyes as irritation overtook me. I was an influencer, and he wanted to me to use my brand to promote Damon Lynch. And he wanted me to do it *for free*.

"Yeah, I'm sorry, but—"

"Damon's hosting a private dinner next weekend at the Plaza with his friends and donors. I was thinking you could come with me."

I asked it flatly. "As a date?"

"As friends." He answered so quickly and casually, it was obvious he'd hoped to turn it into a date. "It should be fun, and, hey—free dinner."

Thoughts spun in my head. I'd never get in on my own, and I was pretty sure I was on a no-fly list. The only reason I'd been at the last campaign party was because I'd freaking helped throw it.

Macalister had warned me not to go after Lynch, but this could be my best opportunity.

And the icing on the cake was Macalister would probably be there for support. He could watch as I strolled in on another man's arm then defied his advice. I'd show him how little control he held over me now.

"What do you say?" Ian asked.

Hopefully to Marist, my smile didn't look as evil as it felt. "That sounds good. I'm in."

I wore the gray dress Macalister had bought me, and when Ian arrived at my house to pick me up, his eyes nearly fell out of his head.

"Wow." His lustful gaze stroked over my cleavage. "You look amazing." He wasn't subtle either, and I could see he was thinking his night had just improved big time.

"Thanks." I snatched my clutch off the table and slid my phone into it. "I'm ready."

When we came down the front steps outside, he went to the driver's side of his BMW, not bothering to open my door. It irked me. I liked chivalry and gentlemen and all the things. I was a sucker for romances and the big, grand gesture at the end. It was part of the reason I'd put everything out there with Tate in my catastrophe of a speech, and why I'd confessed my feelings to Macalister so quickly.

I wanted to live large and love big.

That was the plan for tonight too. I'd nearly died three weeks ago, and if I had . . . would Damon Lynch have come to my funeral? Or was I really nothing to him? I needed this town to know the truth. DuBois's book dropped in three days, and it would shine a light on the dark, dirty corners of Cape Hill, but I wanted a fucking neon sign over Damon.

I'd find a way to confront him in front of the cameras and hit him where it'd do the most damage tonight. Like Macalister, he cared about one thing above all else—his precious reputation.

As he drove, Ian dominated the conversation, not letting me get more than a sentence in here or there. He was twenty-nine and had a super impressive life, according to him. There was a line between cockiness and confidence, and he fell hard into the first category. I longed for a man I could sit in silence with, not a boy who humble-bragged the entire car ride into Boston.

A man like that wants to own you.

I scowled. Macalister had said he wanted me, but he'd also told me he wasn't capable of loving me, and other than a bunch of mind-blowing orgasms, the only thing he'd given me was heartache. And yet I couldn't quell the stupid excitement in my body at seeing him again. Maybe it was just to see the look on his face when he saw I was wearing the dress he'd given me, and showed him what he'd lost.

After we'd gone through security, we were funneled with the rest of the guests into the main ballroom of the Plaza, where round dining tables were decorated with alternating blue and red tablecloths. At the front of the room was a stage with a blue curtain backdrop and evenly spaced lighting cast up on it like columns. American flags hung in stands at either side, and the podium in the middle was wrapped with Damon's campaign logo.

"Bar?" Ian asked me, turning to look at the line that had formed with people waiting to get their drinks. It was cocktail hour, but we'd arrived late because he'd been late picking me up and it had taken him forever to find a satisfactory parking space. His car was nice, but it wasn't so nice it required being an asshole and angling it in two spots at the top of the parking garage.

I definitely needed a drink, not just for courage for what I planned to do, but to survive the night. I was already dreading the Uber ride back home since I'd decided I wouldn't be leaving with Ian. I nodded toward the bar. "Yeah."

While we waited in the line, I had a small reprieve. The husband and wife in front of us were big donors, and my 'friend-not-date' spent his time talking at them rather than me. I scanned the ballroom in search of one Hale man and found another instead.

Vance wore a stone blue suit and tie, paired with a powder blue dress shirt, and he stood near the stage, talking to a group of people while he fiddled with the water bottle in his hands. He was so different from his dominating father and brother. He'd always acted as little more than a fuck boy, but I'd seen and heard enough to know there was more to his story than he let on.

I still needed to chew his ass out about giving Ian my number, though. He fucking knew better.

Damon was all the way on the other side of the room, thick with people. It was going to be hard to get close to him, but as soon as dinner was over, I'd strike.

When Ian didn't tip the bartender, I dropped a few dollars into the jar and collected my lemon drop martini but made it only a few steps before my body locked up, forgetting the man before me was no longer its owner.

Macalister wore a black suit and a silver tie, and the refined elegance that rolled off him was so strong, it was overpowering. If I were tougher, I would have kept going and moved past him, but my feet refused to work.

His blue eyes started at my lips, and his gaze slowly worked its way down, sliding over me like a hot knife through butter. I wanted to melt at how sexual it was, especially out here in the open in front of my date, but instead I focused on the full glass of champagne he carried.

When he was done feasting on me, his attention shifted

to Ian, and his expression went cold. He said it politely, but I imagined it was the same tone he'd use if he told someone to fuck off. "Excuse us."

Ian shot me a look that announced I was on my own. "I'll catch up with you at the table."

I narrowed my eyes at his quick exit then turned my attention back to the man I both loved and hated. I jabbed a finger at his glass of champagne. "What are you doing with that?"

"Someone once told me I look better with it."

And, oh, how he did. It completed his look as a powerful, sexy billionaire.

"What are you doing with that boy?" His mouth twisted into a slight smile. "He's so *extra.*"

I pressed my lips together to stop the smile. He didn't deserve one. "He's my date."

"Hm," he dismissed. "I like that dress." His eyes were inescapable gravity. "Did you wear it for me?"

My pulse tumbled, speeding up. "No," I lied.

He didn't believe me.

"What do you want?" I snapped.

"Since you've refused communication, first I'd like to know how you're feeling."

I darted my gaze away, not wanting to see the concern in his eyes. "I'm getting better."

Although there were people talking and laughing around us, and music playing in the background, when his voice went low, it was all I heard. "Does it still hurt?"

When I think of you, it does. It hurts everywhere.

"Only when I move a certain way or take really deep breaths." I'd gone through a strange spike in pain last week, but my doctor said that was common. Peak pain, he'd called it. I tried to look bored as I peered up at him. "Anything else?"

"Yes. I'd like to make a wager with you."

My stupid heart stumbled a second time, but my mind was smarter. "No."

His eyebrow went up and his jaw clenched, and all the moisture in my body rushed to the center of my legs. He both loved and hated hearing that word from me, and his expression went stern. "You quit without warning, which was incredibly unprofessional, so you will at least listen to my offer. You owe me that."

I swallowed hard. "Fine. What is it?"

"If I get him to announce to this crowd, by the end of the night, that he's your father, you'll leave with me."

The sound in the room dropped out, and it became just Macalister and me.

"You don't want that," I whispered. "And it's impossible. He'll never do it."

"Accept my wager and find out," he challenged.

I shifted my weight and took a sip of my martini, considering his angle. "What would I get if I win?"

He tilted his head. "Anything you want."

Anything? It stole my breath. But he didn't mean *anything;* he only meant things that were tangible. I scoured my mind for something he wouldn't like. "I want a job."

"That's it?" He looked disappointed with my lack of creativity. "I've already spoken to the media director about bringing you onboard."

That was surprising, but I downplayed it and gave a wicked smile. "No, you misunderstand. I want a job somewhere else— anyplace other than HBHC. You'll reach out to that vast network you have and recommend me, telling them you wished you could keep me but you're too difficult to work with, and that's why I left."

Fire burned in his eyes so hot, they turned black, and I was giddy with excitement. I had to pinch my knees together to hold in my pleasure. His fingers on the champagne flute were white from how hard he clenched it, and I wondered if it might break under his force.

But layer by layer, he calmed and composed himself. His chin lifted, and then he squeezed out a tight smile. "All right. Do we have a deal?"

He played to win, so I knew he had this rigged somehow, but I also played to win. It'd be hard for him to get Damon to confess if I marched over to him right now and declared it for everyone to hear, rendering the whole thing moot.

My tone was overly bright. "Deal."

Macalister extended his hand, and my confidence flagged a little when I realized I was going to have to touch him. I put my hand in his, and the moment we made contact, sparks burst all over my body. My lips parted to draw in a deep breath, and the dull ache banded across my ribs.

His eyes turned to liquid, pouring over my face. "By the way, you're the most beautiful woman here tonight. No one can take their eyes off you." He held my hand even as I tried to let go. "You look . . . priceless."

Goddamn him. I tore my gaze away so he wouldn't see the tears he caused to flood my eyes. He released me, and by the time I'd recovered enough to look at him, he had turned his back and was moving swiftly away from me.

He was heading toward Damon.

Oh, no, you don't.

I started off, rounding tables and going as quickly as I could without sloshing my martini everywhere, but then Ian stepped into my path, blocking me. I couldn't stop my frustrated sigh, but he was oblivious.

"Hey, our table's that way." He pointed the opposite direction. "We should probably sit down. They're starting to serve the salads."

I glanced at the table nearest us and saw he was right. And when I looked back at the other end of the room, I watched with disappointment as Damon and two of his staffers disappeared out the side door. They'd probably left to put the final touches on his speech.

I wouldn't be able to get to him now. I'd have to do it right after he was done.

Or maybe you don't, a voice whispered in my head. *It wouldn't be the end of the world to lose and have to go home with Macalister.*

Yes, it would be. He'd kept a secret from me when I'd shared everything with him, including my heart.

"Where's our table?" I asked Ian. "Is it close to the stage?"

Thankfully, it was.

I sat beside him, drank my martini, and picked nervously at my salad while I visualized how I would approach Damon. There were stairs on both sides of the stage, and if he came down the set on the left, it'd spit him out close to my table. I could hop up and ambush him. It wasn't ideal, but it'd get the job done.

As they served the main course, the music suddenly swelled, drawing everyone's attention. Vance appeared on stage from behind the curtain and walked confidently to the podium, flashing a winning smile as he turned the microphone on and adjusted its position. He waited for the music to die down before speaking, and it was undeniable how good he looked up there.

He oozed trust and assurance, and I imagined he was just as comfortable here in front of three hundred people, or arguing a case before a jury, as he was anywhere else.

"Good evening, ladies and gentlemen." His speaking voice was crisp and clear. "First off, on behalf of the entire campaign staff, I'd like to welcome—"

A rustling came through the speaker system, interrupting him, but it was gone as soon it had started.

"I'd like to welcome," he started again, "the volunteers who put in countless hours of work—"

This time, the rustling was louder and longer, and it was followed by a disembodied voice.

"Not now," the male voice said.

Vance maintained his smile and tried to push through. "And to all those who are here tonight to support—"

A different voice interrupted. It was also male, but it was quieter, as if farther away. "You owe me the truth."

People seated at the tables exchanged looks, confused. Was this feedback from a different event going on at the hotel?

On stage, Vance cleared his throat, as if requesting the audience's attention. "We seem to be—"

"Damon, is she your daughter?" the quieter voice asked.

My heart stopped at the question. I recognized that distant voice, just as I was sure Vance did. Oh, my God.

I was about to lose my bet.

But in this moment, it didn't matter. Everything hinged on Damon's next words.

"So she says," his voice answered. "I fucked Colette Alby once, so maybe it's possible, but Sophia can't be mine."

People gasped. Some at the language and some at the content, but I couldn't breathe. I balled my hand into a fist and pressed it to my stomach like it could stop the hole spreading there. There were plenty of people here who didn't know me, but it felt like a million pairs of eyes were suddenly staring down.

Across the room, someone leapt up from a table and dashed to the side door, probably a staff person desperate to switch off the hot microphone Damon had no idea was on. Vance stared at the podium like he wondered if there was a way to switch it off from there.

"Why not?" Macalister's voice demanded. "She's an incredible woman."

"Because it'd ruin me. Kristin knows about some of the affairs, but a kid? She'd cut off my balls."

"Oh, shit," Ian said, dumbfounded.

The rest of the audience was restless and churning with discomfort. The people at my table looked either miserable or outraged by what they were hearing. Vance backed away from the podium like it was radioactive.

Meanwhile, Macalister's voice was louder, as if he'd gotten much closer to Damon, perhaps right in his face. "You're a bastard."

"Jesus, Macalister, like you should talk. And I don't have time for this."

It was so quiet in the ballroom, not a soul was breathing.

I felt . . . strangely nothing. The hole in my stomach grew and consumed me. There was disappointment but not surprise.

But on top of it was also closure. It was out now. Done. Time marched brutally along.

Finally, a new voice punched through the speakers, the person sounding out of breath. "Your mic's on! Turn it off. Oh, my God, Damon. It's—"

"What?"

"—been on this whole time."

Loud, violent thumps played as a hand scrambled over the microphone, muffling any more words, and then it went abruptly silent.

The room sat in tense agony, unsure of what to do, and it only grew when Kristin Lynch rose awkwardly from her chair near the front of the stage. There was no way for her to sneak out unseen, so she tried to hold her head high as she calmly put her purse on her shoulder and walked to the exit. She moved as if each step were painful, and while I wasn't sure she deserved quite so much humiliation, I didn't feel that sorry for her. She wasn't much better than her husband.

She'd had her own infidelities, and although there were tens of millions of dollars in her bank account, she was so cheap, it was criminal. She was the type of person to plant a dead bug in her five-star hotel room to try to get it comped. Kristin was so entitled, she refused to pay full price on anything.

Vance had frozen halfway off the stage, but it was rapidly becoming clear Damon wouldn't be coming out, and so the responsibility to dismiss the audience was going to need to be handled.

Before he could do it, a hero emerged from behind the curtain, and my blood roared loudly in my ears. His master plan executed, he looked effortlessly composed and powerful in victory.

After a quick exchange with his son, Macalister strolled up to the podium like a king readying to speak to his kingdom. He raised the microphone to his level and surveyed the crowd, and his demeanor reassured the room they were in capable hands. He'd tell them what to do now.

"Ladies and gentlemen, in light of what has happened, Damon has decided he will not be speaking this evening. He'll be using this time to reflect on his actions and discuss them privately with his family. He thanks you for your understanding."

It seemed like a dismissal, and I expected him to walk off proudly, come find me, and gloat about his win. I could begrudgingly admit his plan was good. He'd forced the confession from Damon as if by accident and had come off looking like a friend when it was over. But instead of exiting the stage, Macalister braced his hands on the sides of the podium and leaned closer to the microphone.

"I imagine many of you are upset and disappointed, but there's someone in the audience who has lived silently with that for quite a while, and if you will indulge me, I'd like to address her now."

His gaze moved swiftly and directly to me, and I clenched my hands instinctively. What was he doing?

"Sophia Alby," he announced, "I wore this suit for you. I came to this event tonight for you." His chest moved quickly, and his eyes were shockingly intense as he stared at me. "I get up every morning and I keep breathing . . . for you."

Holy.

Fuck.

I whispered it to him under my breath so quietly it might not have made a sound. "What are you doing?"

"I'm sorry I didn't give you what you needed and that I let you down. Despite my efforts, I am not a perfect man. I'm far from it. But you have pushed me to want to be a better man. To be a *good* man."

He drew in a deep, preparing breath, and as he straightened, he looked at me with so much power, it obliterated me. I went boneless.

"I don't care who knows or what they may think, or that I'm making a complete fool out of myself, right here, right now in front of all these people. It doesn't matter. It hurts everywhere with you gone," his voice was solid and sure, "because I am very much in love with you."

Maybe people gasped, or Ian balked at my side, but I couldn't tell. I was trapped under Macalister's gaze, unable to experience anything else. If I moved, I'd die, but perhaps that would be all right. He'd brought me back to life once before.

He could probably do it again.

Tingles raced across my limbs with the electricity of our connection. It was hard to heave air in and out of my lungs, and it had to hurt my fractured rib, but I couldn't feel it. We'd spent months restoring his name and reputation, and he was willing to risk it all—just for the chance to win me back.

Because he was in love with me, and because it was win at all costs.

"You once told me you usually get what you want," he said. "So, if you want me, I'm yours." He held my gaze for a final moment, before turning his attention back to the audience. "Thank you."

He turned the microphone off and strode toward the stairs at the end of the stage.

Murmurs at the tables built quickly to shocked conversations that filled the ballroom. Some people stood and prepared to leave in protest, but I was rooted to my chair. The man who was mine was making his approach, and the determination etching his face screamed what he'd told me in my bedroom.

I want you in every way . . . and I will have you.

A tremble worked along my body as emotional overwhelm set it, and then he was there, standing over me with eyes full of love and concern.

"May I touch you?" he asked in an uneven voice.

My bottom lip was quivering, but I was able to get the word out. "Yes."

He reached for me, his fingertips grazing my face to wipe away a tear I hadn't realized I'd shed, but as he'd done it, I'd caught the subtle shake of his hand. I wasn't the only one trembling, and the idea that I could make this legend of a man nervous was absolutely stunning.

"Do you still hate me?" His fingers were cold, but his palm was warm as he cupped my cheek and angled me up to look at him.

"A little," I whispered. "But only because I hate losing."

His smile was breathtaking, and when he began to lean down, I was sure his intent was to kiss me, and I was too impatient. I burst up from my chair, meeting him halfway, and pressed my lips to his.

Our kiss was full of passion, but it was tame and restrained. Like the first time we'd been together in the costume room, this was a taste. A fraction of what we were capable of and just enough to tide us over until we were away from everyone else. Macalister was not one for making a show of affection or a spectacle of himself, and now that he'd done both, I sensed he was nearing his limit.

But I reveled in the connection of our mouths and the possession of his hands on my body, every nerve ending in me singing at his return.

On the table, my phone buzzed with a notification, and since I was pressed against him, I could feel his phone vibrating in his coat pocket. Word was out about what had happened, and the digital world was spreading it.

"We're leaving," he announced to both me and the table, but it was mostly for Ian's benefit.

I snatched up my phone and my clutch and flashed an apologetic smile to my date, but he simply sat in his chair, staring up at Macalister with disbelief.

Like he'd done in his hedge maze, the man I loved walked so quickly, it was a struggle to keep up at first, but when he realized, he slowed and took my hand. I ignored the scowls from people who stared at us like I was some trollop who should be ashamed to run around with a man twice my age.

I'd faced far worse and survived. This was a small price to pay to get what I wanted.

Down the long hallway we went, Macalister towing me toward the entrance to the parking garage, and as soon as we stepped out into the frigid November air, a black Range Rover pulled up. He grabbed the backseat door handle and pulled it open for me.

This car had been waiting for us.

Once I'd climbed in, he shut the door and rounded the back of the SUV to get in on the other side, and I was dying to know how much of this night he had scripted. We buckled our seatbelts, and the car eased away from the entrance.

"How much did you pay the sound guy to turn on Damon's microphone?"

The interior of the car was lit by the parking garage lights overhead, and a smile teased Macalister's sexy lips. "Nothing. Vance did it for me." His casual fist rested on his thigh, and his thumb brushed over the knuckles. "When he cleared his throat, that was the signal he could hear us, and I needed to ask the question."

"What about his career? You wanted this to be his steppingstone."

"He will be fine, and this," he set his hand on mine, "was more important." He hesitated for a moment. "I've spent too much time interfering with my sons' lives and have decided I won't be doing that anymore."

"You mean, other than getting Vance to give Ian my number?" A smile warmed my face. "Did he also encourage him to bring me tonight as a guest?"

"Vance merely pointed out how beneficial it'd be to the campaign if you posted your support of it."

My expression told him I wasn't convinced. "Uh-uh. What else did you do to make sure your plan worked?"

His eyebrows pulled together. "I sometimes struggle to express myself when dealing with emotion. I'd like you to know the things I said tonight were my words, but . . . I had some help drafting them."

I didn't understand why he was cautious about telling me this. Was he worried I'd be upset someone else knew he was in love with me before revealing it to me? I teased him. "You had a speech writer?"

He was serious. "She didn't know it was going to be a speech. I told her it was a letter."

The pieces clicked into place. "You had Marist help you write a love letter . . . to me?"

"I hope that doesn't upset you. She's the most competent person in the family when it comes to feelings."

For some strange reason, I found it both amusing and touching. He'd once given her a speech to woo her and failed, and now she'd helped him write another. This time, he'd succeeded.

"No," I whispered. "It doesn't bother me. It's actually kind of nice."

He exhaled with relief. "I also paid Ian to make sure you didn't arrive too early. I knew if I could get you to agree to my wager, you'd be competitive about it."

I grinned. "I was going to be. Did you pay him extra to be so douche-y?"

Amusement flared in his pale eyes. "Was he?" But he sobered. "I had unease about using him. I remember how he was around you at Damon's birthday party."

I wanted to laugh at how ridiculous the idea was. "You weren't honestly worried I'd be into him."

We weren't in the garage anymore, and downtown Boston flew by, streaking lights across his unsure expression. "He's a much younger man than I am, Sophia."

I set my pointed look on him. "I've made it pretty fucking clear I'm not into younger men."

Enjoyment coated his expression, followed by a playful look, right before he leaned over and swept his lips across mine. "Language."

Now he delivered the kiss he'd wanted to earlier, holding nothing back. He conquered with his mouth and his tongue, both taking and giving pleasure. My heart fluttered in my chest at the way he kissed me with passion, but also did his best to be delicate. He'd hurt me and was intent on not doing it again.

When the kiss ended, it felt like I had to come up for air, and my hands were fisted on the lapels of his suit, holding on. He wasn't faring much better. His hair was wild from my fingers and he was short of breath, and as we recovered, we grinned at our frantic state.

"Can I ask a favor?" I released my grip and dragged my palms down his chest.

Desire thickened between us at my touch. "Of course."

"I'm starving." I'd been too nervous most of the day, and dinner at the party had been canceled. "Could you text your chef and have him make us something?"

"No. We'll have dinner on the plane."

I blinked, and excitement stirred at his meaning. I hadn't been on the Hales' private jet before, and a getaway—anywhere with him—sounded amazing. My phone continued to buzz in my purse like thunder in an electronic storm. We'd need to escape. "Are we going somewhere?"

"My home in Aspen."

I bit down on my lip to keep from squealing, but I tried to play it cool. "I don't have anything with me. What am I supposed to wear?"

He'd anticipated this question, and his smile was sinister. "Do you still have on the jewelry I gave you?"

I swallowed hard as goosebumps burst down my legs. "I couldn't get it unscrewed by myself."

He was beyond pleased with this answer. "Good. You will wear that and nothing else."

EPILOGUE

MACALISTER

I DIDN'T CONSIDER MYSELF A GAMBLER BECAUSE THE OUTCOME was often left to chance and I preferred strategy, but I didn't shy away from taking risks. None had been bigger than the night seven weeks ago when I'd declared my love for Sophia Alby to the world, unsure if she felt the same, and not knowing what it would do to my reputation.

But I had learned, as Damon Lynch was still trying to, that facing a scandal head-on could decrease its fallout. By making myself vulnerable and putting my emotions out there for everyone to see, it made me human to the people of Cape Hill.

It also helped that they were distracted by DuBois's book and Damon's secret daughter and were discovering that no one in our perfect little town was, in fact, perfect. Everyone had a secret to hide or something that filled them with shame. Exposing the dark underside forced people to recognize their social mortality. They couldn't live as gods above consequence anymore.

I sat in my office at the end of the workday, watching snow as it floated past my window, and eagerly awaited the arrival of the girl I loved. Sophia now worked three floors down in the marketing department, and when she had finished her work, she'd come to me and we'd ride home together.

To *our* new home, a secluded estate set back from the coast and hidden in the woods, just beyond Cape Hill's reach. It needed a lot of work, but I looked forward to the challenge of the project.

She'd moved in over the weekend at my insistence, although it hadn't taken much convincing. We already rode to and from work together every day, so this saved time. Plus, with her mother's adulterous past dug up, it was best for her parents to have some time to themselves, and Stephen Alby was in complete support of my plan. He'd be happy to lock up his biggest client as family.

People thought it was too soon for us to live together, and I understood that. I'd once told Marist that people who fell in love too quickly fell out of it just as fast. It had been my experience with Alice, but the way I felt about Sophia was entirely different. It used a part of my heart I was sure had died twenty years ago, not recognizing it was merely lying dormant.

If the rest of my family disliked my new living arrangement, I wasn't made aware. Royce and I had convinced Vance to return home as he studied for his bar exams, and sometimes Sophia and I would join them for a family dinner. Marist seemed pleased to have another woman around, especially since the two of them were becoming real friends.

The Hale home was full again.

Even if it wasn't mine anymore.

Lucifer was adjusting to his new accommodations and was happy to share our bed with Sophia. This morning when I'd awoken, I'd discovered he'd abandoned me for her. I explained loyalty to him while she was in the shower, but he used his indifference to remind me that, as a cat, he was superior to me in every way.

"Hey," Sophia said as she came into my office and shut the door. She wore a cinnamon-colored dress, which I'd picked out for her this morning, and it made the blue in her eyes more vibrant.

I disguised my excitement at seeing her and lifted a sharp eyebrow. "Did you forget where my office is located? It's twenty after five."

"Sorry, I got caught up."

"It'll take more than an hour to get home now with the traffic and snow."

She shrugged, which was something she'd started doing again once her rib no longer bothered her. It'd been both challenging and enjoyable in Aspen finding all the ways to make her orgasm without causing her discomfort during the process.

"Guess I won't try so hard to be good at my job, boss."

Hot pleasure spiraled through my chest at her snarky comment, designed to irritate me. She wanted to play? All right. My order was dark. "Come here."

She practically skipped over to the side of my desk, and I swiveled in my chair to face her.

"Pull your skirt up. All of it, to your waist."

Her breath immediately went short, and she slowly complied, gathering the skirt up in her hands and exposing what she had *not* worn for me. I stared at her nakedness and licked my lips to let her know how pleased I was. When she'd finished dressing this morning, she'd given me attitude, claiming I was trying to rush her, and so I'd made her take her panties off and leave them at home.

She hadn't earned them, I'd told her.

Sophia stared at me now with curiosity, perhaps wondering if I'd make her bend over, put her hands on my desk, and prepare for me to punish her. I gave a wicked smile. That was not my intent today.

I smoothed my hand up her inner thigh, deep between her legs, and touched the diamond I'd given her. My symbol of control, although it worked both ways. When I owned her, she owned me.

She moaned as I gently rubbed her soft skin and her eyes hooded, but her gaze didn't waver from mine.

"I love you," I said, teasing her clit. "Do you love me?"

"God, yes," she gasped.

I rewarded her by moving faster, and she grew slick and damp. She probably wouldn't come standing up like this, but that was all right. My goal was to go until her legs began to shake, and then I'd take her across the desk. I pressed harder and rubbed quicker still as her hands twisted the fabric of her skirt and she gulped for breath.

"Fuck," she groaned, her shoulders slumping as she began to bend at the waist, trying to stay upright during my furious assault of pleasure. Satisfaction filled me as her knees trembled and threatened to buckle. It came from her in a desperate whine. "Macalister."

I stood and turned her so I could ease her down on her back. In a few more weeks, I'd be rougher, but chest fractures were notoriously slow to heal, and I didn't want her thinking about anything other than her desperation for my cock.

Her legs wrapped around my hips, and her hands went to my belt.

"Do you want children?" I demanded abruptly.

She froze, my belt half unlatched in her hands. "What?"

I clenched my jaw. "I believe you heard me, and I dislike repeating myself."

"Uh . . ." Sophia's disorientation was painted across her face. "I mean, yeah, I did."

"Then I suggest you stop taking your birth control. I am not getting any younger."

She scrambled to sit up on the desk, staring at me with her eyes wider than I'd ever seen them. "What?" she gasped. "You already have kids. I thought you wouldn't want more."

I latched my hands on her waist, anchoring her to me. I'd improved dramatically since she'd come into my life, but I still struggled to admit my shortcomings. "I was not a good father my first time around."

She laced her fingers together at the back of my neck and peered at me with cautious hope. "You want to have kids . . . with me?"

"I'd like the opportunity," I said, "to try again, to be better this time. I know it sounds crazy. We've only been together a short while, and I'm going to be a grandfather soon, but if you want this, I'd do my best to give it to you."

Her gaze focused on the knot of my tie as she pondered it. "Let's think about that some more. We have time." She gave me a shy smile. "George Clooney was fifty-six when he first had kids."

"I am not George Clooney."

She sighed dramatically. "Don't I know it."

I grabbed her hair at the back of her head and tugged, forcing her chin up, and gave her the sharp edge of my teeth at the side of her neck. She whimpered with enjoyment, and the sound of it shot straight to my groin. I'd momentarily derailed the mood with my abrupt question about kids, but I'd been anxious about approaching the subject with her, and it had burst from me without warning. Now that we'd discussed it, it was time to get back on track.

I dropped my gaze to my half-undone belt then gave her a pointed look. "Well?"

She grinned and eagerly resumed her work.

Sophia hadn't given me the answer I wanted quite yet, but I felt confident she would. We wanted the same thing and were both accustomed to getting our way. And there was another answer I was certain I would get from her, when the time was right.

She wasn't really an Alby or a Lynch—her surname in Cape Hill was trapped in limbo.

I had a plan to correct that.

THANK YOU

This book was supposed to be 70,000 words. It finished at 110,000 and three weeks later than I wanted it to. That meant my husband Nick once again became my superhero. He supported me by brainstorming, feeding and entertaining our children, and staying up late to read the first draft, even when he had to be up early in the morning for work. I was at a writer's retreat at the tail end of writing this (when I foolishly thought I had 10,000 words left to go and not 30,000) and when I explained how amazing my husband was, it was decided he needs to be cloned. I don't know how I got so lucky but thank God I did. I love him so very much.

Thank you to Aubrey Bondurant for her daily messages of support and her fantastic idea that helped me get unstuck when I was in my 'black moment, all-is-lost' phase of writing this book. I'm sorry for feeding you the never-ending lie that I was "almost done and probably finishing tomorrow."

Thanks to my publicist Nina Grinstead for pushing me to write this book. I was resistant and scared to try to tackle Macalister's story, but you were absolutely right, and I'm so grateful.

Thank you to all the fantastic folks at the writer's retreat in Orange Beach, AL for being so uplifting when I was struggling under the weight of my stress. I loved getting to witness such a positive community of strong, smart women.

And I owe a huge THANK YOU to you, reader. The Filthy Rich American series has been a joy to write, and the love you've shown it has literally changed my life. When THE DECEPTION hit the USA Today Bestseller list, it was the first time my work has been able to do that on its own. Thank you for reading and helping make my dreams come true!

MORE BY NIKKI SLOANE

ABOUT THE AUTHOR

Nikki Sloane fell into graphic design after her careers as a waitress, a screenwriter, and a ballroom dance instructor fell through. For eight years she worked for a design firm in that extremely tall, black, and tiered building in Chicago that went through an unfortunate name change during her time there.

Now she lives in Kentucky, is married and has two sons. She is a three-time Romance Writers of America RITA© Finalist, also writes romantic suspense under the name Karyn Lawrence, and couldn't be any happier that people enjoy reading her sexy words.

www.NikkiSloane.com

CPSIA information can be obtained
at www.ICGtesting.com
Printed in the USA
BVHW032051310320
576533BV00001B/101